# CREEKERS

## BY EDWARD LEE

"These guys they found dead?" Her voice lowered to a dusky croak. "It looked like they'd been...skinned."

Skinned. Phil's pause burgeoned. Just like that other guy we found, the angel dust dealer from out of town. They'd cut his skin off...

"I heard they found a dozen bodies at least," she went on. "Same m.o. each time. Mullins had Adams and North investigating. Then one day—four or five months ago, I guess—both of them just disappeared."

Phil chewed the inside of his cheek. Disappeared, huh? This was the second time she told him something that directly refuted the chief. And when they'd found Rhodes' body? Mullins had seemed genuinely shaken, but he'd also seemed...

Well, Phil wasn't quite sure what. But he didn't like it. Why would Vicki make something like this up? And if it were true, why wouldn't Mullins have told him about it?

Whatever it is, he declared to himself, I'm going to find out.

He got back on track. "So what exactly happened? I mean, to Adams and North?"

That somber croak came back to her voice. "Nobody knows."

Phil ran a hand across his cheek, scruffing stubble. "Okay. But what do you think happened to them?"

Her brow rose wide. "Me? I think they got killed by the same people who did the job on those dealers. They're probably at the bottom of one of the swamps, chained to a couple of manhole covers. You ask me, they got too close, so they got offed."

"Yeah, Vicki, but what did they get too close to?"

"The Creekers, " she said.

Though in debt to many, the author would particularly like to thank the following for their friendship, wisdoms, suggestions, and for picking up their telephones when I most needed them to: Doug Clegg, Dallas Mayr, Stan Tal, and Lucy Taylor. Added thanks to Adele Leone, John Scognamiglio, and Mom. Also thanks to Uncle Dorin and Uncle Fred, Rich K., Tim O'Rawe, Damon, Brian Hodge, Igor T., Don Myers, Micah Hayes, Sarah Blair, Jon and the crew at the Bowie Post Office. And editors Jasmine Sailing, Rich Chizmar, Mike Baker, John Maclay, Doug Coulson, Lisa Jean Bothell. Plus, super double thanks to Wayne Allen Sallee, whose own visions of uniqueness and grotesquerie helped me write this book.

# PROLOGUE

Roughened hands disrobed her before the cracked mirror. "You are the most perfect of all of us," came the equally roughened whisper to her ear. She could feel the heat of the breath, and of the words themselves.

But then more words oozed through her head:

So perfect... So worthy... So beautiful...

"Yeeeeesss," keened the voice behind her.

*So beautiful...for Him.*

Only a few crooked candles lit the downstairs parlor. In the mirror she could see herself, and she could see the Reverend standing behind her like a queer, tall shadow in black raiments and drooping hood which hid his face.

"So beautiful for Him," he whispered.

Beautiful, she thought. Yes, she was. Much more beautiful than the other girls. Clean, they called her, and the few others who were born like her. A clean baby. A clean child. A clean woman. So few were ever born clean...

The Reverend's large hands peeled away her threadbare dress like a shift of rotten cheesecloth. She did not flinch. Being stripped at any given moment was nothing new to her; she was used to it, and she was used to the things that always happened afterward. Now her naked flesh shone starkly in the mirror's dark veins: sleek, womanly curves, unblemished skin, long legs and high, full breasts. Hair shiny and fine as black silk framed her youthful, striking face. Once she asked why the men from town paid so much less for her. "'Cos you're clean, child," she was told. "You ain't all uglied up like most the others. Cain't hardly even tell you're Creeker, 'cept fer yer eyes..."

She never understood this at all. They should pay more, shouldn't they, since she was so much prettier?

But tonight was different. Somehow she knew that. There were no men from town in the house, and something in the air made her skin feel all crawly like that time she fell asleep out near Croll's field and woke up covered with ladybugs.

"We've finally done it, after all this time—"

"—finally," whispered the Reverend.

And then the other voices continued to churn in her head:

*On-prey-bee! Us-come-too! On-prey-bee!*

When she'd been fully stripped, the Reverend's hand stroked her raven-black hair, brushing it off her brow. She gazed back at herself in the mirror...

Her eyes were bright and clear, their large irises revealing only the slightest tincture of red...

Next, she was being ushered...up. She felt dizzy and strange. The old wood stairs creaked beneath her feet as the Reverend's hands guided her toward the landing. The hands of the others reached out to touch her as she passed.

And the heat of this midsummer midnight drenched her in sweat in moments.

"Yes, you are the most perfect of all of us—"

—*so go forth now and bless us.*

The door closed behind her. All that lit the long, high room was the moon in the window. She smelled something funny, and as her vision grew accustomed to the dark, she noticed strange shapes inclined on the dusty wood-plank floor.

Then something stirred.

And the man walked out of the great gulf of darkness.

He was the most handsome man she'd ever seen. Tall and slender, with chiseled muscles, strong arms, sturdy legs. The kind face looked back at her.

He never said a word.

He was nothing like the men who usually came to her: men who slapped her, pulled her hair, spit on her and bit her nipples till she shrieked. This man was sweet, gentle. His soft hands on her breasts filled her with warmth, not revulsion.

And when he kissed her...

Visions swam. Sensations. Waves of love more intense than the heat of the noonday sun. His caring hands lay her down on the floor; his smile seemed lit, like a halo. Without ever talking, he told her things. He told her how beautiful she was, how important, and how he loved her more than he'd ever loved anyone. All the things she'd yearned to hear for so long: the dreams buried in dust, the promises that never came true.

But now they were true. Now...he was with her.

Her pleasures were untold. Her orgasms quaked. Each release of his semen into her sex was a gift to be revered. It filled her to overflowing—with rapture and compassion and real love. I'm in love, she thought with each beat of her heart, and with his. He delved into her far deeper than any man of her past, and far longer, unlocking sensations of joy she'd never thought possible. At one point, he knelt upright between her spraddled legs, the beautiful penis throbbing yet again for her. It was huge, curved, and gorgeous. In anguish, her hands reached out to touch the reality of its hardened flesh.

So hot, it nearly burned.

Her eyes pleaded to him. She was crying, she was so happy, so replete in her love. Without words, he assured her that he would love no other woman but her, ever.

You are the one, he vowed.

She grasped the stout, hot shaft, then guided it down to enter her again. Her breasts heaved; she gasped aloud, squealing her bliss to the night. Her arms and legs wrapped about the fine, hard body, and pulled him deeper into her.

*Give me your love*, her thoughts panted.

*Oh, yes*, his own thoughts answered. *I will...*

Hours later she lay exhausted in her own ecstasy. Her sweat drenched the warm wood floor beneath her, and his seed trickled from her. He'd rolled off her now, and gently kissed her throat and breasts. Then he moved away...

Her plea sounded powerless, feeble; she could barely speak at all. "Don't leave me!" she cried out.

He stood near the corner by the window. The sweat on his muscles shined in the moonlight—he looked silver.

He looked like an angel.

*Alas, my curse...*

Then she noticed the odd shapes again in the corner. What were they? Why were they there?

The door opened quickly. The others came into the room bearing candles, and the meld of voices rushed:

*On-prey-bee! Redeemer...*

Thanks we give you! Bless us...

The Reverend stepped forward in his coal-black robe and hood, then knelt before the naked man at the window.

*Bless us and sanctify us. Show us your way and keep us whole, we beg of Thee.*

Her eyes shined wide in the wavering candlelight as her lover very slowly turned. He seemed to have changed. His radiance— that lovely halo—had darkened to a sour hue, and the beatific muscles turned ruddy now, swollen and coarse. The handsome face shifted into corrupt angles, while deep, lumpen furrows grooved the high forehead.

*It can't be,* she thought. It must be the darkness. Of course, the darkness, her blissful fatigue, and the strange way the candlelight tinted the room.

*Give us this day our daily flesh...*

The others lifted her up. They were carrying her out of the room now, but not before she was able to finally detect the odd shapes in the corner.

They were—

*Bodies,* she realized. *Dead...bodies...*

*On-prey-bee!* rejoiced the twisted voices. *Give-ona-us-beg-thee-wee!*

Aloft in the others' arms, she stared, caught one last glimpse, then fainted dead away, for in the previous moment, her lover— once beautiful, now hideous—had knelt down before the fresh dead bodies and begun to eat.

# ONE

Lt. Philip Straker double-checked the cylinder of his Smith Model 65. Paranoid, Phil? he asked himself. What, the rounds are going to disappear? The good fairies going to take them when you're not looking? The stainless-steel cylinder shined, still full of six Remington .38s. It snapped shut with an oiled click. At least rank had its privileges; everyone else packed Glocks.

Phil was cooking in his Second Chance Kevlar vest, but a guy'd have to be crazy not to wear one on a narc bust. Red night-vision lights bathed the inside of the tac van—they called them "War Wagons"—one wall lined with commo and DF gear, the other with an array of weapons: AR-15's, a sniper rifle with a night-scope, MP-5's, and enough pistols to start a gun show. Two tac guys from S.O.D. waited with him: Eliot, one of the team leaders, and the "shooter," some ex-Marine with the unlikely name Cap, who sat stolid as a carved-wood figure, cradling a 15A2. Phil had heard this kid could pick cherries at 800 yards—a grim assurance tonight—because Phil realized full well there'd probably be some shooting. There always was during a lab bust. The bastards know they're caught, but they fight anyway. When you shoot at tac men, you die, and the fuckers don't even seem to care. It was like a VW Bug playing chicken with a D8 bulldozer. The Bug will always lose...

"Commo check, Bob," Phil instructed Eliot. "What's Dignazio doing all this time—"

"Probably spitting on his dick, sir," Cap, the kid-sniper, suggested. "Or consulting Mr. Johnny Black first."

"He keeps stalling, I'm gonna miss the Yankees game."

Eliot pulled a squad communications check. Dignazio's team was going in first, to block the exits they'd gotten off the building's blueprints. Then Phil would take his guys in the front and break bad. Dignazio had always ticked him. Probably stalling on purpose just to make me cook a little more in this vest, Phil thought.

Phil Straker, at thirty-five, would be up for captain next month; it went without saying that he'd make deputy chief by forty. He had three valor medals, plus a Distinguished Service, not to mention the half-dozen letters of commendation from the mayor. Hard work on a B.A. in Criminology had taken him out of the depressed, redneck burg he'd been born in and gotten him his dream job with a major metro police department. He'd taken it from there, grabbing his Masters at night, using his brain on the street, and moving up the ranks faster than almost anyone in the department's history. He'd busted his ass for the transfer to District Narcotics, and now he was calling the shots.

Phil hated dope.

Five years driving a beat in District 3 had shown him the truth. Movers and shakers who didn't give a shit about anything. Street gangs hiring fucking lawyers from the biggest firms in the country. Crack stools hung upside down and gutted like deer for spinning, and distro rings addicting six-year-olds to skag. Phil had never conceived of such evil in his life...

"Roger on the commo check, sir," Eliot announced from his perch in the red-lit van. "Sergeant Dignazio says five more minutes, then they ram the door."

"He's just busting our chops, sir," offered the kid.

"I know," Phil said. "It's because of me. The old bastard's had a hard-on for me since the day I met him. I guess I'd be a little ticked myself if it took me nineteen years to make sergeant."

"Word is, sir," Eliot jumped in, "Dignazio sees it he should've gotten your job."

Phil laughed, reholstering his piece. "Tell me something else I don't know, like gorillas are hairy."

He didn't care. If Dignazio deserved the promo to luey, he'd have gotten it. *I ain't crying for him, for Christ's sake, the busted hump. Maybe if he spent less time drinking and more time busting his ass, then I'd be taking the orders from him.*

"Green light," Eliot interrupted the thought, and dropped the headphones.

They burst out the van's back doors. "Technical Services has already cored the lock. We go in quiet and clean," Phil said, leading his men. "Watch your target acquisition and watch for crossfire. And for Christ's sake, watch for kids."

The U-Street Crew, like all the dope gangs, used kids for spotters and dealing because their testimony wasn't admissible, and they could not be tried as adults. A couple years in juvie and they were right back out on the street again. You had to be careful.

"What if some eleven-year-old points a piece at me?" Cap asked.

"You're an ex-Marine sniper, Cap, not a creamcake," Phil said. The question ruffled his feathers. "You scared of kids?"

"No, sir."

"Then you fire over their heads. Aim for hips and shoulders if you gotta, but don't be killing any kids while I'm running this team. Shit, Cap, you're wearing a titanium-plate vest that'll stop a seven-point-six-deuce, and you got one-mile kills in the Gulf War. Ain't no excuse for you to be dropping kids. You gotta problem with that, Cap?"

"No, sir."

"Good."

Then Eliot, charging his Heckler-Koch MP-5, said, "These U-Street assholes pack Uzis and MACs and all kinds of other shit. What about adults?"

Phil stared at him. "This is a PCP lab, Bob. These fuckers trash lives faster than Dignazio goes through pint bottles of Scotch. Either of you guys—any adult who even looks like he's gonna point a gun at you, redecorate the wall with his brains."

Cap nodded. Eliot said, "Gotcha, sir."

Then they slipped in through the door.

The stench of hydrocarbons kicked Phil in the face. The intelligence boys called this one right. Unless they got a license to manufacture ether in a closed warehouse, Phil thought. All the signs were here; this place was a lab.

And darker than all hell.

"Quiet," Phil whispered. He had his 65 at the ready. "And don't scuff your feet. We don't want to ring the doorbell, do we? And, Cap, keep that laser-sight down till we get into the shit."

It was almost too easy. Down the main corridor, then a left and a right, just like the intel blueprints read. At once, they were on a ten-foot catwalk overlooking the biggest PCP lab Phil had ever seen. About a dozen skells were hard at work below, beneath flanks of fluorescent lights. "Don't fire if they run," Phil whispered, "only if they start popping caps at us. Dignazio's crew is at all the exits."

Phil's two tac men nodded in silence, and acquired protected firing positions behind the roof and catwalk props. Time to grow some balls, Phil thought. He stood boldly in the middle of the cat, raised his megaphone, and calmly announced: "EVERYBODY FREEZE. MY NAME IS LT. PHILIP STRAKER OF THE METRO POLICE NARCOTICS SQUAD, AND IT TICKLES ME PINK TO INFORM YOU THAT YOU'RE ALL UNDER ARREST. I'VE GOT FIFTY TACTICAL POLICE OFFICERS SURROUNDING THIS BUILDING AND TWO GUYS JUST ITCHING TO KILL SOMEONE AT EVERY EXIT. PUT YOUR HANDS IN THE AIR AND STAND STILL. ANYONE WHO EVEN THINKS ABOUT MOVING LEAVES IN A BODY BAG." And then he thought, These guys must be getting soft in their old age. Each and every skell looked up, gaped, and raised their hands. Nobody moved. And not one gun was fired.

It was like a freeze-frame. I ain't gonna miss the Yankees after all, Phil thought. Several seconds later, the tac team moved in, covering the paddy boys. No one moved, and not one gun was grabbed for or even seen.

"Shit, sir," Eliot commented. "We'll be out of here in time to catch all ten dancers at Camelot."

"I think you're right, Bob. And I'm buyin'. Just give me a minute to find Dignazio. We'll let him do the paper, and we'll blow."

More labware than a college chemistry class, Phil observed after taking the stairs down and walking through the aisles. The paddy boys from District 6 were cuffing the skells so fast they'd honed it to an art form. Guess they're Yankees fans, too. Dignazio, sided by a pair of golems with MP-5's, stood back by the delivery concourse.

"Hey, Dig," Phil said, trying to be at least cordial. "Looks like we pulled this one off without a hitch."

"My guys pulled it off. All you did was take a walk and talk shit."

Phil smirked. Typical. "Fine, Dig. Look after the cleanup. Your guys check all the halls?"

"You ain't gotta tell me how to do my job, Straker." Dignazio glared, torqued-up, wiry, and with a face with more cracks in it than the original Mona Lisa. Then the sergeant walked off, taking his two gunners with him. Then:

*Chink!*

Phil jerked his head.

He strained his eyes down the concourse and thought he saw something flutter. A shadow? No...

A glint?

*What the hell is that?*

Not a dozen steps into the dark concourse, and Phil realized it wasn't what but who.

A small shadow seemed to whisk from one open doorway to another.

*A spotter,* he thought. *A kid.*

Phil slid his Kel-Lite from his belt, then began down the dusty, linoleum corridor. His light roved. Then—

"Jesus!"

The kid popped out of one of the storage rooms and sprinted toward the dead EXIT sign, his feet scuffing frantically.

TSD had already chained that exit from the outside.

"Come on, kid. You can't get out that way. Let's you and me have a talk, all right? I won't hassle you, I promise."

It was sad, the way these dope-gangs indoctrinated kids into their business. Of course they grow up to be criminals—it was the only thing they knew. And how old was this one? Ten? Twelve? Christ, Phil thought drearily. The kid hit the door, found it locked, then turned around, wide-eyed in his terror.

This kid looked about seven or eight.

"Don't worry, I won't hurt you," Phil assured. "But you're gonna have to come out here now so we can get you squared away."

The kid's face looked like a dark skull in Phil's Kel-Lite beam. Tears glistened on lean, dark cheeks. He's shit-scared, all right, Phil realized. The worst part was the district court'd just stick them in an orphanage, and nine times out of ten they'd just run back to the streets at the first opportunity.

"You're gonna have to come with me now," Phil said.

He never saw what was coming—he never even saw the gun. At once, the ever-familiar sound of a small-caliber pistol clapped his ears

*pap! pap! pap!*

The moment was mayhem. Fierce tiny lights blinked in his eyes; Phil only had time to let instinct haul him behind an empty refuse drum. His Kel-Lite rolled across the cement floor when another bullet pinged into the drum. Phil drew his service revolver.

"Goddamn it, kid! Are you nuts?"

Then he fired a shot high over the kid's head.

The kid stopped shooting.

*How could I have been so stupid? Too busy worrying about the goddamn Yankees.* A second later, two S.O.D. men were aiming lights down the corridor. "Don't shoot!" Phil hollered. "It's just a kid!"

Now more cops were trotting into the hall. "You all right, Lieutenant?" Eliot was asking, and helping him up.

"I'm fine," Phil replied. "But I'm not sure I can say the same for my shorts."

"What happened?"

"Just some shit-scared kid. I popped a cap over his head."

But Eliot was giving him a funky look, and then Phil thought he heard some guys down the hall calling for an EMT.

*No, no,* Phil thought, and sprinted down the hall himself. "I swear to God I fired over his head!"

More cops spilled into the hall, flashlights bobbing...

"Fired over his head, huh?" Dignazio was striding loudly behind. He glared at Phil. "That's a real piece of work right there, Straker. The deputy comm's gonna love this."

The words groaned in Phil's mind like an old house in the wind: *Good God Almighty...*

The kid lay at the foot of the chained exit doors, blood pumping from the bullet hole in his upper-right chest. He was dead before they could even get him on the stretcher ...

Phil peered into the memory. *Six months ago I was a metropolitan police lieutenant about to make captain, and now I'm a nightwatchman making minimum wage.* The death of the kid had been ruled a justifiable homicide by Internal Affairs, even though Phil swore up and down that he'd fired well over the kid's head. "Not high enough," the chief investigator had told him. But that wasn't why he'd resigned...

*Dignazio,* he thought.

*It had to have been Dignazio.*

The IAD chief investigator was an anal-retentive stoneface named Noyle. "Lieutenant, what kind of ammunition were you using in your service revolver on the night in question?" he asked.

"Thirty-eight plus P plus," Phil answered, taken slightly aback at the undue inquiry.

"Thirty-eight plus P plus. Hmm. And what type of service ammunition does the department authorize for sidearm use?"

"Nine-millimeter hardball, and thirty-eight—"

"Thirty-eight plus P plus?"

"Yes."

"And does the department authorize the use of any other type of service sidearm ammunition, Lieutenant?"

What the hell is he driving at? Phil pondered. Why this roundhouse of irrelevant questions? "Only for S.O.D. personnel," he replied, "but only when specifically authorized by Special Operations Division Deputy Commissioner."

"And are you an S.O.D. officer, Lieutenant?"

"No," Phil said. "I'm in Narcotics."

"And on the night in question were you for any reason authorized by the Special Operations Division Deputy Commissioner to use ammunition in your service revolver other than thirty-eight plus P plus?"

Phil was hard-pressed not to frown. "No."

Noyle leaned back in his chair, centered at the long conference table like a low-rent Caesar, with Cassius and Brutus to his left and right. His steely eyes never blinked. "Lieutenant, do you know what a quad is?"

Why's he asking me about quads! This was getting aggravating. "Yes," he answered, perhaps a little testily. "A quad is a special kind of bullet."

"And why is it 'special'?"

"Because it fires four cylindrical slugs instead of a solid, one-piece projectile."

"And what is the purpose of this?" Noyle asked.

"Increased stopping-power. On impact the slugs separate in the target and disperse. Quads, in other words, do a lot more damage than standard one-piece projectiles."

"A 'dum-dum' bullet, so to speak."

"Yes," Phil answered. "A factory-made dum-dum, I guess you could call it... But, sir, if you don't mind, what's the purpose of these questions? If you want to know about tactical ammunition, you'd be better off talking to the rangemaster or the S.O.D. armorer."

Noyle outright ignored Phil's query. "Lieutenant, do you know of any occasion when quads have been or would be authorized for use in this department?"

"No," Phil said.

"No, Lieutenant?"

A pause followed, then Noyle was whispering with his IAD counterparts. Phil took the opportunity to probe their faces. They all looked the same: similar suits, similar blank expressions. They looked like inquisitors, and Phil felt like a warlock on trial for heresy. What in God's name is going on here?

Noyle's rodent eyes returned to Phil's face. "Lieutenant, you've just admitted to myself and the other hearing officers that quads are unauthorized for use in this department."

"Right," Phil said. He was starting to feel itchy, hot.

"Then why were you using them?" Noyle asked.

The question fell on him, like a wall collapsing. His temper had begun to simmer. He wrung his hands in his lap.

"I was not using quads," he affirmed very slowly. If he didn't speak slowly, he'd get mad, and one thing he didn't want to do was pitch a fit in front of three IAD investigators. These three poker-faces were the department's ball-cutting crew. Instead, Phil took a breath, exhaled, and repeated, "I was not using quads. I've never loaded quads on duty or off. And if you want to know the truth, I'm getting really confused right now. I can't make any sense out of this line of questioning."

"Nor can we," Noyle inserted, "make any sense out of your testimony today, Lieutenant Straker. It seems to us that you're lying."

Phil leaned forward across the conference table. "Pardon me?"

"Lieutenant, isn't it proper protocol for an officer to be placed on administrative leave after a shooting?"

"Yeah," Phil answered, "just as I was placed on administrative leave after this shooting."

"And what else did you do? Isn't it also protocol for an officer to turn in his or her service weapon upon such an instance?"

"Yeah, to the next ranking officer on the site. I did this, too. Immediately. And if you think I was using quads on the night of the shooting, just check my service revolver. It's locked up in the property room. Open it and look in it, check the ammo."

Noyle cleared his throat—for formality, not because he needed to. "We did exactly that, Lieutenant, and we found one expended cartridge in the number one chamber. Chambers two through six were loaded with 38-caliber quads."

"That's bullshit!" Phil stood up and yelled.

"No, Lieutenant, it's evidence," Noyle informed him. "And so is the autopsy report filed by the district medical examiner."

"What the hell are you talking about?" Phil asked as though each word were a stone being expelled from his throat.

"That boy you shot?" Noyle paused a moment to adjust his tie. "According to the autopsy report, he was shot in the high chest area, just above the right lung. Upon impact, the projectile dispersed as, and I'll quote, 'four-point-three-eight-inch fragments, two of which exited the body from a high-right anterior position. A third fragment tumbled down the dorsal-side of the spinal column and lodged in the left calyx cavity of the left kidney. The fourth fragment penetrated the aorta.'" Noyle cleared his throat again, then looked back at Phil. "The Special Operations armorer positively identified the referred-to fragments as 'dispersed missile debris' from an unauthorized bullet known as a quad, Lieutenant. Records and Ident verified that the weapon which fired this bullet was your own. And the district medical examiner concluded that the victim's death can be directly attributed to the particular ammunition that was used. In other words, Lieutenant if you'd been using standard, department-authorized ammunition on the night in question, that eight-year-old boy would still be alive..."

Still be alive. Noyle's final words reverberated in Phil's head now, months after the fact. At first he'd tried to fight IAD's findings, but it didn't wash; Phil knew he'd somehow been framed by Dignazio, but how could he prove it? A week later, Phil was standing before the commissioner himself, and was told, "You've got two choices, Straker. You can stick with this ridiculous story about being framed, in which case the district attorney's office will charge you with negligence, premeditated use of dangerous and unauthorized ammunition, and at the very least, second-degree manslaughter."

"What's my other choice?" Phil grimly inquired.

"You can resign. The incident, of course, will go on your department record, but no charges will be brought against you. Use your head, son. Turn in your papers."

Which Phil did. The comm was right—there was no other choice for him. If he challenged the accusations, he'd be formally charged and prosecuted. And since he had no solid proof that Dignazio had framed him, he'd be found guilty. He'd get sentenced to a year at least, and if there was one thing he knew, cops rarely lasted a month in the joint.

So here I am, he thought now, standing in the middle of a textile factory at two in the morning. Blackballed. Washed up. No police department in the country would touch him, not with the bullshit in his metro personnel file. At age thirty-five, his blazing career in law enforcement was over, his degree useless, and over a decade of hard work had been reduced to nothing more than a small pile of ashes.

He almost laughed. *All right, so my cop career is over. Now I've got a new career as a security guard working midnight-to-eights and pulling in chump-change. It's better than being in the joint...*

The job itself required very little in the brain department; a well trained chimp could do it, he supposed. Security work was about the only thing he could think of that was relative to his education and interests, and Preventive Security, Inc. was the only company in the state which offered him a job despite his rep with the metro cops. The job was simple: he punched a Latham round-clock every hour in the factory. The rest of the time he sat in an office, drank diet Pepsi, and read novels. "It's a cinch," his new boss promised. "We haven't had a break-in at this place in twenty years."

Interesting work.

Then the perimeter alarm went off.

"So much for the boss's twenty-year record," Phil mumbled to himself. Probably an alarm malfunction. He checked the jack plate on the Sparrow/Jefferies alarm system. ZONE TWO, the light blinked. ENTRY BREACH.

I don't believe it! I've got someone busting into the place! He cut the office lights and screwed the red lens on his Kel-Lite. Then he grabbed his GOEC Mace—Preventive Security was an unarmed company, no gun permits—and slipped out into a secondary transport aisle. He kept his light low; he didn't want to scare anyone away, he wanted to catch them, if only to relieve the boredom. Walking through the dark factory, though, put him on edge. What if the intruders were armed? Just be careful, skillethead. Flanks of nameless machines led him around the production area. At the other end of the building (designated ZONE TWO) he could see the exit door ajar.

Someone's in here, all right, he realized. But who would want to break into a freakin' textile factory? What's to steal? Spools of thread?

Down the aisle and another turn, and his question was answered. How stupid can crooks be? he wondered. Someone had turned on the lights in the automat, and right this instant he could see a shadow leaning over one of the machines. A coinbox jockey, it seemed obvious to him. Why work a job when you can make a living busting into vending machines? On Metro, this would've been an easy collar, but Phil's new boss reflected some very serious sentiments for situations that actually involved a burglar. "Remember, Phil, you're not John Law anymore, you're just a guard. You see anyone actually break into that place, you call the county cops and get out. No playing hero. Christ, in this state if a guard injures a crook during a crime, the crook sues and wins. I don't need any lawsuits or liabilities." Phil saw the man's point, especially given the fact that he didn't have a gun or police powers any longer. But—that didn't mean he couldn't have a little fun...

"Freeze! Police!" Phil shouted. "Don't move or I shoot!"

"With what? A paper clip and rubber band?" the "intruder" replied and casually turned away from the vending machine. Then he smiled. "How's it goin', Phil? It's been a long time since I've seen Crick City's favorite son. I guess you're not too keen on keeping in touch."

Phil couldn't believe it. The man who faced him stood short and fat. The bald pate glimmered in the automat's buzzing fluorescent light, and his mustache was like a stout caterpillar on his lip. Those features, plus the tidy, starched municipal police uniform, were all Phil needed to recognize.

"Lawrence Mullins," Phil identified, "Chief of the Crick City Police Department. Would you mind telling me what in the hell you're doing here?"

"What's it look like? I'm getting a cup of coffee," Mullins said and raised the steaming Macke cup.

Phil closed his eyes and took a deep breath. Calm down, he commanded himself. Don't blow up.

Then, as was usually the case, he...blew up.

"You broke into my factory just to buy a goddamn cup of coffee!"

Mullins chuckled approvingly. "Still got that temper, I see.

Good, good. And, you know, you sure got some cheapie locks on this place. Shit, I had that door open in less time than it takes to use the key. Oh, and how about reholstering that 44-magnum can of Mace, huh? What, you get a lot of mean dogs around here?"

Phil sighed. "Please, Chief. Don't screw with me. I've had a bad day—or I should say, a bad year."

"So I've heard. Back in town, we all heard about that shooting when you were with Metro. But we can talk about that later. That was a smart move, resigning voluntarily instead of fighting them. You fight with any big city IAD, you lose your ass. Then you really would have been washed up. Shit, a former cop with convictions… You wouldn't have been able to get a job cleaning the greasehole at Chuck's Diner."

One thing Phil didn't need to be reminded of was the Metro frame. And another thing he didn't need was a load of wisecracks. "Chief, look, it's good to see you and all that, but are you going to tell me why you're here, or are you just trying to piss me off while you stand there sipping coffee?"

Mullins sipped more coffee, just barely smiling over the steam. "Oh, is that what you want to know? You want to know why I'm here?"

"Yeah, Chief, I do."

"Well, we're friends, right? From way on back? Shit, I practically raised you myself. And when I heard about the Metro thing, and you taking this pissant security job, well… I was a little concerned, that's all. I mean, it's not like you've seen fit to stop by your old hometown once in a while, you know, just to say hello to some of the folks you grew up with. But of course I guess you been too busy for the last ten years, what with the highfalutin' big city job with Metro. A narc lieutenant, ain't that what you were?"

Were, Phil slowly thought. Not am. Not anymore. "Chief, are you trying to make me feel guilty? All right, so I haven't kept in touch. Sorry. But you still haven't told me why you busted into my gig."

Mullins laughed. "Well, I wanted to see if you were keeping on your toes, now that you're not a cop anymore." The chubby man grinned at the open service door. "Pretty slick lock-picking, huh?"

"Chief!"

Mullins was getting a real kick out of this. "Okay, Phil, I'll level with you. The real reason I came all the way out to this bumfuck yarn factory is because, well… I want to talk to you."

Mullins' cat-and-mouse games got old fast; this was the first Phil had seen of him in nearly a decade, and he was already sick of him. Some guys never change, he dully realized. "Fine, you want to talk to me. About what? Please, Chief, tell me before I have a stroke."

Mullins finished his coffee and pitched the cup in the trash. Then he got a Milky Way out of the next machine.

Then he said, "I want to offer you a job on my department."

And that was about all Mullins had elaborated upon, which was pretty typical; Mullins' hedging sense of humor was part of his overall psychology—he'd always make his point by taking subtle shots. Phil had been born and raised in Crick City. His father had run off a week after he'd been born, and his mother died about a year later when the laundromat she'd been working in caught fire. So Phil was reared by an aunt, who received a subsidy from the state, and about the only thing he ever had that came close to a father-figure was Mullins, the chief of Crick City's police department for as long as anyone could remember. Mullins, now, had to be close to sixty, but to Phil he'd always looked the same, even back when Phil was in junior high and hanging out at the station after school.

Mullins was a decent man, or at least as decent as any shuck-and-jive backwoods police chief. Crick City, with a population of less than two thousand, wasn't exactly Los Angeles in its law-enforcement needs, and since nothing in the way of serious crime ever seemed to occur there, the town council never had any reason to appoint a new chief.

Phil had a confused regard for the man. As a kid, it was Mullins who always had an encouraging, if not gruff, word when Phil was down, and it was Mullins who kept him out of trouble. Mullins looked after Phil when no one else could, and it was Mullins, too, who had inspired Phil's interest in police work.

But on the other hand…

It was the town itself that always rubbed Phil the wrong way, and Chief Mullins was a constant reminder of that. Crick City was a backward, run-down pit of a town—a trap. No one ever seemed to get anywhere, and no one ever seemed to leave. It was the sticks: low-paying jobs, lots of unemployment, and the highest dropout rate in the state. Dilapidated pickup trucks ruled the pothole-ridden roads, at least those trucks that weren't propped up forever on blocks in the front yards of one seedy saltbox house after another. The only crimes that did seem to occur with regularity were drunk and disorderlies, and the hallmark: spousal abuse. In all, Crick City unfolded as an unchanging nexus. A nowhere land inhabited by nowhere people.

Phil didn't want to be one of those people.

But there was one thing he did want to be—

A cop.

And now here was Mullins, appearing like a decade-old ghost, and offering Phil the job that had been taken away from him by Dignazio and his blackball battalion.

Of course, police work in Crick City wouldn't be anything at all like his job on the narc squad. At Metro he had rank, he had respect and credibility, he had goals to pursue, and an important job that utilized every aspect of his education and fortitude. Going from Metro to the Crick City force was the same as going from a Lamborghini to a Yugo.

Quit complaining, he reminded himself. It's better than punching a clock at a yarn factory. At least he'd be engaged in a job he'd been trained at.

At least he'd be a cop again.

*Don't look a gift horse in the mouth*, he thought, *even when the horse is dressed in a chief's uniform.*

Mullins had left the factory shortly after he'd arrived, planting only enough seeds to keep Phil's brain working for the rest of his shift. "Stop by the station tomorrow afternoon," the rotund man had bid, "and we'll talk some more."

"I will, Chief. Thanks."

"Oh, and watch out for them burglars. You never know when the buggers might want to bust in here for some coffee."

"You're a laugh a minute, Chief. See you tomorrow."

And now, hours later, after he'd signed out of his guard post at the textile plant, Phil dogged through morning rush-hour in his clay-red '76 Malibu. He'd picked it up for $500 at Melvin Motors; now that he was no longer drawing lieutenant's pay, it was all his purse strings could handle. The early summer sun glared between tall buildings; the air reeked of exhaust. And as he made his way home, he couldn't stop thinking about Mullins' off-the-wall appearance at the plant, and the surprise job offer. What would it be like to go back there now? Crick City, he mused. Christ, even the name sounds redneck. Had the town changed? Was Chuck's Diner still owned by Chuck? Did the rubes still race their pickups on the Route every Saturday night after tying one on at Krazy Sallee's, the roadside strip joint? Was the coffee still terrible at the Qwik-Stop? Who's still there that I remember? he wondered. Then, more morosely:

Who's died since I've been gone?

Yes, the prospect of going back to his hometown goaded many questions. And…Vicki? What about Vicki? High school sweetheart, his very first girlfriend. She could've gotten out, too, but had chosen to work for Mullins instead, the department's only female cop.

I wonder if she's still around…

But then Phil's stomach turned queasy as he parked the Malibu in his littered apartment lot. Because there was one more question, wasn't there? Remembering the town and the people tricked him into remembering something else…

The voices, and—

The House, he thought.

There'd never been a name for it. Just…

The House.

Was the House still there?

Moreover, had it ever been there?

Just hours afterward, he'd gotten so sick. The doctor had said that a fever so severe often caused delirium and hallucinations. His aunt must've thought he was crazy, just a crazy little ten-year-old boy…

*Maybe I was crazy,* he reflected now, trudging up his apartment steps. *Christ Almighty. I hope I was crazy…*

Because, whether it had been hallucination or reality, it was one thing Phil Straker would never forget—

The House, he thought yet again.

And the hideous things he'd seen there.

# TWO

Cody Natter's shadow looked like a crane lowering as he leaned over the open trunk. So young, he thought. The girl, bound and gagged, shivered as the shadow crossed. Her lovely red eyes looked lidless in her sheer terror.

"What happened?" he asked.

"Upped and split right out the house last night," said Druck, whose right eye—which sunk lower than the left—had a way of ticking when he was excited about something. Druck was the only creeker Natter trusted to remain competent; and he could talk right. "Took us awhiles ta find her. Caught her runnin' 'long Taylor Road just 'fore the sun come up."

Pity. Natter couldn't take his own red eyes off of her. She was shivering, and she'd wet herself. Of course she's afraid, he considered. These are frightening days. Their stock grew worse and worse. Could they even last another generation before…

*Never mind*, he thought. *Faith…*

"You must be good," he whispered to her in a voice that sounded like old wood creaking. "You must trust your providence. Do you understand?"

Certainly the meanings of such words would elude her, but nevertheless she nodded, gasping through her gag.

There was more to understand than mere words.

Druck would expect to handle the usual punishment—hence, his obvious ticking enthusiasm. Sometimes the boy drooled.

"Untie her," Natter said.

"But ain't we gonna—"

"Untie her, and remove the gag."

Druck, dumbfounded, did as he was told. The girl heaved in her tattered clothes.

Cody Natter's long, bony hand touched her cheek. "Go now,"

he allowed. "And be good. Remember your providence."

Tears of gratitude ran down her warped face. She squealed something, some inner words of thanks, then climbed out of the trunk and scampered off into the woods.

Natter turned back to Druck, whose own warped face reflected his disappointment.

"Kill her later," the gaunt man whispered. "Kill her tonight. And be kind."

Druck smiled as a line of drool depended off his chin.

"I needs ta kill me somethin'," Scott said, and he said this with no particular emphasis or intensity—just an everyday, no-big-deal kind of comment. Scott "Scott-Boy" Tuckton rode shotgun today, slouched back on the big bench seat, Lotta ass been on this here bench seat, he mused for no reason. Lotta fine razzin'. Gut drove, Gut being the nickname for one Lowell Clydes, who was called Gut on account of a considerable girth about the waist. Both had cans of beer wedged at their crotches, while Bonnie Raitt sang away on the radio in that hot, cock-stiffening voice of hers.

"Yeah, Bonnie's tonsils shore make my dog hard," Scott-Boy commented, giving his groin a nonchalant rub. "Ain't that right, Gut, my man?"

"Uh, yeah," Gut replied.

Scott stroked his burns in the mid-afternoon sun. "And I say, it's a great day, ain't it? Yes, sir, a great day ta kill us somethin'."

"Uh, yeah."

"'Course, we'se'll probably have ta wait till tonight. Night time's always the best time fer killin'."

Scott liked to kill things. He liked to run down animals in the road. On several occasions he'd run down people. Once they'd plastered a little girl on one of them fancy 10-speeds, then dumped her in the woods up near Waynesville. Another night one of the retard kids from up on Prospect Hill was loping along the Old Dunwich Road just as pretty as you please. Scott had been driving that night, too, and he'd run the kid right smack dab down-Ka-BUMP! "Scott-Boy, why'd you wanna go and do a thang like that?" Gut had inquired.

"Fer the hail of it, I s'pose," Scott had replied.

Scott-Boy and Gut were what clinical psychiatrists would label as "affect stage sociopaths." They harbored no organic brain defects, nor were they subject to any mode of reactive or cerebro-chemical maladaptations. They were capable human beings who knew right from wrong, who had never been sexually abused, and who had never been locked in closets as children. Both were born of decent, hard-working parents and had been raised in an accept-able fashion. Their conduct could not be liberally excused by envi-ronment, abuses incurred during the formative years, or abnormal brain chemistry. Instead—and to put it more simply—they were two bad, evil, shit-kicking, redneck motherfuckers.

For instance, they didn't work. They were perfectly capable of working, they just didn't. "Money's walkin' all over!" Scott-Boy had once postulated. "Uh, yeah," Gut had agreed. Best thing about the south counties—most were unchartered, which meant they didn't have police departments. So they came down regular from Crick City (razzin' too close to home Scott likened to poopin' where they et); a thirty-minute drive up or down the Route easily carried them to any number of remote townships where they enjoyed complete anonymity. Everyone drove big pickups this part of the state, and everyone wore the same duds: boots, straightleg jeans, and jean jackets over T-shirts. Redneck fashion was also great camouflage.

Their lives were happily without direction; Scott-Boy Tuckton and Gut lived week to week in pursuit of their joys. But such pur-suits, regardless of their nature, generally required some mode of finance. Beer cost money, after all. So did truck payments, trailer rent, and insurance. Bar whores were the easiest pickings. The south counties had more roadside watering holes than you could shake a busted camshaft at, and each and every one of the joints had at least one parking lot head queen to take care of a fella's business. Wait till about one a.m. any Friday night, entice one of these fine young ladies into the truck with the typical promise of cash for services rendered, let her do her thing first, of course, then crack her upside the head with the brass knucks. What you were generally left with for your troubles was a purse chock full of tens and twenties. An even better gig was the fellas. Any Friday night (Friday nights were best 'cos the first thing these peabrains did before heading to the bars was cash their paychecks) just hide yourself in the woods behind the bar or poolhall, wait for some homeboy to stumble shitfaced into the parking lot, then crack him a good one upside the head with the brass knucks. Drag him back into the woods, tie him, gag him, then pluck the wallet, which was almost sure to contain half of the dupe's cashed paycheck. A few minutes later the next sucker drags ass out, then you repeat the process. Scott and Gut could commonly take out six or eight guys like this at the same parking lot, in like, about the space of an hour.

Lately, on the side, they made even better money running angel dust for a couple of local dope dealers. Not exactly a job, but it was something. They didn't use the stuff; they just helped sell it a few nights a month. A thousand dollars a drop, not what you'd call chicken feed. So between that and ripping folks off, Scott-Boy and Gut did all right, yesiree.

Once the money was had, their joys remained. "Razzin'," Scott-Boy liked to call it. "What say let's razz up some splittails tonight, ya reckon," he'd suggest. Hitchhikers provided prime razzin'. Lordy Jeez, in this day and age you'd think gals'd be a tad smarter than to get into a vehicle with a perfect stranger. Just the same, if you cruised around long enough, there she'd be, skippin' along some road darker than the devil's buttcrack. She'd be pretty more times than not, and she'd always be alone. And Gut would just pull the pickup right on over. Scott-Boy always did the talkin', in his laid back, farm boy sort of way. "Hey there, purdy lady, where you headed this fine night? Well ain't that just plumb dandy, see, 'cos it just so happens me and my buddy here, we'se headed fer the 'zact same place. Just slide right on in, and we'll git ya where you're goin' safe an' sound."

Safe an' sound, indeed.

Scott-Boy and Gut knew every dell, grove, hillock, and backwood hideyhole anywhere they might happen to be at any given time.

All's it took was one turnoff, and the unsuspecting gal realized that something wasn't right, but of course by the time this realization had been made, it was already too late. Way too late. Way on back deep in the woods, no one could hear them scream, and scream they did—like holy everlivin' heck. Diversity proved requisite to any venture of uniqueness, and Scott "Scott-Boy" Tuckton was a very diverse young man. He liked to hear them scream, and his powers of imagination spared no possibility through which they might do so. Ol' Scott-Boy, yeah, he had himself a headful of visions that would make Ivan the Terrible look like fuckin' Bambi.

Gut supposed they'd killed at least a dozen people. They'd never really set out to, it just happened once by accident. One night they'd been jacking drunks as usual, and Scott-Boy had cracked one poor fucker a tad too hard upside the head with the brass knucks. Exit muggers, enter killers. The poor fucker's head had split, showing pink brains. "Well, hail, would ya look what I just up and done?" Scott-Boy remarked with dull fascination. Like they say, accidents will happen. But for Scott, murder was like potato chips; ya couldn't eat just one. That same night, Scott had sliced open a bar whore's throat after she'd fellated him in the truck. "Jesus ta Pete, Scott-Boy!" Gut exclaimed. "What you go and do that fer?" "Dunno," Scott chuckled his remorse. "Dag good thang we got the vinyl pole-stree." He scratched his head. "Gals shore do got theirselfs a lotta blood in 'em, huh?"

Gut pretty much just helped out or watched. It was Scott who was the virtuoso. He had a thing for slowly stranglin' gals during coitus, fashioning a tourniquet around their necks with sisal twine and a dowel rod. He had also buggered, then beaten to death, a hippie boy he'd first thought was a hippie girl; he'd carved up a yuppie couple he'd found camping in the woods; and then there was that redheaded hitchhiker who must have been at least eight months and twenty-nine days pregnant...

But, never mind what they did to her.

# THREE

Home, sweet home, Phil thought as mordantly as he could. Was it shame? How would it look? Christ, a Master's degree and over ten years on a major metropolitan department, and now I'm coming right back to where I started, back to good old Crick City, the moron mecca of the world.

A few minutes after exiting the interstate, the road funneled down, plummeting with his spirits. This was State Route 154, known to locals simply as "The Route," a winding 30-mile patch-job of asphalt that cut a swath through south county's rolling hills and forest belts. It also cut a swatch through some of the poorest and least developed townships in the state: Luntville, Tylersville, Waynesville, and Crick City. Soon the massive scape of the metropolis faded behind him, only to be replaced by bridged ravines, famished tracks of farmland, trailer parks, and one rundown shack after another. The pits, Phil reflected. Waynesville, Luntville, Crick City—it didn't matter what these towns were called; to him, they were all the same. Bustedville. Even the woods looked destitute—sickly vegetation and ancient garbage clotted between dense masses of trees, some scrawny and skeletally thin, others stout as sewer pipes and hundreds of feet high. Rampant fungus shined like green-white snot over diseased and grossly knotted tree trunks. Most of the road signs could no longer be read thanks to the pockmarks of midnight shotguns; shattered glass littered the shoulders like halite, along with the innumerable carcasses of small animals—"Road Pizza" in police parlance. "Possum Pie"— which were forever being run down by motorists to be scavenged of course by still more small animals, which were then promptly run down by still more motorists. Cyclic carnage.

The easterly ridge loomed to Phil's right, a great wall that seemed to keep the entire Route in perpetual darkness. He passed one town called Lockwood where, several years ago, most of the tiny population had disappeared seemingly overnight, and another, Prospect Hill, where dozens of residents had died or gone blind all on the same weekend from bad hootch. Yes, hootch, moonshine, panther piss—some of these communities made the stuff like it was the Prohibition era, from stills back in the woods. Phil had tried it once, and one sip had about knocked him on his ass.

Abrupt turnoffs periodically marked the Route, roads with absurdly redneck names. Turkey Neck Road, Furnace Branch Road, Old Mill Road—there was even a Tick Neck Road, and as far as Phil knew, ticks didn't even have necks. Ah, sophistication, he thought. A used car dealer's called Lucky Lee's, Fast Eddie's Pool Hall, and a roadside diner that seriously sported a sign: GOOD EATS.

In between the towns, Phil knew, were even more remote communities—actually sub-communities—that existed in complete obscurity, loosely knit hamlets known as "hill towns," where the populace remained unknown to public record. "Hill folk," they were called, and "hill squatters." There were more conventional names, too.

White trash. Crackers. Uncensored settlements of the catastrophically poor. People who lived off the land and had never had a real job, never been to the doctor's, had never owned a television. Children who'd never been to school. The Third World of America the Beautiful. They lived in lean-tos, tarpaper shacks, and abandoned trailers with no running water and no electricity. A cliché to the average person, but all too real in these parts. But Phil knew that all states had their rural poor, and all states had their hillfolk, tiny flecks of humanity swept aside by the world. For cash they sold scrap metal and moonshine; for food they took to the woods. It was hard to believe that in a society of computer chips, banana chips, and anti-lock brakes, of sitcoms, Home Shopping Clubs, and pay-per-view, and of surround-sound stereos and microwave ovens—it was hard to believe that such destitution could exist at all, much less under the very nose of the same society...

He'd see them all the time as a kid, picking through garbage bags dumped in the woods, or wandering down the Route in rag-patch clothes and homemade fishing rods slung over their shoulders. Sometimes the children, filthy and smudge-faced, would beg for pocket change in front of the Qwik-Stops and general stores, until the proprietors ran them off. Yes, he'd seen them many times.

And maybe that explained Phil's unease about returning to Crick City. The hand of fate often dealt from a bad deck. How close had Phil come himself to being one of these people?

Christ, he thought.

The Malibu's corroded ball-joints shimmied through the next long, winding turn. To his right, up on the hill, stood the Fletcher place, a bedraggled old antebellum house that was leaning with its own weight. There were holes in the roof, but the Fletchers still lived there—they refused to move. And to Phil's left sat a trailer on blocks at the edge of Hockley's pond; it had been there for as long as he could remember, and during heavy rains the creeks would fill and the water would rise up past the trailer's floor. Yet the inhabitants never moved.

*I moved*, Phil pondered. *I moved out of here over a decade ago...and look where I am now.*

Past the next bend, the sign appeared:

## CRICK CITY TOWN LIMITS

There was no main drag per se; the Route blew right through Crick City like a spit through a kabob. Decrepit houses passed sporadically, as if shoved into the woods. A small trailer park here, Hull's General Store there. Every so often the woods receded, opening up into tracks of hilly, unkempt farmland, some with great barns off in the distance so rotted you could see through them and vermiculated wooden crosses on which scarecrows had once been crucified until they, like the barns, had eroded away. Phil swerved twice to avoid waddling possums at the centerline; a third possum had not been so lucky, already crushed by a previous car to a plop of meat. A crow lifted off as the Malibu swooshed past, carrying with it a string of entrails a yard long. Phil grimaced as the pink ribbon sailed away.

Didn't the Romans or someone read the future in animal guts? It was an absurd circumspection but one that fit with the image. What did the future hold for him? How could his future be a productive one, now that he was coming back here? My fortune told in possum guts...

Past the next plot of farmland, a rising plane of disheveled corn, he spied Krazy Sallee's, the town strip joint. The bulb-bordered sign promised GO-GO GIRLS AND BEER TO GO! Even this early, several pickups spotted the great gravel lot. A mile past was Bouton's Farm Supply, and another mile Crick City's sumptuous four-star hallmark of cuisine, Chuck's Diner. They didn't have terrine of duck foie gras or roasted quail with porcini mushrooms, but the hash wasn't bad. Several stragglers walked along the shoulder as Phil drove on, a couple of rednecks in overalls, and the infamous Armless Man, whom Phil remembered from early childhood. Every day the guy would walk from the Crownsville trailer park to Snoot's Liquors, pick up a bottle of Bushmills, and walk back. Every day, like clockwork. And it was a good five-mile clip each way. The guy must be a hundred by now, Phil thought, amazed. Some things never change.

And around yet another bend...

A third pedestrian ambled down the shoulder. Hillfolk, Phil deduced the instant he got a good look. The boy, in his late teens, looked tall and lanky, and he seemed to walk at an awkward pace like someone with a trick knee. Long black hair hung in greasy strings, and from afar the kid's face more resembled a smudge of dirt. *I hope this hill kid's on his way to the store for some soap.* And his clothes offered another vestige: they clung to his body like fetid rags, patched up with oilcloths, old towels, pieces of other garments. Yeah, he's hill folk, all right, Phil felt certain, until—

Phil shuddered.

—until he'd approached close enough to recognize the giveaway details.

*Christ, his face...*

One half of the kid's face swelled forward, the other half seemed collapsed. A bent nose showed one nostril tiny as a pegboard hole while the other nostril seemed flared out to the diameter of a quarter. And the ridge of the forehead was totally bereft of eyebrows.

And the eyes—

*A Creeker...*

—showed maroon irises.

That's what they called them around here. Creek people. Creekers. The utmost extremity of the hill dwellers. Though often talked about, they were seldom actually seen. (Phil had only seen them himself a handful of times in all the years he'd lived out here.) The creek people were inbred over multiple generations, to the extent that nearly all of them displayed drastic physical deformities. Malformed heads and faces. Arms and legs all different lengths. One eye larger than the other. Phil had heard some were born with no eyes at all, and no mouths. To intensify the tragedy, mental defects were just as apparent. Some Creekers couldn't speak at all, and many of those that could were only able to mumble globs of words that made no sense. Like the hill folk, Creekers were the secret of any backwoods town—unacknowledged, as if they didn't even exist.

"Well, there he is. I was beginning to think you were gonna stiff me," Chief Mullins said from behind his huge, cluttered desk. Phil was taken aback; the Crick City Police Station seemed much smaller than he remembered it, compressed and stuffy. Through the back window he could see the tiny jailhouse, and parked next to it was Mullins' Pontiac Bonneville fitted with a siren horn and red and blue lights. Hunting trophies lined the top of the chief's banks of beaten file cabinets, along with his framed certificate of appointment as the town's head law enforcement officer. The certificate, once bright white, had yellowed from the countless years it had been propped there.

"You gonna sit down, or you got poop in your pants?"

"Actually, Chief, I've got poop in my pants, but I'll sit down anyway." Phil pulled up a metal folding chair, then quickly declined Mullins' offer of coffee, remembering that it generally tasted like caffeinated turpentine.

*I can't believe I'm sitting here*, he thought.

Mullins' corpulent face and balding head shined in the sunlight. He sipped his coffee and sighed. "Bet'cha never thought in a million years you'd ever be working for me."

"Look, Chief, you said you wanted to talk, and I'm here to listen. I haven't taken the job yet."

"'Course you'll take the job. Once a cop, always a cop. Shit, you'd rather spend the rest of your life guarding piles of fabric?"

Good point, Phil admitted.

"Besides," Mullins added, "I need ya."

"All right, so what's the scoop?"

"The scoop is I ain't got no cops, and though Crick City ain't exactly big, I ain't a one-man police force."

Mullins, as Phil remembered, always had two or three officers working for him. Phil struggled to recall their names. "North and Adams, they've been with you for years. What happened to them?"

"What happened?" Mullins chuckled in despair. "The fuckers quit, that's what happened. They turned in their notice and walked, got better paying jobs with other departments. North's driving a sector beat in Fairfax, and Adams got snagged by Montgomery County."

"They were good men, Chief. You should've given them more money."

"Yeah, and the mayor should be fucking Santa Claus. There was nothin' I could do. I can't offer the money and bennies of a county department. All I could do was watch and wave bye-bye."

*Hmmm,* Phil thought. *North and Adams left for better departments. But I wonder what happened to—*

"What about Vicki?" Phil asked.

"I figured that'd be your next question. Well, she left too, years ago. You'd be more informed about things if you'd keep in touch."

"Hey, I sent you a Christmas card, didn't I?"

"Yeah, back when Reagan was in office." Mullins scratched his chin. "Or was it Carter?"

"Funny, Chief. I'm laughing hard, see? Now what were you saying about Vicki?"

"I wasn't saying nothin'. You were asking... Still got a torch burning for the old sweetheart, huh? Still got the hots for that red-haired little cutie-pie..."

Phil frowned, but he couldn't help but think back. He and Vicki Steele had dated from high school through college—his first love...well, his only love in reality. *Guess I didn't love her enough, though,* he considered now. When they'd gotten their degrees, they'd had the most awful fights. Phil had been hired at once by Metro. She didn't want to leave. He did.

He left. She didn't.

End of story.

"But," Mullins rambled on, "there's one thing I never understood. How come you dumped her?"

Phil frowned again. He had a feeling he'd be frowning a lot if he did indeed take this job. "I didn't dump her. Things didn't work out so we broke up, and are you going to tell me what happened to her, or are you gonna jerk my chain for the rest of the afternoon?"

"She quit, just like the others. Walked right out on me."

"What department picked her up?"

"I never said she quit to go to another department," Mullins took the opportunity to be cryptic. "She's still around, though. I'm sure you'll run into her sooner or later, so put it back in your pants and let's get down to brass tacks. It just so happens that those turn-coats North and Adams boogied on me right in the middle of a crisis..."

But Phil's attention phased out; he was still musing upon Vicki. Christ... Where was she working now? Where did she live? Did she still look the same? And when—

*When was the last time she thought about me?* he dared to wonder. *Grow up!* he ordered himself. *She probably doesn't even remember who you are anymore, you smug, pompous ass...*

"What's that you were saying?" he finally got back to reality. "A crisis?"

"That's right, I got big problems here all of a sudden, and if I don't fix it, the town council might give me the boot."

Phil couldn't imagine any kind of genuine "crisis" out here, much less one severe enough to depose Mullins' seemingly end-less reign. The guy had been chief here longer than Caesar had ruled Rome. "What," Phil jested, "You got stoners ripping off park-ing meters from the town square?"

Mullins didn't laugh, or even smile. It was hard times when this man got serious. "No, smart boy. You remember Cody Natter, the Creeker?"

"I remember Cody Natter, vaguely." Rumor had it that Natter was sort of the governor of the Creekers, the tribemaster.

"Well, the ugly fuck and his Creeker cronies are givin' me problems like to make me shit my pants."

Phil, if only indistinctly, remembered the tall, gangly, and incredibly ugly Cody Natter. Yeah, ugly as all hell but smart as a whip. The guy, it was claimed, was either psychic or could count cards, since he'd cleaned out many an illicit poker game in the back of Sallee's after hours, and he had this subtly twisted smile that, the few times he'd seen him, sent shivers up Phil's back. His own childhood's version of Hannibal at the Gate; Phil's aunt always told him, "If you don't go to sleep, Cody Natter'll be stopping by for a visit tonight." The guy always drove a souped, rebuilt '69 Chrysler Imperial, dark-red, and was always blowing money all over town, though no one knew how he earned it. And he was ugly, sure, the ugliest Creeker of the clan.

"Oh, so it's Cody Natter who's ripping off the parking meters from the town square. Sounds like a crisis to me."

"I thought Sam Kinison was dead, funny man," Mullins responded. "Take my word for it, Cody Natter and his Creekers are a pain in my ass."

"But the Creekers always pretty much kept to themselves," Phil said. "At least that's what I remember."

"Yeah, well, they're all over the friggin' place now. Shit, he's even got the less-fucked-up-lookin' ones working around town."

"Christ, Chief, I lived in Crick City twenty years, and I don't think I saw more than a dozen Creekers in all that time." But then Phil paused, reflecting. I just saw one ten minutes ago, didn't I? Walking down the Route? The image remained: the swollen head, the uneven arms and legs, and—

—*The red eyes*, he remembered.

"I don't care what you seen when you were a punk," Mullins articulated. "Things have changed in ten years. Natter's trying to take over the town, and the ugly motherfucker's doing a great job since I ain't got no cops on my department."

Phil still couldn't quite believe this. The Creekers had always been harmless, and so seldom seen that most people didn't even believe they existed. This sounded like bullshit to him; he stood his ground. "Okay, Chief. How's Cody Natter taking over the town? Tell me that, will you?"

Mullins' fat face turned dark, and his little eyes narrowed in puffy slits.

"He's dealing drugs now," he said. "Right here in town. Right now."

"Drugs, huh?" Phil jeered. "Cody Natter? In Crick City? So what kind of drugs is he dealing? Laughing gas out of empty whipped cream cans?"

"No, funny man," Mullins said. "He's dealing PCP."

# FOUR

When darkness fell, Scott and Gut's spirits rose. Well, at least Scott-Boy's did. All of a sudden, Gut wasn't feelin' too good...

A little later, they had a big dust drop to make; they'd be making a big pick up of product—in this case, pure, distilled PCP to later be turned into "flake"—and drop it off at one of the primary points just out past Lockwood. It would be their biggest run yet and, hence, their biggest payoff.

Gut ordinarily would've been pretty keyed-up at the prospect of making such a fine grab of money for so little effort. But...

He drove the big pickup with authority, down the Route and out of town. It was feigned authority, actually, though he tried hard not to show it. Somethin' bad in the air tonight, his thoughts swayed. And he felt sure it didn't have anything to do with their dope run later.

They weren't due to make the pickup for another couple of hours; they had time to kill, in other words, and Gut knew too well how Scott liked to kill time.

"Hey, Scott-Boy? What say we do somethin' different tonight 'fore we make the pick up."

Scott Tuckton was lounged-back in the big bench seat, swigging his can of Red, White & Blue. It was a warm, balmy night, and everything was perfect. A high, bright moon. Cold beer. Crickets makin' a ruckus. Warm air rushed in through the open windows while Elvis crooned "Blue Moon" on the radio.

A perfect night, in other words, for killing.

"What'choo mean different?" Scott-Boy inquired, stroking his sideburns. "We'se goin' on a razz first, ain't we?"

"Uh—" Gut replied. He steered through the Route's next bend. "How 'bout we go to Sallee's instead? Gander us some knockers and tail."

"Sheeeeee-it," Scott came back. "Why's look at it—at a tittie bar—when we'se can have it fer real in our face?"

"All rights, then how 'bout we go there and buy us some whores? They gots whores at Sallee's. Or maybe stop by Crossroads fer some. We'se can afford it, 'specially with the green we'se be makin' later after the drop. We'se can afford a bunch of girls."

Scott-Boy gaped. "Sheeeeee-it," he repeated with typical verbal eloquence. "Bein' able ta afford it ain't the point, Gutter. We'se razzers, man. We never pay fer it. We'se gonna have a nut tonight, fer sure, and if you wants ta razz some bar whores 'fore the run, well, that's just dandy. We'll pick 'em up, lay some peter on 'em, then bust 'em up and take their green likes we always do. I don't know abouts you, but I needs ta get my dog in some bush in a big way, but they'll be sellin' snowcones in Satan's place before I pay fer it.' Fact, I could go fer some serious razzin' too, like ta crack me up some bitch's head with my hickory pick handle, or maybe like that time out near Nalesville.' Member that, Gut? When we snagged us that pixie with that real purdy long dark hair hangin' all the way down past her ass?"

Gut remembered that one, all right. They'd been killin' time before a run that night too, and there was this hot brunette they picked up thumbing it down the Old Governor's Bridge Road. Gut wanked hisself off in her face while Scott-Boy pooped her dog style in the dirt and took a whizz up her tail after he blew his nut. She had a right purdy body on her though, but she weren't purdy fer long. See, she had real long hair on her too, just like Scott said, long straight dark hair hangin' to her ass, so's they tied her hair to the trailer hitch on the back bumper of the truck and then lead-footed it down St. Stephen's Church Road at about a hunnert miles an hour. Weren't much left of her time they was done. 'Course, that didn't stop Scott-Boy from havin' another roll-around with her 'fore they dumped her off at the big stinky Millersville landfill...

Razzin' could be had just about anywheres that had hitch-hikin' gals and bar whores and the like. But Gut and Scott-Boy never razzed in Crick City, their home town, on account of Crick City, unlike most of the burgs along the Route, had theirselfs their own police department and a ball-breaker chief the likes of which Gut and Scott preferred not to fuck with. Plus they didn't want ta bust up no whores at Krazy Sallee's 'cos Krazy Sallee's, they'd heard, was owned by some big ugly fella named Natter. Now,

Gut had never hisself seen this dude Natter, but the word was he weren't no one ta fuck with eithers.

But that were not the problem Gut was a'contemplatin' as he drove the big pickup onward. There was many, and one were the critters. Gut hisself wanked at least once a day, an' several times durin' a fine razz. It wasn't that Gut preferred the feel of his own hand to the feel of girly works—he just didn't want to catch no critters an' such, what with the crabs that were now as big as the crabs the watermen hauled out the bay, and the penicillin-resistant gonorrhea, and this new syph they was talkin' 'bout that'd put a pusser knot the size of a walnut on a fella's knob, and a'corse the AIDS. It seemed a prudent concern in these times, but Scott-Boy didn't seem ta give a tiddly. "Aw, all this AIDS ballyhoo, a bunch of hype, it is. Everbody knows ya only catch it if yer a queerboy or a drugshooter. 'Fact, I was just readin' 'bout it the other day in The Enquirer, says the Army invented AIDS to take care of the fudge-packers and druggies 'cos they'se don't gen'rally amount ta nothin' noways, or work jobs or pay taxes an' contribit ta society."

"But, Scott-Boy," Gut interjected, "just 'cos we'se ain't queer-boys or drug-shooters don't mean we couldn't get it from some gal who's been with one. Lots of these by-sexshools runnin' about these days."

"Aw, Gut, that's just a load of the horseflop," Scott came right back. "Sorry day when a natural man can git a killer bug just by makin' proper love ta a woman."

Sometimes Scott-Boy could be the shit-stupidest fella to ever walk, but Gut kept quiet. Gut hisself was shore no model of moral-ity or Christian goodwill. He'd cut a fella's throat for a tenspot any-day. He'd crack a splittail upside the head and wank on her milkers without a second's reservation. And drivin' for flake dealers weren't no problem with him either; if they didn't move the shit, someone else would. But he did possess one sensibility that Scott "Scott-Boy" Tuckton didn't, and that was somethin' called common sense.

Scott-Boy didn't give a pig's wink about much of anything. It was like he thought he was invincible. He didn't care about the herpes or the AIDS. He didn't care that someday someone might see 'em on a razz and tell the cops, nor were he afraid that someday the cops might nab 'em on a dust run. And he didn't seem to give an outhouse grunt that if they kept going like they been going, somethin' even worse might befall 'em...

Sooner or later we'se gonna pick the wrong folks ta razz, Gut thought fairly grimly.

It could happen, shore. One night they might be jacking a drunk with the brass knucks, and the fella might pull a knife, or next time they set to razzin' a bar whore, well, what's ta keep her from shucking one of them Saturday Night Specials from a purse and pumping him and Scott-Boy up with .25s? Gut shore didn't want to do life up in the state slam, no sir, not where a fella couldn't even take a shower without a bunch of bigger fellas givin' it to him up the tail or making him get down and do the mouthjob on five or ten guys. Likewise, Gut shore didn't want to wind up screamin' like a stuck pig in some parking lot some night with a belly full of Stingers or hollowpoints. Just one mistake and that could be the end of some fine times indeed...

And it was just then, just that very minute whiles he was steerin' the big pickup down the Old Dunwich Road that Gut's ponderins socked home, and all of a sudden he had this really low, sicklike feeling way down deep in his breadbasket, and this was either ironic or terribly portentous considering what was about to happen to the both of them.


Phil's boss at the security job cut him loose without demanding any notice, which was quite considerate; Phil had guarded enough fabric shanks and spools of yarn. He spent the rest of the evening unpacking his things in his new room at Old Lady Crane's boardinghouse. Moving hadn't been too much of a hassle; he'd rented a U-Haul trailer for his furniture, and stuffed everything else into boxes. Then he was on the road, out of the bustling metropolis he'd lived in for the last decade.

And back to Crick City.

The room was no Buckingham Palace, but it would do for now. The rest of his conversation with Mullins earlier in the day had been pretty cut-and-dry, mostly tying up loose ends:

"Cody Natter's dealing PCP?" he asked in disbelief. "Here in Crick City?"

"That's right," Mullins said. "And that's why I need you, 'cos you got experience. Besides, I ain't got no one else."

This comment didn't exactly make Phil feel like Cop of the Year, but he could see Mullins' point. "So what about my rep with Metro?" he asked.

"You resigned, you were never charged. I don't give a shit what's on your record there. Just don't pop any more kids with quads."

"Wait a minute, Chief," Phil felt obliged. "Let's get one thing clear: I never shot anyone with quads or any other illegal ammo. It was a frame. Some guy named Dignazio set me up because he wanted my job. Hell, the only caps I popped were over the kid's head. It was Dignazio who shot the kid with quads, then he made it look like it was me."

"Yeah, right," Mullins rushed. "Whatever."

"You don't believe me, do you?"

"'Course I believe ya," the chief said, smiling. "And even if you did it, I don't care. What, I'm supposed to give a rat's ass that you snuffed some pissant ghetto kid who was spotting for a PCP lab? You ask me, they should've given you a medal. Only thing I know is I got Cody Natter pushing the same shit in my town, and if I don't take care of it, you and me'll both be punching the night clock at the bedsheet factory. So do you want the job or not?"

"Yes," Phil said without even thinking. But he didn't really even need to think. The peanuts pay here was still more than he made as a guard, and at least he'd be a cop again.

But it wasn't so much the job as the issue. Phil had a big problem with drugs. In the city, he'd seen what the stuff did to people, to their bodies, their minds, their whole lives. It was the most integral evil he'd ever imagined. They sold the shit to 6-year-olds on the playground, for God's sake. The younger they got them hooked, the better, then they'd have the kids robbing liquor stores or turning tricks on the street. It was an industry that perpetuated slavery, and the goddamn courts seemed more concerned with the rights of the dealers than the innocent lives they destroyed. Crack, heroin, PCP—take your pick. They were all different but all the same, all part of the same machine that preyed on people's weaknesses and used them up until there was nothing left. PCP in particular. They cut the shit with industrial solvents to make it cheaper; each drag caused brain damage, made you crazy. Phil thought if he could ever do anything useful in his life, it would be sending these evil motherfuckers to the joint for life. And here was Mullins, offering him another chance...

"Yeah," Phil repeated. "I'll take the job. When do you want me to start?"

"Right now," Mullins said, pouring more rank coffee into his NRA mug.

"Chief, I can't just walk off my security job. I gotta give my boss some notice."

"Fuck him. I'm your boss now. Tell him to hire some other monkey for that no-dick job. I need you here more than he needs you guarding yarn."

"All right, but my apartment's over forty miles away. You have to give me some time to find a closer place to live."

"I already found you a place. Old Lady Crane, you remember her? The old bag's still got that hole-in-the-wall boardinghouse out off the Route, and she's holding a room for you. Thirty-five clams a week—you think you can swing that, Daddy Warbucks? And I already paid your first month's rent. So quit jacking your jaws and get out of here. Go load up that piece of shit you got for a car and get moved in tonight. I'm putting you on eight-to-eights, the night shift, and I'll even pay you overtime for anything over forty until I can get a couple more men hired on."

Phil felt winded. "Chief, we're moving way too fast, aren't we? First off, I need clearance from the state training academy, don't I?"

"You're already cleared through Metro."

"And I need uniforms, I need a piece, I need—"

Mullins pointed to the corner. "See that big box sitting there? Those are your uniforms. And see that little box sitting on top of it? That's your service revolver." Mullins got something out of his desk drawer. "And see this teensy weensy box right here?"

Phil took the little box from Mullins' fingers, opened it, and removed its contents:

A brand-new Bianchi police badge.

"There's your fuckin' tin," Mullins finished. "You're a big bad policeman again. We'll send in your new print cards to the state tomorrow. Only other thing I need from you is a passport photo for your department ID, and you're all set."

"Christ, Chief." The badge flashed in Phil's hand bright as 24-carat gold.

"Now shag ass out of here and get your shit squared away," Mullins remarked, unconsciously flipping through last year's Swank calendar. "Can't you see I've got work to do?"

Phil picked up the boxes and headed for the door. "Okay, Chief. See you tomorrow."

"Yeah. Oh, and one more thing."

Phil turned.

Mullins' mustached lip twitched up in a smile. "It's good to have you back...Sergeant Straker."

Sergeant Straker, the words drifted. He was staring out the window now, of the tiny room in Old Lady Crane's boardinghouse that was suddenly his home. Yeah, Sergeant Straker, back in the tin...

Outside looked strange—trees and fields and hills instead of skyscrapers and traffic. Cricket sounds instead of sirens. Pine air instead of smog. Crick City was abed, and the night bloomed in a kind of beauty he'd forgotten even existed. Maybe this won't be so bad, he considered.

Or was that just wishful thinking?

Because when Phil went to sleep, he dreamed...

He dreamed of his childhood.

And the vague, half-seen horrors of The House.

*Yes, sir, sooner or later,* Gut thought, *we'se gonna pick the wrong folks to razz...*

Scott-Boy crumpled his empty beer can, tossed it out, and cracked open another. They could go through a case a night, no problem, healthy young livers and constitutions and all. But Gut was nursing his.

"What's buggin' you?" Scott inquired, never one to sit calm whiles his only razzin' buddy displayed signs of psychic distress. "You done look plumb et up with a case of the blahs tonight, Gut."

"Aw, it's nothin'. Just feelin' a tad spotty's all."

"Well, we'se shore gonna put a fixin' to that right soon enough. Coupla bad razzers like us, we gots it all, ya know? Good beer, good set of wheels, plus laters on we'll both have ourselfs a horse-choke-size wad of cash in each our pockets after we're done with our run. Yes, sir. We'se plumb got it made."

"Uh, yeah," Gut replied with little enthusiasm. But then he decided it couldn't hurt to air his feelings. He felt weird tonight, he felt really bad. "But I'se been thinkin', Scott-Boy. Like maybe sooner or later we'se gonna pick the wrong folks to razz."

"Sheee-it!" Scott whooped. "Yeah, and if worms had guns, birds wouldn't fuck with 'em! Ain't no one on the good earth with a pair brass enough to take us on. We're bad razzin' fellas, Gut.

Ain't no one can touch us. Why—I'll show ya! Just lookit this!" And then Scott-Boy shucked his daddy's big Webley .455 and cocked that sucker.

Scott-Boy laughed, guzzlin' his brew, and givin' his crotch a rub now and again on account of the idea of killing gave him as much spark in the loins as seeing a real looker in the buff or a nice big jiggly set of milkers, but Gut still had that low sicklike feeling way down deep in his belly. The feeling deepened as he drove the truck on down the road. The moon went right along with them over the trees, kind of funny-colored and not quite full, and there weren't a cloud in the sky, just a big glittery bunch of stars, and the harder Gut looked into them stars, the worse he felt.

He just didn't feel like killin' anyone tonight.

"Scott-Boy, look, I really don't feel up to a good razz right now. I means like we'se got that run ta make soon. So why don't we do somethin' quick, like buy us some whores or somethin'?"

"'Cos, Gut, see, I already told ya, there ain't no kick to that. That's like drinkin' Yoo-Hoo instead of the good beer like we'se always drink," Scott explained, and cracked open another one. "Can't have no fun unless we'se into the really groaty hobknob-bin', ya know? And why waste time? We ain't due fer the pick up fer a good spell, so let's have us a hoot till then."

"Uh, yeah," Gut came back. He could see there was no point; once Scott "Scott-Boy" Tuckton had his mind set, there weren't no swayin' him. And what Scott meant by "groaty hobknobbin'" was his usual kind of razz, the kinky, down 'n' dirty kind like he was used to. The really wild, un-Christian kind of stuff like the time they did the job on that old lady walkin' on crutches, or that time last summer when they'se spotted that gal in the wheelchair waitin' fer that special bus at the junction, and they stopped and just throwed her in the back of the truck and droved off to one of their fave-urt clearings back in the woods, and Scott-Boy did all kinds of rowdy things to that poor gal 'fore he got ta snuffin' her. That's what Scott meant by groaty hobknobbin'. That's what gave him his biggest kick: the really pree-verted stuff.

And that gave Gut an idea.

Yeah, pre-versions. Some really plumb bad, down 'n dirty groaty hobknobbin'...

It was something he'd heard about since he was little, something about the Creekers. His daddy'd tell him about it when he was on a drunk which was most ever night, yeah, stories about this place the Creekers had way on back in the woods where a fella could buy hisself a Creeker woman, and these Creeker gals, they'se were all fucked up an' deformed an all, and it was a place where a fella could go fer some really groaty hobknobbin'. 'Course, Gut hisself hadn't seen many Creekers ever, and as for this Creeker whorehouse, well, he didn't know if the place really existed at all, like maybe it was just a bunch of shit his daddy was spoutin' ta scare him, but if Gut could sell Scott-Boy on the idea of tryin' ta find the place, then they wouldn't have ta kill no one tonight, and that sounded just fine to Gut 'cos he still had this really bad feelin' 'bout killin' right now, and that feelin' was a'growin' in his belly like that time he et some bad squirrel pie, and he was just sick as a dog fer two weeks. So Gut just then, he decided to make his pitch:

"Say, Scott-Boy, ya know, fer longer than I can remember I been hearin' stories 'bout some really wild whorehouse back up the boonies somewhere, but this whorehouse, see, it's different from the reg-lar kind 'cos they say it's a Creeker whorehouse where the gals have funny-shaped heads and a couple more tits than they'se supposed ta and fucked-up stuff like that, and I mean I bet if we found it we'se could have us a real rowdy time, some real groaty hobknobbin' like we'se never had before, don't'cha think?"

"Aw now, Gut," Scott dismissed, "I heard them stories too since I was a kid, and it's just a load of horseflop, and I ain't seen me five Creekers in my whole life I bet. So quit tryin' ta spoil my night of razzin'. There ain't no Creekers, and there shore's shit ain't no Creeker whorehouse."

That idea shore went bust, Gut concluded. He couldn't even reckon where he was drivin'; he just cruised down one road after the next while Scott-Boy chugged more beer. The moon kept followin' him, flashin' at him through the trees like an eye blinkin'. Then:

"Hot-damn," Scott-Boy leaned forward and whispered. "You see what I see, Gut?"

Gut saw her, all right. Some chick walkin' along the Old Dunwich just as fast as her legs'd carry her, wearin' some real ratty clothes, and she never turned as the big truck approached, not hitchhiking but just walking, and it was kind of creepy, her just walkin' along with that funny colored moon hangin' over her.

And Scott snickered. "We'se gonna pluck us this one."

Gut groaned in his mind, that low feeling in his belly getting
hot. He pulled the truck up just ahead of her and stopped, and
Scott-Boy was out lickety-split. He cracked her a good one upside
the head with the brass knucks and just as quick was hauling her
into the truck, and then Gut was stepping on it again just like that,
like maybe five seconds was all it took to pluck her off the road.

"Oooo-yeah-mama!" Scott-Boy exclaimed. "I just knowed we
was gonna find ourselfs some splittail tonight." He was pushing
the barely conscious girl down into the footwell, giving her a few
slaps on the head, and he was just laughing away as usual, all riled
up now. "Yeah, Gut, let's git off this road right quick 'cos I gots ta
slip into this skinny bitch 'fore my pecker busts, ya know?"

"Uh, yeah," Gut nearly moaned. Up a spell came a dirt turn-off
they'd used fer razzin' in the past. Scott-Boy turned on the dome
light, saying, "Let's have us a gander first," and he was hauling
her up between them as Gut parked in the moonlit clearing. The
girl was still out of it from the shot with the brass knucks; her head
just kind of lolled like she had no neckbone. But they got a good
gander as Scott-Boy got to pulling them ratty duds off her. She had
a decent body on her, and a good-sized set of milkers fer a chick so
skinny, but kinda limp, straggly black hair, and—

"Jaysus!" Scott-Boy exclaimed.

Gut saw it, too. This gal, she had some weirdnesses about her,
like, first, she didn't have no bellybutton, and she had six fingers on
her left hand and not but three on her right. She was fully hairless
on her plot, too. But that weren't the cause of Scott-Boy's exclama-
tion. It was her face...

"Jiminy Peter, Gut. You believe this?"

This girl, her face looked kinda lopsided. A kind of smushed
nose, and one ear lower than the other, and that dog-dirty black
hair hangin' over a forehead that looked really queer and round.
But queerer still were her eyes.

"Gander them eyes," Scott-Boy whispered.

They was real big, but one was surely bigger than the other
and higher on her head, and the eyes too were a real funny red-
dish color almost like blood. Gut had never in his life seed eyes this
color on anyone.

"Gut, this shore is the fucked-upest gal I ever seen," Scott-Boy
observed.

"She's a inbred."

"A what?"

"A inbred, Scott-Boy. Like what I was talkin' 'bout before. This here's a Creeker."

Scott-Boy's face became a study in fascination. "You know, I never seen me one up close like this. How they get theirselfs so fucked up?"

"Kromerzomes," Gut answered. "My daddy told me alls about it once. We all gots these things in us called kromerzomes and genes—"

"You means like Levi's?"

"No, Scott-Boy, I'm talkin' 'bout some other kinda gene, and these things are real fragile-like. And what happens is, see, these dirt-poor families of hillfolk livin' way up the boonies, they get to doin' the bop with everyone, fathers knockin' up their daughters like it was nothin', and brothers gettin' together with their sisters, and mothers gettin' pregged up by their sons over and over for a long time. And what happens is the genes and kromerzornes get messed up, and the kids come out all wrong like this here gal. And they calls 'em Creekers."

"Creekers," Scott murmured, gazing at the girl. "Ain't this a kick?"

The girl began to rouse, making strange noises that sounded like "allup, allup, allup-harup." And those big red eyes of hers seemed to be looking up without seeing much of anything, and Gut, in his undeniable erudition, explained, "And most Creekers are real slow in the head on account of their brain's all fucked up, too. Can't barely talk, most of them, and those that can just mumble like they'se got their yaps full of backer. It's 'cos they're Creekers is why they're so shit-stupid."

Then the girl's twisted mouth began to work, and she blinked those big red eyes and jabbered, "Skeet-inner, come no-hurt."

"What's that, girlie?" Scott mockingly asked. He guffawed and slapped her in the face. "What'choo sayin'?"

"Skeet-inner," she said.

"Yeah, she's stupider than dogshit, all right," Scott-Boy determined, grinning in the dome light. He began to take his pants down. "Got a big cooze on her too, don't she? Sheee-it, I'm gonna blow me a dandy of a nut up them there works, I am. 'Fact I'll blow me several, feisty as my dog's been of late."

Gut felt even shittier now. He figured this Creeker gal had

enough problems, but he didn't dare raise the suggestion that they let her go. Scott-Boy's intent was plain as barn paint, and once he got his dog up, there was no gettin' it down. Hell, Gut had even seen him do it with some sheep up on Miller's pasture a couple times they couldn't find no gals to razz. "A nut's a nut, hail," he'd said and then got to it. Gut felt sorry for the sheep.

And Gut surely felt sorry for this gal right now. Scott pushed her on her back, not even needing to wank a little to get his dog hard. The gal just lay there on the bench seat, blinking her big lop-sided red eyes every now and again, and then Scott-Boy pushed her legs apart. "Gut, how's 'bout waitin' outside on account there ain't room fer the three of us, huh? I wants ta fuck with her some and fire me a coupla nuts up this bald pussy of hers. Then you can take a turn if ya want, 'fore we kill her."

"Uh, yeah," Gut obliged, and he shore didn't have no trouble obliging. He could razz with the best of 'em, but he didn't want no part of this. Just weren't natural to be doin' it with a Creeker. So he moseyed around the clearing, finished his beer, and chucked the can. He could hear Scott whooping it up fierce in the pickup. Sheee-it, he thought morosely. He knew Scott-Boy real well, and knew how his head worked, and he figured that the girl's deformities added a lot of extra spark to Scott's razz.

*Groaty hobknobbin'*, he mused. *Jaysus…*

He looked around the grove, up at the moon, up at the sky. He didn't want to think about what was going on in the truck, but it was a spot hard not to. Scott kept the dome light on, and Gut couldn't help but catch a few ganders. He could see the Creeker gal's funny feet sticking up, then he could see her head hangin' out the window as Scott-Boy turned her over and gave it to her in the behind. Then she started pukin', and Scott-Boy was just laughing away and slapping her around and all in the truck. "Got's ta get rid of this dog-dirty hair so's we can see yer purdy face, jabber-puss," he was saying, and then he started cutting her dirty coal-black hair off with his buck, right close to the scalp and throwing it all around and laughing it up real good, and this poor Creeker gal looked a sight when he was done, just tufts of scrap sticking up on her big, cockeyed head.

Gut sat down on a stump to wait. Hurry it up, Scott-Boy, he thought. We got a run to make later. These dust dealers they drove for, they wouldn't take too kindly to he and Scott bein' late, but 'acorse that was really just an excuse, bein' late fer the run. He wanted to get out of here was all. The low, sicklike feelin' in his breadbasket was still there, not just from what Scott was doin' to this poor Creeker gal, but from a bit of everything. The whole night just had a bad feel to it.

"Ah-no-save-me!" he thought he heard the girl shriek from the cab. "Ona-prey-bee!"

Who knew what the gal was tryin' to say. Hell, she probably didn't know herself, so et up she was with the messed up kromerzomes. Gut guessed it must've been some scientist fella named Kromer who discovered 'em. These kromerzomes, see, was so deller-kit, if families hobknobbed together long enough over generations there never weren't no babies born right. No, none at all. 'Least, that's what his daddy'd told him.

"Ah-no! Lep! Evernd! Peese! Ona!" the gal wailed.

Scott's whooping voice echoed through the grove. "Hot damn, Gut! This is a reg-lar hoot, this is! This splittail's box is shore somethin'!"

Uh, yeah, Gut thought. He was fidgetin' like he had ants on him, the bad feel of the night or the cryptic whispers of the augurs of ancient Rome. He got back up then and began to pace about the moonlit dell, and every time he glanced toward the truck all he could see was Scott-Boy's devil-grinnin' face whiles he continued to put serious blocks to this Creeker gal, and then Scott was guffawing, "Oh yessiree bob, I'm gonna blow me a nut so dandy it'll be squirtin' out this jabberin' bitch's fucked-up ears, it will!"

"Hey, Scott-Boy?" Gut feebly called out. "Hurry it up, how 'bout. We got that run to make, don't ferget."

But Scott-Boy, so busy he was just then, didn't even hear what Gut had said.

The presage thickened; Gut was sweating now, itching and rubbing his face in some unnamed dread, and the pickup truck was rockin', and the Creeker chick still jabberin' away whiles Scott-Boy set to bangin' her warped head bam bam bam! against the door a country mile a minute, and suddenly—inexplicably—Gut felt a fear like he couldn't 'magine, and he ducked behind a tree for no reason he could really put a name to, and that was when Scott-Boy started screamin'...

In an eye's wink, big, quick-moving shadows were crunching around the pickup, and Scott-Boy, he was screaming right away—it didn't even really sound human, like the sound Cage George's 'Cuda made that time he was red-lining it and the oil pump went— and next off, another pickup truck was pulling up in the grove, not from the road but from a dirt lane in the woods, only this pickup was real old and beat to shit, with real dim headlights, and then these shadows was dragging Scott-Boy out of the truck, and he was still screaming bloody murder. Other shadows took the Creeker gal out and then carried her to the truck with the real dim lights, but dim as these lights was, Gut could also see Scott-Boy and what happened to him to get him screaming like that

*Keeeeee-riiist...*

Scott-Boy had no works left at all 'tween his legs, just a crotch-full of blood pouring like a faucet. One of them shadows had cut Scott's dog and bag clean off, and Scott was still screaming and flailing away in the dirt as several of these big shadows got to holding him down, and one of them was smack smack smack! bringing a tire iron or something down fast and hard on Scott-Boy's arms and legs, breakin' bones like they was pencils, and another shadow whipped out a buck bigger than Gut had ever seed in his life and started scalping Scott-Boy alive right then and there.

More of that Creeker jabber shot up into the grove, only this weren't the gal, these were guys by the sound of 'em:

"Ah-no-prey-bee!"

"Ah-no-for-blood!"

"Skeet-inner this one!"

"Ona!"

But then there was another voice Gut coulda swore he heard, but, see, he seemed to hear it in his head instead of his ears, and what he heard was this:

*Redeemer Sanctifier, bless us...*

*Ah-no ah-no!*

*To thee we bring this gift of flesh...*

*Ona!*

Gut felt like part of the tree he was lookin' past; he couldn't move at all. These shadows was really doin' the job on Scott-Boy, the likes of which turned even Gut's breadbasket. "Gut, Jaysus ta Gawd ya gotta help meeeee!" screamed Scott-Boy, crushed and scalped but still alive. One of the shadows was givin' it to Scott-Boy something fierce up the tail, while the one with the shank took to cutting off Scott-Boy's ears, and whittling the skin off his fingers, and chopping off his toes like they was carrots for stew on a butcher block. Gut shuddered frozen behind that tree, not able to move but knowing if he didn't, these fellas would surely do the same to him.

*Gotta move gotta get out of here right now!*

When the one fella finished havin' his nut up Scott-Boy's tail, he slid that tire iron right up the same hole and jiggled it around fierce up there, and that other fella with the big buck cut Scott's throat so deep you could hear the blade scrapin' bone, and that was about it for Scott "Scott-Boy" Tuckton, yes sir.

He shore did pick the wrong folks to razz tonight.

Then them shadows, what they did next was they hauled what was left of Scott-Boy back to that beat-ta-hell pickup of theirs and throwed him in the back like he was a sack of farm feed. And then—

Another fella stepped outta the shadows.

Fuck, Gut thought.

This fella was taller than the others, and Gut guessed he'd been standin' back in the dark whiles his buddies did the job on Scott-Boy. He stood there a speck and kind of made to sniff the air, and then he turned in the moonlight and—

Fuck! Gut thought.

—looked right at Gut squattin' behind that there tree.

Gut's eyes bugged like they might jump out his head as this big killer dude took to staring at him, and Gut figured he'd just up and die, but what he did instead was piss and shit his pants both at the same time. He only saw the big fella's face a second but a second was enough, a face squashed up worse than the gal's with one ear twice as big as the other and fucked-up teeth stickin' out of his smile, and then he pointed right at Gut with a long, crooked finger, staring back at Gut with eyes just like that gal's.

Eyes that were blood-red...

*Run, boy*, Gut heard in his head. *We'll getcha next time...*

And Gut ran, and he didn't stop runnin' till the sun was comin' up over the ridge about five hours later.

# FIVE

Phil slowed as he passed Krazy Sallee's, flagged by its great flashing road sign. Place is jam-packed, and it's barely 7:30, he observed. Sallee's wasn't just the only strip joint in town, it was the only bar—period. Phil had only been in there once or twice back when he was eighteen, the old days before the drinking age went up to twenty-one, and all he recalled were a few docile-looking women with bad tattoos and floppy breasts clopping around a strobe-lit stage; he'd be more aroused watching pigs snort in a mudhole. But as he passed, he realized he'd be paying some close attention to the place. Vices, he'd learned on Metro, always tended to mix together. Booze begat dive bars, which begat strippers, which begat prostitutes, which begat drugs. Sallee's would be the most logical place for Cody Natter to use as a distro point. Phil couldn't imagine punks stopping by Bouton's Farm Supply or Chuck's Diner to pick up their weekend angel dust.

He parked in the little gravel lot behind the station. First day on the job, he reminded himself. Look sharp. He adjusted his gunbelt and Sam Brown strap—Mullins had purchased good leather—and the starched uniform (navy-blue shirt, powder blue pants) fit pretty well. The gun on his hip, a Colt Trooper Mark III, dragged annoyingly; its hot dog six-inch barrel made it weigh more than the Smith 65 he'd carried on Metro, but of course it was better than carrying a lone can of Mace, which was all he had as a security guard. Just as he turned to enter the station, he heard a door chunk shut, and saw Chief Mullins coming out of the small brick building which sat on its own behind the station house—the town lockup. As Phil recalled, it had only three cells and was rarely used for anything more than a place for drunks to dry out.

"All ready for work, I see," Mullins remarked, loping heavily across the lot. His bald pate shined like a crystal ball of flesh.

"Lookin' like a regular Dirty Harry."

"I didn't know Dirty Harry was a town clown," Phil came back. "And who you got in the jail?"

"The jail? Oh, no one," Mullins said, hauling, open the back door to the station house. "For your info, whenever we book some-one, we use the county lockup in Mayr now. You know where Mayr is, right? Down past the mobile home dealer on Route 3?"

"Yeah, I know where County HQ is, Chief. And if we don't use our own jail for prisoners, what's in there now?"

"Supply room. I was checking the inventory."

Inventory? Phil couldn't imagine a small-town department like Crick City needing any significant supply space. "Oh, the SWAT and riot gear, huh? You keep the department helicopter in there, too?"

"No, funny man, I keep the really important cop stuff in there, like coffee filters, which we're out of, by the way. So that can be your first mission as one of Crick City's finest. Sometime tonight during your busy and dangerous watch, run on by the Qwik-Stop and pick up a box of filters. The boss needs his coffee in the morning."

"Ah, so that's why you hired me. Sergeant Straker the errand boy."

"Damn straight. Now why don't you shitcan the jokes for a minute and let me brief you."

"Sure, boss."

Phil took a seat in the fold-down as Mullins rummaged through one of his desk drawers. The man's stomach bulged to the extent that if he leaned over any further, his shirt would more than likely burst. "One thing you need to learn fast, Adam 12, is we use the county signal sheet, not the fucked-up codes you had on Metro." He passed Phil a copy of the set of radio signal designa-tions. "Learn it fast."

"Gee, Chief, I don't know. I've only got a Master's degree; this might take me a while to get in my head—like about thirty seconds."

"See how hard I'm laughing?" Mullins replied, poker-faced. "Just learn it and quit the wisecracks, unless you want to get fired your first day and go do amateur comedy for tips every Friday night at Rudy's Tavern."

Phil smiled. "So we're on the county commo band, huh?"

"Fuck no. We've got our own frequency and our own

dispatcher. Her name's Susan, and she's in the other room. Make sure you touch base with her before you start your shift."

"Susan, dispatcher. Right."

"She's nice, so don't break her chops like you do mine."

"Oh, one thing I wanted to ask. Does the department supply a bulletproof vest?"

Mullins looked back in grim hilarity. "What do I look like, fucking Santa Claus?"

Actually, with white hair and a beard... "Hey, you know, cops get shot at all the time," Phil pointed out.

"You're a Crick City cop, not the warrior of the apocalypse. Only thing you need a vest for around here is to keep the mosquitoes from stingin' your tits when cooping out by the swamps. You want a fucking vest, buy it yourself."

"Hey, I was just asking."

"You want to ask questions, fine. Just don't ask dumb questions."

"Okay. What's the department policy on impeachment use of statements obtained without Miranda warnings during spontaneous field situations after probable cause has been previously determined?"

Mullins glowered. "Just whatever they taught you in the academy."

Phil kept his smile to himself. *He steps on my tail all the time, it's only fair that I step on his every now and then.* It seemed only fitting. Plus it was *a lot* of fun.

Mullins packed a pinch of Skoal under his lip, then spit into the old coffee cup he was using for a spittoon. Phil hoped to God that the chief never actually drank out of it by mistake. "What I want you to do," Mullins said, "is refamiliarize yourself with the town first couple of nights. That shouldn't take too long considering you grew up here, unless of course all that smog you breathed on Metro for ten years rotted your brain. After that, everything's pretty routine. First part of your shift, keep on your ass. Cruise all the TA's and residential areas real slow, let the lokes know we gotta night cop again. And keep an eye on the Qwik-Stop 'cos it's open all night. And whatever you do, don't fuck up the cruiser. It's brand-new, and it took me years to get the mayor and the town council to requisition it." Mullins spit again into his cup. "And I guess that's about it."

Phil's eyes narrowed. "That's it? I thought you were going to brief me."

"I just did."

"Yeah, sure, Chief, but you must have some particular operating procedures you want me to follow."

"For what?"

Phil sighed. "For the PCP thing. You say that's your biggest problem in town. What ideas have you got? How do you want me to handle it?"

Mullins looked momentarily confounded. "Oh, yeah, well naturally I want you to check it out. Buzz around, look things over. Just do all that good cop shit you did on Metro."

Phil wanted to laugh. Was the man naive? If the town's biggest problem was Natter's PCP ring, didn't Mullins have any kind of plan? He seemed not to have thought about it at all. Phil could see he would have to use his own initiative; waiting for Mullins to come up with a strategy on his own would be less productive than waiting for his own hair to turn gray. "Well, the way I see it," Phil began, "is we have to isolate Natter's distro point, and the most logical distro point in Crick City is probably Krazy Sallee's. I mean, what else have you got here? Not only is Sallee's your only watering hole, it's your only strip joint, and chances are half the girls working there are turning tricks, so it's a good bet that's where the local dustheads go."

"Right," Mullins conveniently agreed. "Sallee's is where you'll want to keep your biggest eye out. So start staking the place out each night close to last call. What, I gotta tell you everything?"

This guy's something. Must be getting too old for the job. Phil didn't bother shaking his head. "You want me to stake out Sallee's every night in the patrol car?"

"Sure. Why not?"

Now Phil did shake his head. "Chief, if Natter and his people see a cop car sitting in the parking lot every night, they're just going to move someplace else and make it that much harder to step on their tails."

"All right, smart boy, big city narc, what's your plan?"

"You want to catch these guys red-handed, I'll have to go undercover. First couple of weeks why don't I check the place out in plainclothes and my own car? Nobody's going to remember me 'cos I never hung out there, and if anyone does, I'll have a cover story ready. It'll give me a chance to get some names, tag numbers, and some kind of a read on what's going on out there. If I'm lucky I might even be able to cultivate an informant or two."

"Well, sure, a little undercover work, that's what I was going to suggest next."

Yeah, right. "Okay, so that's what I'll do. Each night about an hour before last call, I'll change into plainclothes and check the joint out. You'll pay me mileage for use of my own vehicle, right?"

"Yeah, yeah, fine," Mullins complained. "Just go do your thing. Report to me in the morning. Oh, there's one more detail you should know, too. Natter owns Krazy Sallee's now."

How in the hell? Phil thought. "How'd a Creeker manage to buy a strip joint? Most of them have no incomes."

"No legal incomes," Mullins augmented. "I had IRS investigate the buy, and the records were legit. Somehow he laundered his dope money and bought the place."

Phil nodded. Makes sense, he realized. There were all kinds of financial loopholes that seemed to exist solely for criminals—this was nothing new.

"Okay." Phil got up and prepared to leave, but Mullins, after spitting again into his cup, added, "And whatever you do—"

"I know, be careful."

"Well, that too, but don't forget to pick up those coffee filters either."

That's what I like, Phil thought, a police chief with real priorities. He went out into the front of the station to check in with the dispatcher Mullins had mentioned. Probably some old ditty on social security, he speculated. Looks like Old Lady Crane on a bad day.

"In here," he heard.

Phil turned toward a cubby of a room off to the side of the front door. Boy, did I call this one wrong, he realized. Sitting behind a big county scanner and Motorola transmitter was a pretty blond woman who looked to be in her late twenties, dressed simply in jeans and a plain pink blouse. Opened in her lap was a textbook of some kind.

Phil extended his hand in greeting. "I'm Phil Straker, the new cop."

"Well, I sure as hell didn't think you were the new Good Humor Man dressed like that," she replied, and strangely did not shake his hand. "My name's—"

"Susan, the night dispatch," Phil cut in. "The chief told me to check in."

She seemed exasperated, though Phil couldn't fathom why. *I guess I better change deodorants.*

"We use the county signal sheet, so familiarize yourself with the codes, and do it fast," she said. "One thing I can't stand is a green cop who doesn't know his radio codes."

Phil frowned. "Do you know what a signal 72 is, by the county signal sheet?"

Her face darkened. "A 72? No."

"It's a juvenile complaint call. You can check on your sheet there you got taped to the wall. And if you got some problem with me, fine. Just don't break my chops for nothing, all right? And for your info, I'm not green, I've been a cop for ten years."

"Yeah. I know," she said choppily and went back to her book.

Phil walked out of the station, as discomfited as he was confused. He wasn't anti-social, but he didn't see any reason why he should take a load of crap from some woman he'd just met.

It wasn't her rudeness that bothered him nearly as much as the look in her eyes…

They were probably the prettiest blue eyes he'd ever seen, yet in that last moment before he'd left the station, he sensed beyond a doubt that those same blue eyes were burning with outright disdain.

# SIX

Such a precious little thing, Natter mused, assessing the new girl with his uneven eyes.

"How old is she?" he asked.

"'Bout sixteen, I thinks."

Such a precious harbinger...

"You think she's ready, Cody?"

But what did ready mean? What did it really mean, in the light of everything? Have faith, he told himself. He was, after all, a faithful man. These little people, his own kin, served in their own way. They didn't realize how, but what did that matter? They all fed the meaning of their providence...

She'd been cleaned up. Her straight black hair hung long and shiny black, shiny as a wet grackle. She was missing one ear, but that wasn't particularly noticeable, and her eyes were very nearly the same size; she almost looked good enough to use at the club.

Almost.

*This curse,* he thought in a deep despair. *When will it end?*

Druck stripped her, to reveal her flesh. Her red eyes cast down during Natter's perusal. Full, healthy breasts, despite a dual nipple on the left. The multiple navel was barely discernible, and though one leg was longer than the other, her limp, too, could barely be noticed.

*Such a lovely thing...*

Sometimes, he could cry.

"When?" Druck asked.

Natter's elongated hand stroked his chin. His red eyes, though dull, looked full of—something. What?

Hope.

"Break her in first," he said. "Break her in easy."

As per instructions, or rather instructions based on his own suggestions to a boss he was beginning to suspect of either senility or just plain absent-mindedness, Phil occupied the first five hours of his first shift cruising Crick City in the department's patrol-vehicle. It was a decent ride—a new white Chevy Cavalier—with a standard Visibar, cage, Lecco gun-rack, and commo gear. For some hotdog reason, Mullins also had a Smith & Wesson tear gas gun locked in the trunk, plus an AR-15 with what looked like a quality scope—but, of course, no ammo. Phil called in 10-8 with Susan, the snooty dispatcher, then went about his patrol, cruising the local TA's—TA's were private businesses—the few small apartment complexes, and the trailer parks. He also ran by Chuck's Diner, Hulls General Store, the farm supply before they closed, and Hodge's tiny mart, which was the only thing close to a mall that Crick City would ever have. He stayed away from Sallee's on purpose. *There's a new cop in town, and I'm sure not going to broadcast that,* he determined.

But driving through the town at large filled him with something almost akin to sentimentality. Yes, this was quite different from the city. It was spacious, laid back, lazy. Long open roads, rolling hills and meadows, plush woods—

So why did he feel so uneasy?

New job jitters, he tried to tell himself. But he knew it was a lie.

It was the memory that he'd been burying for most of his life…

Was the House really out there?

Did it really exist, or was it just something he'd imagined all those years ago?

He'd tried to forget about it—and he had—until…

*Until I came back here.*

The sedate hum of the engine merged with his resistance—memory was hypnotizing him, seducing him like a tittering sprite on his shoulder, and then—

*Christ, no…*

—slim shards of the imagery glittered back in the eye of his mind. It was a child's eye, wasn't it? A sputtering, nightmarish bogeyman flashback of a terrified little boy:

*…no…*

Open doorways.

Slats of sunlight cutting through sluggish darkness.

Then that same darkness…began to move.

He could see things there. Shapes. Moaning. Moving. In the thin tines of sunlight, he could see—

People…

Flashes of faces.

Flashes of flesh.

A twisted hand here, a crooked bare foot there.

Squirming o's of mouths opening, closing, gasping. Lines of drool swinging off cleft chins, and tongues struggling like fat pink sea worms between rows of broken teeth. And—

…*God, no…*

Phil pulled over onto the shoulder, squeezing his eyes shut against the mudslide of images. His stomach felt shriveled to a prune-sized clot, and pain raged at his temples…

*You never saw any of it!* he screamed at himself. *It wasn't real! It was all hallucination!*

But as hard as he tried to convince himself of that, he knew he would never be sure.


Phil went in the back way to change, then popped into the common room. "I—" he began.

Susan, the dispatcher, frowned in dismay. "Your shift doesn't end till eight in the morning," she told him. "What are you doing in civilian clothes?"

"I'm staking out Sallee's for a little while," Phil bluntly replied.

"Oh, yeah? Says who?"

"Says Chief Mullins. You know, for a dispatcher, you're not very well informed."

Her frown deepened. "Well, how can I be informed unless you inform me?"

"I'm informing you now," Phil said.

Susan hesitated, putting up her book. Now she was reading a text called Forensics 1994. "The chief didn't tell me anything about you going undercover to Sallee's tonight."

Phil sighed. Organization, yes sir. "Actually, Susan, I'm making the whole thing up. I'm gonna go drink beer and watch strippers on the clock."

"That wouldn't surprise me. Sallee's is probably your kind of place." She paused again, tapping her finger against the lit transmitter. "I don't know about this. I better check with the chief."

"Go ahead," Phil invited. "I'm sure he wouldn't mind at all being woken up at one in the morning by a dispatcher who doesn't even have enough initiative to inquire about any daily SOP changes."

"Asshole," she said, glaring through blond bangs.

"Hey, that's my middle name. Look, you go ahead and do what you want. Call the chief, call the mayor and the town council. You can even call the Little Mermaid and Steven Spielberg if you want, but I'm 10-6 to Sallee's."

"Don't forget your radio."

Phil held up the Motorola portable. "What's this look like? A toilet tank cover? Log me in 10-6," he snapped and left the station.

*God, she gets on my nerves!* Phil got into his Malibu, updated his DOR, and pulled out. *How come she hates me?* the question nagged. Sure, he was new, and cop folks routinely took a while accepting new hires, but—Christ, *she acts like I pissed on her dog. Must be a permanent case of PMS.*

*Or—*

*Maybe it's me,* he considered. *Maybe it's my karma or something.* Phil could recognize no reason at all for Susan to treat him with such ill-will, but he had to admit women seldom took to him, and he never knew why. He'd had his share of relationships during his time on Metro. *Yeah, and they all went bust, with me looking like the heavy. But maybe he* was *the heavy.* The longest one had lasted maybe eight months, and by the end of it they were arguing worse than the schmucks on *Crossfire. Be real, Phil,* he ordered himself. It was easy to be real about one's self when driving alone at just past 1 a.m. *Self-realization, man. There's something about you that rubs women the wrong way. Maybe she's right. Maybe I am an asshole.*

On that note, he decided that self-realization might not be the best thing to ponder right now. *Why rub your face in your own shit if you don't have to?* he reasoned. *Worry about Sallee's, Natter, the PCP ring—that's what you're here for. Not to bellyache to yourself about why women act like you're the Boston Strangler.*

Around the next bend, the great lighted sign flashed: KRAZY SALLEE'S. Gravel popped under the tires as he pulled into the lot and hunted for a strategic place to park. Certainly the beat-up Malibu wouldn't be conspicuous, but some guy parked right up front with a portable police radio would be. He edged into a space

toward the back which afforded a pretty wide survey of the building and the lot.

Plates, he reminded himself. All he wanted to do the first few
nights was get a log of all the vehicles that remained in the lot
till past closing, descriptions, tag numbers, physical makes on the
owners, then compare them at the end of the week and see who the
regulars were. He also wanted the tags of any out-of-state vehicles.
This would be slow, but slow was the only way to start.

Pickup truck paradise, he thought. Half the vehicles occu-
pying the lot were, unsurprisingly, pickups in various states of
bad repair. The rest were equally beat cars like the Malibu, and a
smattering of souped hot rods. No, this ain't the parking lot at the
Hyatt-Regency, he joked and began jotting down tag numbers with
his lit CRP "NitePen." He'd also brought a tiny pair of Bushnell
7x50's with a zoom for the plates out of eyeshot. This didn't take
long, which left him with nothing to do but watch blue-jeaned and
T-shirted patrons come and go. He guessed last call would come
at about one-thirty, then the lot would clear out and he could see
what was left. Weed out the louts, he thought. Whoever's still here
are the folks to check out.

Boredom set in quick.

Undecipherable C&W boomed through the lot each time someone left. Most who left were clearly drunk, harping about the "hot
babes." Many saw fit to urinate between cars before leaving. *If I
had a nickel for every redneck I've seen piss in public tonight,* Phil
reflected, *I could probably fill my gas tank with high-octane.* He
tried to divert his thoughts, but every time he did, they kept roving back to himself: the topic of the evening.

Working in Crick City would never earn him a silver star, but
at least it was a job and one that fit his college and career goals.
So he supposed he should be grateful. Beats sudsing fenders at
Lucky's Carwash. Despite Dignazio's frame at Metro, Phil realized
things could be worse—a lot worse. It didn't even matter that no
one here would ever believe he'd been set up. At least he was working, at least he was getting a paycheck for something more fulfill-
ing than punching a clock at the yarn factory. Lots of people these
days didn't have jobs at all.

*So what am I moping for?*

Like an undertow, then, his thoughts took him back to earlier
contemplations. Women. Relationships. *I've struck out more times*

with women than Boog Powell struck out at the plate. Maybe he'd never taken things seriously enough. Maybe he'd taken things for granted. Human compatibility wasn't supposed to grow on trees. It can't all be me, he, well, pleaded with himself. To think so was quite a condemnation, wasn't it? Shit, he thought. Two more rednecks staggered out of Sallee's. They both relieved their beer-strained bladders before piling into a primer-red Chevy pickup and driving off.

*What the hell's wrong with me?* Phil thought.

Vicki had been his only genuine, long-term relationship. He knew that he'd loved her—he'd loved her more than anything. *Only on my terms,* he regretted now, and then his thoughts turned mocking. *Yeah, the woman of my dreams. Only thing she didn't do for me was change her whole fucking life. What a dick I am.*

But why think of this now? Ancient history. This was over ten years ago, and here he was doing stakeout in a redneck strip joint parking lot, and all he could think about was some girl he dated through high school and college, and who probably hadn't thought about him since *Three's Company* was still on the air.

*Get your head together! You haven't been back in town two days and already you've turned into a moron!*

Again, he tried to refocus, on his job, on the stakeout. And on Natter. How well had the guy held up over the last decade? Phil had only seen him a few times in his life, and that had been a while back. Must be uglier than ever now, he concluded. Natter was an inbred—a Creeker—yet the man, despite his physical deformities, also spoke with great articulation and seemed keenly intelligent. Was Natter's car here now? And was he himself in Sallee's this moment? These were things that Phil should've considered previously, but he hadn't. It was getting close to two—closing time; the cars in the lot had begun to clear out. Christ, Phil thought. I should have at least asked Mullins if Natter was still driving the same car...

More locals stumbled out, jabbered, and drove away. "Man, that back room's somethin', ain't it?" one frightfully large redneck remarked, expectorating a plume of tobacco juice.

His companion, even larger, did a rebel yell. "Man, those chicks got me all fired up," he replied. "We'se comin' back here ever' night!"

Please don't, Phil thought. They were just stoners, not dope dealers. And what had they said? Something about a back room? I don't remember any back room, Phil thought. They must've expanded the place—

Then...

*Here we go.*

Phil jerked alert and raised the tiny pair of binoculars. Only a few vehicles remained in the lot now, a couple of pickups (one of which looked absolutely ancient) and a fully refurbished '63 Chrysler Imperial, an eerie dark, dark red.

And next, in the building's front entry, a figure appeared. There he is, Phil realized. There could be no denying the identity. Faces like that you don't forget, and Phil actually gave a quick shiver when he focused the Bushnell's. Inhumanly tall and thin, Cody Natter stepped out into the lot, dressed in jeans, an embroidered button shirt, and a black sports jacket. The bastard must spend a fortune on custom-made clothes, Phil thought. Forty-five-inch inseams weren't easy to come by at Wal-Mart. Slivers of gray looked like webs of frost in the man's shoulder-length black hair— of course, all Creekers had black hair—and they all had red eyes too, irises as red as arterial blood, which momentarily glinted now as Phil squinted on through the binoculars. Then a second shiver traipsed up his spine, like a procession of spiders, when he took his first good, hard look at Cody Natter's face...

It looked runneled, warped; waxpaper skin stretched over a gourd of jutting bone; Phil swore he could actually see veins beneath the thin sheen of skin.

Lips so narrow they scarcely existed formed a mouth like a knife-cut in meat; a sprawl of uneven teeth outcropped from the depressed lower jaw. One big earlobe hung an inch lower than the other, and seemed to depend in a way that reminded Phil of a shucked softshell clam. Several crevices ran across the enlarged brow, deep as gouges made by a wood chisel, and, lastly, the four fingers on each of Cody Natter's hands each displayed an additional joint.

*Christ, what a living wreck,* Phil observed.

A pair of uppity blondes filed past, short skirts, tattoos, and an excess of makeup. Strippers. They each seemed to bid Natter a downcast goodnight, but Natter did not reply. Instead, he stood just outside the entrance as if in perturbed wait.

*Who's he waiting for?*

Then another male Creeker came out, limping toward one of

the pickups, his forehead so defective it seemed to possess a bolus. And, next—

Phil zoomed in.

Three women made their exit, keeping their heads down as they filed past Cody Natter. They were dressed similar to the blondes: high, racy skirts, glittery blouses so tight across their bosoms Phil was surprised the rhinestone buttons didn't fly off. They all wore straight, raven black hair shiny as oil, and they all had red eyes...

Creekers, Phil realized.

The realization carried more weight when he recognized more telltale traits, however slight:

Misshapen heads, uneven limbs, queerly thin lips. Trace veins could be seen running beneath skin so pale it could've passed for white Depression glass. One woman walked with an obvious impairment, while another seemed to have two elbows on one arm. Natter stopped the third, speaking to her as her scarlet eyes remained leveled to the ground. During this pause, Phil noticed that her mouth was so tiny it was hardly a mouth at all but something more semblant of a puncture.

*They've got Creekers working in there,* Phil couldn't help but deduce. *Creeker girls doing a strip show...* He couldn't imagine anything so exploitative.

The first two women got into the back of the Chrysler, while the third clopped awkwardly across the lot and got into the dilapidated pickup truck with the second man. The truck pulled out, and was followed by a second pickup, whose tag number Phil had already logged.

*What the hell is going on here?* he wondered.

And what was Natter waiting for?

The tall man remained by the entrance, inspecting inch-long nails on his multi-jointed fingers. Then the front door swung open again. A sleek shadow crossed the entry, high heels ticking on cement, and then the shadow materialized in the pallid yellow light, a curvaceous redhead in a skintight black-leather skirt and black-leather bra. Obviously another stripper, but—Not a Creeker, Phil knew. She looked flawless, and her tousled red hair shined like spun cinnamon silk in the flashing lights of the large bar sign. The stripper paused, coyly tossed her head, then took Natter's arm and got into the Chrysler with him.

A moment later they drove away.

But by then Phil was nearly in shock, nearly in tears, and nearly sick to his stomach.

The thought cracked like a stout bone in his head:

*My God...*

—because he easily recognized the redheaded stripper as Vicki Steele, the only woman he'd ever been in love with in his life.

# SEVEN

"Where's the girl?" Jake "The Snake" Rhodes asked the kid with the fucked-up head.

"She went on inside. Wants to freshen up a tad—you know how gals can be."

Yeah, well, she ain't gonna be fresh for long, Jake promised himself. He was feeling mean tonight.

The kid grinned; you could count the gaps where his teeth were missing. Jake had parked right behind the kid's rust bucket pickup, surprised how long it had taken to get out here. Didn't know the roads went back this far into the hills. The kid drove like a maniac—Jake had barely been able to keep up—and at one point the road narrowed so severely he could hear branches scraping either side of his own pickup, which pissed Jake off more than a little. In these parts, it wasn't a man's home that was his castle, it was his truck—in Jake's case, a midnight-blue GMC full-size with slot-mags and about ten coats of lacquer and the last thing Jake needed was some fucked up rube road fucking up his paint. But he was so hot tonight, he didn't pay it much mind. One good thing about dealing dust, the money was so good you didn't worry about your paint job if it got scratched up. I'll just buy another paint job, he concluded, his springs bouncing over the road's deep ruts. And I'll sure as shit take an extra piece out of that Creeker girl's ass...

Yeah, Jake was feeling mean tonight, real mean.

Sallee's was a good place to hang out after a gig, have a few beers, eye some pussy, plus sometimes he'd get a line on a good buyer. He'd been there plenty of nights, but this was the first time he'd heard anything about that back room. One look was all it took.

"Well, what'choo waitin' fer, Jake?" said the kid with the knot on his head. "She gonna die of old age 'fore you get up there."

The kid was pissing him off; Jake didn't like that wiseass, busted-tooth grin, and he had a mind to slap it right off his fucked-up face. Of course, that wouldn't be such a hot idea, not back in these parts. Hill folk looked after their own, and—

Jake caught something funky. "Hold on a sec," he said. "How do you know my name?"

"Oh, we'se know all about'cha, Jake Rhodes." The kid thumbed his overall straps, leaning back against his rusted fender. "If we didn't, then you can bet yer ass you wouldn't be here."

What the fuck's that supposed to mean? Jake thought. And why did he sense the kid was mocking him? Crickets trilled during the impasse. Then Jake blew it off. These inbreds are weird, that's all. How can they not be, fucked up as they are? And the kid said they'd heard of him—they, no doubt, meaning Cody Natter. Maybe Natter had an interest in Jake's "enterprises." Maybe this was his way of suggesting they get together to do some business.

*Now there's a thought,* Jake considered.

"I'se just funnin' with ya, Jake," the kid told him, grinning away. The knot on his head looked as big as a baseball, and when he scratched his belly, Jake noticed he had two thumbs on his hand. "Just mosey on up and go right in, she'll be waitin' fer ya. She cain't talk much, but she'll suck yer dick so hard yer asshole'll inhale. Best head in the county, and a good tumble, too." The kid chuckled, a high-pitched titter. "Just don't 'spect no rousin' conversation."

I ain't interested in talking, Jake reminded himself. "All right," he agreed. "I'll be done in a spell."

"Take yer time, Jake. Have fun."

Jake left the kid at the old pickup and followed the short, rutted drive. He didn't see any other cars or trucks around, and no people either. The moon hung just over the trees behind him, and up ahead he could see the big house sunk back in the woods against the clearing. Faint amber light glowed softly in the shuttered, lower-level windows. The steady chorus of crickets and spring peepers rushed in his ears like gentle ocean waves breaking on a beach.

As Jake climbed the wood steps to the porch, he thought, Aw, yeah, for at the same time the stripper appeared in the entry and held open the screen door. She'd changed into a frilly white robe-like sort of thing sashed at the waist. It was so sheer she practically looked naked standing there, the outline of her body cut sharp as a freshly stropped blade against the lamplight behind her. But when Jake came into the parlor, he saw that the light came from several old oil lanterns. They ain't even got electricity in the joint, he thought. The parlor was stuffy with old furniture, old framed paintings, and old avocado wallpaper that was peeling at the seams. An enormous oval throw rug covered the hardwood floor.

"All right, hon, let's get to it."

The screen door flapped shut. Then the girl turned abruptly, took one of the lanterns, and padded barefoot down the hall. Jake followed.

Christ, it's hot, he realized, but that's the way Jake "The Snake" Rhodes liked it: hot, humid, the air thick in its own heat. A hot night for some hot fucking. They called him the Snake because he was as mean as one, and he needed to be. Nice guys didn't last in Jake's business. When someone ripped you off, you had to get rough. And when new guys tried to move on your turf, well... You had to do what you had to do. Jake had knocked off more than his share of cowboys—that was the only way to keep the word out that he wasn't one to fuck with. Every now and then his distro people got greedy and thought they'd make a few quick extra bucks by stepping on his raw product with turpentine. Jake didn't need his customers dying, so sometimes he'd have to break a few bones or pop a few kneecaps. That got the message across loud and clear: Don't pull shit on Jake Rhodes.

And chicks? Shit, it's easier this way. What did he need a steady squeeze for? He'd never met a woman in his life he could trust. They all turned on you eventually; they all sold you out when they thought they could get a better deal somewhere else. He remembered one splittail he kept around a few years back, fucked him anytime he wanted and seemed straight up. Then Jake started losing some of his point distributors, and he found out it was the chick selling his points to some cowboy from Tylersville. Well, Jake had set the guy's trailer on fire—with the guy still inside, of course, conveniently gagged and handcuffed to the drainpipe under his bathroom sink. And he had a good old time cutting up his squeeze with the stainless-steel Seymour machete.

He followed the Creeker girl into a cramped room off to the right. Here several more lanterns glowed, and their dancing flames made the drab wallpaper look alive with pulsing swirls of light; the room seemed to breathe. No bed, just a big old scarlet scroll couch and a highback armchair with cracked upholstery. "How about gettin' that shit off," Jake said, and sat down in the chair. "Lemme have a look at ya."

The girl paused and blinked, then falteringly stripped herself of the veil-like robe. She just stood there, blinking stupidly out of her pale nakedness.

"Now how's about layin' down on the couch and playin' with yerself awhiles, like you were doin' at the club?"

She stared a moment, then mumbled something that sounded like "lay-ply-self? Ah." But evidently she got the gist because then she lounged back on the couch and began to run her hands up and down her sides and inside her legs, and Jake noted that her right hand was much smaller than the other, like a toddler's, while her left was as big as his own. And then he noticed something else: when her flat, thin-lipped face inclined to look at him, he saw that the color of her eyes very nearly matched the dark strawberry-red of the velvet couch.

"Thlyke thisssss?" she asked.

"Yeah, baby, just like that."

Jake pulled out a roach; he saw no harm in taking a hit of his own stuff every now and then. What he did, like most, was spray the raw dust in liquid form on mats of Old Bugler tobacco, then roll it up into joints. Just a nip. His lighter flashed, and he took a quick snatch down his throat and held it. The sharp, edgy buzz hit him quick, unpleasant at first, but then it smoothed out in his head and left him gritting his teeth in a tight grin. Jake wasn't into nice gentle lovemaking; he wanted a nasty, down and dirty fuck, and a good toke of his own product got him in the mood right quick. He tamped the roach out with his fingers and went on watching the girl through the hard, glitterish buzz.

"That's it, you little mushmouth. Rub up on them funny tits of yours awhile."

Jake had chosen this one for just that. Her breasts. Small, like cupcakes, but fascinating in their imperfection. Two dark pink nipples sprouted out from the center of each breast, large as the end of Jake's thumb. I'll be biting on those big suckers real hard, he thought. But first...

Jake stood up and walked to the couch. "Get'cher face right on up here, retard. Yer brother outside says you give some good head—or is he yer father?" Jake cut a laugh. "Guess he's probably both, huh?" Then he grabbed the girl by a rough handful of her shiny black hair—the tiniest shrill leaked out of her throat—and lifted her to a sitting position. Then he dropped his jeans.

"Go on, uglypuss. You know what to do. Bet you been sucking yer relatives' cocks since you was in kindergarten," and then he laughed again. "'Course I guess you never went to kindergarten 'cos I don't imagine they take Creeker retards like you into kindergarten."

But the girl, if she understood them at all, gave no reaction to Jake's ugly remarks. Instead, she simply followed suit.

Jake moaned, leaning his head back. He watched the queer squiggles of light rove the ceiling. It was like a sea up there, a churning, stormy sea of shadows and firelight, and again he thought of the sound of the surf as the night sounds pulsed in from the opened window. The sensation, backed by the buzz of his angel dust, brought an excruciating pleasure he'd never felt anything like before. Gawd almighty, he thought. I've had bitches suck my dick hundreds of times but never like this. That lumphead outside was right. This gal gives the best head in the county and then some...

In fact, the sensation was so remarkable that he pushed her face off a moment, and pushed her lower lip down with his thumb. Then he cracked off another laugh.

The girl had no teeth.

*Don't that just beat the bushes! No wonder she sucks such a good cock—she ain't got a single chopper in her yap!*

Jake grabbed her hair again, giving it a hard twist, and urged her to get back to business. His penis felt caught in a hot, wet trap which seemed omnipresent over every inch. "Where'd you learn to suck cock so good, honey? Your daddy teach you that? Yeah, I bet he did. I bet you were suckin' dick the same time you were suckin' milk out your mama's tit." Jake gave her hair another twist, then reached down with his other hand, to her breast. At once his fingers found that remarkable, jutting dual-nipple. From then on it was instinct; he began to squeeze the gorged, pink double-knot of flesh between his thumb and forefinger, hard enough that the girl whined immediately from deep in her throat. The harder he pinched the more she whined, and this bizarre vocal sensation only added to the mounting pleasures of her mouth. "Honey," he gasped, "your cock-sucking's so good I'm afraid I'm gonna have to blow my first squirt right down yer throat." His laughter hitched up. "You won't mind none though; in fact you'll thank me 'cos it'll probably be the best meal you had in weeks," and at that same moment everything Jake Rhodes felt converged to a pinpoint of irrevocable, demented lust. The firelight on the ceiling swirled into chaos, the night sounds rushed, and the girl continued to whine in her pain as the moon glowered in through the window, and Jake's climax broke like a wild ferret let out of its trap...

His eyes crossed, and all that dust-edged lust poured out of him as he squeezed the girl's face to his groin by tight fistfuls of hair. She was gagging, but Jake didn't care. The sensation seemed impossible. As good as it was, it just didn't seem quite right—

Eventually he released her hair, and she fell back gasping against the couch, her chest heaving. "That was real good, mush-mouth," Jake complimented her, "but something's really fucked up here, and I aim to find out what 'fore I fuck you so hard you'll be shitting out your nose."

He grabbed her head, turned her face up, and jammed his fingers into her toothless mouth. "Open up, retard. Open yer yap unless you want me to punch your lights out."

The girl's panic had nowhere to go. Tears smeared her cheeks along with the bewilderment and terror in her scarlet eyes. Then she let her mouth yawn open.

Jake squinted. The fuck? he thought. He grabbed her slender throat and squeezed.

"Stick out yer tongue, ya cumbucket."

The girl resisted, whining, gagging. Her eyes seemed lidless as she stared up in total incomprehension.

Jake squeezed her throat a lot harder, till her face began to tint pink. "Stick it out, ya Creeker freak. Right now."

The pink tint began to darken. Then, tremoring, she stuck out her tongue.

Jake stared back.

It was not a tongue that stuck out of her mouth, but a pair of them, both roving like fat worms on a hotplate.

She's got...two...tongues, he marveled in the most grotesque fascination.

And that's about all Jake Rhodes had time to marvel over because at the same instant the fidgety shadow slid up behind him and—

Ka-CRACK!

—brought a yard-long two-by-four straight down on top of his head.

"Where's the chief?" Phil asked brusquely when he returned to the station at the end of his shift.

"You didn't call in 10-6 for shift change," Susan smirked in reply.

Phil fumed. "Straker, Philip, ID 8, reporting 10-6 from eight-to-eight shift. Out of service," he said. "Now, where's Mullins?"

"If you mean Chief Mullins, I believe he's back in the supply building—"

*Probably checking coffee filters*, Phil thought.

But Susan Ryder continued from her console, "And one thing I've been meaning to ask you. What kind of service ammunition are you loading...Sergeant Straker?"

"What's that supposed to mean?"

"It seemed like a pretty cut-and-dry question to me. But just let me remind you that sabot, teflon, liquid-filled, and especially quad ammunition is illegal for all law-enforcement use in this state."

So that's it, Phil realized. That's why the Ice Bitch hates me. "I get the gist of what you're saying, Ms. Ryder, and not that I'm in the habit of reporting the nomenclature of my service ammunition to radio girls, I'm loading Plus P Plus .38 wadcutters, which is what I've always loaded."

"That's not what I've heard," she said, and redirected her gaze into her textbook.

"Yeah, well, you've probably also heard that I'm a kid killer, and I wouldn't be the least bit surprised if you've heard that Jesus Christ is really an astronaut from another solar system and that Elvis is alive and well and has lunch regularly at Chuck's Diner, nor would I be surprised if you actually believed those things." Phil leaned over her console desk. "But let me make a suggestion, Ms. Ryder. I really think it would be prudent for you to not only get your snooty nose out of other's people's business, but you also might find life a lot more agreeable if you put a lid on that outrageous ego of yours, and—" Suddenly Phil pounded his fist—BAM!—down on her desk, whereupon Susan Ryder's derriére lifted at least an inch from her seat in complete surprise. "—and let me tell you one more thing. I've never loaded quads, and I never killed a kid. That whole Metro mess was a sham, Ms. Ryder; I was set up. And if you don't believe that, I don't give a flying fuck. But I do have one more suggestion, you rude ego-maniacal bitch. Don't make judgments about people until you know all of the facts."

Then, in utter calm, Phil turned around, walked into Chief Mullins' office, and closed the door very quietly behind him.

God, I hate women so much sometimes, he told himself. Through the window, he saw Mullins coming out of the lock-up-turned-supply building and the man did not look happy.

When the back door swung open, Phil beat the chief to the punch. "Look, Chief, I'm sorry, but I forgot to pick up the coffee filters. Bust me."

"Christ, you kids," Mullins griped and sat his girth down behind his desk. "Can't trust ya to take care of your own bowel movements, huh? Looks like I'll have to waste valuable tax-dollar-time getting the friggin' filters myself."

"Guess so," Phil said. "But I suspect the world will still continue to revolve while you're gone."

"That's what I like about you, Phil. You're a smartass after my own heart." Mullins raised a paper cup and spat tobacco juice into it. "You stake out Krazy Sallee's in plainclothes last night?"

"Yeah," Phil replied. "Got some tag numbers, descriptions, stuff like that. It's a good start."

"You see that ugly fuck—Natter?"

"Yeah, Chief, I saw him."

"You see anyone else?"

Phil rubbed at minute stubble on his chin. "Yeah, Chief, I did. And right now I got a burning question for you."

"Lemme guess, hot stuff," the chief said, "You saw Vicki Steele coming out of there, and now you're pissed at me 'cos I didn't tell you she was stripping up there."

"Bingo," Phil said.

Mullins spat again. "Well, I figure there's things a man has to learn on his own, especially when it's about a woman he's still got the hots for."

"I don't have the hots for her. But I think it would've been pretty civil for you to warn me in advance. And you expect me to believe that Vicki Steele quit the department to do a strip show at Sallee's?"

"No, I don't expect you to believe that," Mullins said very quickly. "So let's make a little bit of an amendment to what I told you beforehand. Vicki Steele didn't quit like North and Adams. I fired her."

"For what?"

Mullins let out a stout chuckle. "Shit, Phil, you're the one who dated her for five years. I gotta tell you?"

"You're losing me, Chief. And you're pissing me off more."

"I fired her for dereliction of duty on the grounds of overt sexual misconduct."

"Bullshit," Phil said at once.

"Believe what ya want, son. But it's true. You think I wanted to tell you about the shit she pulled?"

"Tell me," Phil asked.

"She was fucking her boyfriends on duty, Phil. And since you asked for it, she had a lot of boyfriends. Or maybe I'm using the term 'boyfriends' out of respect—"

Phil glowered. "Be disrespectful, Chief."

"She was fucking just about anything that moved," Mullins pulled no punches. "Hey, you're the one who asked. She was picking up guys at the Qwik-Stop and doing them right in the patrol car. She'd pull rednecks over at night for speeding, and she'd wind up fucking the guys. You want more?"

"Sure," Phil said.

Mullins shrugged. "One night I came in and caught her blowing a prisoner in the lock-up. I got half a dozen complaints that she was rousting patrons at Sallee's, pulling them over and threatening to DWI them, and then fucking the guys and letting them off. You want more, son?"

"Sure," Phil said, a bit less enthusiastically this time.

"I have good reason—documented reason—to believe she was actually turning tricks while on duty. Threatening to write guys up for drinking behind the wheel, then fucking them for money in exchange for not writing them up. Christ, one night she even put the make on me, and I haven't had a hard-on in about fifteen years."

Phil sat back in his chair, reflecting. Vicki? A sex maniac? A... whore? Then he reflected further. She'd always been pretty feisty—and sometimes downright kinky—in bed. But that doesn't mean she's a nympho, he thought. Mullins seemed straight up about this—at least as straight up as he could be—but Phil had a hard time seeing Vicki Steele changing so drastically that she would actually blackmail traffic offenders into a scenario of prostitution.

"I just can't believe it," Phil said. "I just can't see her doing things like that."

Mullins' brow raised as he took another spit. "Neither could I, until she told me the reason. And please don't ask me to tell you what she said."

"Tell me what she said," Phil directed.

"You can't handle it, Phil."

"I can handle it. So quit fucking with me, will ya?"

Mullins set his jaw. He appeared genuinely distressed, which was something Phil had never recalled seeing. He cleared his throat, did a fidget in his seat, and said, "When I fired her, she said it was all because of you. You taking off without her. You dumping her."

Phil stared. Could this really be? I cannot believe this, he told himself very slowly. Then his words grated, "I didn't dump her."

"Bullshit, Phil. When you leave a girl for a job, and she doesn't want to move with you, that's the same as dumping her. After you left she went nuts. She turned nympho. And when I shitcanned her, the very next week, she was stripping up at Sallee's and turning tricks every night. Still don't believe me?"

Phil's voice turned black when he said, "No."

Mullins, with a sour look, hoisted himself up, retrieved a folder from one of his file cabinets, and turned. "Buck North, Pete Adams, before they quit for the other departments, this PCP headache was just starting up. So I had them doing the same thing you did last night. Staking out Krazy Sallee's, trying to get a read on what's going on up there. Only these guys didn't just take down tag numbers. They took pictures."

Phil gulped as if a chunk of broken glass had stuck in his throat...

"Take a peek at your own risk," Mullins warned. "But don't get pissed at me for showin' ya, 'cos you're the one who asked."

Then Mullins dropped the folder in Phil's lap.

It was some presage, a hideous one: Phil refused to believe any implication, yet his hands hitched toward the folder like someone about to unveil an as-yet unidentified cadaver on a morgue slab. He opened the folder—

No, he thought very simply.

—and stared. His face felt as though it had fused into a mask of impassive stone. A small stack of 8x10 black and whites showed him first several nondescript women leaving Sallee's hand in hand with various rubes. All tackily dressed in tight skirts, glittery blouses, high heels. Some were clearly less-defected Creekers, like the ones he'd seen last night. Next, a few grainy telephoto shots, obviously taken with fast film through a low-light lens. The discreet snapshots depicted the same women engaged in various sex acts with rough, jean-jacketed men. In pickup trucks and souped hot rods, behind the building.

One photo showed a Creeker woman—with one arm undeniably longer than the other—lying on her back on the garbage dumpster behind Sallee's, her legs wrapped around some anonymous redneck's back. Natter's Imperial was seen in several of the shots, and so was Natter himself, tall, gaunt, and crevice-faced as he leaned to speak to several patrons in the entry.

And the last four photographs showed Vicki Steele performing the act of fellatio in the cabs of different pickup trucks. A final photograph showed her flashing a wicked smile as she stuffed paper cash into her bra. Something shiny splotched her blouse and hair, which could only be semen...

"Told ya so, didn't I?" Mullins harped. He loaded a fresh pinch of snuff and immediately spat. "But you wouldn't listen. That's your problem, Phil. You never listen to anyone. You always gotta know more than the next guy about everything."

Fuck you, Phil thought, but now, as he closed the folder, he knew the chief was right.

*I asked for it, I got it*, he thought. *Happy now, you asshole?*

"Now you know the score," Mullins informed him. His desk chair creaked as he shifted his significant weight. "Sometimes the world really can be a piece of shit, huh?"

Phil didn't say anything. He coldly placed the folder up on Mullins' desk, his face still stiff as plaster.

"Go on home. Get some sleep."

Phil rose as if climbing out of a tomb. The imagery swarmed behind his mind: Vicki's head buried in some slob's lap, semen shining like diamond-points in her hair, and like jeweled studs on her blouse.

A whore, Phil thought as he walked out of the station.

*I dumped her, and she turned into a strip-joint whore...*

# EIGHT

It was a fascinating sound, a slick wet clicking, like duct tape being pulled off something tacky.

The world seemed to hum in his head: glories, wonders.

*Mishmash words ricocheted in his brain. My poor brethren, he thought. I bless thee in thy error. I love thee...*

*Ah-no-prey-bee!*

*Skeet-inner!*

*Ah-no, slave-luss!*

He watched, in reverence, in faith. *What an honor to behold sights such as this...* He felt heady and warm. He felt exuberant. *The flesh of the world... My God, we are blessed...*

That slick, wet sound resumed. Colors glittered, contrast flashed. It was just so beautiful! Red running over white.

His eyes turned to the window, to the sky.

And the wet sounds continued.

Soon, the Reverend thought. His heart burned like an ember, an ember of love, a hot, glowing ingot of molten truth.

*Yes. Soon it will be time again...*


He was a little boy. Bugs buzzed at his face, some of them sinking stingers. Dead branches and leaves crunched beneath his blacktop Keds as the sun blistered through the trees.

He didn't feel good. At school, Miss Cunningham mentioned that a real bad flu from China was going around. I won't get it, he remembered thinking. I'm not Chinese.

But his skin felt cold in spite of the drenching heat. His stomach felt dry—he'd thrown up earlier, hadn't he?—and he knew it must be the stuffed peppers his aunt served for dinner last night. He hated stuffed peppers. Why couldn't they eat Pop Tarts every night instead? The cinnamon kind were great, and the strawberry kind with the white icing…

He didn't want to go home. He didn't want to believe he was sick. I'm not sick, he convinced himself. I don't have any Chinese flu! So on he marched, wandering as children do in a pent-up glee, in a curiosity that was as honest as it was without direction of any kind. This gully here, he'd played in with his G.I. Joes. And over here by the stump that looked wide as a manhole cover, he and Dave "Cave" Houseman had shot at Nehi bottles with the BB gun that Cave had borrowed from Eagle. And they'd hit plenty of the bottles.

His Keds crunched on. He didn't know where he was going, and he didn't care. One night he'd stayed over at Eagle's house, to watch the Alfred Hitchcock show, and a lady on TV had killed someone with a frozen leg of lamb. And Eagle's Uncle Frank had come in—he built houses—and said to never go in the woods because there were "things" in the woods that ten-year-olds shouldn't see. So naturally the next day he and Eagle Peters had gone into the woods, which they did almost every day from then on. One time they'd found a warm can of Miller beer, and they even drank it once they found what Uncle Frank called the churchkey. Another time they found a dead cat behind Buckingham Elementary, and the cat's belly was moving from a bunch of worms that got in it. And then there was another time they found a big dark-green plastic bag full of moldy magazines, only these magazines had lots of pictures of naked ladies in them, and they laughed because it reminded them of a show called Naked City. One of the ladies was pouring honey between another lady's legs, then she was licking it off! In another magazine a lady was sticking a gun in another lady's hole. And after that she was sticking cucumbers and bananas and things in her. And in one other magazine there was a caption that said "WENDY LIKES TO SUCK," and that reminded them of the song they heard all the time, called "Wendy," or was it "Windy"? The lady had a black man's thing in her mouth!

He and Eagle roamed the woods whenever they could, but they never found the "things" that Uncle Frank said ten-year-olds shouldn't see.

"Uncle Frank said a girl got raked out here once," Eagle told him one day when they were shooting slingshots at bottles by the creek. "He said it said so in the paper."

"A girl got raked? What's that?"

Eagle seemed to know everything, and, as he lined up his next shot—at a Briardale Cola bottle—he spoke like it was nothing.

"It's when a man puts his pee-er in a lady, and she doesn't want to."

This confused him. "Why would a man want to do that?"

"'Cos it feels good, stupid. Don't you know anything? He squirts baby-juice in her, and it feels good."

"Oh... What's baby-juice?"

Eagle laughed. "You're stupider than Larry on the Three Stooges! Baby-juice is the stuff that comes out a man's pee-er when he puts it in a lady. It makes 'em have babies. But when rake-ists do it, they do other things too." Eagle pulled the slingshot back. "Bad things."

This made him wonder. When Eagle hit the Briardale Cola bottle, it exploded. "What bad things?" he asked Eagle.

They called him Eagle because he had blond hair, but his father always made him get a crewcut, so he looked like a bald eagle. And Eagle said, "Well, they beat the ladies up too, and sometimes they kill 'em."

Something bloomed in the little boy's head, a curiosity like the time he broke his arm, and it itched under the plaster so bad he stuck one of his aunt's knitting needles up there to scratch it. When Doc Smith took the cast off, he cried 'cos the doctor did it with a little saw that sounded worse than Doc Verib's dentist drill. And when the cast fell away, his arm was covered with white flakes, and all the hairs on his arm had turned blacker than Lisa Cottergim's eyebrows. She was an Oriental girl who got 'dopted by her parents, and her pretty eyebrows were blacker than a crow's feathers. Maybe she was Chinese, and that's why they had this Chinese flu going around that his teacher had told him about. But, anyway, Doc Smith told him his hairs turned black only 'cos the plaster had covered the hairs from the sun for six weeks. And anyway something itched in his head just like the way his skin itched under the cast.

"What kind of...bad things?" he asked.

Eagle hogged the next shot at one of his G.I. Joes that had busted 'cos a rubber band broke inside and made his head fall off. "Like really bad things," he said. His eye opened behind the rock. "Like this lady? After the man squirted a lot of baby-juice in her peehole, he squirted some in her butt, too—"

"He did not!" the little boy exclaimed, appalled.

"Yes he did, 'cos I heard my dad and Uncle Frank talking about it one night they thought I was asleep. They were watching Naked City and talking about the lady who got raked. And the rake-ist squirted baby-juice up the lady's butt, too, and then..."

"What!" the little boy nearly shrieked.

"Then he tied her to a tree and hit her with a monkey wrench, and then he stuck the monkey wrench up her peehole. And after that—" Eagle seemed to pause, like he did when he was making something up—"he hit her in the head with a rake and kilt her."

"With a rake? Why?"

"Why?" Eagle laughed at him again. "Because that's what rake-ist's do, stupid. That's why they call it rake."

The little boy wondered about this. It didn't make sense. "But why would a man ever want to do that to a lady?"

"Don't really know," Eagle said. "But Uncle Frank said there was lots of folks in the world who were sick in the head, and I guess that's why. And, anyway, Big Chief Mullins 'vester-gated the rake, and he told the papers it was a Creeker who done it."

Creeker, the little boy thought. He let Eagle hog another shot 'cos he was too busy thinking. Creeker...

The word slid down his belly hot and ugly and worse than his aunt's stuffed peppers, and even worse than her corned beef and cabbage with the lumpy tomato sauce that he hated even more. He'd heard a little bit about the Creekers, just little bits. No one talked about 'em much, like they was some bad secret or something, or like the way nobody ever talked much about Mrs. Nixerman, who got sick in the head and would run around buck naked at night with her big fat boobs flapping. She had to go to a special hospital in Crownsville that was only for people who were sick in the head. But even though he'd heard a little bit about Creekers, he asked Eagle anyway, 'cos he figured Eagle might know more. And that's what fascinated the little boy, like about the rake-ist, and the "things" in the woods, and all that.

He wanted to know.

"What's a Creeker?" he asked.

"Aw, you're stupider than Larry and Shemp!" Eagle guffawed. "A Creeker is someone who got born by their father or brother's baby-juice. And there's somethin' about it—I'm not sure what—but if a father like puts his pee-er in his daughter and squirts his baby-juice in her peehole, the baby comes out all wrong. And the same if a mother lets her son squirt his baby-juice in her. Uncle Frank said it's 'cos you're not supposed to do it, and God gets so mad, he makes the babies come out wrong."

Wrong, the little boy thought. It slid down his gut just like the word Creeker, and just like his aunt's corned beef and cabbage and the stuffed peppers. "How you mean...wrong?"

The headless, naked G.I. Joe took Eagle's rock right in the chest, and pieces of plastic flew everywhere—

WHAP!

"The babies come out like the hippie, peacenik babies Uncle Frank told me about. These hippies take LSD and it messes up a man's baby-juice, and it makes the babies real ugly and wrong. Same as Creekers. They'se just hillfolk who only squirt their juice into their reller-tives. And their babies get, like, real big heads like a fishbowl and giant red eyes that are crooked, and ten fingers on each hand instead of five. And girl Creekers sometimes had extra boobs and nipples like a hog and stuff. Sometimes they get born without no arms or legs, so the Creeker fathers kill 'em. They eat 'em."

"They do not!" the little boy wailed.

"Shore they do, 'cos Uncle Frank told me. And lots of 'em got teeth like Kevin Furman's bulldog."

The little boy shuddered. He wasn't feeling too good to begin with—on account of his aunt's stuffed peppers, he was sure—but this made him feel even worse. 'Cos Kevin Furman's bulldog Pepper had the gnarliest, ugliest yellow teeth, and he couldn't imagine anything scarier than a person with those same kind of teeth in their mouth...

'Cos there wasn't nothing uglier than Kevin Furman's bulldog.

"And there's something worse," Eagle said, lining up the next hogged shot.

"What?"

"I don't know if I should tell ya, 'cos you'd probably cry like a baby."

Eagle missed the next target, a big dead toad they'd found by the creek. But one time Dave Houseman told them his friend Mike Cutt would take live toads and shoot 'em with the slingshot, and he'd even play baseball with live toads. He'd swing the bat, and the toad's guts would spray way out. And the little boy couldn't think of anything grosser. And then Eagle continued, "the Creekers, you know, they got their own whorehouse out here somewhere."

"What's—" the little boy gulped. "—what's a...whorehouse?"

Eagle rolled his eyes. His next shot, too, missed the big, dead toad. "It's a place where men pay money to squirt their juice into ladies, ya moe-ron. Don't ya know nuthin'? And sometimes the whores put a man's pee-er in their mouths and let 'em squirt their baby-juice there—"

"In their mouths?" the little boy shrieked.

"That's right, in their mouths too, not just their peeholes. But anyway, I heard Uncle Frank and my dad talkin' 'bout it one night, and the Creekers have a special whorehouse, where men can pay to squirt their juice into Creeker ladies, like the kind I was tellin' you about who are all messed up and wrong and gross-looking and have big heads and ten fingers on each hand..."

*And teeth like Kevin Furman's dog,* the little boy remembered.

SPLAT!

The little boy looked up. Eagle had finally hit the big dead toad with the slingshot.

The toad's insides splattered everywhere, in a wormy red mist.

That day Eagle had gone on to say that this Creeker whorehouse was supposed to be a secret. Nobody talked much about it just like they didn't talk much about Mrs. Nixerman. Not just any man could go there—'cos it was special—but only men who were friends with the Creekers. This all fascinated the little boy. That ladies—they were called whores—would let a man do these things to 'em for money, and 'specially Creeker ladies...

But now the curiosity itched, much much worse than the way his skin itched under Doc Smith's plaster cast.

The next day Eagle got grounded by his dad, for beating up his brothers Ricky and Billy 'cos Ricky and Billy had called him "bald eagle," and only Eagle's friends were allowed to call him that.

But the little boy still itched with curiosity, with the innocent quest for knowledge. He wanted to see...the "things" Uncle Frank had talked about.

So for the whole time Eagle was grounded the little boy wandered around the woods anyway. Right after school. Sometimes he'd stop by the police station and say hi to Big Chief Mullins,

Edward Lee

who chewed gross-out tobacco but seemed like a very nice man, and sometimes he'd give him licorice sticks; he even offered him a "chaw" once but the little boy didn't want to put that stuff in his mouth.

Summers made the town—his entire world, in fact—a wonderful, lazy dreamland. School was out; he did his paper route in the mornings, mowed lawns in the afternoon, and sometimes Big Chief Mullins would pay him a few dollars to wash the police cars or clean up the station. Most of his money he gave to his aunt, to help out with the bills, but in the summer he always had some left for Cokes and models. And when his work was done, he'd wander.

In the woods.

Maybe Eagle's Uncle Frank was just kidding them. So far he hadn't even come close to finding the "things." There probably aren't any, he thought one day, trudging through the wooded hills up behind the creek. Probably just said it to scare us...

But why would Uncle Frank do that?

It was mid-August, and the hottest day of the year. His belly didn't feel right that day. "Too much of that ice cream," his aunt told him that morning when he got back from his route, but he knew better. It was those stuffed peppers she'd served again last night. But like most ten-year-olds, he wasn't about to let a belly-ache keep him cooped up at home. He felt even worse mowing that day's lawns; a couple times he thought he might upchuck. Mrs. Young would fire me for sure, he thought, puking stuffed peppers on her lawn! He should've stayed home when he was done, but he couldn't help it. Bad as his belly felt, after he'd cleaned up the mower and put it back in the shed, he headed for the woods.

He crossed the rushing creek, carefully stepping on the stones he and Eagle had thrown in last year. Some green slimy stuff had grown on some of them—he had to be careful. Clumps of frog eggs clung to sticks in the water, and on the bank he almost stepped on a big brown snapping turtle he thought was a pile of mud. Uncle Frank said they'd bite your fingers off if you got too close. On the bank, he kicked over a log. Two fat shiny salamanders sat there, and they had yellow spots, which was neat. But his heart jumped when he kicked over another log: a nest of baby snakes slithered in the damp spot, six of them, but to him it looked like a hundred. And they were brown with tiny diamond heads. Harmless in reality—they were just hognose snakes—but to a ten-year-old boy, any brown snake was surely a copperhead.

He scaled the embankment up a fallen tree, then pushed into the woods. Eech! he thought when he also pushed through a sticky spiderweb suspended invisibly between two trees. Several trails branched out (he and Eagle hadn't taken all of them) so he took the one to the far left and just started walking…

Maybe one of the trails would lead to the "things."

He couldn't imagine exactly what kind of things Uncle Frank meant. Maybe he'd find more of those moldy magazines that had pictures of naked ladies. Or maybe—

His heart jumped again.

*Maybe I'll find a lady who's been raked,* he fretted.

He hoped not. What would he do? And what would he do with the rake? Take it to Big Chief Mullins?

The sun blazed through the trees; sweat dripped in his eyes, and his T-shirt stuck to him. He passed another creek he'd never seen before and was suddenly swarmed by mosquitoes, and when he tried to run on he—SPLAT!—accidentally stepped on a big toad. Aw, gross! he thought. The toad's plump body burst under his shoe like a baggie full of pudding.

The bugs were biting him all over, and the harder the August sun beat down, the worse he felt. Not just his belly now, but his throat was hurting too, and his head felt stuffed up, and there were a couple more times he thought he might upchuck. I'm never eating those stuffed peppers again, he vowed to himself. Ever!

After another twenty minutes his belly got to feeling real bad. This is stupid, he thought. There aren't no things in the woods. Uncle Frank's full of dog poop! And just as he was ready to turn around and go back home, something snapped. A branch? he wondered.

He stood still.

Then he heard a voice:

"You. Hey."

Another branch snapped. Behind him.

His eyes darted around. It was a lady's voice, he could tell, but it sounded sort of…funny. Sort of like the way his aunt sounded on Friday nights when she drank out of that big bottle of wine she kept in the icebox.

"Wha'choo fer lookin' ah? Lost ya?"

At first he couldn't see her; the old stained sundress she wore blended right in with the woods. But then she seemed to appear like magic while he squinted toward the direction of the voice. A girl stood a few yards away between two trees. She had real black straight hair, but it was all kind of mussed up in her face, and she wasn't wearing any shoes, and her legs looked real dirty. She stood there a bit looking at him through her hair, and when he took a few curious steps, she took a few too and suddenly the sun was on her. She looked older, like maybe twelve or thirteen, 'cos she had little bubs pushing against the top of her dress like most of the sixth-grade girls had at school, and he could even see little buds poking through! "Bub-buds," Dave the Cave called them. "Tittie buds. Milk comes out of 'em when ya suck 'em." Milk? That sounded pretty silly. Why would milk be in a girl's bubs, he remembered thinking, when you can get it right out of the icebox? But that was a while ago when the Cave had told him that, and it didn't matter now. He could see this girl's boobs real good because her dress top was all stuck to her with sweat just like his Green Hornet T-shirt. He could tell he liked her, though, even though she was all dirty and all, and her messy hair was hanging in her face. Yeah, he could tell he liked her, and he could tell she was pretty. And there was one other thing he could tell:

*Hillfolk!* he realized. *She's a hill girl. Probably lives in a shack somewhere. Probably doesn't even go to school...*

"Hi-yuh, ya," she said, and black strands of hair hanging over her mouth sort of puffed out when she spoke. "What's-er-yer name, er-ya?"

He squinted at her, not quite sure what she'd said. "Uh, Phil," he said. "Phil Straker. What's yours?"

"Dawnie, me." She glanced around, like maybe she was nervous about something. "I'm me name Dawnie, me," and there her hair went again, puff-puff-puff.

This hill girl fascinated him, and he kind of thought he fascinated her too because then they stood there some more just looking at each other, but all that looking made him feel dumb, like he should be saying something, so he just said the first thing that came to his head. "I go to Summerset Elementary. Where do you go?"

"Whuh-ut?" she replied.

What a dumb thing to ask her! he immediately regretted it. Hill kids don't go to school! Then he said, "I live off the Route in my aunt's house. Where do you live, Dawnie?"

"There yonder, out." And she pointed behind her, into the woods, and the little boy wondered exactly where and in what. Did she really live in a shack or a lean-to? Hill folk didn't have any money at all so they couldn't buy houses. They couldn't even buy food, so they had to eat animals they caught in the woods. At least that's what Uncle Frank had said...

"What's, huh?" she said, stepping right up to him. He turned rigid as she abruptly put her hands on him, feeling his T-shirt. "What's this hee-ah?" she asked.

"It's the Green Hornet," he mumbled back. Dawnie probably didn't know who the Green Hornet was 'cos she'd probably never seen a comic. But then he felt flushed, instantly prickly. "What's this?" she asked again, fingering at the rim of his underpants which stuck up over his belt. Then she pulled at it...

"It's...underpants!" he replied, feeling hot and mushy, and suddenly his thing was stiff.

Her hands felt strange on him, but they felt good. Her breath puffing through her hair smelled sort of like milk. Then he looked at her hands—

*Holy poop!*

—and saw that one hand had seven fingers, and the other had four but was missing a thumb. And then he looked at her feet—

*She's a—*

—which had at least eight little toes on each.

*—Creeker!*

She tugged curiously up on the edge of his underpants, and all at once his pee-er felt funny, like something was going to happen. The little boy couldn't imagine what, though. He stared at her, never moving. She's a Creeker, he thought more slowly this time. She had to be, just like what Eagle said. They were wrong, they were messed up. Why else would she have so many toes if she wasn't a Creeker?

Her coal-black hair swayed in front of her face...

"You kin kiss me, ya want," she said, and in that next second she was kissing him, real sloppy like, and putting her tongue into his mouth. At first he was grossed-out, but very quickly he started to like it. Then—

"Dawn!" a voice cracked out of the woods like a rifle shot. "Dawn! Hee-ah! Now, girl!"

Dawnie jerked back. "I go gotta now," she whispered in panic, glancing back. "Bye!"

Then she ran off into the woods.

"Wait!" his voice broke. He wasn't even thinking. He didn't want her to go. He wanted to...kiss her some more. But off she went, her feet carrying her away.

What should I do? he thought quite dumbly. The answer was simple.

He ran after her.

She'd got a good head start. Leaves and branches crunched under his sneakered feet as he pedaled forward into the brush. Vines and thorn bushes scratched at his arms and face, but he didn't care, he didn't even feel it. His eyes darted forward. Where had she gone? All he saw up ahead were trees, woods, spiderwebs. Then he pushed through more thicket and sunlight broke on his face...

Suddenly he was standing at the end of a dirt road which led up a hill. At the end of the road stood a house.

A big three-story rickety farmhouse. Gables stuck out of the upstairs rooms; old gray wood showed through old whitewash, and some of the shingles on the roof were missing, which reminded him of Mrs. Nixerman's missing teeth. The roof seemed to sag...

He still wasn't thinking. He was running up the road. He didn't see Dawnie, but he knew she must live there 'cos there weren't any other houses around. The house got bigger as his feet stomped along the dusty dirt road. Big bugs zapped at his head.

Weathered planks creaked as he moved up the steps. He stood on the porch a moment, then took very slow steps to his right—

Toward the first window.

He placed his hand above his brow, to shield the sun from his eyes.

Then he put his face to the window and looked in...

# NINE

D ream, the parched thought throbbed in his head.

Phil was staring up into an abyss he eventually recognized as his bedroom ceiling. Threads of sunlight strayed through the gaps in his blackout curtains, spoiling the makeshift nighttime that his work schedule forced him to create. Despite the room's beastly heat, he felt buried in cold mud.

*A dream...*

Not a dream as much as a replay, a mental towline dragging him back to that day twenty-five years ago. The rekindled images, now, made it seem like yesterday...

The humid, bug-buzzing woods. The little Creeker girl. The long dirt road leading up the hill he'd never seen before, and...

The House, he remembered.

And that was all he dare remember—the House. Not the things he'd seen or at least the things he thought he'd seen. Thank God he'd awakened before the dream had replayed all of that, too...

He groaned, swung out of bed, and frowned fiercely upon opening the curtains. Working at night, of course, meant sleeping during the day, something he was accustomed to by now, except for that first rude jolt of sunlight. It seemed weird getting up at three or four in the afternoon when the rest of the world rose in the morning. But at least, he reminded himself, I never have to put up with rush hour.

The bedroom and cubbyhole den he rented from Old Lady Crane was no Trump Towers penthouse, but the price was right; it was all he needed, at least for now. The only killer was the place had no air-conditioning, and that fact drove home right this minute; he turned on the behemoth window fan, then grabbed a towel and headed for the shower. He paused at the bathroom mirror, though, long enough to mock, Looking good, Phil. Nice tan, too.

He supposed he was in decent enough shape for thirty-five, but ten years of police work—not to mention his security stint on the graveyard shift—left him white as a trout belly. His image in the mirror made him laugh: palely naked, stubble on his face, his dark-blond hair in ludicrous disarray from six hours of sweat-drenched sleep. You better forget about that GQ cover, he thought. Even his normally clear hazel eyes had dark circles under them. The dream had worn him out, along with the grueling memories…

The cold shower felt lukewarm in the ninety-degree heat. By the time he dried off, he was sweating again. He still had several hours before he needed to get ready for work, but he had no idea what he was going to do. What? Hang out at the fire station? Go for a leisurely spin through beautiful downtown Crick City? Christ… He knew he needed to divert himself, or else he'd start thinking about the dream again, or he'd start thinking about the business with Vicki Steele. He needed to get his mind off all of that, but how could he, now that he was back in the same town, with all the old familiar sights and people? Start by shaving. He lathered up with Edge Gel, then nearly dropped his razor when someone knocked on the door.

*Who the—my rent's not due, is it? I've only been living here three days. Maybe it's* Reader's Digest *bringing me my fifteen mil.* Shave cream jiggled on his chin as he wrapped a towel around his waist and answered the door.

"I gave at the office," he said when he saw who it was.

The pretty face offered a snide smile. The blond icebitch, he recognized all too fast. Susan, our amiable, upbeat dispatcher.

"Nice towel," she said.

"If I'd known you would be knocking on my door, I'd have dressed black tie. Okay, so how much are the Girl Scout cookies?"

"You really are horribly sarcastic," Susan Ryder said.

Phil could imagine how silly he looked: green Edge Gel fizzing on his face, and a towel as the only thing keeping him from being stark naked. "All right, let me rephrase. What the hell do you want?"

"Well, I think I'm already regretting this, but I thought I'd offer to buy you dinner."

*Dinner,* Phil thought nebulously. *This woman hates me. She thinks I kill ghetto kids. Now she wants to buy me dinner.*

"Or I should say," she corrected, "whatever it is we night-shifters call the first meal of the day. I guess it's our breakfast." She seemed shaky suddenly, or even nervous. "Sort of a, you know, peace offering."

"Peace offering," Phil stated dumbly.

"Is your head made of bricks?" she suddenly snapped. "I'm trying to apologize! Jesus!"

"Apologize," Phil stated dumbly. The shave cream continued to fizz. "Uh...apologize for what?"

Exasperation, or rage, thinned her pretty blue eyes. "For treating you shitty this morning. But if you're going to be an asshole about it, then forget it."

"Oh. Uh," Phil brilliantly replied. This whole scene caught him off guard. "Well, in that case, your apology, and your invitation, are accepted. Can I finish changing, or do you want me to go like this?"

"You can go like that if you want," she said, smiling. "But if that towel falls off, you'll have to arrest yourself for indecent exposure."

"Or unlawful display of shaving cream in public," he said. "Come on in, I'll just be a minute. It's the maid's day off, so you'll have to forgive the current disarray of my estate."

Susan Ryder walked in, and immediately went to peruse the bookshelf in his broom-closet-sized den, mostly law enforcement, judicial, and criminology texts from his Master's courses. "All my Aquinas and Jung are still packed up," he said, "but I do have every Jack Ketchum novel ever printed." He quickly grabbed some clothes and slipped into the bathroom. He shaved haphazardly, realizing his own nervousness when he nearly sprayed Glade Air Freshener under his arms. What do I have to be nervous about? he joked. I have beautiful blondes in my room all the time. She was certainly attractive; perhaps he hadn't fully noticed that when they'd met, considering the circumstances. He left the bathroom door cracked an inch, and in the mirror he could see her stooped over his put-it-together-yourself fiberboard bookshelf: simply dressed in jeans, sneakers, and a faded lime blouse. Yeah, she's pretty, all right, he acknowledged as he began to brush his teeth with one hand and haul on his jeans with the other. Unfancified white-blond hair shimmered at her shoulders. Nice behind, too, you sexist pig, he noted of the way her pose accentuated her rear end. He knew what it was, though—not her good looks but the whole apology business. Apologies didn't seem like her style at all, but—

He didn't really know her, did he? So how could he make a judgment like that, when only this morning he'd ranted on her for prejudging him about the Metro fiasco. Who's prejudging who? he admitted with a mouthful of Crest.

"Oh," she commented from the den. "Did you know you talk in your sleep?"

Phil instantly spat toothpaste into the sink. "What!"

"You talk in your sleep," she repeated, still leaning over his books. "You're a bigtime ratchetjaw."

Phil stared into the mirror, toothpaste smeared on his lips like a drunken clown's whiteface. Of course he knew he talked in his sleep on occasion—the women in his past had always pointed that out—but how on earth could Susan know that?

"Either you're psychic, or you've got a microphone hidden in my room."

"Neither," she said. Now, in the mirror, she was flipping through his stack of LEAA journals in a box on the couch. "I rent the room right above yours."

Phil almost spat his toothpaste out again. "You live here?"

"Yeah. Isn't Mrs. Crane great? Anyway, eventually you'll discover that the heating ducts make for a very effective in-house intercom. So you better gag yourself whenever you go to bed, unless you want me to know all your secrets."

That's just great, Phil thought, pulling on a Highpoint College T-shirt. He tried to think of a funny comeback.

"The heating ducts, huh? So that explains the loud vibrating sound I hear everyday from upstairs," which he immediately regretted. He didn't know her well at all, and certainly not well enough to be making jokes like that.

"If you must know," she came back just as fast, "I use imported ben-wa balls, not vibrators."

Jesus. He guessed she was joking, or hoped she was. He came back out then, was about to speak as she turned in the den, but hesitated. Though his pause lasted only a second, it seemed like full minutes to him. God, she really is beautiful. No makeup, just a simple, pretty farm-girlish face, a slender yet curvy body, and high B-cup breasts that looked firm as apples. For a moment her face seemed brightly alight in the frame of pure-blond hair. Her eyes, a beautiful sea-blue, sparkled like chips of gems.

"You can take me out to dinner now, or breakfast, or whatever it is that us night-shifters call the first meal of the day," he said. "I'll put on my best sports jacket if you're taking me someplace expensive."

"Is Chuck's Diner expensive enough for you?"

Phil held the door open for her, then followed her out. "Chuck's Diner? I guess I should put on my tux."

They went in her car, a nice Mazda two-door, for which Phil was very grateful. It wasn't that he was embarrassed by his dented, rusted, clay-red '76 Malibu, it was...well, something probably worse than embarrassment. Immaturity notwithstanding, no real man wanted to drive an attractive woman anywhere in such a vehicle. Susan's car was clean and unadorned, like her, attractive in its lack of frills. He watched her bright-blond hair spin in the breeze from the open window. "No valet parking?" he joked when she pulled into Chuck's.

"Only on weekends," she said. Inside they took a booth in the back. Another blast from the past, Phil considered. It had been over a decade since he'd last set foot in here. Chuck's Diner was your typical greasy spoon, though cleaner than most. A middle-aged waitress in an apron and bonnet took their orders.

"So what are you packing?" Susan asked.

"Packing?" Phil queried.

Susan, frowning, rephrased. "What kind of weapon do you carry off-duty?"

"Oh, that kind of packing." But what a strange question. "A Beretta .25."

"That's a peashooter!" she exclaimed. The waitress set their orders down, then Susan continued. "What are you gonna shoot with a .25? Gnats?"

Phil appraised his hash and eggs. "Well, actually I'm not planning to shoot anything, except maybe the waitress if she doesn't bring me some salt and pepper."

"Cops are supposed to be prepared for trouble round the clock. What if some coked-up scumbags try to take you down?"

"In Chuck's Diner? Look, if they want my hash and eggs, they can have it."

"I wouldn't be caught dead with anything less than a hot-loaded 9mm," she told him, then nonchalantly bit into her cheeseburger sub. "Right now I carry a SIG .45."

"You carry a gun?" Phil asked.

"Of course. Mullins got me a carry permit, told him it was the only way I'd dispatch for him. It's a crazy world, there's a nut around every corner."

Phil nodded. "Two on every corner is more like it." And he'd seen them all on Metro. He felt inclined to tell some stories, but before he could, Susan said, "Take a look," then abruptly opened her purse and withdrew a large, clunky automatic.

"Put that away!" Phil said. "This is a diner, not an armory."

She shrugged and put the gun back. "I'm thinking about buying one of those H&K squeeze-cockers, or maybe a used Bren-10."

How do you like that? Phil mused. Dirty Harry's got a sister. "If you want my opinion, stick to simple pieces."

She glanced across the table as if slighted. "Oh, because I'm a woman? Women can't handle sophisticated handguns?"

Phil sighed in frustration. "Simmer down, Annie Oakley. Wait till you're neck-deep in a shootout one night and your fancy auto stovepipes a round. You'll sell your soul for a Colt revolver."

Again she shrugged, almost as if she couldn't decide whether or not to agree. "How's it feel to be back?"

"Okay, I guess. A job's a job."

She fidgeted with a French fry, glancing down. "And, again, I really apologize for the way I treated you this morning. I had no right to say things like that."

"Don't worry about it," Phil passed it off. Actually, it was kind of funny now. A few hours ago she was practically accusing me of murder, and now she's buying me hash. "I guess we all have a bad day every now and then." But he thought it best to change the subject quick. "So what are all the books I see you reading at the station? You in college?"

"Yeah, slow but sure. I'm majoring in criminology, minor's in history. This is my last semester, thank God. Evening classes a couple nights a week."

"That's great," Phil acknowledged. "What are you going to do when you get your degree? Work for Mullins?"

"Not on your life. I'll shoot for DEA or maybe Customs. And there're always the county departments up north. Last thing I want to be is a Crick City cop—" Then she caught herself, brought a hand to her mouth. "Sorry. No offense."

"None taken," Phil laughed. "It's the last thing I want to be, too, but I don't have much of a choice at the moment."

Her gaze moved absently to the window. "It's the town, you know? It's so slow and desperate and backwards. It's depressing. The minute I get a decent job, I'm out of here."

"I know just what you're talking about, believe me," Phil related, but at once he felt dried up. He'd said the same thing to Vicki, hadn't he? No way he was going to work in a nowhere town like this. He was too good for Crick City. And now Vicki was a prostitute and Phil was—

The thought didn't even need finishing.

"How long have you been working for Mullins?"

"A little under a year," she said. "He's a decent man, if a bit ornery, and he offered me the dispatch job when he heard I was looking for something to help me through school. He knew my parents when they were alive."

Better not ask about that, Phil told himself, though he did note their commonality. "So you grew up here, too?"

"Yeah," she said despondently. "My father was on disability; he got shot up in Viet Nam. My mother worked lots of odd jobs to get us by, but it just seems the harder she worked, the harder things got."

There seemed to be a similar variation of the same story for just about everyone around here: poor people struggling just to make it, and never quite succeeding. Phil had been too young to really even remember his own parents—but the tale was the same. He could tell the conversation was draining Susan; her luster was gone, her bright-blue eyes not quite so bright now. He struggled for something more upbeat to talk about, but nothing came to him until he remembered that she seemed enthused about guns and cop talk in general.

"What do you know about Cody Natter?" he asked.

She pushed her plate aside, leaving the fries. "Not a lot. About the only place he's ever seen with any regularity is Sallee's. He owns the place now, you know."

"Yeah, Mullins mentioned that. Don't you think that's weird?"

"Sure it's weird. A guy like Natter? No visible income, no bank account. I don't guess that Sallee's sold for much, but still, you have to wonder where he got the cash to buy the place."

"I'm even more curious as to why?"

"I have to agree with Mullins," Susan said. "An out-of-the-way strip joint like that is the perfect contact point if you're networking dope. Last year Mullins had the Comptroller's Office audit him, but the guy's books were picture perfect. No way we can nail him on taxes. I don't know how he did it."

Phil didn't care. "I don't want to get him on tax fraud or ill-gotten gains; I want to bust him for manufacturing and distribution."

"Then you're going to have to have solid evidence linking him to his lab, which'll be tough," Susan reminded him, "and finding the lab itself will be plain impossible."

"Why?"

"Natter's a Creeker; his lab's got to be up in the hills. You ever been back there? It's a mess. You're talking about three or four thousand acres of uncharted woodlands. There are roads back there that aren't even on the county map grid. Finding Natter's lab will be like looking for the needle in the haystack, or try ten haystacks."

She had a point, and Phil was no trailblazer. "Yeah, but maybe one of his people will spin."

"Don't hold your breath. Natter's people are all Creekers, too; they're never gonna talk, first, because they're all terrified of Natter—he's like their god—and another reason they'll never talk is simply because most of them can't. Let's just say you catch one of them dealing dust; no judge in the world will accept their testimony. Why? Because technically they're all retardates—they're legally mentally impaired."

Phil frowned. She was right again. "But what about Natter himself?" he raised the issue. "You ever talked to the guy? He's sharp as a tack. He's smart, he's well-read, he's articulate. I wouldn't call him mentally impaired at all."

"Phil, be real. The guy's a Creeker, he makes Frankenstein's monster look like Tom Cruise. You get him into court on shaky testimony, all the guy's gotta do is play dumb and the judge throws the whole thing out. The only way you're gonna get Natter is to bust a bunch of his point people or bag men—people who aren't Creekers—and get them to testify. You're gonna have to make a positive link between Natter and known PCP dealers. At least Mullins has you on the right track. Staking out Sallee's over a period of time, getting a line on Natter's out-of-town contacts— that's the only way you'll be able to get Cody Natter on a distro bust that'll stick."

Phil saw no point in telling her that the whole idea was his, not Mullins'. But she was right on all counts. This would probably wind up being as complicated as any of his PCP cases in the city, if not more so since the circumstances were so atypical. "I still want to find that lab, though," he muttered, more to himself. "No judge will argue with hard photographic evidence."

Susan's expression turned bemused. "What, you think you're gonna get a picture of Natter at the lab?"

"Why not? It'd be an open-and-shut case."

"Never happen, Phil. Natter's way too smart for anything even close to that. He's probably never set foot in the lab, you can bank on that."

Phil grumbled. Again, he knew she was right. Yeah, this sure ain't the city, he thought. On Metro, he'd been one of the best narc cops on the force, but his expertise felt like a white elephant now. Everything was different here; things worked different ways. This was another world.

"Phil!" Susan was suddenly whispering. "Look!"

He glanced up from the remnants of his hash and eggs. Susan was gazing fixedly out the window. Along the shoulder of the Route, a teenage boy and girl were walking, both dressed in little more than rags. Both had shaggy heads of dirty black hair, and they ambled along unsteadily, even crookedly. The boy wore rotted workboots, while the girl was barefoot, oblivious to the shoulder's sharp gravel. In the bright, hot afternoon sun, they looked like bizarre ghosts.

"Creekers," Phil uttered under his breath.

"God, I feel sorry for them," Susan remarked, still staring out. "Talk about getting a bum deal from life."

Phil gulped. Her observation made him at once feel selfish; in all his reflection upon his own problems, here were two kids with real problems. They walked at such a distance that he could discern little of their physical features, but even that was more than enough. The boy's neck appeared twice as long as it should, which caused his enlarged head to droop to one side, while the girl didn't seem to have any jaw at all, and though her left arm looked normal, her right was grievously shortened, the hand sprouting from the elbow.

"I wonder how many of them there are?" Phil said.

Susan's gaze never strayed off their backs as they grew tiny beyond the bend.

"Who knows?" she answered.

# TEN

Back in Black, Paul Sullivan thought along with the pounding juke music. Right now this hotter-than-hell redhead was dancing up a cock-stoking storm on stage. Big tits, like a Penthouse Pet, and legs that looked a mile long. Vicki Steele, her name was. He and his buddy Kevin Orndorf just got off a bag run out near Waynesville; Krazy Sallee's was the perfect place to drop a few beers after a sale. It was also a good place to meet their partners and point men, talk some quick business and make arrangements. Of course, they'd never actually sell the product here—that'd be crazy. Paul and his people, after all, were big time runners, not dime-baggers. Kevin himself was a little cranked up; he'd lit up a dust roach in the parking lot and he was hopping. Paul had lit up himself, but just a toke; he didn't want the shit turning his brain to mush. Just a quick hit once in a while.

The joint was packed. This redhead on stage was pure fucking dynamite, the best bod he'd seen in the house all night. Wonder how much a gal like that'd cost, Paul's thoughts strayed. Couple hundred at least. Maybe five.

But it would be worth it.

"Too bad they gotta wear them fucked-up g-strings here," Kevin postulated, stroking his goatee. "Bet she's got a snatch redder than a pit fire."

"And them tits?" Paul added. "Christ. You could hang your hat and coat on 'em."

"Be right back, partner. Gots to drain the love-snake." Kevin drunkenly rose, then wended through the jammed aisles. The music was so loud it seemed to swell Sallee's old plank-wood walls. Strobe lights throbbed to the beat, along with the redhead's sultry dance moves. Her firm, big breasts jiggled as those long legs traipsed across the stage. Dollar bills fell like confetti...

*Man, she could tease the cock out of the Pope's pants just with her smile,* Paul theorized. *What I wouldn't give for just a half hour with that piece of pie.*

Not that he could complain. Darleen, his current squeeze, was tough stuff, and almost had a set of tits to match. And she could get down on the rod like Sandra Scream in them porn films he watched sometimes on card night. But, Christ, there was so much out there... For a guy to confine himself to one girl, well, that was like going to McDonald's every fucking day and having a Big Mac. Every now and then a fella might want some McNuggets or a fish sandwich.

Right?

The music compressed in his ears; he could barely hear himself think, not that Paul Sullivan ever needed to think all that much. He lit a Lucky and looked up. Kevin, clearly half shit-faced, was talking to some creepy looking kid by the john door. That dumbass better not be trying to move any dust here, Paul fretted, but then Kevin disappeared into another door off to the side, while the creepy kid hung out another minute, then went up the stairs.

"Hey, what's in that back room?" he asked the waitress when she came along. Typical beat redneck mama, probably dropped eight kids by the time she was thirty, and now she looked fifty.

She emptied a clogged ashtray and asked, "You want another Carling?"

"Yeah," Paul said. "And what's in that back room? I just seen my buddy go in there."

"Pinball machines," she quickly replied. "You said you wanted another Carling, right?"

"Right."

A half hour later, Paul was getting drunk, and Kevin still hadn't come back. Pinball machines? He ain't into that shit. Never been. The redhead had long since finished her set; some skinny tattooed brunette—who looked pretty drunk herself—had replaced her and was now feebly dancing to some bass-ripper by Motorhead. Sheets of cigarette smoke wafted before the lit stage; at one point, the brunette lost her footing and fell down, which brought a burst of laughter. This was getting dull; Paul wasn't even looking at her. He didn't like tattoos on women, and this gal in particular wasn't dancing for shit anyway. And—

*Where the hell is Kevin?*

It was almost last call, plus they had a run in the morning. Havin' to drive the first runs themselves was a pain in the ass, but it seemed like every time they hired some new drivers, the fuckers disappeared. Scared off, he figured. Kids, most of 'em. Come to think of it, a lot of point people had run off lately, too. Can't find good people fer shit...

Just as Paul was about to get up and go find his partner, Kevin appeared at the door by the john and headed for the table. He seemed antsy with excitement when he sat down, or maybe it was just the dust he'd toked. His goateed grin leaned forward. "Man, you won't believe what they got back there, partner! They got—"

"Pinball machines," Paul didn't let him finish. "Big deal."

Kevin Orndorf's broad, goateed face ticked, perplexed. "Pinball machines? What'choo talkin' about? What they got, they got another stage, and more dancers. Thing is, though, the girls back there are Creekers."

"Creekers?" Paul exclaimed. "Stripping?"

"Yeah, man. You wouldn't believe it, it's great!"

Great? He couldn't figure what could be great about a bunch of Creeker women dancing in a strip joint. He'd seen Creekers plenty of times; they were inbred, deformed. Had heads that looked like balloons and lopsided eyes. "Man, are you nuts? Them Creeker girls are ugly as all hell. They got faces on 'em like pigs."

"Not these, man. These girls are hot, let me tell ya. They're a little fucked-up, sure, but they're still lookers." Then Kevin, his face still lit up in some arcane thrill, put his half of the tab down on the table. "Here's dough to cover my beers. I gotta go."

Paul's face pinched. "Go where?"

"I'm buyin' me one."

"You've got to be shitting me!" Paul thought he might puke up his eight Carlings right there at the tabletop. "You're payin' for a Creeker whore?"

"Yeah, man," Kevin tittered. Suddenly, the wicked, pumped-up smile within the sharp goatee made him look like a redneck version of Lucifer. "They got one gal—you ain't gonna believe it! She's got four tits..."

"Aw, man," Paul complained, "you can't be doin' shit like that. We got a big drop to make in the morning."

"I'll be there, man, don't worry." Kevin rubbed his broad

hands together in perverse glee. "I can't wait to get me a piece of this bitch. See ya in the mornin'."

Paul frowned after him. Kevin went out with that kid he'd seen talking to him earlier, who Paul guessed must be a Creeker too, on account of the funny-looking head. And… Did the kid have two thumbs on one hand? It looked like it. Ain't that the dumbest shit I ever heard, Paul thought, and drained the foam out of his last Carling. The juke cut off then, the last dancer stepping drunk off-stage to not much applause, and the house lights went on. "Last call!" shouted the barkeep, a thin balding guy in a T-shirt which read Shut Up And Do Me. "Order up or get out!"

I'll get out, Paul decided. He was, after all, a drug dealer possessed of a professional sense of responsibility. Got a big drop tomorrow, got to get up early. Ain't got no time to be fuckin' around with whores. Sometimes he just couldn't figure Kevin out. The guy was a wild man. And who the hell would want to fuck some deformed Creeker girl with four tits? Now that redhead, Paul surmised. That's different, that's natural. But…a Creeker? That kind of kinky shit just wasn't Paul's speed…

Paul shuffled out through the thinning crowd. Headlights swarmed the parking lot as one pickup after another started up and pulled out. The hot night seemed static; the big blinking KRAZY SALLEE'S sign winked off. The moon peeked over the tree tops just past the ridge, an ugly, cheesy yellow like the color of his daddy's skin when the old fuck had checked out from pancreatic cancer. Paul got into his own truck and idled out of the lot. He looked around for Kevin's truck but didn't see it anywhere. Guess he's already gone, him and his Creeker whore with four tits.

And Paul Sullivan was right about that. Kevin was gone, all right.

Kevin Orndorf was gone forever.

For the next week, Phil did pretty much the same thing: he'd maintain a visual surveillance of Krazy Sallee's—in plain clothes, and in his own car—until after closing, snap a few pictures, and log every tag number in the lot each night, for a future cross-reference. Then he'd change into his police uniform, and finish his night shift in the department's patrol car. Routine police work in Crick City was unsurprisingly dull, but at least this stake-out operation each night helped breakup an otherwise grueling 12-hour shift. On a few occasions he'd caught glimpses of Vicki Steele, leaving Sallee's with Natter in the mint Chrysler Imperial. But at no time did he witness Vicki or any other woman engaging in any parking-lot prostitution. Still, though, the snapshots Mullins had reluctantly shown him continued to stick in his mind...

Between rounds, he'd hang out at the station and shoot some bull with Susan, whom he was beginning to like. She seemed made from a different mold, not a typical Crick City woman at all, but enlivened to pursue an education and career that would one day take her away from this place. (And he hoped she had better luck than he had.) The variety of her intellectual facets intrigued him; she was very smart, she knew a lot about lots of things, yet she clearly possessed a persona which transcended her bookishness. She was sassy, opinionated, even hot-tempered at times; when they disagreed on a particular topic, she wouldn't hesitate to be in his face about it. Phil admired that.

He also admired her looks. She's beautiful, it occurred to him every time he'd come in for a coffee break. She struck him as idyllic in a way; her beauty—a very real, unassuming, and unaugmented kind of beauty—made her shine in his eye. How do you crack a woman like this? he wondered almost constantly. He'd asked her out three times, and three times she'd politely declined, citing her evening classes would not permit it. Perhaps Phil was paranoid, but it felt to him as though she liked working with him, but had no desire to date a municipal cop. He could only hope he was wrong.

Chief Mullins remained typically oblivious, chewing his tobacco, chugging atrocious coffee, and bellyaching about anything that suited his redneck fancy. He never seemed to ask much about what was going on, but this was typical Mullins: as chief he didn't expect to have to ask, he expected to be told, and in all honesty, aside from a few SRO's and traffic citations, Phil had nothing to put on the so-called "blotter."

But after his second week on the job, Mullins did indeed ask one morning: "So how're things going with your stakeout?"

"All right, I guess," Phil answered, transferring his surveillance notes to an official log. "Too early to get a decent read on things just yet."

"Yeah?" Mullins seemed to grumble, pouring the black ichor he thought of as coffee. "I thought you were supposed to be moving on this."

Phil frowned up from the desk. "I am. Rome wasn't built in a day, you know."

"Bugger Rome. This is Crick City. You making any headway out there or just gandering your ex-girlfriend through the binocs?"

Sometimes I could kill him, Phil thought. "Chief, I'm doing this the way we talked about. I'm logging the plates of the regulars so we can eventually get a decent cross-reference. Things like this go slow."

"Yeah?" Mullins packed a wad of Red Man, then chased it with coffee. "Too slow if you ask me."

Phil all but threw his hands up. "All right, boss. You're the one who wanted me to check out this PCP net in town. You think I'm doing this wrong, then tell me how to do it right."

"Don't bust out into tears yet, Phil. I didn't say you were doing it wrong. I just said you're taking too much time."

"Yeah, well, like I said, Rome wasn't built in a day," Phil repeated and got back to his writing.

"You're right, it took a thousand years, which is fine for Rome. But I ain't got that kind of time myself. You sure you're not stalling a little?"

This time Phil's frown creased his face. "Stalling on what, for God's sake?"

"Well, you're sitting out in Sallee's parking lot every night, writing down tag numbers like a good little boy, sure. But don't you think it's time for you to get a move on? I mean, how many tag numbers can you write down before your hand starts to hurt?"

Phil leaned back in the chief's office chair, arms smugly crossed. "Chief, save us both some time, will ya? What are you implying?"

"Implying? Me?" Mullins chuckled, scratching his formidable belly.

"Yeah, you."

"Well, maybe I'm merely suggesting that it's time for you to move on to the next step. After all, this whole procedure was your idea."

"Fine. The next step. What have you got in mind?"

"See? You are stalling. You've got enough tag numbers, Phil. You're staking the lot in your POV, you're in plain clothes, and nobody knows you're back in town, and even if they did, nobody would remember you anyway. It's high time, ain't it?"

Phil still didn't know what the chief was talking about. "High time for what, Chief? For the Yankees to win the pennant?"

"No, high time for you to get your ass into Sallee's and check things out from the inside."

"Sure," Phil agreed, "but don't you think it's still a bit early for that?"

"Hell no. Why don't you just admit it, you're stalling. You don't want to go in there 'cos—"

"Because why, Chief? Because I know I'll run into Vicki? Is that what you're driving at?"

"Well, yeah," Mullins said, and spat into his ubiquitous paper cup. "I think you're a little bit chicken to run into her again. Christ, you dumped the poor girl like a load of heavy diapers."

Phil simmered in his seat. "I did not dump her, Chief. And keep in mind I've been a cop for over ten years. I do know how to keep my personal past separate from my job." Phil felt convinced of this, but he also felt...a sudden distant queasiness. "You want me to go in there, Chief. Fine, I will."

Mullins packed a pinch more Red Man into his jowl—if it was tobacco, he chewed it: snuff, leaf, plugs. "Glad to hear it, Phil." Then he spat a big one. "Get your ass in there tonight."

# ELEVEN

"What are you nervous about?" Susan asked behind her Motorola station base.

"I'm not nervous," Phil asserted. He'd just changed into his street clothes in Mullins' office, then came out to the commo room. It was just past midnight.

"Not nervous, huh?" Did she smile? "Looks to me like you're about to tinkle in your jockey shorts."

"How do you know I don't wear boxers?" Phil quickly changed the topic. He changed it, he knew now, because he was nervous, and he also knew why.

Evidently so did Susan. "It must be the girl, huh? Vicki what's-her-name, your ex-fiancée?"

Phil seethed. "No, it is not. Christ, can't Mullins keep his mouth closed about anything?" He shuddered to think what else the dubious chief had told her.

"Did you really dump her 'cos she wouldn't move?"

"No, I did not! Jesus!"

"Don't get whipped up. I was just asking," she said, adjusting the frequency modulator on the radio. "And if you don't mind my saying so, you make a great-looking redneck."

"I've never been more flattered." But he supposed she was right. Tight, tapered Levis over pointed shit-kicker boots, a big buck knife on his belt, and a black-and-red flannel shirt. It astounded him how the societal contingent colloquially thought of as "rednecks" insisted on wearing flannel shirts even in the middle of summer. He'd also slicked his hair back with Score.

"Look at the bright side," Susan added, cueing her mike once. "How many guys actually get paid to sit in strip joints?"

"Hmm, you're right. It's a dirty job, but someone's gotta do it. Might as well be me. Anyway, I'm out of here. I'll be back around two."

"Wait, wait," she was suddenly complaining. She got up from behind her console. "Don't you know anything about redneck fashion? You've got to show some hair."

"Pardon me?"

She walked right up to him, so close he could smell her herbal shampoo. Phil was six-feet even, while Susan stood about five-seven. He looked down at her, instinctively noting the lean compactness of her body, the sudden proportion of her waist and hips, and the stunning white-blond hair. In the small "v" of her blouse, he spied a breast satcheled in a plain beige bra. The simple, beautiful image nearly shook him.

Then she began unbuttoning his shirt.

"What, uuuuuuh," he asked, "what are you doing?"

"I told you. You have to show some hair. It's the redneck's version of a tie."

"Oh," Phil replied.

She unbuttoned his shirt all the way to his solar plexus, then fluffed it out some. "There, that's much better," she said. "Now you look like a true Crick City redneck." Her eyes thinned momentarily, and her mouth turned up in the slightest grin. "Nice pecs, too. If you don't mind my saying so."

*Jesus*, he thought as she went back to her commo cubby. "That's all? Just nice?"

"Get out of here," she said, laughing.

Nice pecs. Well, he thought. He hadn't touched a barbell in five years, but at least Susan's remark, even if she hadn't been serious, offered him a welcome diversion during the drive. He realized, most fully now, that what Mullins had accused him of this morning was absolutely on the mark. I'm a fucking nervous wreck, he admitted after parking in Sallee's dusty gravel lot. And he realized two things more, just as fully:

*Vicki's going to be in there, and she's going to see me.*

He left his off-duty Beretta locked in the glove box; the last thing he needed was some, drunk redneck spotting his piece printing in his pants. And there was another consideration: Vicki knew that Phil had worked for Metro; he had a phony line all planned about a new job—a non-police job. Another thing he didn't need was everybody in the joint knowing a cop lurked amid the clientele.

That would blow the whole stakeout right then and there.

KRAZY SALLEE'S, the high road-sign blinked as he disembarked. His boots scuffed gravel as he traversed the lot. Lurid light bathed him in the entry; a bull-faced bouncer gave him the eye at the door, then let him pass through. Phil expected thunderous—and awful—heavy metal or C&W. Instead he walked into a half-full bar full of similarly flannel-shirted 'necks talking over tables flanked by beer bottles and ashtrays. *I thought this was a rowdy stripjoint,* he reminded himself when he took note of the empty stage. Loud music and near-naked women were what he had prepared himself to be in the midst of. What he found instead was a lethargic gathering of good old boys shooting the shit over bottles of Black Label and Schmidt's.

No one seemed to notice him when he scouted the floor; he tried to make it appear that he was looking for someone. The only thing he was looking for in reality was a seat. Sallee's layout hadn't changed an iota from what he remembered. Cheap tables packed around makeshift aisles, a carpet of crushed peanut shells and beer slime, warped wood walls with tacky upholstered booths in back. Every possible beer-ad-plaque hung in evidence: Budweiser mirrors, Schlitz wall lamps, Michelob neon squiggles, a Killian's mural, and an illuminated Miller clock. What else hung in evidence was a shifting—and nearly living—wall of cigarette smoke. Phil had never taken up the habit, but he suspected he'd be getting more tar and nicotine just breathing the air here than chaining a pack of Camels. *Next time wear a gas mask with your flannel shirt, bud.*

He wanted an inconspicuous seat from which to observe, but then the barkeep, a thin blond guy wearing a Jeff Dahmer T-shirt, waved him over. "Plenty of seats up at the bar, brother."

Good enough, Phil thought. At the bar corner he wouldn't be obvious. Another thing he knew he had to do was order a beer, despite his being on duty. When working undercover in a strip joint, ordering Pepsi didn't emphasize one's credibility.

Only problem was, Phil hated American beer.

"Heineken," he said.

"Ain't got it, brother," enlightened the keep. "We're all Americans here. You want your money to go to Holland? What they ever do for you besides balk out of World War Two while your daddy was probably getting his ass shot at by the Waffen SS."

"Bottle of Bud," Phil fairly groaned.

"Comin' right up."

Phil glanced up at the TV mounted high at the back corner of the bar. He wondered what the Yankees were doing but saw only dismal pro wrestling on the color screen: a black guy and a big blond schmuck suplexing each other to a slavering crowd. When the keep brought his Bud, Phil asked, "How about switching on some baseball? The Yanks are on tonight, hopefully whipping the shit out of Baltimore."

"What, grapplin's not good enough for ya? It's the all-American sport." The keep seemed offended by Phil's suggestion. He gestured toward the screen. "We got Ric Flair tusslin' with Bruce Reed here, brother. You'd rather watch the Yankees?"

Don't make waves, Phil warned himself. "Oh, shit, man, I didn't realize it was Bruce Flair. Keep it on, man."

The keep frowned. "That's Ric Flair, brother. He's only been heavyweight champ ten friggin' times."

"Yeah, yeah, Ric Flair. Best black wrestler in the sport."

The thin keep frowned again. "Reed's the black guy."

"Right," Phil faltered. "It's been a while since I've caught any... grapplin'."

The keep slid away, leaving Phil feeling like a horse's ass. Can I help it I don't know who Ric fucking Flair is? Right now, on the TV, Mr. Flair seemed to be getting his clock seriously cleaned by the black guy. But then Phil noticed the obvious incongruity: both wrestlers looked like they had three-pound rockfish stuffed in their trunks. Either those guys both have ten-inch dicks or they're big fans of Idaho potatoes.

So this was what rednecks did? Hang out in strip joints with no girls on the stage and watch wrestling and drink Budweiser? There must be more to life than that. "Hey, man?" Phil flagged the keep again.

"Yeah, brother?"

"This a strip joint or a social club?" Phil indicated the empty stage. "Ric Flair's fine, but I was kinda hoping to catch some chicks."

"You're not from around here, are ya?" the keep sideswiped the question. "Haven't seen you around."

"Actually I am from around here, but I just moved back to town. Name's Phil." He extended his hand.

The keep didn't shake it. "Wayne. We're in between sets right now. You want women, just keep your shirt on a few. We got women comin' out that'll mow you down like a county-prison weed-whacker crew."

"Sounds good," Phil feigned. But—*A county-prison weed-whacker crew?*

"And we got a two-for-one special on hot dogs tonight," the keep added. "Best dogs you've ever had."

Phil got the gist quick. A lighted rotisserie hosted a lone hot dog that looked like it had been cooking in there for about a month. Rule Number One, he thought. Never cut down wrestling in a redneck strip joint.

The Bud tasted awful. They should pay me to drink this swill. He was so bored so fast, that he contemplated paying up and leaving right now, but that would blow his cover too, wouldn't it? Try to fit in, he insisted to himself. He glanced up at the wrestling and saw Mr. Flair hitting the black wrestler over the head with a metal chair, then pinning him. The crowd roared in a glee that could only be described as sociopathic. But then Phil started; at the same time the patrons of Krazy Sallee's began to applaud with equal enthusiasm, and it wasn't because of the wrestling.

Phil craned his neck back, eyed the stage.

Amid applause as loud as cannon fire, a woman in sheer crimson veils stepped up onto the lit stage in five-inch-high heels. Tousled red hair shimmered around her head like a halo of fire. Long coltish legs rose to join a zero-fat body of perfect curves and awesome contours. With feet apart and hands on hips, her eyes scanned the crowd in a predatory glare. Her breasts jutted beneath the sheer material, tight chiffon orbs the size of grapefruits.

The juke kicked on a loud, obnoxious heavy metal cut, and the girl on stage began to dance.

"Happy now, brother?" the keep asked, wiping a glass off with the edge of his Dahmer T-shirt.

Phil felt like something shrinking, like a robust plant being drained of all its water by a parasitic taproot. The woman on stage was Vicki Steele, and what was worse, after her first stage-spin under the pulsing strobe lights, she skimmed off her top veil, stopped on a dime and looked right into Phil's eyes.

The night—a beautiful night—unfolded to Cody Natter's inbred crimson eyes. "Beautiful things are made for nights like these. Glorious things. Powerful things..."

"Huh?"

It was no matter. So many of his clan were weak0headed; how could he ever expect them to understand the things he saw? God had cursed them all, hadn't He?

*Ona,* he thought idly. *Mannona, come to us...*

One day, he knew, he would sit in equal glory, and piss in God's pious face.

"Fireflies!" Druck exclaimed. "Look-it!"

"Yes. They're beautiful, aren't they? Like the night, like the moon above us. Like the world."

"Like Ona?"

Yes.

Druck scratched his stubbled cheek with the two thumbs on his left hand. In his right hand, he held the knife.

Natter looked down at the corpse. So beautiful, too, he realized. Even in death, she lay beautiful, despite the flaws of their Godly curse. The sallow moon shone faintly on the still-warm breasts, the sleek legs, an black hair. Her open eyes reflected the night back like the pristine face of the cosmos.

Druck, on one knee now, appraised the hollow gourd of her abdomen. His blade glittered with blood, and he passed his other hand through the detached pile of her entrails...

The boy got carried away sometimes.

"You'd best bury her now, Druck."

Druck looked confused. "But... What's 'bout skeetinner?"

"No, Druck. Just bury her."

The seemingly eternal night-racket—peepers, crickets, grackles—throbbed around them. Druck's simple idiot face gazed upward, a question struggling in the warped, uneven red eyes. The sweetmeat of the girl's spleen drooped slack in his hand. "Kin I eat some of her first, then? 'Fore I put her in the ground?"

"Yes, Druck," Cody Natter granted. "You may eat some of her first."

The Budweiser was killing him. And so were the flashing lights and the infernal music. Last call approached; Vicki had seductively danced a four-song set, then disappeared, only to be replaced by other women who likewise twirled and spun and gyrated until they'd stripped themselves down to their g-strings. Phil paid them no mind; seeing Vicki had been impact enough. He was sure she'd noticed him, but at the end of her set, she'd merely walked off the stage and retreated to the dressing room. Seeing her again, after all this time, was like seeing a ghost.

The last dancer bumped and grinded to Twisted Sister, baring her breasts as a wolf bares its teeth. She was attractive enough, but Phil preferred to stare into his beer. *What am I doing here?* he asked himself disgustedly. He certainly wasn't making any observations relevant to the case. And where was Vicki? What was she doing? What was she doing right now?

*Probably blowing some redneck scumbag out in the parking lot,* came his worst considerations.

"Last chance, brother." It was the keep, meandering behind the bar now as Sallee's crowd quickly thinned.

For some reason, the keep's head reminded Phil of a big sweet potato. "No thanks, no more beer for me."

"No, I mean the hot dog." The keep pointed to the wizened grease-sheened thing revolving lazily in the lit rotisserie. "If you don't want it, I'm gonna have it."

Phil thought of a lone car on a dilapidated ferris wheel. "It's all yours, brother," he said.

"Suit yourself. Don't know what you're missing."

*Time to get out of this hole in the wall,* Phil concluded. *I got better things to do than talk to this guy about hot dogs.* He was about to reach for his wallet, to pay for the wreckage of this dismal night, when suddenly—

"Hey! Hey, man!"

A hand was shoving him from behind. *Did I get made already?* he feared as the hand continued to jostle him.

"Aren't you Phil Straker?"

*Christ.* Phil turned on his barstool to face a tall guy, dressed in similar redneck garb, with blond hair down past his shoulders. "Yeah, I'm Phil Straker," Phil admitted.

The half-drunk grin heightened. "I guess you don't remember

me—gotta admit, it's been awhile. We went to school together. I'm—"

"Holy shit," Phil said when the recognition finally sparked. "Eagle? Eagle Peters?"

"That's right, man."

What a mind-blow this was. They shook hands vigorously. "Christ," Phil said. "I haven't seen you since high school. So what've you been up to?"

"Nothin' much, same old dickin' around," Eagle answered. "Got into some trouble up north a few years back, but I'm squared away now. Hangin' sheetrock in north county when there's work. I heard you were a city cop."

Phil figured Eagle had probably "heard" a bit more than that, so he tailored his spiel. "Not anymore. I got fired, but the job sucked anyway. That cop shit wasn't for me. I'm working for a landscaper now."

"Planting bushes and pulling weeds doesn't seem your style."

"It ain't, but a buck's a buck."

Eagle laughed. Phil paid his tab—a whopping six dollars—and walked out to the lot with his childhood friend. Gravel dust flurried as countless pickup trucks idled toward the exits.

"Must've been a bummer, huh?" Eagle said.

"What's that?"

"You know. Walking into the joint and seein' your ex up on the stage doing a strip routine."

"It was no big deal," Phil lied. "I'd heard she was working here. She still looks good, I'll tell you that."

"She's the hottest ticket in the joint these days," Eagle informed him. "But she really took a nosedive since you left town."

"What do you mean?"

"Forget it, man. Let's just say that she's into a whole lot of shit that you don't want to hear about."

Yes I do! Phil wanted to yell. But he held back. Eagle was just the kind of information source Phil needed to get a line on the underside of the town. It was best not to press the guy, better to slowly cultivate his trust. Besides, all Eagle probably meant was Vicki's plummet into prostitution, which, thanks to Mullins' photographic enlightenment, Phil already knew about. I hope that's what he means, Phil thought. What could be worse than that?

"Gotta get rolling," Eagle said. "Got an early job tomorrow, hanging rock in Millersville."

"It was great seeing you again, Eagle. You hang out here much?"

"Most nights. Let's get together soon and shoot the shit."

"Will do. Take care of yourself."

They forked off. Eagle got into a beat-up Chevy four-runner—Phil memorized the plates, an occupational instinct—and filed out of the lot. How weird. Phil hadn't given Eagle Peters a thought since the dreams had recurred, and now here the guy was in the flesh. And what had he meant about getting into trouble up north? And that stuff about Vicki—could Eagle have been implying that she was into more than just roadside trick-turning, or was Phil just being paranoid?

I'm being paranoid, he insisted to himself. He got into the Malibu, started it up, and sat a moment. So much gravel dust rose in the lot he could barely see, just as too many thoughts cropped up in his head, too much marauding him at once, from too many tangents: Mullins' PCP case, Eagle, Susan, the Metro sham, and, of course, Vicki.

Vicki…

*…she's into a whole lot of shit that you don't want to hear about…*

"God," he muttered. This was no good at all. He'd only had two beers, but he felt drunk in drenched images. Her dance routine ground in replay in his mind, like a lewd, overbright film loop—garish strobe lights pawing at her flawless body, her red hair a shimmering dark fire about her sleek shoulders, and the large breasts—which he'd once caressed in total love—displayed on her chest like prime raw meat in a butcher's case…

Bait, no doubt, for her new trade.

"Yeah, the hottest ticket in the joint, and I used to be in love with her."

He felt pathetic, a putz, a wimp. Pining over a relationship that didn't work. But—

Why didn't it work?

*Because of me*, he thought. *She's a stripper and a whore now… because I abandoned her in this shit-pit of a town.*

He flicked on his headlights, prepared to pull out and head back to the station. But through the mist of dust, he spotted Cody Natter's big maroon Chrysler rumbling up to Sallee's entrance, and out of that same entrance Vicki Steele emerged, high heels at the ends of her long legs, a skin-tight blue sequin dress tight as frost about her body. She leaned over, was about to get into Natter's car, then she paused. Erected herself. And turned around... Through the gray dust, she stared. She was staring right at Phil's headlights. Phil's heart sank. More dust rose in the wake of another pickup truck, and when it eventually cleared, Vicki, along with Natter's long dark-scarlet car, was gone.

# TWELVE

Phil came in off his shift at about seven a.m., to take care of the night's paperwork and, much more importantly, to get the coffee brewing before Chief Mullins came in at eight. Susan hadn't asked him how things had gone at Sallee's when he'd come back to the station last night to change back into his uniform; perhaps she sensed his mental disarray.

*What a night...*

The entirety of his shift was haunted by thoughts and images of Vicki Steele.

He tried to clear his head, and sat at Mullins' big desk to finish off his DOR, but then he noticed the sheet of paper on the blotter. MISSING PERSON'S REPORT, it read; somebody named Orndorf had been reported missing by somebody named Sullivan. "Hey, Susan," he called out. "What's this missing person's report here on the chief's desk?"

Susan, from her commo cubby, answered rather snidely, "It's...a missing person's report."

"Funny. I mean, what's the scoop? You know either of these guys?"

"Nope."

"How'd this guy Sullivan look?"

"Like a typical creep. He came in about an hour ago, filed the report because he said he hadn't seen his buddy Orndorf in several weeks."

Phil's eyes scanned down the sheet of paper. "Why'd he file it here? These guys don't even live in Crick City."

"Yeah, but the last place Orndorf was seen was in our juris. At Krazy Sallee's as a matter of fact."

Sallee's? Hmmm. But why should Phil even care? Nine times out of ten, a missing persons was nothing. The guy probably owed a bundle in alimony or child support, so he blew town and didn't tell anyone. Happened all the time.

He went back to his DOR, but still, something was bothering him. Eagle's words: She's into a whole lot of shit that you don't want to hear about.

"Hey, Susan," he called out again. "Do me a favor and run a rap check on Vicki Steele, will ya?"

Did she actually chuckle? "Checking out the ex, huh?"

"Don't break my chops. Just do it, okay?"

"All right. Give me a minute."

Phil waited, tapping Mullins' blotter with a pencil-end. From Susan's cubby, he heard computer keys clicking. Then:

"Nothing," she said when her terminal responded.

He tapped the blotter some more, thinking. "Run a check on Eagle Peters," he said next.

"Who?"

"Eagle Peters. Long-time resident, he might be into something. His real first name is James."

Another flurry of clicking keys. Probably nothing on him, either, he supposed.

"He might be into something, huh?" Susan came back a minute later. "This guy's got three outstanding traffic warrants, three suspended sentences, and four narcotics busts."

"You're kidding me. Eagle?"

"Yeah, Eagle. And that's not all. He served three years on a five-year sentence in Clay County Prison."

Phil fell silent, tapping the desk more rapidly. This information left him partly excited, partly disappointed. But it wasn't for another moment that the most pertinent question of all occurred to him.

"The jail stint—that was narcotics?"

"Yep," Susan answered. "Possession, transport, and intent to distribute."

"To distribute what?"

"Your pet peeve. Synthetic phencyclidine."

PCP. Paydirt.

Phil sat a moment more; now he felt geared up. Eagle would be the perfect schmooze. He didn't know Phil was a cop, plus they were childhood friends. If Eagle was in deep, he could lead them right to Natter…

"Hey, Susan?"

"Yeeees," she groaned.

"Do me a favor and run raps on these guys too, Orndorf and Sullivan."

"You know, whenever we run a rap check through the county mainframe, the department gets charged."

"I don't care," Phil almost snapped. "Just run the raps...pretty please."

"Well, in that case..." More clicking, more waiting. Then: "You got some sense of foresight. Both guys have several priors, same thing. Possession with intent to distribute."

"PCP?"

"Ten-four."

Well well well, Phil thought. This was getting downright interesting. Phil poured some coffee, oblivious to its acrid tang. Three rap checks in a row, three base hits on PCP busts. He couldn't wait to tell Mullins.

Mullins...

Then Phil looked at the cracked VFW clock mounted above the chief's shooting trophies.

"Hey, Susan?"

"What now! You want me to run a rap check on Snow White?"

"No, but how about the Easter Bunny? He hangs out at Sallee's, too... Where's Chief Mullins? It's almost eight-thirty."

A pause, then, "You're right. He's never late."

"Maybe he's hungover."

"Naw, he quit drinking years ago."

"Maybe you should call him. Maybe he forgot to set his alarm clock or something."

"I doubt it," she said, but then he could hear her dialing anyway...

"No answer."

That's weird. Then he shrugged. "He'll be in. He's probably waiting in the donut line at the Qwik-Stop."

"Now that's a possibility."

Well, looks like I'm stuck here till he comes in. He killed some time calling the county hospital, the lockup, and the morgue, but no one by the name of Kevin Orndorf had checked in. Then he called the state and had them run the name on their blotter program.

Nothing.

"Hey, Phil?"

*We really should get an intercom,* he thought. "Yes?"

"You ever gonna ask me out again, or should I just give up?"

Phil almost spat his coffee out all over Mullins' desk. He tried to recover as quickly as he could, but what could he say? The smart-ass approach, he decided, might be best. "Hey, I already asked, but you were too busy. Remember? My rule is to never ask more than three times. Women have to stand in line to go out with me, I'll have you know. Sometimes they pay."

Susan shrieked a laugh.

"And if my memory serves me correctly, Ms. Ryder, your three chances have already been expended." Phil smiled at his own cockiness, even though, from her commo cubby, she couldn't see him. "It's like baseball," he told her. "Three strikes, and you're out."

"Hey!" she shot back. "I can't help it if you only ask me out on days I have class."

"Well, I suppose you're right, so just to show you I'm a man of character and fairness, I'll give you an unprecedented fourth opportunity to be graced by my presence." He paused for effect. "You want to go out tonight?"

"I can't. I have class."

Phil winced. "You evil, toying, malicious—"

"But tomorrow would be great," she interrupted. "Call me when you manage to drag your behind out of bed."

"Why bother calling? I'll just yell up through the heating duct."

"Don't forget," she warned him. "You ever heard the line 'Hell hath no fury like a woman scorned'?"

Forget? Phil nearly laughed. Yeah, like I'm gonna forget I have a date with you. "You needn't worry, Ms. Ryder. In fact I'll have my itinerary director mark it down on my calendar, posthaste."

"Posthaste, my ass," she came back. "Don't stand me up."

*Jesus, she's serious,* Phil realized.

"And speaking of getting stood up, I think we've both been," Susan said.

"What?"

"The chief. He's really late."

"You're right," Phil agreed when he noted the clock again. Chief Mullins was a lot of things—arrogant, biased, stubborn, crotchety. But there was one thing he wasn't: late.

"He's got a radio in that big land yacht of his, right?" Phil asked. "Try giving him a call."

"Good idea." Susan keyed her base station mike. "Two-zero-one, relay Signal 3 immediately."

The only reply was static.

"Two-zero-one, do you copy?"

Nothing.

"Chief Mullins? Do you copy?"

Still, no reply.

"To hell with this," Phil said and got up, grabbing the cruiser keys. "I'm gonna go look for him. Something's not right here." But before he made it to the back door, Susan called out, "Wait! He just came on line."

Phil stepped quickly into the commo cove. Mullins' voice, even more gravelly through the airwaves, was grumbling, "...yeah, Susan, I'm 10-20'd north on 154, just past Hockley's Swamp..."

"We were getting a little worried. Are you all right? Do you need assistance?"

"You might say that—Christ. Is Phil still at the station?"

"Yeah, Chief, he's right here."

"Good. I want you to lock the place up and get out here," Mullins directed. "But first, Susan, I want you to get several pairs of plastic gloves, some forceps, and a handful of evidence bags." Static crackled through his next pause. "And tell Phil to bring a Signal 64 report."

Holy shit, Phil thought.

Susan turned off the base station. Her face looked grim. "You heard him," she said as she opened the small drawer they kept their evidence collection materials in.

Yeah, I heard him, all right. Phil then, just as grimly, went to the file cabinet and retrieved a Signal 64 form, otherwise known as a Uniform Jurisdictional Standard Report for Homicide.

"What in the name of..."

Phil didn't go to the trouble of finishing. In the name of what, exactly? What, he wondered in fragments. Could possibly. Describe. This?

Susan, standing right beside him, gaped down into the ragged ravine, while Mullins lingered several yards off, facing away. He looked on the verge of displacing his last meal into the woods.

If he hadn't already.

The corpse glistened, scarlet hands locked in rigor. A few flies peppered the gore-sheened head; it took Phil a few solid moments of staring before he could even discern it as human. The chief, his bulbous face going pallid, was pointing to the flat front-right tire on his Caddy and explaining "...so just when I come around the bend, I get a blowout. Brand-new friggin' tire, too. And anyway, I'm lugging the jack out of the trunk, I turn to take a spit in the ravine, and the first thing I see is that."

Hell of a way to start the day, Phil thought. His stomach felt as though it were shrinking to something the size of a prune as he looked more closely. It was still early; the sun hadn't yet cleared the ridge, which left them in dappled shade. This lent a strange purplish hue to the corpse's glittery scarlet. At first Phil surmised that the body was merely nude and covered in blood, but when he stooped over, hands on knees, he realized it was something far worse than that.

"My God," Susan croaked. "It looks like it's been—"

"Skinned," Phil finished. "And a humdinger of a job, too. This is some serious, calculated work here, Chief."

"Tell me about it."

The corpse lay in the ravine as if haphazardly dropped there, its arms and legs canted at impossible angles. Probably pushed out of a moving car, Phil guessed, though he pitied the poor chump who had to clean the car out afterward. Sinew, tendons, and even veins remained flawlessly intact along the flensed musculature. "Yeah," Phil mumbled. "Somebody really did the job on this guy... if it even is a guy."

This observation was pertinent; though the corpse appeared to possess a male frame, its obvious loss of genitalia left its gender in question. And there was no hair either—it had been scalped. What remained of its head grinned back liplessly at them, a crimson meaty lump.

"It's a guy," Mullins said. He pointed ten yards to his right. "Those ain't a woman's duds."

Further along the ravine, Phil spotted clothing—a pair of men's straight-leg jeans, a large flannel shirt, and a pair of decent-looking cowboy boots—strewn about as recklessly as the corpse. Then Susan, squinting, noticed something else.

"Is that a wallet lying there, too?" she asked.

"Yeah," Mullins said. "That's why I wanted you to bring gloves and evidence gear. Check it out."

Both Phil and Susan slipped on pairs of polyvinyl evidence gloves, and approached the strewn garments. A braided wallet sat next to one of the boots. Susan knelt and, very gingerly, opened the wallet with a pair of Ballenger forceps. "No cash," she discerned. "But—"

Just as gingerly, then, she slipped out something else.

"Driver's license," Phil noted. "Not surprising."

Mullins, in spite of his obvious nausea, grew excited. "Ain't that some luck? We got an instant ID."

"It's not luck, Chief," Phil said. "This is a hit, and I'll bet my next paycheck it's drug-related."

"How the hell do you know that?" Mullins testily asked.

"It's protocol for dealers," Susan told him. "They left the wallet on purpose."

"Exactly," Phil added and shook open an evidence bag. "Whoever did this wants the word to get around that this guy got whacked. I saw stuff like this every other day on Metro."

"Jake Dustin Rhodes," Susan read the name off the license. "Waynesville address." Then she dropped the license into the bag.

"And I'll bet another paycheck," Phil went on, "that this guy's got dope busts on his record."

"You seem to know an awful lot," Mullins grumbled. "I still don't know what you're driving at."

Phil frowned. He kept forgetting that this wasn't the city anymore. "This guy Rhodes is a cowboy, ten to one, and some other cowboys did this to him for moving on their turf. This is how dealers put the word out: deal on our territory, and this will happen to you."

"That's a hell of a way to leave a message," Mullins commented.

"Yeah, but it always works." Phil bagged the wallet next, and then he and Susan began putting the clothes into larger evidence bags. "On Metro, they'd do this all the time, decapitations, dismemberments, blow-torch jobs, then leave the body with the ID so word will get around. This guy was dealing dope on somebody else's territory. And since they left the body within Crick City town limits, we can safely assume that the territory in question is Crick City itself."

"Natter," Mullins said.

"It's a good bet, unless your previous intelligence is wrong."

"It ain't wrong. It all fits." Mullins pulled out his bag of Red Man, grimaced, then put it back. "I'll bet that sick, ugly fucker had one of his Creekers do this."

"Let's not jump the gun just yet. We still gotta check everything out. I could be wrong. I just doubt that I am."

Mullins ran a squab hand over his pasty face. Phil sympathized; Mullins was a down-home, laid-back town police chief—he didn't know how to deal with situations like this, and since the office of police chief was an elected post in Crick City, that was a further worry. Mutilation, murder, drug assassinations came as alien to Chief Mullins as bottles of Seagrams at MADD meetings. Mullins was trying hard not to fall apart, and he wasn't doing too keen a job of it. He didn't want to look weak in front of his employees, which presented a side of the man—vulnerability—that Phil had never fathomed.

"I-I gotta wait for the M.E.," Mullins wavered. Every time he glanced into the ravine, he looked like he might keel over. "You two get back to the station and start a rundown on this Rhodes character."

"I'll wait with you, Chief," Phil offered. "Help you change that tire."

"No, get on back, the both of you. I ain't a baby, you know. I been at this business since you were wearing diapers."

"Look, Chief, I'm not saying you're a baby, for God's sake. But you're obviously a little shaken up."

"I ain't shaken up," Mullins insisted. He steeled himself then, and stuffed a chaw of the Man into his cheek. "Take the evidence back to the station," he ordered. "Run a rap check on Rhodes. And whatever either of you do, don't tell anyone about this, not the county cops, not the state, not any-fucking-body. We're not town clowns, you know. We're a police department just as good as anyone else, and I don't want some outside agency hogging our case. This is our problem, and we're gonna be the ones who fix it."

"Chief, look—"

"Get on back to the station with Susan," Mullins commanded, more resolutely this time. "I'm your boss, so don't give me no lip. You don't like it, go work someplace else."

"Got'cha, Chief," Phil obeyed. "See you in awhile."

He and Susan put the evidence bags in the trunk, and without further word, took the cruiser back down the Route. In the rear-view, Mullins' discomposed reflection shrank as they drove away: a fat, old, broken man.

"I've never seen him like that before," Susan said from behind the wheel. "He was in pieces."

"It's hard for him to cope with—shit—getting out to change a flat and finding somebody skinned in his juris? He just doesn't want to let on that he's shook up. And he's right about one thing. We can handle this ourselves. We don't need the county cops wiping our noses."

"Yeah, but—"

"But what?" Phil asked.

Susan's pretty face looked in complete disarray as she steered the cruiser through the Route's weaving bends. "This is serious business, Phil."

"We'll handle it."

"I mean, Christ, you saw what they did to that guy. Who could possibly do something like that?"

"Psychopaths, that's who. The only thing worse than a psychopath is a psychopath who's a businessman. Drugs are just like any other business: you succeed by cutting out the competition. I guarantee, the people who did the job on that guy, it was all in a day's work to them. They don't give a shit."

And then, without any warning at all, as his hair sifted in the breeze from the window and the first streams of sunlight peeked gloriously over the ridge, the most macabre question occurred to him.

*What the hell did they do with the guy's skin?*

# THIRTEEN

Both Phil and Susan got out of the station by noon. Mullins had returned earlier, after fixing his flat and signing the corpus of one Jake Dustin Rhodes off to the morgue; it hadn't taken the M.E. very much time to officially pronounce Rhodes dead. It was hard to be much deader...

Phil's estimation had been right on the mark; Susan's rap check on Rhodes had revealed a profusion of arrests, convictions, suspended sentences (famous in this state), and even some time in the county slam—all for possession, distribution, and sales of PCP. He'd even been held as a suspect in a couple of drug-related murder investigations but had been released due to insufficient evidence. The world would not miss Jake Dustin Rhodes. After being a cop for a decade now, Phil was not surprised by the sense of detachment that overcame him shortly after seeing the state of the corpse; the sensibility went along with the job: when you see dead people, you don't take it personally, and when you see dead drug-dealers, you care even less. Nor was Phil surprised by the strange and accelerated manner in which this narcotics investigation had bloomed. For weeks he'd been on the case and uncovered nothing to suggest a PCP operation in Crick City. Yet now, and literally overnight, he had Eagle Peters with a PCP history, a missing person named Orndorf with a PCP history, and a corpse named Rhodes with a PCP history. Another aspect of police work—sheer spontaneity—that he was well used to by now. Dumb luck was frequently a cop's most reliable friend.

"Don't forget our date tomorrow," Susan reminded him when they both got out at Old Lady Crane's boardinghouse.

Are you kidding me? He'd sooner forget his name. "I know, hell hath no fury like a dispatcher scorned."

"See you at work tonight," she said, skipping up the old carpeted stairs.

Phil smiled in spite of his fatigue, and walked down the first-floor hall to his own room. He felt a numb elation; he hadn't been on a real "date" in some time. And what pleased him much more was the growing attraction he felt for Susan. It seemed easy and honest, not just his physical attraction to her—each day, though, she did seem even more beautiful, her eyes more blue, her hair more silken, her physique more alluring—but his personal attraction as well; he liked her in too many ways he could name, and she clearly liked him. I must be doing something right, he gave himself credit. Why would she want to go out with me if she didn't think I was a cool guy?

Right now, though, he was a tired guy. Night shifts skewed his metabolism to begin with, and worse was the fact that, thanks to today's unavoidable overtime, he was getting to bed hours later than he was used to. The simple prospect of sleep never seemed more luxurious as he closed and locked his door and began to undress.

He only had one wish.

*No dreams today, okay, Mr. Sandman? No nightmares.*

The dreams were subtly haunting him now. It seemed that the instant he dozed off, his mind took him back to that byway of his childhood. Like a grainy, ill-exposed movie: his ten-year-old self wandering through the humid, vine-tangled woods. The little Creeker girl, pretty in spite of her deformities, running away into the blistering sun. The high hill surrounded by dying grass that was as tall as he was, and atop the hill—

The House.

*Christ...*

And its marred, narrow windows set into whitewashed wood. Windows like eyes glaring straight into the throbbing heart of the nightmare itself...

He hung up his gunbelt in the closet, unfastened his badge and pulled off his shirt. A moment ago he'd been in a great mood—now it was ruined. The nightmare festered even when he was awake; it sabotaged him. Why should he remain so obsessed with the memory? That had all been over two decades ago, if it had even been real at all. I should see a shrink, he considered. It wasn't fully a joke. The nightmare was stressing him out now, making raids on his sleep, and pecking at his waking thoughts like some demented, needle-beaked grackle gorging on a pile of delectable worms. It was now to the point that, exhausted as he was, he felt afraid to go to bed. For he knew the specter would be waiting to feast on more of his memory, the grim, blade-sharp images of the things he thought he'd seen in the House that day...

*Jesus Christ, can't you quit thinking about that shit!* he hollered at himself. *What the hell is wrong with you, you basket case!*

And at the end of this self-explosive thought, the tiniest rap of knuckles sounded at the door. His mind felt so disarranged at that moment, he didn't even at first contemplate who it might be. Susan, maybe. Maybe she forgot to tell him something. Or maybe it was his landlady, or Mullins. But when he answered the door he saw, in smothered shock, that it was none of these people.

"Hello, Phil," came the subdued and slightly sultry voice. Slightly sultry, yes, but more than slightly familiar.

Phil gulped as if swallowing dry oatmeal.

"Hello...Vicki," he replied.


*Ona...*

The thought came like a single sob of joy. Like a herald, like a breath of—

Of what? he wondered.

Of hope?

No. Deliverance.

Enraptured in the tainted dark, the Reverend stood poised in the opposite corner. The darkness dressed him as if in a holy man's mantle. He was, after all, a holy man. He gave succor to holy things. He bid blessings and cast absolutions. In his own cloak now, weaved of the most austere sackcloth, he stood in pensive, undeniable worship.

*Save us.*

From the shuttered window, the tiniest leakage of sunlight hung in the dark chamber like brilliant web-strands. The light of day provided its oblivion—didn't it?—as it did their own souls, their own spirits, a sanctuary from the misery of their cursed and most obscene blight.

Like their savior, their only real freedom was the glorious dark...

*Save us, I beg of thee,* the Reverend thought.

A tear welled in his eye.

And past the minute webwork of light—in the haven of its own darkness—

Something stirred.

"I wasn't going to come by, but—"

Vicki's words seemed to die of their own starvation, as though each were a little shrew expiring in its tracks.

"But what?" Phil asked after he let her in. He'd asked the question more out of his own mental famine. Her presence assailed him. Why had she come? What did she expect him to say? How did she perceive him?

*She has every right in the world*, he reminded himself, *to hate my friggin' guts.*

Had she come to tell him off? To unload on him in an outburst of anger and betrayal that had simmered in her for years? Most women would, he thought. He was the guy who had professed his love, and then abandoned her.

Yet she seemed composed, if not a little nervous. In her manner and the shades of her voice, Phil could not detect anything of the rage he imagined.

"Didn't want to bother you—"

"It's not a bother, for God's sake," he replied so quickly he may have seemed irritated. "Christ, we almost—"

He bit the rest off. We almost got married, he nearly finished. And what a catastrophic thing that would have been to say. A pause, hard as concrete, floundered between them.

"You look good, Vicki," he said. "And it's good to see you."

He expected some equally benign reply, but then he thought, *How good can I look in crumpled pants and an old T-shirt? Yeah, dickhead, how good can it be for her to see me? The guy who walked away from her life and never looked back?*

"I saw you last night," she said more quietly, "and I'm sure you saw me—at least I guess you did." She made a morose chuckle. "It's probably pretty hard not to notice your former fiancée up on stage in a strip joint. I was going to come over to the bar and say something to you, but, well... Complications, you know?"

Complications? That could, mean anything, but to ask her to elaborate now would only make things more difficult for her; just coming here had to be difficult enough. "You want something to drink?" he asked instead, and opened the refrigerator. "I've got-uh..." The fridge was empty. "I've got some great imported sparkling tap water."

"No thanks," she laughed. "You remember me—I never touch the hard stuff."

Phil took a few seconds to really look at her then, though those few seconds ticked by like full minutes. She was dressed revealingly: a short, tight denim skirt and a glittery vermillion tanktop, very sheer and as tight. Where Susan was attractive in a plain and simple sense, Vicki's looks could be likened to a caricature, every stereotypical trait of feminine desirability all flawlessly converged into one woman. Her light red hair hung straight just past her bare shoulders; whenever she turned her head, the hair shimmered like fine tinsel. Trace makeup accentuated the lines of her model's face. Her deep sea-green eyes seemed huge, gemlike, and the faintest pastel lipstick highlighted a pert, full mouth. She was more beautiful than even Phil could remember. She seemed more fit, more trim, more toned of muscle than ever before, which made sense— dancing, even in a strip joint, proved a vigorous exercise. Long legs, sleek shoulders and arms, the keen neckline, all bare and a creamy white. Even the mistlike spray of freckles just above her breasts seemed a perfect embellishment, while the breasts themselves, obviously braless beneath the sparkling tank, were firm and full. In Phil's long absence from Crick City, Vicki Steele had become a sexist's dream, a living monument to the numbers 38-24-36, a paragon.

And in all her beauty, perhaps that was the saddest part of all. That's all she was now, in a sense, a body. Crushed by backwoods subjugation, trapped by her own upbringing and the indoctrinated fear to leave, her real womanhood had all but evaporated. The lot of her life had left her nothing else.

A queer smile came to her lips. Had she noticed Phil's momentary appraisal of her? He hoped not; the last thing she needed in her life was another chump gaping at her, especially when the chump was her ex-fiancé. She sat down in the ragtag chair by the dresser. Her skin seemed to whisper as she crossed her legs; she sat back lazily, looking at him.

"I heard you're working for a landscaper now," she said.

Evidently Eagle had run his mouth, which was just what Phil wanted. And it was a damn stroke of luck he'd hung up his shirt and gunbelt in the closet before she'd come in; his cover would've been blown before it started. "Yeah, part-time for now," he said. "Until I find something better."

"Around here? You're lucky to have that." Her big green eyes took in more of the cramped room. "I guess it was about six months ago or so, I kind of heard that things didn't work out for you on Metro."

"I got canned," Phil admitted immediately. "It's a long story, and a boring one."

"Must have been a real bummer for you. Being a cop was what you wanted more than anything else in the world, wasn't it? I mean, for the whole time we were together, that's all you talked about."

Phil swallowed a lump. It was almost innocuous, the way she'd said for the whole time we were together. "It's no big deal, all for the better really," he rebounded, lying. "Took me ten years to realize that being a cop wasn't for me. I got tired real fast of seeing people get hurt, ripped off, and killed every day. You must know what I'm talking about, you were a cop, too."

"I was a town cop," she corrected, then recrossed her legs. "Not the same thing, really. But it was a good job."

This seemed the oddest of remarks. According to Mullins, there'd been no choice but to fire her for all manner of sexual misconduct. She was obviously not cut out at all for police work; she'd made the transition from cop to prostitute all too easily. Mullins' photographs proved that.

Didn't they?

A grim smile surfaced on her lips. She relaxed back, closed her eyes, and sighed. "You always were such a gentleman, Phil. Aren't you even going to ask?"

"Ask what?"

"Aren't you the least bit curious even?"

Phil read what she was driving at, but to admit that would only increase the severity of this weird circumstance. Instead, and with not much conviction, he said, "I don't know what you mean, Vicki."

Her frown drained all the prettiness out of her face at once. "I used to be a cop, Phil, and now I'm a stripper. Most people would think that's a little bit weird, wouldn't they? Don't you want to know what happened?"

With more conviction this time, he replied, "Hey, that's your business, none of mine. As long as you're happy doing what you're doing, then that's all that matters."

In part-whisper, part-croak, and with her eyes still closed, she responded: "You think I'm happy doing this?"

Phil sat down on the edge of his bed, brows raised. He couldn't summon a reply.

"I was like you, remember?" she continued. "I wanted to be a cop, and I was a good cop." A hesitation, an uneasy gulp. "You want to know why I'm not a cop now?"

I already do, Phil thought, but of course he couldn't say that, not without blowing his cover completely. "So tell me what happened."

"Mullins blackballed me. From day one he was trying to get into my pants but, you know, I figured it was all a joke. Country bumpkin small-town chief, just acting the part like any good ol' boy. But soon the joke stopped being funny. One night he tried to rape me, told me if I didn't put out he'd fire me. I filed an harassment complaint with the state liaison office, but Mullins got it nixed, trumped up a bunch of crap and phony documentation, and then he fired me."

Phil stared at what she was saying as much as he stared at her. He'd like nothing more than to believe her, but how could he? Mullins' own claims of her on-duty sexual negligence provided an undeniable corroboration with the photos that had been taken after her separation from the department. There could be no denying what the pictures showed—sexual acts in public—and there could be no denying that Vicki Steele was the woman in the pictures.

"But I'll bet that's not what you heard, huh?" she whispered on. "I'll bet you heard some snowjob about me turning tricks on duty, huh? Is that what you heard?"

"I never heard anything, Vicki," Phil lied again, protecting his cover. "I've only been back in town a month."

"Yeah, well, that was the word the bastard put out all over town and in my personnel file, that I 'demonstrated social behavior unbecoming of an officer in general' and 'engaged in acts of sexual solicitation and prostitution while in uniform.' He even had 'witnesses' turn in written statements and promises to testify if I took him to court. Next thing I knew I was on the street with no place to go. And no way any police department in the country would even consider hiring me. The son of a bitch ruined me, all because I wouldn't fuck him."

The word fuck clanged like a cracked bell. But, again, Phil couldn't believe her story. *I saw the pictures,* he grimly reminded himself. Too often in life, he knew, people changed for the worse, and Vicki Steele had to be a prime example. That's why she came here today. To save face, to make an excuse now that she knew I was back in town. All he could do now was feel sorry for her.

And it made him feel ultimately shitty, too, not just the tailspin her life had taken since he'd ended their relationship, but the acknowledgement of what he was doing to her right now. He was using her, wasn't he? There could be no other word for it. Phil was pretending to be someone he wasn't, and he was using her misfortune as a means to get deeper into his PCP leads.

*She's a perfect information dupe,* he told himself. *And I'm a perfect asshole...*

Vicki finally straightened up and opened her eyes. "You don't believe me, do you?"

"I believe you," he lied yet again. He didn't want to contemplate how many lies he'd told already. "I know all about getting blackballed, Vicki. One day I'll tell you what happened to me on Metro. Same thing, different circumstances."

She sighed silently. Relief? Resignation? "I'll bet you think I blame you, though, right?"

Finally here was a question he didn't have to answer with a lie, though the topic was not an enlightening one. "You'd have every right to, Vicki. The main reason things went to hell for us is because I wanted out of this town more than anything. I know that. And I don't feel too good about the way things ended for us."

"Yeah, but at least you knew what you wanted, and you went for it. I was too insecure—too afraid—to think I could do better than Crick City. And look at me now..."

"I'm not exactly doing great myself," Phil tried to lighten things. "I gotta goddamn Master's degree, and I'm making peanuts planting rosebushes and laying manure."

"You always manage to get around the issues, don't you?" she said. "I guess that's your way of being polite."

"What's that?"

Her face hardened. For a moment she wasn't pretty at all; she was ugly in a raving glare of self-disgust. "I'm a roadside stripper, Phil. I'm not gonna lie to you." The big gemlike green eyes struggled against sudden tears. "I'm a whore."

In an unbidden instant, part of Phil felt transported back to another time not really that long ago, a time when they were in love with each other and when the current state of their lives was so remote as to be unthinkable. He wanted to argue with her, to shake her around and bellow in her face that she should stop indicting herself and step out of the seamy ditch her life had fallen into. Stop feeling sorry for yourself and get your shit together! he wanted to rant. All right, you fell down, so get the fuck back up and make a real life for yourself before it's too late!

But he could say nothing of the sort, and he knew it. He needed her, for the case. He was a cop, and he had a job to do. He had to play along, or else he'd lose his best lead yet.

*Yeah, my best lead. A girl I used to love. A girl I almost married...*

"Excuse me," she said and abruptly stood. "I need to use your bathroom."

"Right in there," he pointed.

She went in and closed the door. He knew she was crying, which made him feel even more despicable. He was low enough to use her for the profit of the investigation. But beyond that, no matter how hard he rationalized it to Mullins or even to himself, he knew he would always be partly to blame for what had happened to her.

After several minutes, he began to pace his room. Several more and he began to worry.

He knocked on the bathroom door. "You okay, Vicki?"

"Yeah."

"You sure?"

"Yeah. I'll be out in a sec."

And when she did indeed re-emerge from the bathroom, she seemed back in control, but—

Oddly so.

Again, she looked neat as a pin, her posture perfect, every shining red hair in its place, but her eyes bore a glint now like ice. She seemed stolid, hard, when only a few minutes ago she'd been falling apart.

"Look, I'm sorry about that," she said.

"We all have bad moments, Vicki."

"I guess the real reason I came here was because I wanted you to know what happened, that's all. I didn't want you to think—"

"Don't worry about it. I'm glad you stopped by."

Their eyes locked. For a moment the green ice cracked. "Really?"

"Sure. Look, the past is the past, right? We both got bum raps, that's life. Why don't we try to put the past behind us, forget about all that and leave it lie? Let's be friends, okay?"

Something like a repressed despair threatened to collapse her entire face, but she seemed to stave it off. "I'd really like that, Phil. I'd like that a lot, but—"

"So what's the problem?"

"It'll have to be a secret."

"A secret? Why?"

She steeled herself. "I'm married now, Phil," she said very coldly. She raised her left hand, flashed the wedding ring with a diamond on it the size of a pea. Then:

"I'm married to Cody Natter."

He tried to manage his shock, tried to keep it from getting out and molesting the memory of how he used to feel about her.

"Still want to be friends?" she asked.

"Sure. I don't care if you're married to Elvis."

She let a smile eek out, gave him a final glance, then kissed him very lightly on the lips.

"See you around," she said and left.

His bewilderment held him in a momentary check. When he looked around the doorway and down the hall, she was already gone.

Cody. Natter's. Wife. Each word smacked like a piton into stone. How could any man, however irredeemable, let his own wife dance in a strip joint and turn roadside tricks in pickup trucks. When Phil closed the door, he wanted to punch a hole in it. His anger raged like a huge beast trapped in a tiny cage. He thought he would explode.

And the emotion doubled when he went into the bathroom. Perhaps his cop's sensitivities had tuned him in; anyone else wouldn't have noticed it in a million years. But—

"Oh, my God, Vicki, no no no—"

At the corner of the old porcelain sink, the faintest sprinkling of diminutive white dust lingered. He knew what it was even before he rubbed a trace across his upper gum and felt the numb, cold tingle.

*Cocaine. No wonder Natter got her stripping and turning tricks so fast. He got her hooked on coke...*

# FOURTEEN

Phil walked into the station at five of eight, keyed up by an array of emotions: despair, perplexity, and anger...

Mostly anger.

"Hi, Phil," Susan said from the commo niche, her nose buried in a textbook.

"What?"

She vaguely smirked, looking up. "I said hi. It's a colloquial Modem English interjection commonly used to denote a greeting."

"Oh, yeah. Hi. Where's Mullins?"

Susan obviously sensed his disheveled mood at once. "He's eating sushi on the Ginza in Tokyo. You know, like he does every night at eight."

"Huh?"

"He's in his office! Where else would he be?" She closed her book somewhat testily. "What's wrong with you? You get out on the wrong side of the bed today?"

"Sorry, Susan. I—" He didn't know how to properly explain it, not that he would want to anyway, not to her. What? My ex-fiancée stopped by today and enlightened me to the fact that she's married to Cody Natter. She claims Mullins tried to rape her. Oh, and she's also a prostitute and a coke addict. No, that wouldn't wash, and it would certainly put a damper on their date tomorrow.

"Just feeling a little out of it today. Talk to you later."

Phil's frown widened when he stepped into the chief's office; Mullins wasn't there, but an instinctive glance to the back window showed the chief lumbering out of the disused lockup behind the station, bearing a can of coffee.

"Bright-eyed and bushy-tailed I see," the big man said when he came in.

Phil didn't waste time. "That was real cool of you to not tell me

Vicki Steele was married to Cody Natter. I guess you just forgot that minor detail, huh?"

"I can tell you're in a great mood." Mullins started another pot of coffee, then sat down at the cluttered desk. "I figured it was best you found out on your own. Didn't want to shake you up before I had to."

"Oh, I appreciate that, Chief. I'm not a school kid, you know. I don't let personal stuff get in the way of my job."

"I can tell." Mullins' chair creaked like a keening hinge when he lounged back. "You haven't even been in the office ten seconds, and you look about as happy as a mad dog. I didn't think you could handle that information right off the bat."

"Well, fine. But next time fill me in, all right? How can I do a good job on this case if you withhold pertinent facts?"

"Sorry, dear. It won't happen again. I take it you ran into her."

"Yeah, this afternoon before I turned in."

"Were you in uniform?"

"No, no, my cover's intact."

"Good." Mullins hand-pinched a few choice leaves of tobacco from his bag, then stuffed them into his cheek.

"Takes the cake, don't it? That ugly scumbag is married to the best-looking woman in town, and he's got her doing a strip show and turning tricks."

Yeah, it takes the cake, all right. But now that he'd had time to think about it, it wasn't terribly surprising. "Actually it's pretty common in criminal networks. Drug kingpins frequently take a beautiful wife for status, then use them for business. The dust honchos in the city do it all the time. It's like buying a $500 silk shirt and using it to check your oil. It's street machismo."

Mullins chuckled grimly at the simile. "Ugly Creeker slime. I can't wait to bust his ass."

"We got a lot of very positive leads real fast, and Vicki's the best lead yet."

"You figure you'll run into her on a regular basis?"

"Sure. She works at Krazy Sallee's; I'll be hanging out there every night. And I'll be seeing a lot of Eagle Peters, too. I should be able to infiltrate the entire scene at Sallee's if I play my cards right."

"Yeah, but if you play 'em wrong, you could wind up looking like that chump we found in the ravine this morning. So be careful."

"But," Phil went on, "a secure cover is the key, and there's no way I can expect to maintain a secure cover by staking out Sallee's for a few hours in plainclothes and then touring the town in uniform for the rest of my shift all night. There's only one way to do this right, Chief."

"You want to go undercover full time, in other words?"

"There's no other option, Chief. Say I'm hamming it up at the bar with Peters one night, and a couple hours later the guy sees me cruising around in the patrol car. Or any of the regulars at Sallee's. Not only would that destroy my cover for good, it would tip Natter that you're eying him. He'll move his distro point somewhere else, and then we're worse off than before we started."

"You're right," Mullins grumbled and spat. "But I'll have a hard time selling it to the town council. This ain't Miami Vice, you know. They won't like the idea of paying an officer for full-time undercover and not having a uniform on duty during the nightshift."

Phil gave a smirk. "Piss on the town council, Chief. They want you to solve this PCP business, you gotta do it the right way. Those loudmouth assholes shouldn't even know about it. And, shit, you don't really even need a patrol cop out here at night. All I ever get are smoochers parking out on some of the old logging roads. Anything hairy goes down, Susan can call you, or dispatch the county. If you want me to get into Natter's shit, I can't be seen anywhere near this station or that cruiser. And no one, not even the town council or the mayor, can know about me being undercover. They could blab, and I wouldn't be surprised if Natter's greasing one of them for tip-offs. You trust those guys?"

"Wouldn't trust 'em to walk my dog, and I don't even have a fuckin' dog." Mullins festered a moment more, then conceded. "All right, you're the big city expert, we'll do it your way. Work your own hours, do your own thing, but keep me posted each day. And be fuckin' careful. These people don't fuck around; you saw that Rhodes guy this morning."

I sure did, Phil remembered. Seeing a skinned human being wasn't easy to forget. He got up to leave, but hesitantly.

"Ain't you even gonna stay for a cup of coffee?"

Phil raised a brow at the bubbling pot. "No thanks. But look, Chief, there's one thing I gotta ask."

"What?"

How could he phrase the question without looking absurd? He'd wind up proving that he couldn't keep personal feelings separate from the job.

Still, though, he had to ask.

"Vicki said—" he began.

Mullins laughed immediately. "Let me guess, supercop. She told you I fired her on bullshit, right? What'd you expect her to say? 'Phil, honey, big bad Chief Mullins fired me 'cos I was fucking a bunch of stoners for twenty a bang in the back of the cruiser.' Get real, Phil. Bet she also told you I tried to rape her."

"Well—"

"Check the file, lover boy. It's all documented. Sure, I'll bet she also told you I fabricated the charges and the witnesses, and if you're stupid enough to believe that, then you need to turn your brain in for a new one."

"I didn't say I believed it," Phil stumbled. "I just—"

"How am I gonna jink affidavits and sworn testimony? It's all filed through the county. The county investigated the whole schmear. What, they're making it up, too? I'm buddies with the fuckin' county? Those fuckers hate municipal departments. Go down to the county hall of records with a FOIA request, see for yourself. Christ, I showed you the pictures. She was turning tricks in the parking lot for God's sake. She was giving blowjobs, behind the fucking dumpster. And that was just one stack, Phil. You want to see the rest?"

Phil felt he was shrinking from embarrassment. Yes, he'd made an idiot of himself even bringing it up. "No," he said. "It's just, like—"

Mullins spat tobacco juice into one paper cup and swigged rancid coffee from another. "Look, I know it ain't an easy thing to admit, but no matter how you look at it, there's no way you can tell me otherwise. Vicki Steele's a hooker now. A roadside fuckin' whore turning tricks for her old man, who's the biggest angel dust supplier in the county and probably a murderer to boot. Back in the old days, sure, she was different then, she was a decent person, but that was a long while ago. People let their lives go to shit every day, and sometimes they're people we know, even people we used to be in love with. But as cops, we have to forget it. We can't let that shit get to us 'cos if we do, we ain't worth shit ourselves. You hearing me?"

"Yeah, I'm hearing you, Chief." Phil walked out, dejected, asi-nine. Mullins was right. Vicki Steele was a whore now.

A whore, he told himself and let the word sink in. And noth-ing more.

"Go ahead, Druck," Cody Natter granted permission. No one, naturally, could touch his wife without permission, no one dared. "Just take care not to leave any marks. She must always look good on stage. Few would want to purchase her services with her lovely face all bruised, yes?"

"Please, Cody," his wife pleaded. One of the Creeker boys held her elbows behind her back, inclining her up on her tiptoes. "What is wrong?" she sobbed. "What have I done?"

Natter sat down to watch. "Hmm. Wrong. I suppose that's for you to tell me, yes?"

Druck cracked the knuckles of his two left thumbs, then very delicately untied her tanktop. Vicki whined as the Creeker boy behind her exerted a bit more pressure against her elbows, which jutted her bosom. "You shore are pretty, Ms. Vicki," Druck made the compliment. His crooked eyes fixed on her breasts. "Now what'cha wanna go jerkin' Cody 'round fer. He's a right fine hus-band to ya, seems ta me."

"I didn't do anything!" she shrieked.

In the corner, a third Creeker boy drooled, rubbing the crotch of his overalls, while the boy behind her drooled even more pro-fusely onto her bare shoulder. "Don't'cha bite now," Druck sug-gested. "Otherwise Ise'll have to have the boys do ya twice, and you wouldn't want that, would ya? 'Specially Scooter there. I'se sure you'se heard how big he is. Last time he assed a gal, she plumb up an' bled ta death."

Druck then inserted his two long thumbs into Vicki's mouth. He wriggled them gently, smiling his warped, broken-toothed smile as the Creeker boy holding her began to jibber in enthusiasm, spittle bubbling at his lips. Vicki's own lips squirmed in revulsion. Tears smeared the fine-lined mascara down her cheeks like trails of black blood.

Cody Natter made a single, resolute nod.

"Time ta listen up, Ms. Vicki, and ya's best listen good—" Druck slid his double thumbs all the way to the back of her throat and pressed down. He pressed down hard.

Instantly, Vicki was gagging, her green eyes widening, her body in tremors. "Don't'cha bite," Druck kindly repeated, "an' don't'cha dare puke. Just listen." Beads of sweat welled on Druck's protuberant forehead; his scarlet eyes focused intently. "You tell Cody here what'cha were doin' today. You tell Cody where ya been."

He pressed down hard one more time until she nearly retched. Then he removed his thumbs.

"Go on."

After a violent coughing fit, she managed to catch her breath. Tears and sweat pasted shocks of her red hair to her paling face. "I just—went—for a drive," she croaked, then whined when the boy behind her resumed the clenching pressure on her elbows.

Cody Natter blinked. His own eyes, though keen and clear, were uneven, one lower than the other and noticeably larger. His ears, too—each the size of a pastry—pressed the sides of his head so unevenly they scarcely appeared real. And in spite of the monstrously malformed face—long, bony, runneled—a sane and even considerate sense of deliberation seemed suffused through his twisted features.

"A drive," he said. "That's all? And where did this drive take you?"

"Nowhere, Cody, I swear!" she exclaimed, her teeth gritting against the pain of being chicken-winged. "I just went for a drive 'cos I was bored!"

"Hmm. Well." Natter steepled his triple-jointed fingers in his lap. "What do you think, Druck? Is my fair wife telling the truth, or is she lying?"

"Well, jeez, Cody, I don't rightly know, ya know?"

"How about you, Scooter? Is there a liar in our midst?"

The third Creeker boy babbled excitedly, tossing his squashed head and rubbing briskly at the obvious erection in his trousers. A foot-long line of drool depended off his bulbed chin.

Natter sighed. "Perhaps a trifle more convincing is in order. Yes, I think so."

"No, please!" Vicki shrieked. "I didn't do anything, I swear to God!"

"You needn't swear to God, my dear. Not here."

Natter nodded then to the third boy, who quickly appeared and returned a moment later, dragging along a gagged and blindfolded Creeker girl. Immediately, he clutched her by strings of jet-black hair and threw her to the floor.

"Lovely wife, please. Come sit with me."

Vicki was released and shoved forward. Natter's queerly long arms and hands shot out, grabbed her about the waist, and pulled her in, forcing her to sit in his lap.

His grip tightened, and his big grouper lips whispered in her ear: "So many choose to stray from our fold. Shanny tried to run away again last night. Such a pity. The poor thing doesn't realize."

Scooter, the third boy, stepped clumsily out of his overalls, clucking like a psychotic chicken. The second boy pinned the girl's shoulders with his knees while Druck, drooling himself now, opened a buck knife and cut off her gag and blindfold. Then Scooter—sporting an erection so large and genetically malformed it more resembled a loaf of French bread—climbed atop the girl and began to rape her.

The girl's screams were dizzying.

Each time Vicki tried to turn her face away, Natter's claw-hand vised the back of her head and forced her to return her attention to the madness on the floor. "You must watch, my love," came his shredded whisper. "You must see. Everything that we see makes us more real in the face of our faith. Do you understand? Some sights aren't so pretty, but they're real just the same…"

Vicki looked on from her husband's lap, paralyzed, nauseous. Druck and his two dutiful attendants took turns raping the screaming girl. Her shrieks rattled the windows and pierced Vicki's ears. All manner of molestation and sodomy ensued until the sheer gravity of shock robbed what was left of her senses, leaving her silent, bug-eyed, and convulsant on the wood floor. Blood poured freely as if dumped from a bucket.

"All things serve a higher purpose, wife. Even terrible things. One day you'll see that as clearly as I do."

Again, Natter nodded.

Druck slit the girl's throat to the bone. She twitched feebly once or twice, then died. The two boys jabbered on, their bulbous heads bobbing in glee. Druck's knife flashed, cutting an expert seam from the girl's pubis to her chest.

"Soup's on, boys!" he exclaimed.

The three of them, then, sloppily disemboweled the girl where she lay, reveling in a wet, noisy festival of gore. Hands dipped down and came away red. Jabbers of enthusiasm rose above the sounds of evisceration. Organs were promptly scooped up and consumed...

Natter's hand released the back of Vicki's head; her eyes fled away.

"Oh, my love," creaked the monstrous man's voice. "Never lie to me, or else they'll do the same to you."

# FIFTEEN

"No Ric Flair tonight?" Phil asked when he pulled up a stool. The bizarre barkeep gestured toward the TV. "Flair, the Nature Boy, the Champion of Champions? Naw, ya missed him. He's already been on, whupped the tar out of Rocky Johnson. Like he says, to be the man, you have to beat the man. Right now we got Terrific Terry Taylor mixing it up with Rick Morton."

"Ah," Phil said. "Of course."

"Bottle of Bud? Hot dog?"

"Just…a bottle of Bud."

Sallee's was buzzing, the crowd waiting for the next dancer. Phil glanced around. Well-bosomed waitresses in ludicrously tight tops wended orders between tables like tight-ropists. Same crowd as last night—Generic rednecks, Phil thought. Is that all these people do? Bum around in strip joints? Lights throbbed idly above the vacant dance stage, through lolling sheets of cigarette smoke. Hoarse laughter erupted every so often, and the bar, in its casual discourse, was not lacking in foul language and bad jokes. "Hey, what are two words you never wanna hear in the men's locker room?" "What?" "'Nice dick.'" "You got ten gals with PMS and ten gals with yeast infections, what've ya got?" "What?" "A whine and cheese party!" Brilliant, Phil thought. He didn't see Eagle anywhere, nor Vicki; he felt immediately foolish sitting at the bar by himself. He frowned up at the wrestling foolery on the TV. These guys probably spend more money per year on hair bleach than I spend on car insurance. The keep was peddling shriveled hot dogs at one end of the bar, while two bearded guys at the other end nearly got into a fight arguing over whether cast aluminum engine blocks were more durable than cast iron. Next, they'll be arguing over who should win the Nobel Prize for Literature, Phil joked over his beer. But this night was no joke. His lame distractions coaxed him to forget he had a job to do, yet he continued

to do exactly what Mullins—and professionalism in general—
warned him never to do: Take things personally. His mind kept
homing back—to Vicki, and the dusting of cocaine she'd left in his
bathroom.

Addict, the word kept haunting him.

Eventually the next dancer came on, a blond who was surely
half-inebriated as she plunged her routine into another nondescript heavy metal tune. A snake seemed to peer from her navel,
but then Phil realized it was a tattoo. Small, weathered breasts
jiggled with each high-heeled step, like slackened bags of gel, and
wires of black pubic hair leaked from the seams of a flesh-colored
g-string.

One thing Phil eventually came to notice, though, in spite of
his despondency, was an influx of patrons crossing the bar toward
the men's room but never returning, and as he became more aware
of this, he tried to pay more attention without being conspicuous.

*What the hell's going on back there?*

A cramped hallway in the corner led to the men's room, and
right next to it stood a door. A funny-looking kid in overalls waited
beside the door itself, arms crossed and stone-faced. A Creeker,
Phil ascertained. The gaunt features and enlarged head left no
doubt. One periodic redneck after another approached the kid,
bypassed the men's room, and after a moment of discussion, was
granted permission to pass through the cryptic door. It seemed
almost as if the Creeker kid was guarding it.

Maybe it's a billiard room or arcade or something, Phil suggested to himself, but that wouldn't make sense.

Why would the kid be guarding it? Then Phil thought back:
When he'd first started staking the lot, hadn't he heard several
patrons mention something about a back room?

A hand slapped on his back. Phil jumped.

"Hey, man. How's it going?"

Eagle, his long blond hair in his face, pulled up the next stool
and ordered a beer.

"Can't complain," Phil answered. "Well, I guess I could, but
why bother? What's up with you?"

"Same old, same old." Eagle craned to view the current dancer,
then quickly frowned. "Looks like she's dancing with cinderblocks
tied to her feet."

"Give her a break, Eagle. She probably just got out of Harvard

Law School but hasn't quite found the right firm."

Eagle chuckled and swigged some beer. "I don't know where they dig some of these girls up. Sure, some of them are all right, but most of 'em look like death warmed up. Vicki blows them all away."

"Yeah," Phil replied but thought: *Yeah, I'll bet she does, when she's not blowing Natter's coke up her nose.*

Another thrashing song thumped on the juke, waves of grinding guitars like chainsaws in tempo. The crowd haphazardly applauded when the dancer stood on her head and parted her long, pale legs, no easy task for a drunk. Phil and Eagle small-talked a while, but in the corner of his eye, Phil detected still more scruffy patrons shuffling rearward, to the door beside the Creeker kid.

"Hey, Eagle? What's in there?"

"Where?" Eagle asked.

"That door back there. I keep seeing guys walking over and talking to that kid. Then the kid lets them in."

"You don't want to know, man. It's a gross-out."

"A gross-out?" Phil pondered this, and came up with nothing. "Come on, what gives? They got pool tables back there or something? Let's go shoot a few games."

Eagle chuckled again, more darkly this time. "Ain't gonna shoot no pool in there, man. It's the back room. I been in there once, but I'll tell ya, I wish I hadn't."

Phil couldn't figure this one out. Gambling? Cock fights? He wanted to find out what was cooking. "What? I gotta guess? Fill me in."

Eagle swept some of his shoulder-length hair out of his face, to reveal the sourest of smirks. "They got a second stage back there," he replied.

"What, you mean more girls?"

"Yeah, man. More girls," he said, dour.

Why's he balking? Phil wondered. "Well, this gal here isn't exactly setting the world on fire; looks like she might die before the next set. Let's go check out this other room, see these other girls."

"It ain't like out here, Phil," Eagle finally confessed. "They got Creeker girls working the back."

Phil's beer went flat in his mouth; he nearly gasped. "Creeker girls? Stripping?"

"That's right, partner. The cream of the crop. They all look great—till you take a second glance. Believe me, man, it's a gross-out. That's the draw. The only people who go back there are kinks and sickos."

Phil eyed the door. Creeker strippers. He'd already seen some, that first night of his stakeout, with his binoculars. He couldn't imagine who would want to witness such a thing, but then he remembered what Eagle had just said. Kinks. Sickos. Yeah, Natter's really got himself a prize here. Shit. It seemed ultimately perverse, and an even more ultimate exploitation, but Phil doubted that the girls were underage. Natter would never be that stupid.

So why was there a doorman?

Only one way to find out, Phil. Ask. "How come that kid's watching the door?"

"It's private. Cody Natter doesn't let just anyone go back there, only friends or regulars. Things would get too rowdy otherwise. The kid's name is Druck, one of Natter's gofers."

This sounded too fishy to resist; Phil finished his beer. "Come on, let's go check it out."

Eagle rolled his eyes. "I just got done telling you, man, regulars only."

Phil leaned over. "Yeah, and you're a regular. You could get us in."

"Sure, I probably could, but I'm not going to." Eagle seemed exasperated by the topic…and a little nervous. "Listen to me, Phil. You'll blow chunks if you even take one look behind that door. They've got girls in there with three or four tits, triple belly buttons, triple nostrils. Hunchback girls, girls with no ears, girls with ten fingers per hand and two elbows per arm. The one time I went back there"—Eagle swallowed hard—"this one Creeker chick walks out on the stage, and she had a body on her that would make Vanna White look like Dr. Ruth—"

"Sounds great! Let's go!"

"—but all she had for arms were these little twigs with fingers on them." Eagle paused to gulp again. "And a head the size of a basketball. I'm tellin' ya, man. It's a fuckin' freak show back there."

These, of course, were not things that Phil wanted to see… But *I have to get into that room,* he determined to himself. *See what else is cooking back there.* He persisted, feigning more enthusiasm. "What's the matter, Eagle? You scared of a few inbreds? Christ, this is Dullsville out here." He shrugged at the stage, and at the next narcoleptic dancer. "These girls are tripping over themselves, for shit's sake. They look like they're ODing on 'ludes. But I'll bet there's plenty of spark in that back room."

"Spark, huh? That's what you want?" Eagle shook his head. "All right, you pay the tab here, and I'll try to get us in back."

"Solid," Phil said, and left a ten on the bar. "Let's go."

They got up and squeezed past the waitress station. Phil's curiosity blended with abundant disgust; butterflies went mad in his belly. But he had to keep playing the part; he had to prove to Eagle that he'd changed, for the worse.

"Hey, Druck," Eagle greeted the Creeker kid at the door. "This here's my buddy, Phil."

"Hey, Druck," Phil said.

"We'd like to go in back," Eagle added. "Phil's a townie, he's just been away a while. But he's all right."

The kid's expression, if it could be called that, didn't waver. His stout, muscled arms remained folded like a sentinel; the scarlet eyes never seemed to even blink. He looked Phil up and down, his enlarged jaw set, the swollen front of his head shining in mushy colors from the dance strobes.

Then he nodded.

"Thanks, Druck," Eagle said.

"Yeah, man," Phil added. "Have a good one."

The music grated on. The strobe lights flashed behind them.

Then Eagle led Phil into the back room.

# Sixteen

Kinks. Sickos. Kinks. Sickos...

The words spun round Phil's head like a ring of scavenger birds. What he and Eagle walked into was not so much a different room but a different realm. A circumference of grainy darkness seemed draped around the single, elevated stage. Faces could not be discerned—just half-formed suggestions of faces signaled by the orange tips of lit cigarettes. Weird electronic music resounded in place of the typical fractious heavy metal, and there was none of the rowdy bar-talk, boisterous laughter, and perverted jokes.

Just human silence, and the steady electronic drone.

As a limping waitress took them around to a table, Phil nearly tripped. "Christ, this is like wearing a blindfold—I can't see a thing!"

"Shhhh!" Eagle replied. "Quiet in here. Rules of the house. They don't want no loud talk, clapping, shit like that."

They were seated several rows back; the waitress or hostess or whatever she was seemed to evaporate. Eagle ordered two beers from another waitress who trolled through the unlit aisles; the darkness revealed only enough of her face to hint at deformities: overlarge eyes; flattened, uneven cheekbones; a bifurcated nose. She made a wan grunt in reply, and slid away. Then Eagle leaned over and whispered, "You're the one who wanted in. Beers are ten bucks a pop back here."

Ouch! Phil thought. Some scam. But was that really all that was going on here? The dusty darkness unnerved him; he wished he could see the faces of the other patrons, to compare them with the pictures he snapped while staking out the parking lot over the past few weeks. But what unnerved him more was the crowd's utter silence. Anticipation thickened in the air; Phil could feel it, he could nearly breathe it...

The stage existed as a single colonnade of dark, roving light.

Then the light went out.

Jesus, Phil thought. They were now sitting in pitch dark; all that his eyes could make out were myriad cigarette ends rising and lowering. The music—or noise really—plunged into a barely audible suboctave note which Phil could feel rattling in his throat. Very slowly, it rose and grew louder.

And even more slowly, the stagelight—now a deep blood-red—revived itself, increasing in a lapse of time that seemed minutes long.

But now the lone stage had a host...

A woman, draped in diaphanous veils, stood immobile as a chess piece in the axis of scarlet light. The music began to throb in a diastole, like blood through a heart; the sound was somehow gelatinous.

And the woman on stage began to move.

It wasn't dancing; it was more like some macabre kind of performance art. Dexterously, she drifted along in the midst of the arcane music and light, invisibly shedding the segments of her veil. In the meantime, and in imperceptible increments, the light adopted new colors—algae greens, yolk yellows, livid purples—so languorously the entire spectacle took on the texture of a dark dream.

Eventually, the girl was naked save for a pinkish, translucent g-string.

The sludge-like light played with Phil's vision, while abyssal noise-works distracted him further. It was a trick. At first he could note nothing abnormal about the girl, but as he trained his gaze, details began to surface as uncannily as magic. Features seemed to appear rather than be noticed. The girl's left eye was tiny as a marble, the right large as a scarlet billiard ball. Otherwise her face was flawless.

But the rest of her, Phil could soon tell, was not.

*Aw, God...*

Her bare splayed feet divided in two but with a pair of squab toes. Her hands were the same: two-fingered. As she swayed her head to the sonic dirge, shimmering black hair fell momentarily away to reveal that she had no ears at all, not even holes or indentations where the ears should be. Her navel, too, was fully missing—no suggestion of any such thing on her midriff. Pert breasts danced in the light, each topped by a perfect, dark nipple, yet more nipples—a half-dozen on each side—tracked down her sleek torso and abdomen like teats on the underbelly of a wolf.

Phil never tasted his ten-dollar beer. The grotesqueries onstage chained his gaze; repelled as he was, he couldn't look away for the life of him. More dancers came and went, each harboring accelerated genetic deformities, which, if anything, exceeded even Eagle's previous descriptions. One girl had three arms (two of them normal, but a third tiny arm sprouting from her armpit like a dead branch), another none, and a third possessed arms that appeared totally boneless—slack tubes of flesh swaying this way and that, with shriveled fingers at their ends. Another dancer displayed multiple breasts, four per side, stacked like pancakes, not to mention a head that seemed cloven.

Each girl finished her set with an obligatory—and masturbatory—floor show. The three-armed woman openly caressed her pubis with two hands, while the third hand—atrophied at the end of the shortened arm—plucked at her nipples.

Phil thought he might vomit any minute.

The evening's progress seemed to drip. The dark grew more murky as cigarette smoke thickened, and eventually the room became sweltering. Phil felt narcotized, shocked to numbness, as though in the aftermath of being bludgeoned in the head. On a few occasions, his eyes had acclimated sufficiently to see that every seat in the back room was taken. What a show, he thought despondently. A packed house. Eagle was right; this was where the denizens came. People who found arousal in the tragic misfortune of others. The kinks. The sickos.

One thing he noticed right off was that each dancer wore a garter, and attached to the garter was a small white card with a number on it. What's with the numbers? he managed to wonder. What purpose could they serve?

When the show was over, Phil felt winded. *I thought I'd seen everything on Metro. Boy, was I wrong.* Stepping outside, into the fresh night air, made him feel released from a long sentence in jail. But he couldn't let on how revolted he was; he must maintain the pretense to Eagle, and to everyone here, that he was just another busted, bent-out-of-shape redneck looking for kicks. Obviously the back room was a magnet for Crick City's most jaded, and would provide a very serviceable fuel for his investigation. To infiltrate a crowd such as this, he must pretend to be a part of it.

"Happy now?" Eagle asked.

"That was pretty wild, man."

Eagle shook his head. "You're into that kind of shit?"

"These days I'm into anything that's not dull. And that show definitely wasn't dull, you gotta admit."

"Christ, man, I couldn't believe that one chick with no bones in her arms."

"The gal with the eight tits was a kick, too."

Eagle gaped at him. "Man, I never would've guessed you'd be into that. Lookin' at those girls makes me wanna blow chow."

Phil feigned a nonchalant shrug. "Different strokes, like they say. One thing I didn't get, though. Why did they all have numbers on their garters?"

Eagle's smirk creased his face. "Why do you think? They ain't just dancers, Phil. They're hookers. A guy sees one he likes, he gets the number and talks to the pimp after the show."

"Who's the pimp?"

"That Creeker kid at the door, Druck. He makes the arrangements. All the money, of course, goes to Cody Natter. That fucker's something; he's got himself a gold mine here. The girls who work the front stage are hookers too, but I guess you figured that. Anything for a buck. Ain't that the American way? Natter's even got his wife turning tricks. You did know that Vicki's married to him, didn't you?"

"Yeah," Phil said. "I heard all about that." His next question, however morbid, wouldn't let go. "How much you think she costs?"

"Vicki? Shit, she's the prime beef of the front room, probably a hundred at least. Natter's pretty selective about who he lets buy her."

*Buy her.* The two words hit him like a kick in the chin. *Probably uses her to finish off deals with his point men and dope distributors. Typical.* "What about those Creeker girls?"

"From what I've heard, they're even more expensive, 'cos this is the only place you can get 'em. Hard to believe guys would want to pay to fuck a Creeker."

"But where? Where do they turn their tricks?"

"Right in the parking lot, in your car mostly. For a little extra, they'll go home with you." Eagle looked at him. "You're not thinking of—"

"Naw, I'm just curious. This town's changed since I been gone."

"Yeah, man." Eagle laughed. "And so have you."

You got that right. Phil fished in his pocket for his keys. He'd made a lot of headway tonight; Eagle was a veritable tap of information, and he seemed to know a lot about Natter. Phil wanted to hit him up for more info but—Don't push your luck. You ask too much too soon, he'll get wise. Taking it real slow was the name of this game. One day at a time, he told himself. "You coming here tomorrow night?"

"I got a late job tomorrow, so probably not," Eagle said. "But I'm sure I'll be in the next night."

"Okay, take care."

They branched off to their separate vehicles. Phil was thinking. Late job? Eagle said he did construction work, but then Phil remembered his rap sheet; he'd done time for dealing PCP. Maybe he's bullshitting. Maybe he really runs dust for Natter. These considerations were pertinent, but there was no point jumping the gun. Only time would tell. Phil knew he'd need to work on Eagle with great care, or else his cover was gone. He also knew it would take a lot more than a couple beers in a strip joint to gain complete trust.

Dust rose in billows as the parking lot began to empty. Following Eagle tonight would be a dumb move, but he thought it might be a good idea to tail one of the regulars for a while, just to see which direction he was headed. He set his sights on one of the pickups that frequented the lot, waited a moment, then pulled out. The pickup turned north on the Route, away from town. In fact, most of the vehicles pulling out headed north.

And another thing occurred to him. *Natter wasn't at the club tonight. His car wasn't in the lot...*

But before Phil could contemplate that any further, a shadow rose up behind him from the back seat.

The dream was a proffering, a blessing...

It was a gift.

In the dream, he was vapor, an unholy ghost. Bodiless. Perfect. Spiraling down perfectly into perfect black.

But it wasn't really a dream, he knew that. They were never really dreams...

They were summonings.

*Ona. Oh, blessed flesh of Ona*, he thought. *I am so unworthy...*

He ascended, somehow, downward.

He soared.

Bereft of the flaws of his curse, he was perfect now, the vessel of his being light as air, his wisdom heavier than all the earth.

He knew where his wisdom had come from.

The darkness smeared, soaring past. He felt terror at first—so quick was his flight. He breezed through massive stone channels pocked and blackened by the age of all of history. He wisped through crevices no more wide than a fraction of an inch.

On and on. Down and down.

Into the blessed black.

Soon the great ebon wall approached. He soared right into it——then through it.

Greater blackness bloomed beyond the wall. Blackness that was brighter than the sun. He could smell the sound of screams. He could taste the dense stench of burning human muscle and bone. He could smell pandemonium, a scent sweet as fresh-cut roses.

And with his ethereal eyes, he saw the field.

A field of flesh, of people. Acre upon acre, prone humans lay naked and alive, awaiting the field's noxious attendants, its pious harvesters. And they squirmed in their wait. Screaming. Shrieking. Convulsing in spastic tremors.

Soon the harvesters arrived: squat, rough-skinned figures plodding forward into the screaming field. Above them, a blistering black moon shined, offering light to their sacred tasks. Dutifully, then, and steadfast, they began to farm the field.

With unholy tools, they plowed and tilled; great blades and hewers and trowels, rose and methodically fell to turn the hearty human soil. Skulls burst under the blows of mallets. Breasts, buttocks, and faces threshed raw. Bellies riven open by scythes which swept this way and that like clockworks, baring fresh, fertile entrails, ripe organs, and rich, fecund blood. Some of the harvesters worked barehanded, crawling along the squirming horde to punch out eyes with stub fingers, twist genitalia out of shivering groins, crack bones and unseat limbs. Hands and feet were bitten off by glassine teeth, then spat out. Talons raked throats. Palms and heels crushed bodies and heads like grapes in a wine vat.

Hard work. Eternal work.

*Tending the fields of the father!* he thought in utter, rushing joy.

Acres and acres, miles and miles, he continued to soar above the wondrous spectacle. Oh, how he prayed that on some great day he, too, would join the harvesters in their divine and hallowed labors.

But even eternal farmers needed reprieve. They needed sustenance. They needed recess. So at the granted time, they set aside the tools of their industry—

*Such wonders!*

—and began to feast.

Some took their meat raw, others preferred it cooked. Plump organs were plucked from opened abdomens as fruit might be plucked from vines. Eyeballs were swallowed whole like grapes, lungs eaten like bread loaves, intestines consumed like so much robust salad. The living dirt screamed forth. Whole heads were cooked to perfection over open flames, then prized apart and picked clean of their delectable meat. Testes were roasted on skewers, severed breasts fried crisp, uteri and placenta, fetuses and kidneys, human bowels and human hearts—all flame-broiled and lustily munched.

It was a hearty meal, and a well-earned one.

And once the reverent harvesters had sated themselves of the belly, they next proceeded to sate themselves of the groin. Demonic erections rose, to plunder every conceivable orifice, and some not so conceivable. Vaginas were routed with gusto, rectums were sodomized raw by perverse organs sunk to their hilts. Unwilling jaws were pried wide till their tendons tore—the only way the pitiful human mouths could accommodate the tumescent girth of such nether-worldly members. Trowel punctures and scythe rents, too, provided fine pockets of release, and such release poured forth in copious volume, gouts of lumpen semen flooding bowels and wombs, stomachs and entrails, emptied eye sockets and cracked-open cranial vaults.

A romp indeed.

Slaked now, the field hands took up their tools and finished the dark work they'd started.

The field was tilled red. Rich, fresh blood drenched the chopped soil, the finest of fertilizers. More attendants followed behind, bearing sacks of strange seeds. The seeds were sewn liberally into the verdant, warm soil, and beneath the light of the caliginous moon, they began to sprout at once. Soon stalks rose high, heavy with succulent fruit, and the fruit was then expeditiously threshed and taken away to market.

The harvest was over, only to begin again and again and again...

His vapor siphoned back, wisping fast as light through stone cracks and rabbets, back up the charnel earthworks, back from whence he came.

He didn't want to go back; he could soar here forever, and revel in these holy sights and many more.

*But I must go now,* he realized.

He had his own fields to farm...

Back, back, he sailed. Back out of the hot meat of the earth, back to the lackluster terrain of his forebears, back to his wretched human vessel.

Back—

Like blood sucked up by a sponge, his flesh reclaimed his glorious vapor.

*Ona. Ona. I give thanks to thee for such sights, such heralds, such righteous and holy gifts.*

*I live to serve thee...to the ends of the earth.*

The Reverend opened his eyes.

And sighed.

"Jesus Christ!" Phil shouted. "You scared the—"

"The shit out of you, I know. Sorry."

Phil, in his shock, had weaved across the yellow line, then veered back over to the shoulder. When the shadow had risen from the back seat, he freaked...

But the shadow...was Vicki.

"I just—I just needed someone to talk to," she explained. "I'm sorry if I startled you."

Phil put the car in park on the road's shoulder. "Yeah, fine," he acknowledged. "But did you have to hide in the back of my friggin' car?"

She hesitated. "Well, yeah. I guess so."

"Why?"

She swept shining red hair off her brow. "Let's just say I had a bad day."

Phil gave his heart a moment to slow down—actually, several moments. "I didn't see you in the club tonight. What, day off?"

In the rearview, he saw her glance down. "Something like that. It's best if you don't ask."

All right, Phil instructed himself, Don't ask. But he had to ask something. "I was hanging out with Eagle Peters. Do you know him?"

"I know who he is," Vicki said. "When you're in my line of work, you don't really know anybody. You're not allowed to. It also makes things a lot easier." Then, as if premonitory, she asked, "You made it to the back room yet?"

"Uh, yeah," he admitted. "That's some show. Jesus. Kind of feel sorry for the girls."

"Don't bother. No one else does." She got out of the back and then got into the front. The door chunked closed.

Christ, Phil thought.

She wore cut-off shorts, sandals, and a tight, bright-pink halter top. Coltish, perfect legs inclined. Her hair shined like some kind of rare metal.

"I didn't see your husband at the club either," Phil pointed out.

"He's busy tonight."

"Yeah?" he queried, though a hundred other questions occurred to him. Like, Busy? Busy doing what? Dealing with a dust distributor? Killing cowboys moving on his turf? Buying your next rail of cocaine? But none of these questions could he ask. Not without jeopardizing his cover. He'd have to deal with Vicki the same as he was dealing with Eagle. Slowly, discreetly, for snippets of information.

"I just wanted to talk," she said. "Maybe that sounds pathetic, but you don't know how long it's been since I've actually had a normal conversation with someone. It's not easy, you know. Under the circumstances."

Phil could imagine what she meant. A good-sized chunk of her humanity was erased now, or turned into something fairly useless. She wasn't a real person anymore as much as she was a pretty painting hanging in a rogue's gallery. Only these paintings you could rent, if the price was right. As a prostitute, and a stripper, how could she ever really relate to anyone anymore? And being married to someone like Cody Natter? It must be hell...

"Why don't you just tell me what's wrong?" he said.

She was looking out the window, into the woods and the night's profusion, but he knew what she was really looking at was herself. "Sometimes I feel like I'm falling apart," she said more under her breath than to him. "Sometimes I wake up, and I can't believe what's happened to me. I can't understand how I could ever let this happen to me. It must've been a pretty big shock for you."

"What do you mean?"

She laughed cynically. "Oh, come on, Phil. Stop trying to be such a gentleman all the time. The last time you saw me, I was a police officer. Ten years later, you come back to town to find out that I'm working in a strip joint and turning tricks. Probably not quite what you expected."

"Well, if there's one thing I've taught myself, it's that I should never have expectations about people. Especially about myself."

"Yeah? And what's that supposed to mean?"

Now it was Phil's chance to laugh. "You're not the only one who's taken a fall since the old days. I didn't exactly come back to Crick City better off than when I left. I came back because there was nowhere else to go."

"What happened?" she asked him. "You never really told me. All I remember is hearing bits and pieces. Something about a shooting. Something about a kid."

This was Phil's chance. Here he knew he could mix lies with truth and have it work to his advantage. He could win her confidence, like he did tonight with Eagle, by pretending to have turned into a typical town scumbag. Working undercover, that was his job. Time to let some bullshit fly. "We were taking down a PCP lab one night. It was cut and dry; in fact, the whole thing went off without a hitch. Only problem was there was this prick named Dignazio who had it in for me. He shot a kid, a spotter, with illegal ammo and made it look like I did it. It was a sham, a frame-up. But I got shitcanned all the same."

She looked at him sympathetically. "Why did this guy have it in for you?"

Here was his cue, the perfect place to start his cover story, his lie. "I was stringing out; Dignazio was the only guy who knew that, and he wanted me out of the picture. Only problem was he couldn't prove it without turning on his own stools."

Her stare fixed on him in the dark. Sure, she was a prostitute, but she was also an ex-cop, and she knew the language. "You were strung out? You?"

"That's right," Phil lied. "By then, I'd been free-basing crystal for a few years. Then I switched to dust 'cos it was the only way I could get off the ice."

This fabrication, he knew, would build a new bond between them, however phony. By demonstrating a weakness that she could directly relate to. Vicki knew she was on a road to ruin; if she believed Phil was on the same road, he'd have her. And from there—with some luck—he could get a real line on Natter's lab and operation.

"Now," he continued, "I'm trying to get off the dust, but I can't. It's a real bitch."

"Tell me about it," she said. "I've been trying to get off coke for two years now. Can't do it. I try real hard all the time but…"

"I know," Phil said. "You don't have to tell me. I guess it's all the same in a way. Coke, dust, ice, booze—it's all a kick in the ass, but what can you do? A habit's a habit."

A pause drifted between them, but Phil sensed it was a natural one. She was letting some serious things air out here, another good sign that his pitch was working. They lounged back in the darkness, watching the fireflies, listening to the crickets. Phil thought he'd delivered his lines well, and he knew that she believed him when, a moment later, she snapped open a small wrist purse.

Was she testing him? No, if she thought his recital was a fake, she'd never take so open a chance as this.

So, it could only mean one thing:

*She trusts me.*

*If she didn't trust me, if she even suspected for a minute that I was really still a cop, there's no way in hell she'd be doing something like this.*

In the moonlight, he couldn't see much, but he could see enough. The purse contained the typical provisions of a prostitute: lipstick, eyeliner, a small pack of tissues, and, of course, condoms. He also noticed a small amount of cash. But from beneath it all, she extracted the tiny glass vial…

*No, she'd never be snorting coke in front of me if she thought I was working undercover…*

"You want some?" she distractedly offered.

"Naw. That stuff makes me break out in hives. Like I said, dust's my bag."

A tiny silver spoon and chain depended from the vial. With expert quickness, she sniffed two shots out of the spoon, and then the stuff was all back in her purse before either of them could so much as blink.

"Jesus," she whispered.

I guess that says it all, Phil thought. She rested back against the bench seat, her eyes closed. Her chest, arousing in the tight halter, rose and fell. And the look on her face...

He'd seen it a million times. The source of the habit didn't matter in the least (cocaine, PCP, crystal meth, heroin), the expression was always the same. There was no pleasure in it, but an articulate and very abstract intertwining of relief, disgust, and self-capitulation.

All addicts had it. It was the look of someone who had surrendered to their own slavery.

The night's stillness enveloped them. The high, two o'clock moon cast shadows about the car. Lightning bugs shifted in legion, and the trill of crickets throbbed hypnotically.

Vicki fidgeted a moment, and sighed.

Hitting her up now with questions about her source—would be the worst thing he could do. As with Eagle, he knew he'd have to walk on eggshells a day at a time. He must prove to her that he was one of her ilk, that his life had turned to garbage just as quickly as hers had.

"Maybe it's all for the best," she said with a grim joke in her words. "You're on dust, I'm on coke... Not what you would call model cops."

Phil laughed. "You got that right." Then he shrugged as though it didn't mean much. "Guess we just weren't cut out for it. Big deal, you know? I was a shitty cop anyway."

"I don't miss the job, either. It got too scary."

"Scary? What could be scary about driving a beat in Crick City?"

"You don't know the half of it, Phil." Lethargically, she lit a menthol cigarette and watched the smoke drift out the open window. "Let's just say you got out of town at the right time. Remember Adams and North?"

"Yeah. Town boys. I never knew 'em, but I'd seen them around. They worked for Mullins too, didn't they?"

"Um-hmm. After I got fired, some pretty serious shit started to go down around here."

"Like what?"

"Never mind what. Just take my word for it, it was hairy. Mullins had Adams and North working on it, though."

Phil could guess what she was talking about: Natter's PCP

operation, but of course he couldn't let on that he knew about that, at least not yet.

"All right," he said. "But what about Adams and North?"

"They disappeared," Vicki said.

Disappeared. It took a moment for the word to sink in. Mullins had told him that Adams and North had merely left the department for better-paying jobs elsewhere. *Fairfax and Montgomery County*, he thought. And as he recalled, they were decent guys and fairly tough customers.

"There were some murders," Vicki finally admitted. "Drug dealers from out of town, PCP guys mostly. It was really gross; they were mutilated. It looked like..."

Phil's patience ticked. He didn't want to push her, but he did want to know what she was talking about. He let a few more seconds pass, then: "It looked like what, Vicki?"

She was clearly distressed, but was it the coke or something else?

"These cowboys they found dead?" Her voice lowered to a dusky croak. "It looked like they'd been...skinned."

*Skinned.* His pause burgeoned. *Just like that cowboy we found, Rhodes. He was a dust dealer from out of town. And he'd been skinned.*

"I heard they found a dozen bodies at least," she went on. "Same m.o. each time. Mullins had Adams and North investigating. Then one day—four or five months ago, I guess—both of them just disappeared."

Phil chewed the inside of his cheek. Disappeared, huh? This was the second time she told him something that directly refuted Mullins. And when they'd found Rhodes' body? Mullins had seemed genuinely shaken, but he'd also seemed...

Well, Phil wasn't quite sure what. But he didn't like it. Why would Vicki make something like this up? And if it were true, why wouldn't Mullins have told him about it?

*Whatever it is*, he declared to himself, *I'm going to find out.*

He got back on track. "So what exactly happened? I mean, to Adams and North?"

That somber croak came back to her voice. "Nobody knows."

Phil ran a hand across his cheek, scruffing stubble. "Okay. But what do you think happened to them?"

Her brow rose wide. "Me? I think they got killed by the same people who did the job on those dealers. They're probably at the bottom of one of the swamps, chained to a couple of manhole covers. You ask me, they got too close, so they got offed."

"Yeah, Vicki, but what did they get too close to?"

"I don't know," she wavered.

*I know,* Phil thought. *They got too close to your Creeker hubbie's angel dust bizz. That's what they got too close to. So he murdered them. I gotta funny feeling you know that, Vicki. But you're not gonna say it because you're covering for your husband. The same guy who's using you for a piece of meat to show off to his dope friends. The same slimy, ugly motherfucker who strung you out on cocaine and has you turning tricks at a low-rent strip joint.*

She was reaching into her purse again, repeating the phantom ritual of her curse. Two minute scoops of the white powder disappeared from the spoon up her nose, and again Phil felt torn between two opposing poles. The part of himself that still cared about her, and then the other part, the cop part, the part that knew if he objected, he'd be letting personal feelings obstruct the integrity of the case.

*Holy shit,* he thought very slowly. *What am I going to do?*

The coke was wiring her up now. Her face flushed. She was breathing faster, she seemed antsy. She kept sniffing at nothing but the air, and was rubbing her hands unconsciously up and down her nearly bare white thighs. That must be some first-class blow he's feeding you, Phil thought. Probably pure. The purer the better, right, Vicki? The easier to keep you in line, to keep you destroying yourself for his wallet and status. Then the saddest reflection of all hit him in the head...

Coke addicts never lasted long. They used themselves up. What would Natter do when there was nothing left of her?

The same thing he probably fucking did to Adams and North and Rhodes and all those other people...

That's the way it worked. Eventually coke-queens outlived their usefulness. Then they became a liability.

A guy like Natter? He'd toss her out like next week's garbage.

This was hard. This was a woman he used to be in love with, and here he was sitting in a car with her, watching her coke herself to oblivion. And knowing there was nothing he could do about it made him feel even worse.

But what could he do? Spill it all? Reveal the entire undercover operation to her? She'd squeal in a heartbeat. Or what else? Quit the department, drag her into the county rehab program knowing there was only a ten-percent success rate?

*All I can do right now,* he commiserated, *is play the game.*

"Phil?" she asked.

"Yeah?"

He supposed he should have known this was coming. Why hadn't he foreseen it? She was wired now, coked to the gills, and even though she had undergone a catastrophic change since their relationship had ended, her feelings for him probably hadn't changed. *I'm the only reminder she has that her life hasn't always been the hell it is now,* he figured.

Her hand was on his leg. He could feel its subtle heat.

"How did things get so screwed up?" she asked in the most forlorn voice he ever heard.

"I don't know," he said.

Her hand slid up. Her body slid closer. "Why don't we, like, pretend...that nothing bad ever happened to either of us?"

An impulse reached him, like an alarm. The urge to push her hand away, to berate her, to tell her there was no going back. But instead, he did nothing to dissuade her.

He made no reply at all.

Which, in this particular circumstance, was the same thing as a clear consent.

There was no breaking of any old ice. Instead, some weird, inexplicable current in the air drew them closer...

The night joined them.

She was kissing him immediately. Her slender bare arms at once slid about his neck. *I cannot do this!* he ordered himself. *This is crazy! I'm a cop! I'm on a case!*

Her tongue licked across his lips.

*No more! This is where it ends! I'm going to stop this right now!*

She untied her halter, slipped it off...

*No!* Phil thought.

She slipped off her shorts—

*No.*

—then her panties.

*Nnnnnnn...*

Phil's resolve died flat, like a machine whose tank had just run dry. His eyes opened on her. His heart surged. She sat facing him, her back against the passenger door. The soft moonlight buffed her marble skin; her perfect body glowed.

"You used to say I was beautiful."

"You still are," he replied with no forethought at all. The words didn't even sound like his own. "More than I ever remember."

She came over to him again, sliding along in the moonlit darkness. Her mouth opened over his, and all he could do was lie back as if comatose. The moon seemed to peer at him, either as an accuser or the very face of his id.

Her warm hands roved all over him, gradually in their travels unbuckling his belt, unfastening his pants, lowering his zipper.

Their tongues slid together.

Her large breasts slid against his chest.

Into his ear she whispered, "I still love you."

*Aw, God, no, don't say that. Say anything, but don't say that...*

"I-I never stopped," she finished.

Her hands found his waistbelt and began to work at getting his pants off.

I can't be doing this, his thoughts made one last waning effort. Then the effort flitted away, like the fireflies outside.

No, he knew he shouldn't be doing this, but by this point he knew he was going to do it anyway.

# SEVENTEEN

Phil parked behind the local Qwik-Stop, about a half-mile away, then cut through the woods up to the station. It was perhaps an extreme precaution but a worthwhile one. Now that Phil was insinuating himself among the locals, he couldn't take the chance of letting his car be seen anywhere near the station. True, he could've called Mullins on the phone, but—

Not good enough, he thought, hoofing it past the old lockup and across the back lot.

This has got to be face-to-face.

Phil didn't like loose ends.

It was just past 9 a.m. when he slipped in through the back door. Mullins, as usual, was pouring himself an acrid cup of coffee and chewing tobacco at the same time.

"Well, look what the cat dragged in." Mullins chuckled. "Ya know somethin', Phil? You're startin' to look like a pure-bred red-neck. Maybe this plainclothes business is bringing out the real you."

"I hope to Christ not," Phil said, but he knew what Mullins meant. Boots, old jeans, flannel shirt, plus he hadn't shaved in two days. To play the part, he had to look the part.

"How come I can always tell when you're pissed off?" Mullins asked. "You don't even have to say nothin'. I can tell just by lookin' at ya."

Phil sat down. "You know what I did this morning, Chief?"

"Hmm. Let me guess—"

"Don't bother. I called up the personnel office of the Fairfax Police Department. I also called Montgomery County PD. And neither of them ever heard of North and Adams. Said those guys never even filed applications."

"Oh, jeeze." Mullins sat down himself then, behind his desk. His belly stretched his police shirt to its absolute physical limit.

"How come you lied to me, boss?"

Mullins chewed on the accusation. "I wouldn't exactly call it lying. Let's just call it—"

"What? A tactical circumvention of facts?"

"Well, yeah. That sounds good. I kinda like it. A tactical circumvention of facts. You got yourself a dandy vocabulary, Phil."

"Fuck my vocabulary," Phil said. "How come you told me North and Adams left for better-paying departments?"

Mullins gusted a big sigh. "'Cos I needed ya, Phil. This PCP shit is turning the whole town to garbage, and it's makin' me look like the garbage man. You might not've taken the job if I told you up front why North and Adams left."

"So tell me now. What happened to them? Are they dead?"

"Dead?" Mullins gaped. "No, they ain't dead, but they sure as shit ain't here. Things started to get too hot, so they both threw in the towel. Turned in their badges and boogied."

Phil smirked plainly. "Come on, Chief. The whole story."

"All right. North and Adams were working on the PCP thing for a couple months. Then they got a lead on Natter's lab, so the three of us checked it out one night. We was told he had the works back up in the hills past Hockley's."

"Who told you that?"

"Let's just say an anonymous tip."

"Okay. What happened?"

Mullins suddenly flinched, as if at a bad memory. "What happened was we nearly got ourselves killed. The whole thing was a set-up. There must've been two dozen of those fuckers waitin' for us, a fuckin' army of 'em."

Phil didn't quite get it. "An army of who?"

"Of Creekers. And they were all packing rifles and shotguns. We walked right into Natter's ambush. I got myself an assful of 16-gauge buck. Wanna see the scars?"

"I'll pass," Phil said.

"Adams took a .308 in the upper leg, shattered his thigh bone. The bullet fragged and tore the living shit out of his knee, poor bastard'll never walk right again. And North got nicked in the ear. Another two inches, and he would've got his head blowed off. By the time we got out of there, the patrol car was so full of holes it wasn't even fit for the demolition derby."

Phil leaned back in his chair, assessing his boss. Mullins had broken out in a light sweat, and when he took another sip of coffee, his big, fat hand was noticeably shaking.

"So North and Adams freaked?"

"That's right," Mullins said. "Said they couldn't hack it no more, and I can't say I blame 'em. North quit right away. And Adams quit the day he got out of his cast. Had to pay the fucker ten weeks of workman's comp."

Phil folded his arms. "That's funny, Chief. I heard that neither of these guys quit. I heard they disappeared and were never seen again."

Mullins' lips puckered as if he'd just sucked a lemon. "You seem to be hearing a lot these days, and I think I know who you're hearing it from. Don't let Vicki Steele make a horse's ass out of ya, Phil."

"Shit, Chief. You haven't leveled with me. Give me one reason why I shouldn't believe her."

"I'll give you a bunch," Mullins replied. "She's a sexfreak, a stripper, a dopehead, and a whore. Plus she's Natter's wife." Mullins hocked his chaw into the wastebasket, then loaded up another. "North is walking a mail route in Bowie, Maryland—after he took fire, he said he never wanted to be a cop again. Adams and his brother got a small-business loan and bought a liquor store in Whitehall. If ya think I'm bullshitting ya, then go right ahead and look up their names in my Rolodex and give 'em a call."

Skip it, Phil thought. Mullins was coming clean now. But there was one more thing...

"All right, so you pulled my leg about what happened—"

"Naw," Mullins interrupted. "I made a tactical circumvention of facts."

"Fine. But why?"

"I told ya. I was afraid you wouldn't take the job if I gave the full scoop right away. I was fixin' to tell ya; I was gonna tell ya this week as a matter of fact. Figured you'd be agreeable once you got on the case awhile."

"That's pretty shitty, isn't it?"

"Well, sure," Mullins admitted. "But face it, Phil. Once a cop, always a cop. This case was cut out for you; I just wanted to give you some time to ease into it. You'd have taken the job anyway, right?"

Phil didn't answer, but he knew the chief was right. He knows me better than I thought. "One more thing," he said.

"Let me guess. Your ex-sweetheart blabbed shit about North and Adams. Stands to reason she'd blab more shit to boot. The bodies?"

"Yeah, Chief. The bodies. Vicki said there were over a dozen, all with their skin cut off like Rhodes."

A wave of Mullins' hand dismissed these mere details. "It wasn't no dozen, shit—maybe seven or eight, and yeah, they were all done up like Rhodes pretty much. All dust cowboys from out of Crick City. I figure Natter's got his Creekers hitting anyone who tries to compete with his own operation."

"That's what it sounds like to me, but that's also beside the point," Phil posed. "It would've been helpful for me to know about these murders before you sent me out on an undercover investigation, don't you think?"

Mullins shrugged. "Keep your shirt on. I was gonna tell ya all about that too, just like I was gonna tell ya about North and Adams. But I thought it best—"

"To give me some time to ease into things."

"Right."

By now Phil's frown seemed like a permanent fixture on his face.

Mullins spat again, sipped more coffee, and scratched his belly. "That night we got shot up, that was because none of us knew what the hell we were doin'. North and Adams, sure, they were decent cops, but they were town cops, Phil. They didn't have the know-how to get on with a serious dope and murder investigation, and neither do I. But you do know what you're doin'. You're an expert at this kind of job; Christ, that's all you did out on Metro. If I'd thought for a minute that you weren't experienced enough to hack the heat on a case this hot, then I never would've rescued you from that brain-dead goin'-nowhere yarn factory you were rotting in uptown. I gave you a chance because I figured you deserved it. Not many chiefs would"—Mullins paused to stretch—"considerin' the shit on your record at Metro."

This little reminder took some of the punch out of Phil's petulance. The chief had a point; Phil knew dope networks like the back of his hand, and he knew what to expect. But Mullins? And hicks like Adams and North? No wonder they almost lost their asses. Those guys don't know PCP from a PCV valve.

And another consideration began to smolder. Who am I to get pissed off at him for not exactly following protocol? Last night relit in his mind: Vicki.

They'd made love in his car for over an hour.

*I haven't exactly been following protocol either,* he had no choice but to remind himself.

"So let's get it all right out on the table," Mullins began again. "Without you on this case, it won't be long before the whole county knows about it, the papers, the news shows. Sure, I got a vested interest, I ain't sayin' I don't. My fuckin' job, you know. Natter and his Creekers are turning Crick City into a pile of shit, and I'll be the one goin' right down the crapper with it. But it ain't just the job— this pissant, redneck burg is my home and it's yours, too, whether ya like it or not. You don't owe me nothin', and I don't expect you to stick your neck out to save my job as chief. But, shit, Phil, you must care a little about what Natter's doing out there. He's getting kids turned onto his shit, nippin' 'em in the bud before they even get half a decent chance at life."

"I was a narc lieutenant for several years, Chief," Phil refreshed the big man's memory. "I know what dope does to kids."

Mullins spat another streamer. "And don't forget about what Natter did to your ex."

Another reminder.

Phil hitched uneasily in his seat.

"So like I was sayin', if you feel I done you wrong, then I apolergize. And if you wanna turn in your badge right now and tell me to get stuffed, then I'll understand. Shit, I guess I'd deserve it. Sure, it might get real hot out there on a case like this, but you knew that from the start. I wasn't stonewallin' ya, Phil. I just didn't want to hit you up with too much at once, that's all."

"Relax, boss. I'm not going to turn in my badge. Just try to keep me a little more informed in the future."

"'Course I will." Mullins rubbed his hands together. "So are we friends again?"

"Sure, Chief."

"Good. Now tell me what'cha dug up at Krazy Sallee's last night."

"I hung out with Eagle Peters—"

"Your buddy with the rap sheet full of angel dust?"

"Yeah, but I didn't push him for anything. It's too early for that just yet. I have to pin the guy's confidence before I can expect him to trust me. And, yes, I ran into Vicki last night, too," Boy, did I run into her, he thought. "I figure if I get in good with both of them, they'll spread the word that I'm cool. Then I'll be able to get closer to Natter's net. I've got Vicki thinking I'm a dust-head, and Peters probably reads me as a kink."

"A kink?" Mullins asked. "Why's that?"

Phil's stomach gave a minor quake at the memory. "Natter's got a back room open at the joint. They only let certain people in."

Mullins made a face. "A backroom? What's he got going back there? Blackjack, craps?"

"Nope, that's what I thought it must be at first. But then Eagle got me in; he's a trusted regular. It's another dance stage back there. They got Creeker girls tricking."

Mullins nearly expectorated coffee and tobacco simultaneously. "You're pullin' my leg, right?"

"Wish I was, Chief. It was pretty gross, but I played along like I was into it."

"Smart move." Mullins wiped brown juice from his lips with a napkin. "Only whackos would want to see that kind of shit, and I'll bet half of them are Natter's distributors."

"That's what I'm betting, too," Phil said. "I'm gonna try to get into there whenever I can, and try to cross-reference the regulars with my parking lot photos. I should be able to link some of them to their vehicles, then I can run their tags with MVA, get their names, and run rap checks from there. That way we'll know who to keep a special eye on. Plus I'll be keeping my ears open for anything I might pick up along the way."

Mullins nodded. "All right, sounds like you're on the mark. Keep it up, and for Christ's sake be careful."

Phil stood up, got ready to leave. "Don't worry about me, boss. I may be dumb, but I ain't stupid."

"Yeah?" Mullins said, giving him the eye. "Hobnobbing with Vicki Steele sounds pretty stupid to me."

The comment held Phil in a momentary check. *He's just guessing, there's no way he could know about what went on with me and Vicki last night. Absolutely no way.* "Fishing season's over, Chief. What makes you think I'm *hobnobbing* with her?"

"Couple things," Mullins came back. "One, there's a saying— old love dies hard—"

"Gimme a break, Chief," Phil complained. "That ended ten years ago."

"Two," Mullins ignored him, "since she got hitched to Natter, she's turned into a right cunning little bitch, and a pushover like you? You'd be putty in her hands."

Phil rolled his eyes and groaned.

"And, three. If that ain't her lipstick on your blamed neck, then whose is it? Eagle Fuckin' Peters'?"

Phil's eyes widened. He's bullshitting, he convinced himself until he ran a hand across his neck.

Aw, no. Aw shit, he thought next.

His fingers came away red—

"So let me tell ya somethin', Phil," Mullins got back into it like a surrogate father. "You ain't the first guy in the world to get teased by a woman, and you sure as shit ain't the first to get teased by her. That's a rough crowd she runs with—they're killers. And the last thing I need is for you to start dicking her and getting yourself all tangled up again. It's human nature, sure—men think with their peckers instead of their brains. But I hope you're too smart to fall for her tricks."

There was nothing Phil could say to justify last night's accident. I fucked up, he admitted. But how could Mullins be so self-assured? "All right, Chief, you got me. I made an error in judgment."

"An error in judgment?" Mullins blurted a stuffed-mouth laugh. "You stepped on your ever-lovin' dick is what ya did. You must've whizzed your common sense out the last time you took a piss. Don't do it again. That bitch'll make mincemeat out of ya. She'll have ya like a regular fool, and you'll wind up blowing your cover and maybe getting your ass killed." Mullins aimed his big finger like a pointing stick. "Use your head, Phil. Keep out of that whore's panties, or she'll wind up hangin' you with 'em."

"Chief," Phil had to object. "You've got her sounding like Lucretia Borgia. What makes you so sure she's so dangerous, huh? Tell me that."

"I will, smart boy." Mullins' heavy face darkened; again he looked like he'd sucked something intensely sour. "That night I was tellin' you about, when we got that tip on Natter's lab and wound up nearly getting blown away by a whole helluva lot of Creekers?"

"The night you, North, and Adams got set up," Phil

remembered. "What about it?"

Mullins' small, hooded eyes glared in the recollection.

"It was Vicki Steele who gave us that tip," he said.

"Nice car, huh?" Phil joked, and opened the Malibu's passenger door for Susan. Untold junk cluttered the back seat, cracks webbed the upholstery, and the paint job looked flat as dried mud. I *should've at least cleaned out the back,* he complained to himself. *She'll think I'm a slob.*

"You're a slob, Phil," she said. "But don't take that as a criticism."

Phil started it up and gunned the old engine. "Never judge a man by his car. The Ferrari's in the shop for a tune-up; otherwise, we'd be going out in that."

"The Ferrari, huh?" Susan smiled at him. "I guess your razor's in the shop too, right?"

"Hey," Phil remarked of the several days' stubble on his face, "you think I like to look this ratty? Working a dangerous under-cover operation, it's my professional duty to look as scummy as possible. And let me tell ya, that ain't easy when you're as hand-some as I am."

"Your diligence is outweighed only by your amazing mod-esty," Susan replied, cranking the window down. "I do have to admit, though, you are the best-looking redneck scumbag I've seen in a while."

"I'm touched by the compliment." Phil pulled out of Old Lady Crane's front drive and headed down the Route. "So now that I've finally got you out on a date, I have one very important question."

"What's that?"

"Where are we going?"

"Hey, you're the one who asked me out, remember? It's your job to make the evening's agenda."

"Okay. I'll surprise you."

Phil actually didn't have a clue as to where to take her, but he knew he couldn't take her anyplace in town, now that he was effectively undercover.

"So are the folks at Sallee's buying your cover story?" Susan asked.

"Yeah, I think so." *If they thought I was a cop, they never would've let me into the backroom.* Then a darker voice, the voice of his own guilt, perhaps, added: *That's right, Phil. And if Vicki thought you were still a cop, she sure as hell wouldn't have been snorting coke in front of you last night, would she? And she wouldn't have fucked you, either. You've got your little stoolie trained real well, buddy boy. The best of both worlds, huh? You're using her for information, and you're using her as a sex object. Give yourself a pat on the back.*

The thoughts soured him. He didn't want to confront them, so he got back to answering her question. "I'd be able to tell if they were wise to me. And hanging out with Eagle Peters gives me more credibility since he's a regular. As long as I keep up a good front, I'm in."

"That might be harder than you think," Susan said.

"Why?"

"What if you have to prove yourself? Say you get deeper into Sallee's crowd. Someone starts smoking dust one night, and they offer you a hit?"

It was something any undercover cop had to consider. "That's a good question, and I guess the answer is I don't know. In the right situation, I could probably fake it. I'll worry about that when I have to."

"Aren't you scared? What about Natter and his people? If they ever got wind that you were a cop…"

"I know, and, yeah, it is a little scary. I'm gonna keep my distance from Natter. You never get the kingpin dead-on, you get to him through his flunkies. I'm used to being real careful."

He took her just out of town, to an old family-owned crabhouse with the absolutely ridiculous name, Captain Salty's. "Oh, this is beautiful," Susan commented when he took her out onto the back deck. Their table offered a vast view of the bay. "I never knew about this place. What a find."

"We lucked out," he admitted. "I wasn't sure if they were even still in business. Great steamed crabs, though, if I remember correctly. I—"

What had he been about to say? Was he out of his mind? *I used to bring Vicki here a lot.* "I used to come here a lot back in the old days," he quickly caught himself. "Sometimes the watermen will bring their boats right up to the dock and unload fresh bushels of crabs and oysters."

Susan seemed taken by the view. A slight breeze played with her pure-blond hair. Phil couldn't help but steal a glance; he, too, was taken by the view—but not of the bay.

Of her.

It assailed him—her plain and simple beauty. Her casual grace. Her unadorned demeanor. Again, it occurred to him that her attractiveness was the opposite of Vicki's. It seemed more honest, more genuine. It seemed to reflect all of her at once with no veneers. No makeup, no designer clothes, no fronts; she didn't need any of that. Phil felt lured to her.

And guilty as all hell.

How much of a chance would he stand with Susan if she knew about what had happened last night with Vicki?

He ordered a pitcher of iced tea, a dozen oysters, and a dozen steamed crabs. "I'll pass on the oysters," Susan said, leering at the plate. "I don't quite have it in me to eat things that are still alive."

"It's all a matter of conception, my dear," Phil said, and then sucked one down whole right out of its shell. "I guarantee you, that oyster didn't feel a thing." When the crabs arrived, Phil gave her a quick lesson in technique. "There's only one way to eat crabs," he cited. "Like a barbarian." He tore one open in his hands, then methodically began removing the meat. Throughout their meal, Phil avoided work-related topics. Instead, they talked more about her classes, her upcoming degree, her plans for the future. In a sense, he envied her; she had things to do and places to go. Just like I did, about ten years ago, he thought dryly. I hope she has better luck…

But she seemed to enjoy the restaurant, and the messy frolic of crab-eating. She also seemed to enjoy his company. Phil knew he needed to take this easy. He wanted her to be comfortable with him, and he wanted her to like him. He wasn't quite sure what he foresaw—he just hoped it would be something good.

But something remote bothered him throughout their meal; he was too distracted by Susan to acknowledge it. He kept pushing it back—whatever it was—shoving it away. But when Susan excused herself to use the ladies' room, the awareness socked Phil in the face—

Vicki.

And the things Mullins had implied…

Was he exaggerating, or did the chief know more about Vicki than he did? Mullins had solidly stated that it was Vicki who'd given them the phony tip the night they'd been set-up. But…

*Could that be true?* he wondered.

Phil slid his last crab away, reflecting. He hoped Mullins' implications were an overstatement, but one thing that couldn't be overstated were the goings-on last night. Christ, Phil thought. Right there on the front seat of my Malibu... Images felt charred into his head like emblems from a branding iron.

Vicki had been voracious.

He'd been surprised, even shocked. Her seduction was an avalanche; she'd assaulted him with her sexuality, baked him with it, smothered him. One minute they'd been sitting there talking, the next they were a naked tumult entwined in the front of the car. Each second seemed to proceed in a breathless succession of images—the shimmering sweep of her hair, the curve of her hips, the lines of her face—like cutaways in manic film. Her bare, hot breasts squashed hot against his chest; her skin sliding over his as if oiled. The darkness cocooned them there, the drenching heat glued them together. Her hands plied at him, desperate, quick, but knowingly precise. Her tongue churned in his mouth, her teeth nipped at him, her arms and legs tied him up securely as a mistress's bedropes. Each touch and each caress, each moan and kiss and lick, made Phil feel another step closer to a precipice. At any second he might fall...

Vicki did things to him she'd never done in the past—things, in fact, that no other woman in his life had done.

She was wild, but—

Too wild...

She was like a predatory beast; Phil's desires, and her own, were things she hunted down and devoured...

And when it was over, he lay exhausted, debauched, wrung out and used up. He doubted that he'd ever felt so primal in his life. As intense as the experience had been, it scarcely even felt real. There'd been no meaning in any of it, no passion. They were just two phantoms run amok in the moonlight.

And now, sitting here amongst a pile of crab shells, watching the late-afternoon sun sparkle on the bay, he regretted it all even more. The last ten years had trained Vicki well. Her life had a new master now—a cold and very dark master, an alchemist of spirits. It had turned her dreams to fodder, and her heart into a desperate, pleading little thing that had nothing to rise to, nowhere to go.

And then the black voice returned, a voice he'd been hearing a lot lately, sniping the truth he'd been aware of all along but never wanted to face:

*She's nothing now but a coked-up whore...*

Phil winced into the sunlight.

*And it's your fault, isn't it, Phil? You left her cold. You threw her to the wolves. You tossed her love back in her face and let Natter turn her into a junkie roadside hooker. Good job, Phil. You're a first-class guy.*

"Get off my back," he whispered to the voice.

*Yeah, you're a piece of work, all right. Not only did you fuck her, you lied to her, you're pumping her for information, you're using her, Phil. You don't care about her, all you care about is your goddamn case.*

"Eat shit, voice."

*And look what you're doing now. You're on a date with a real woman, not some busted whore. What would she do, Phil? What would Susan do if she knew you fucked a whore last night, a junkie?*

"Shut up..."

*Are you gonna fuck her, too? Are you gonna fuck Susan like you fucked that whore last night?*

"Go to hell!"

*I'm already there,* the voice replied. *So where does that leave you?*

Then it drained away.

The voice, of course, was his own, the part of his psyche that couldn't stand himself for what he'd done and was doing. Was he really using her? Were the ruins of Vicki's life really his fault? And was he really using those ruins, taking advantage of them for the benefit of the case?

He didn't want to know.

His guilt stuck to him, like an incessant gnat buzzing round his ear. He felt dried up, as mentally ragged as he'd been physically last night, after his venture with Vicki.

"That was fun," Susan said as they walked back to the car. "We should come here again sometime."

"Yeah, it's a great place," Phil replied, slightly stunned. Maybe her comment was just a casual one, but if she didn't plan on seeing him again, why would she be making such a suggestion? At the very least, he could take this as a good sign that their first date had gone well.

But it was still early, and now that Phil could pretty much set his own hours, he didn't need to be going into work by eight p.m.

*Where do I take her now?*

"Hey, Phil," she said, "I know this is going to sound really lame, but—"

"Let me guess," he said, and opened the car door for her. "You have to go home early tonight."

"No, I have to go to the library."

"The library?" Phil's face crinkled. "What for?"

"I left some of my school books there last night. I want to pick them up before somebody rips them off. Do you mind?"

Phil almost laughed. At least now he didn't have to think of a place to go next. "No problem. Next stop, the library."

He started the car, was about to pull out, when she added, "And thanks for dinner."

Then she leaned over and kissed him very lightly on the lips.

# EIGHTEEN

The trip to the county library, in Millersville, had taken them back down the Route, across town. "Look, more Creekers," Susan pointed out when they cruised past the intersection of the Old Governor's Bridge Road.

Phil spotted them.

Two figures trudged along, a boy in his late teens and a much younger girl, probably his sister. They dragged old burlap sacks behind them, no doubt full of discarded bottles and cans which they'd scrounged from beneath the bridge. Lots of the local punks parked just off the bridge at night, swilling beer and chucking the empties over the side into the water. The litter eventually washed up onto the creek-bed, where hillfolk, mostly Creeker kids, would pick it up and sell it for pennies per pound to the recyclers. Picking up junk was all the employment most of these kids would ever have.

Susan, in remorse, turned her face away as they passed. "Christ, that's sad. Those poor kids."

"Yeah," Phil agreed. "I see them all the time now, collecting garbage, or fishing off the streams with strings in the water."

He'd caught only a glimpse of the pair, filthy, disheveled, in threadbare clothes going to rot. The little girl had no right arm, while the boy possessed arms that were overly long, his hands swinging down past his knees. Their misshapen heads turned, two pairs of tiny scarlet eyes glancing up hopelessly as Phil's car drove past.

"Some Creekers seem a lot worse off than others," he observed. "Like those two there—Christ."

"The way I understand it is it's kind of like a genetic potluck," Susan said. "The more these little societies inbreed among themselves, the more deformed they are. Some of the reproductive genes are more defective than others."

Last night's excursion into Sallee's backroom was good proof of that. The Creeker girls Phil had seen dancing were obviously birth defected, yet they also had inherited plenty of normal, and even beautiful, physical traits. Some of them, in fact, couldn't even be distinguished as Creekers at all, until he'd looked hard.

"And the strangest thing is Natter himself," Phil went on, following the Route down to the turnoff onto the county expressway. "He's so big and deformed, but I also remember him being very smart."

"I don't know that much about it," Susan said, "but I did take a sociology class a few years ago on dissociated cultures. Inbred societies aren't that uncommon, even in this day and age. It's typical for certain members to have extraordinarily high I.Q.'s while being physically deformed at the same time. And it's these people who are always the leaders."

"That fits Natter to a tee."

"Well, if you want to know more about it, we're going to the right place."

Yeah, he realized. The library. Natter was a Creeker, and his PCP operation was run by Creekers. It would be a good idea for Phil to find out as much about them as possible. Then he could deal with them more effectively and with more cognizance.

The library was antiquated: a file card index system instead of a computer, which he was used to from his college days. Susan helped him find his way around after she retrieved her books. They located several titles on the subject, from the very basic—Inbred Life in Appalachia to the very clinical—Genetic Reproductive Defectivity and the Human Genetic Transfection Process.

Phil appraised the stack of books in his arms as they walked back out to the Malibu.

"No Doonesbury for me tonight," he said.
The end of their date had been cut a bit short; Susan, after all, had to work tonight, too, but her hours weren't as lenient as Phil's. A goodnight kiss was all he'd gotten at her door, but it was all he'd expected. To push for anything more would've been a bad move—even a fatal one, if he hoped to continue seeing her.

Which he did.

And, anyway, it was a good kiss.

Yeah, I really like her, he told himself, walking back to his own room. She's...cool. It came hard to believe that they were hitting it off this well, considering her original concept of him. She probably still had some doubts, though; who wouldn't? His Metro record would be a blot on his life forever, despite the fact that the whole thing was a lie. But at least it seemed to him that Susan truly believed him.

*Give it some time,* he thought.

There was no need to change for work; jeans and T-shirt would do for undercover at Sallee's. But he still had some time to kill, so he sat down in his busted chair and began to read.

Just a little bustin' up, Blackjack thought. That's all he had time for tonight; he had to make a major pick-up at Rip's lab out in Tylersville by midnight. But I still got me an hour, he reminded himself, looking at his watch. I'll make it quick.

It never took Blackjack long to put a good busting on a girl.

He followed the fucked-up kid's truck up through an old logging road off the Route. The price was right, and Blackjack had heard that you could buy a Creeker girl once you got to be known at Sallee's. And that chick he'd seen in the backroom?

Yeah, Blackjack thought.

Once he'd gotten a look at her up on that stage, he knew he had to put a busting on her. He'd heard that the kid with the big head was the one you dealt with; Blackjack figured he must be Natter's pimp; that's why he watched the door. "Fifty fer a half hour," the kid quoted. "Sev-tee-five fer a full hour. More fer special."

Blackjack read the scene right. "Special, huh?" He laid two c-notes on the kid. "How's about a little bustin' up?"

"Shore, just don't'cha cut her none, or kill her. Cody'd be pissed."

Cody, Blackjack thought. As in Cody Natter. That big ugly fuckin' Creeker was one dude even Blackjack didn't want to fuck with. These Creekers gave him the creeps, and everybody knew they looked after their own.

When the kid had taken the green, Blackjack noticed that he had two thumbs on one hand.

"Just foller me," the kid had said. "'Tain't far."

The rutted road wound through the woods, then sidelined a long grassy field. It was hot tonight, and muggy, but that's the way Blackjack liked it. And he was getting hot himself just thinking about that Creeker chick he'd seen dancing the first set. A four-titter—He'd heard about them, but tonight was the first time he'd ever gandered one with his own eyes. And the tiniest little mouth, probably not even big enough to stick a cigarette in.

Yeah. Here was a girl he could bust up good.

See, there was no kick if he didn't bust 'em up first. That was Blackjack's style—going for the kick. Of course, sometimes he could get a little carried away. One time he'd picked up this little truckstop whore at the Bonfire. He slapped her around a bit first, and then he gagged her when she started to get too noisy, stuffed a big wad of toilet paper in her yap, then tied one of her stockings through her teeth.

Then he got to really punching her up.

He beat her face down to pulp—it looked like a busted open blueberry pie by the time he was through—then he got to giving her a good reaming. Only problem was she all of a sudden got real loose back there, and when Blackjack flipped her over to see what was wrong, he saw that the busting up he gave that pretty face of hers must've been a bit much 'cos she was stone-cold dead. Oh, well. In fact, he'd wound up killing several gals in the past—all accidents, kind of. And his part-time partner, Jake Rhodes? Now there was a dude who really went for the busting up, killed plenty of gals, and on purpose, too.

Funny, though, now that Blackjack thought about it, he hadn't seen old Jake for damn near a month.

*Probably out roustin' more junkies,* he figured. *Lookin' for a kick.*

That's all Blackjack wanted: a good kick. And this Creeker gal, all fucked-up like she was, that would make the kick extra special...

Blackjack was fully boned when the bighead kid's truck pulled up an unpaved incline and stopped. Up ahead, against the woods, Blackjack saw the house, a big whitewashed old place with a long wood porch and sagging roof. The wash took on a kind of gray glow in the moonlight.

Okay, Bighead, what's the scoop? Blackjack thought when he got out of his own truck.

The kid seemed to be staring up at the house.

"Hey, man? What now?"

"Oh, just go on up, walk right in," the kid said.

"Where's the girl?"

"She up there. She'll be waitin' fer ya in the front room."

Blackjack's rattlesnake boots crackled up the drive. The house looked weird—actually it looked ethereal, but Blackjack himself wasn't the type to conceive of such a notion—the ghostly white wood glowing, fireflies blinking swarms of tiny lights. Oil lamps seemed to glow in the narrow windows, the haloed moon radiating high up in the crystalline sky.

*There she is,* he thought when he stepped into the foyer. *The four-titter. My oh my, am I gonna put a busting on this bitch but good.*

To his right, a long hallway extended into darkness. He heard a distant thumping sound, then what seemed to be a muffled grunt. A tall grandfather clock ticked hypnotically at the rear of the foyer. Tick-tick-tick. Tick-tick-tick.

Oil paintings hung on the walls, but their faces were so dusty and old they looked smeared.

To his left a flight of banistered stairs rose, and halfway up stood the Creeker girl. A plain, very sheer nightgown made her hourglass body appear shrouded in mist. In her seven-fingered hand she held a brass oil lamp.

She didn't speak—of course not. She probably couldn't, not with that tiny, dowel-hole mouth of hers. Instead, she gestured him to follow with her other hand, which sported eight fingers.

Blackjack took the stairs up, his groin thumping with his heart. He was getting antsy to put a good busting on her, and a good tweaking to those four little tits. On the second-floor landing, another more narrow flight of stairs led upward into pitch dark, from which heat seemed to eddie down.

"What's up there?" he asked.

The girl, naturally, didn't answer. She took him down the second-floor hall and turned into the first room.

A big old four-poster bed sat right in the middle. The walls, dark with moldy wallpaper, displayed more blotchy paintings. The girl set the lamp down on an ancient nightstand as Blackjack closed the door.

*click*

"You're right pretty for a Creeker," he said and promptly ripped the nightgown off her body. She trembled only vaguely. The lamp cast indistinct shadows on her paperwhite skin. Blackjack stood back to look at her, and smiled. Yeah, she was a cute little thing, and damn near perfect except for that tiny mouth, them fucked-up hands, and the four tits. But to Blackjack, those traits only increased the kick—they made for a better meal to feast on. Her ink-black hair shined, and those fishblood-red eyes of hers— they just looked at him.

Blackjack cracked her hard across the face with his open palm; he wore fingerless leather mitts that gave an extra snap! to the blow. The girl reeled back, her eyes rolling like little red marbles, and fell on the bed.

"What'sa matter, honey? Bighead outside said it was okay to put a bustin' on ya," he guttered. "And damned if I ain't, what with the green I put in his fucked-up paw." Blackjack's eyes focused to pinpoints; his gaze painted her flesh. "Yeah, your bighead pimp, he told me I could do anything I wanted, 'cept cut ya or kill ya. Well, that leaves a lot in between, don't it?"

He jumped on her.

He plied her breasts. He squeezed them like little bags. Each small breast had another breast underneath, like one pancake lain over another. The nipples were large and dark—pulpy. He bit into the top two, and the girl made a neat squealing sound. Then he lifted the top breasts and bit the more tender nipples on the two beneath. The girl bucked under his weight.

Blackjack liked that. It gave his loins the spark he sought. Her bare, pretty legs splayed beneath him; her flesh was suddenly chaos. It was soft, tender. It was wonderful. Her bristly plot shined like slivers of onyx.

Then those big mitted, boat-hook-sized hands of his girded the girl's slender throat and began to squeeze. He watched her very intently. Each time he squeezed, her little red eyes bugged. Then he let go, and she gasped through her tiny mouth. He did this for quite awhile, pawing her double breasts each time she blinked away. Squeezing a sponge in a pail of water, then releasing it to let the water soak back in—the sponge was her brain.

He stood up. She lolled on the bed, her face looking like a limp freak-mask. Maybe I'll bust that little mouth of yours, he made the serious contemplation. But then he thought better of it; he remembered what the bighead kid outside had said. If he busted her up too bad, Natter would be pissed, and Blackjack sure as shit didn't want that.

"How they feed ya, hon, through that teensy Creeker mouth? What, Bighead outside, he let ya suck pig slop up through a straw?

Bet he does. And I bet he puts a good fucking on ya, too, anytime he wants. Bighead out there, he gotta big dick?" Blackjack laughed. "Shee-it, I'll'se bet he got two, just like you got four tits."

So he slapped her in the face again.

*Whap!*

Then he rolled his big hand into a fist and punched her in the face.

*Whap, whap, whap!*

She moaned as best she could, her eyes fluttering.

"Like that, sweetheart? Bet'cha do. All women do, just they never tell ya. I know the only way ta get any of ya hot is ta beat the shit out'cha."

He punched her a few more times, enlivened by the sound. The girl was barely conscious, so he bit into her nipples again, one at a time, until it put some jump back in her. Couple of times, he bit into them big meaty nipples like ta bite 'em clean off. Give her somethin' to remember old Blackjack by. Yeah, that would be a trick, wouldn't it? Just bite off all four of her nips and eat 'em like big, sweet gumdrops…

Then he flipped her over.

And dropped his jeans.

"Now, hon, I'm gonna choke you out full, and when ya wake up, I'll be giving you an assin' like you never dreamed. And don't tell me ya don't want it, 'cos I know ya do. All you floozy bitches do. Ya act like yer all highfalutin' and snotty, but watch'cha all really want is a good ass-fuckin' after ya been choked out by the Blackjack."

Gonna be kinda like corin'a apple, he thought. Then a different thought ganged up on him.

*Just like my daddy cored me…*

She lay docile on her belly. Blackjack straddled her, and slapped his big hands about her throat. Then he squeezed down.

She bucked at first, then kind of shook.

Then she went limp.

He grabbed a big handful of her pretty night-black hair and pulled it back like horse reins.

A dull whap! resounded behind him.

Blackjack glanced up in a kind of mindless, sudden awareness. But he didn't know exactly what he was aware of here.

*What the goddamn hell happ—*

Then a blossom of pain exploded at the base of his skull.

# Nineteen

Sallee's was rocking. Heavy metal power chords from the juke-box shook the walls. Strobe lights flashed and hammered the stage in multicolored pandemonium. As rowdy patrons barked for more beer, waitresses hustled between the aisles like gymnasts on high wires.

The crowd was in an uproar.

Christ, Phil thought.

It was Vicki.

She danced through her set with an unmitigated prowess, each step of her high heels in perfect synchronicity with the pounding music. Green eyes scanned the crowd like highly faceted emeralds; her carmine g-string glittered. It was clear—Vicki owned the stage, as well as the crowd, whenever she danced. This was her domain, totally. It must be an odd feeling of power for a woman, through her mere sexual presence, to command the attention of everyone in her midst. But it also must be pretty depressing, Phil considered. When she was up there, naked save for spikes and a g-string, she was an icon of flesh. Not really even a human being anymore, but an entity stripped down to its sexual bones.

Phil tried not to stare.

Her red hair spun to a blur. The strobes seemed to highlight her body in split-second fragments which flashed, then disappeared, all within the pulsing, sonic scape of the music. The crowd howled in frenzy at each step, each move, each sweep of a leg and toss of a shoulder. Glitter and sweat sparkled in the cleft of her bosom…

Phil couldn't help but let his contemplations crumble. He knew he didn't love her anymore, yet still, it was not an easy thing to watch one's ex-fiancée dance topless in a strip joint. The crowd's predatory revel rose like waves, while Phil's spirit plummeted. That black voice returned, to ask the question he couldn't stand to face:

*How many guys is she gonna fuck tonight, Phil? Two, three? Five, maybe? Maybe more, huh? A bod and a set of tits like that, shit, I'll bet she bags a bundle off these redneck slimebags. But cheer up, buddy. At least you got to fuck her for free...*

Phil felt even worse when he took a closer look; something glittered more fiercely on her bare chest. Aw, Christ, he thought when he realized what it was.

A tiny diamond on a sheer gold chain.

A Valentine's Day gift he'd given her over a decade ago.

"Another beer, pal?" asked the odd barkeep.

"Yeah, why not?" Phil replied.

"You look like someone shot your dog."

"Well," Phil said, "actually I'm pretty bummed that there's no wrestling on tonight."

"Grappling," the keep corrected. "It was on earlier. Nature Boy Ric Flair knocked Sting's lights out. It was glorious."

"Damn, I miss out on everything," Phil said.

Then the ever-familiar slap impacted his back; Eagle Peters stood up to the rail, his long blond hair swaying. "What's up, man?"

"Just hanging out."

Eagle cast a quick gaze to Vicki onstage. "Yeah," he replied rather darkly, then wisely saw fit to change subjects. "Hey, you feel like going in the back room?"

Phil looked up with a wince. "I thought you hated the back room?"

"I do, but I gotta talk to someone." Eagle paused. "Gotta talk a little business."

A little business, huh? Phil thought. It seemed another great opportunity had just landed in his lap. "I'm always game for the back room," he said, remembering his cover. "Let's go."

"And another thing." Eagle lowered his voice. "You interested in a little sideline work? We gotta little run to make tonight, but we need a driver."

"What are you running?" Phil asked.

"Just don't worry about that. It ain't risky. We can lay a couple hundred on you for an hour's work. You interested or not?"

Was Eagle testing him? Phil didn't know. But what he did know was that Eagle had an arrest record for running PCP, and he'd just asked Phil to be his driver. This was every undercover cop's dream...

"Like I said, man, let's go."

*Just play it cool, Phil,* he told himself.

They got up and wended their way to the entry. Druck, the Creeker doorman, gave them both a hard look, then nodded that they could pass. Inside seemed even darker than last night, and quieter. A deformed dancer moved slowly up on the stage in a veil of blood-red light and droning music. Thank God it was dark in here; Phil didn't care to see the details. All he could tell was that her head seemed bulbed in three humps...

Eagle whispered something to a cryptic waitress with large breasts and one foreshortened arm. Then she seated them in a back booth.

At once, another figure joined them.

"This here's Paul Sullivan," Eagle introduced. "My pal, Phil Straker. Don't worry, he's cool. Says he wants to drive for us tonight."

Alarms were already ringing in Phil's head at the name. Paul Sullivan. That's the guy with the rap sheet for dust, the guy who filed the missing person report. "Hey, Paul, good to meet ya," he said and offered to shake the guy's hand.

The guy didn't shake.

Paul Sullivan had a face like a beaten anvil, a beady-eyed, unpleasant wedge. Shortish dark hair and a toughened build. "I don't know, man," Sullivan complained to Eagle. "I ain't never seen this guy before."

"Relax," Eagle assured. "I told you, he's cool; I known him for years. You said we needed a new man since Kevin blew town."

Sullivan shrugged. "Awright, I guess we can try him out. So long as he don't ask no questions."

"Hey, man, you want me to drive, I'll drive."

Sullivan sort of smirked, then began trading whispers with Eagle. Phil couldn't make out much of what they were saying, but he figured it best to try to pick things up a step at a time. Instead he pretended to watch the stage. The Creeker girl with the cloven head had lain down on her back, her legs rising in a sleek V. Her bare feet, with but three toes on each, roved slowly in the dark-scarlet light.

Earlier Phil had read a little bit about inbred physiology in the books he'd gotten at the county library. The phenomena proved much more intricate than he'd thought.

The more intensive the inbreeding, the more damage to the reproductive genes, and the higher the rate of defective births. Scarlet eyes and black hair were common traits, and so were enlarged heads, missing or extra fingers and toes, and uneven limbs. But Phil quickly assumed that these Creekers were extraordinarily inbred, bad genes passing down not for years but for whole generations, because a lot of the deformities he'd seen were gross extensions of those detailed in the books. One of the books had pictures, and they weren't nearly as severe as the Creekers here.

Phil looked closer at the dancer's head. It seemed split by a hard fissure of flesh. But—

*What's she doing now?*

The dancer remained flat on her back with her legs raised.

Then her hips seemed to…shake.

In a few seconds it became apparent what she was doing.

She's dislocating her hips, Phil thought in grotesque astonishment. It was true. Her buttocks, completely bare save for the tiny g-string, began to flex, sleek muscles churning beneath the white, stretched skin. Phil grit his teeth; the macabre act hurt just to watch.

Eventually her labors alternately worked her femurs out of their hip sockets with a resounding double pop-pop!—

*Hooooly shit,* Phil thought.

—and then the dislocated legs ranged back all the way to the floor.

She lay the back of her head in her feet as one might do with their hands while lying in bed. Phil couldn't imagine anything more unnatural—that is—until he saw what she did next.

Her feet rose back up, turning at impossible angles as the trained muscles of her legs twisted expertly this way and that. Soon, then, she was caressing herself with her feet.

Her toes trailed up and down her abdomen. Her heels rubbed her pubis. And then, with the arches of her feet, she began to caress her breasts as deftly as if they were hands…

Good God Almighty, was all Phil could think.

"Come on, man," Eagle said. "Time to go."

Phil rose, gulping at the final image: the girl slipping her feet beneath the diminutive g-string and fondling her sex. He followed Eagle and Sullivan out the back door.

"Like that Creeker freak-show shit, huh, bub?" Sullivan asked him.

"Yeah, it's a trip," Phil lied. They walked across Sallee's gravel lot. Phil could tell he didn't like Sullivan right off, the tone of his voice, the mean look in his small eyes, but Phil had to keep that at bay. "Yeah, they're all a bunch of fucked-up whores in there," Sullivan continued. "Them chicks up front too, cokeheads, cock-suckers. 'Specially that hot-shit Vicki Steele. You see her, bub?"

"Yeah, I saw her."

"She's the only one of them whores who charges more'n a hun-dred. Fuckin' stuck-up, ritzy cokehead whore is what she is, thinks her shit don't stink, thinks that just 'cos she's Natter's cooze she's somethin' special. Ain't nothin' but redneck scum just like all the rest of 'em. Boy, I'll tell ya, I'd fuck that cokehead whore so hard her brains would slop out her ears."

Phil swallowed these words like a mouth full of rocks.

"Hey, Paul, give it a rest, will ya?" Eagle kindly suggested without elaborating that the woman he so explicitly referred to had once been engaged to Phil. "You wanna fill our new partner in, or what?"

Sullivan chuckled. He solidly filled out his jeans and light flan-nel shirt with a body-builder's physique, and that unpleasant, beat-up face of his only steepened the image. A tough customer. But Phil didn't let that intimidate him; Sullivan was flesh and bone just like everyone, and just as vulnerable. The guy went on. "Okay, bub, me and my buddy Eagle here, we gotta make a pickup tonight, and we need a dupe to drive us, ya know? A dummy who'll dummy up and not ask a lot of questions."

Phil smiled vaguely. Sullivan was testing him, all right, to see just how much shit Phil could tolerate. Fine with me, Phil thought to himself. "Hey look, man, I'm just along for the cash. I could shit care less what you guys are moving."

"Good, bub, and make sure it stays that way, 'cos there ain't nothin' that pisses me off worse'n a nosy chump."

"You can call me chump and dupe and dummy all ya want, brother," Phil told him. "Like I said, I'm just lookin' for the cash, and as long as yours is green, you can call me fuckin' Captain Kangaroo if you want."

Sullivan chortled and slapped Phil on the back. "You know somethin', bub? I'm beginnin' ta like you already—"

Boy, would I like to kick this guy's ass all over the parking lot, Phil thought amusedly. Instead he just said, "We gonna gab all night, or should we get moving?"

"Your wheels, bub," Sullivan instructed. "Cops might be wise to me and Eagle's wheels."

"Fine," Phil said, approaching the Malibu. "I just hope I moved that box of dog shit out of the back seat."

Sullivan guffawed. "Yeah, Eag, this pal of yours, he's a friggin' riot!"

Jesus, Phil thought. *This guy's some mental giant. Bet he's got an I.Q. smaller than his belt size.*

The three of them piled into Phil's clunker, Sullivan riding shotgun. Phil put the keys in the ignition. "Where to?"

"Nowhere just yet." Sullivan's dark angled face turned; he seemed to be reaching for something in his pocket. Is this guy shaking me down? Phil wondered with surprising calm. Does he know I'm a cop? Phil had his Beretta .25 in a Bianchi wallet holster; it would be tough, but he thought he could get it shucked and cocked fast enough to beat Sullivan to the draw if the guy was pulling a fast one. Phil's hand slid along his own leg, inching toward his pocket.

"Hey, Paul?" Eagle asked from the backseat. "What gives? We gotta get moving."

Sullivan's face looked like a mask of baked clay. He'd removed a small plastic bag from his jeans pocket. The bag contained several joints.

Phil sorely doubted that it was marijuana.

"What we got here, bub, is some of the best flake in the county, and just to show you what a class guy I am, I'm gonna let you have a toke."

"Come on, Paul," Eagle objected. "Put that shit away. He's gotta drive for us."

"Yeah, well, if your buddy boy here can't drive with a buzz, then he must be a pussy, and we don't want no pussies drivin' on our runs." Sullivan grinned in the dark car. "And besides, I don't know this chump from a hole in the ground. How do I know he ain't a narc?"

Then Sullivan handed Phil a lighter and one of the joints. Flake, Phil thought. PCP sprayed on pot or tobacco.

Sullivan's voice seemed to flutter. "Go ahead, bub, light up and have a toke. And if you don't, that tells me one thing."

"Yeah?" Phil replied.

"You ain't for real."

Phil rolled the end of the joint in his mouth.

*Here goes nothing*, he thought.

He lit the joint. An acrid, nasty fetor rose with the thread of smoke off the joint's end. The smoke coiled in the air, a ghost-snake, spreading, spreading...

Susan had warned him of this, hadn't she?

He had no choice.

Phil began to take a long drag.


Blackjack came to with a smeared glare in his eyes. The moon, he realized dazedly. Cloying, humid darkness encloaked him, but as he squinted up he noticed the moon in the window.

*Wait a minute! Where the fuck am I?*

Memories straggled back, marching through his mind. Sallee's. The backroom. And—

The trick. The whore.

*That Creeker bitch done set me up...*

When he tried to get up, a parade of pain rewarded him for his efforts. His left arm felt numbed, throbbing, and so did the lower-right side of the back of his skull. The darkness smothered his right hand when he raised it; he brought it down and touched his chest, his hip, his thigh, and realized he'd been stripped naked.

The bare, splintery wood beneath him felt warm; sweat trickled down his sides like crazed ants.

*Good God, I feel like hell...*

The darkness throbbed with his arm and leg, and with the roaring pain at the back of his head.

And more memories flitted back.

He'd been about to put a good busting on that Creeker whore. The four-titter, he remembered. The one with the tiny mouth. But what happened next?

He'd been choking her out, and—

*Fuck.*

That was all he remembered...

He clamped his teeth shut against the pain. *Yeah, some son of a bitch fucked me up good*, he deduced. *It's a scam Natter's got going in there. The whore set me up, then I'll bet that bighead kid snuck up behind me and put a wallop on my head. But what the fuck's Natter got against me? I ain't done shit to that ugly Creeker fuck. Don't make no sense to whack me out.*

One thing Blackjack did know:

*I gotta get the fuck outta here.*

Wherever here was.

The house, he thought. Yes, he must still be at the house. She'd taken him up to a small room on the second floor. But this couldn't be the same room. It was hotter than embers here, and he remembered old carpet on the floor of the whore's room, but this floor was bare wood.

*Get up. Gotta move,* he ordered himself. *Gotta get out of this joint before Bighead comes back to finish the job…*

It was nearly impossible not to cry out when he lifted himself to his hands and knees. He had to rest, shuddering. His brain throbbed like something fit to bust out of his skull. The only bearing he could make for himself was the shutterless, uncurtained window and the moon glowing in its frame. The smudged panes stood just above him to the right, but the pain made it seem hundreds of feet away. He could hear his sweat dripping onto the wood floor as he crawled forward, toward the flaking sill.

*Goddamn, what a job they done on me!*

His left hand was all but useless. His right grabbed the lip of the sill and pulled.

It was a concerted effort; Blackjack never would've thought that simply standing up would be so difficult. Nevertheless, after much wincing, gasping, and grunting, he stood on his own two feet, leaning racked against the wall.

He peered out the window.

*Christ…*

Yeah, this was the same house, all right. He recognized the front yard and that shitty dirt road leading down the hill. But the bighead kid's rattletrap truck was gone—

*Motherfuckin' Creeker motherfuckers!*

—and so was his own.

God knew how he was going to get out of here, and once he did, what would he do? Walk around the woods buck naked? He didn't even really know where he was. Some unmarked road off the Route, then a couple of turns he'd never remember. But—

Fuck it, he concluded.

Better to walk around naked and lost than stay here and buy the farm.

Peering out, he figured he must be on the third floor, not the second. From earlier, he vaguely recalled a narrow flight of steps going up from the floor the whore's room was on. The window was his only way out...

He'd have to crawl out the window, slide down the shingled awning, then drop to the roof. That would be tough in any case, but with his left arm and leg so numb they felt dead, it would be damn near impossible. Still, though, what choice did he have?

*Just gonna have to do it*, he told himself. *Just gonna have to flop outta this window and get the fuck outta this freak-house.*

Just as he tried to push open the window, he noticed—

*Aw, fer shit's sake, no!*

—that it had been nailed shut.

But before he could think further...

*Whuh? What the fuck was that?*

Had he heard something?

Voices, or something like voices, seemed to tickle his mind. He stared back wide-eyed in the dark...

*Ona...*

"Ah-no-pray-bee...

*Redeemer...*

"Mannona-come...

*Sanctifier...*

"Save us—"

They were like words mixed with thoughts. Etched whispers melded to blobs of swarming head-sounds. But one thing was clear to Blackjack: Someone else was in the room.

"Wh-who's there?" Blackjack challenged.

The dark stood before him, impenetrable, a solid black wall.

"I know someone's there, so how's 'bout tellin' me what the fuck's goin' on?"

No reply. Just the grainy dark staring back.

Then—

Blackjack jerked right.

Did he see something? Did he see something moving there in the corner to his right?

Something seemed to have shifted. A wet slither behind something blacker than the darkness...

"Mannona-come..."

"Onnamann..."

*Blessed Ona, we give thee thanks!*

A scream froze in Blackjack's throat when something slimy, humid, and hideous reached out of the dark and very gently touched his shoulder.

# TWENTY

Something hot seemed to insinuate itself along Phil's nerves to his brain, where it then lodged and seemed to hum. At once, he felt edgy, disjointed, but at the same time tranquilized. He knew there was no way to fake it, not around these guys. They were pros. He'd taken most of the drag in his mouth, holding it, then snorting it out through his sinuses, and had actually inhaled only a trace.

But only a trace had been enough.

Goddamn, he thought, flabbergasted. What a buzz...

Sullivan took the joint back. "Hey, bub, don't be a bogart." Then he laughed and began to smoke it himself.

Thank God, Phil thought. The stuff packed a heavy wallop; he knew that if he had to smoke any more of it, he wouldn't be able to stand up, much less drive a car. Got to shake this off, he told himself. He started the Malibu. "Decent flake," he said. "Big buzz. So where are we going?"

"North up the Route," Eagle said.

Once he got going, he began to feel better. He let the fresh air from the open window rush into his face. His brow prickled, dark splinters seemed to twitch at the farthest peripheries of his vision, and every so often he was touched by a chill that was somehow hot.

Sullivan finished the flake joint as though he were eating the dense smoke. "Okay, bub, now I know you're for real. One of our partners beat town a couple weeks ago, so we need a new driver full-time. You're it."

"Sounds good," Phil said.

"What we do is pick up the finished product from our supplier, then drop it off at our points. The money's good, and the cops aren't on to us."

*Oh, yeah?* Phil thought. *I can't wait to send you up to the slam for five...bub.* "What's your circuit?"

"Just north county," Eagle said from the back of the Malibu. "Millersville, Lockwood, Waynesville, thereabouts. Rednecks buy this shit hand over fist. Our product's better and cheaper than the regular supplier. We're gonna cut him out."

"Who's the regular supplier?" Phil asked, but he thought he had a pretty good idea already who they were talking about.

"Never you mind about that," Sullivan griped. "You're just the wheel-man, so get on the wheels."

"Right," Phil said.

Eagle directed him through several turns up roads he never knew existed. Most were dirt roads, rutted and potholed, often so narrow that overgrown brush swiped the car on either side. Eventually they came to a clearing, and Phil was instructed to stop.

"Fuckin'-A," Sullivan complained. "The bastard ain't here. Are we early?"

"We're five late," Eagle said.

"Then where the fuck is Blackjack?"

Phil just sat there and kept his mouth shut. He knew he'd learn more about the network in time. But Sullivan and Eagle seemed overly distressed, pressing themselves into long silences, jerking their gazes constantly about the car.

They sat there a half-hour, and no one showed up.

*These guys are freaking out because their point man's running late?* Phil thought. It didn't make much sense. *Why are these guys shitting their pants?*

Eagle nervously swept his hair out of his eyes, leaning forward from the back. "How many times has Blackjack been this late?"

"Never," Sullivan hotly answered.

"So the guy's late," Phil offered. "What's the big deal?"

"Tell him the big deal," Sullivan said, waving a hand.

Eagle's face in the rearview looked pale. "Lately a lot of our point men and distros have been disappearing."

"Jake Rhodes, Kevin Orndorf, and now Blackjack," Sullivan grimly recited. "And there have been others, and I mean a fuckin' shitload of others."

"Maybe the cops are on to us," Eagle suggested, "and we're just too stupid to see it."

"You guys are moving local dust," Phil jumped in. "The county and state could shit care less about it—dust is small time to them.

They're all out after scag and coke. And the local cops? Guys like Mullins? No way. Those town clowns can't even write parking tickets; they're too busy taking bingo graft and pad money. It ain't cops, fellas."

"The fuck's going on then?" Sullivan shouted.

"Wake up and smell the coffee. You just got done telling me you're trying to undercut the major dust supplier in the area, and all of a sudden your people are disappearing. What's that tell you?"

"Somebody's putting the whack on us," Eagle said. "And we're sitting here like three ducks in a bathtub."

What a couple of dupes, Phil thought, chuckling all the way back. No wonder the idiots had done time; they were just plain stupid. Fuckers couldn't sell shovels to ditch diggers. He'd dropped them off at their trucks back at Krazy Sallee's, and agreed to meet them tomorrow night. Mullins is going to love this. Gotta hand it to the guy, though. He called the whole thing right from the start.

The "other" dust supplier had to be Natter, and it had to be Natter who was putting contracts out on these new movers. So far everything fit.

*Now I just got to plan my own next move,* Phil realized, *and it better be a good one.*

It was past two when he'd dropped Eagle and Sullivan off. He drove around an hour just to make some leeway, then parked the Malibu behind the strip mall where they had the cleaners who did his shirts. Then he made a half-mile walk to the station.

"How was the rednecking tonight?" Susan asked from behind her radio console.

"Not bad," Phil told her. "Maybe I really am a redneck at heart; I'm fitting in just like the real McCoy."

"I was getting a little worried," she said. Her bright blue eyes glittered up at him. Her blond hair shined. "I didn't hear from you over your portable all night."

Worried about little old me? Phil thought. Well, that was a good sign. "It's hard to whip out the police portable when you're driving on a pickup run with two PCP peddlers," he proudly replied.

"You're kidding. Who?"

"Eagle Peters and that guy Sullivan, the one who filed the

missing persons a while back." Phil smiled. "They're both dust peddlers, and I'm their new driver."

"That's great!" Susan exclaimed. "Jesus, you're really getting in deep, and fast."

"It's just my well-proven expertise, my dear. I can't help it—I'm a supercop."

"Yeah, well, Supercop better be real careful. The closer you get to these people, the more dangerous it gets."

"Danger," Phil said, "is my middle name. Oh, and you were right; I had to prove myself tonight."

"What?" she asked very speculatively.

"I had to smoke some dust."

"What was it like?"

"I only smoked a little, but it put a whack on me pretty fast, made me feel kind of mellowed out but hyper at the same time. I don't know what the big deal is, though. The crap just gave me a headache after the buzz. But, anyway, these guys think I'm legit now, so I'm in."

"What are you going to do now?"

"I've got a good idea, I think. What I need right now is for you to punch up Sullivan again."

"Why?"

"I need his address."

Susan looked doubtful. "What have you got cooking, Phil?"

"Just trust me, okay?"

She wavered at her console, then, reluctantly punched up Sullivan's name on the county mainframe-link. Then she gave Phil the guy's address.

"All right, see you later."

"Wait a minute." Susan got up and came toward him at the door. "You're really spooking me. What are you going to do?"

"Hey, I told you, don't worry about it. Let's just say that I'm going to spin some grease and see how fast I can turn a tough guy into a stool pigeon."

"Phil, I don't like the sound of this. You can't be screwing around with these people. At least let me go with you."

"Forget it. I'll talk to you tomorrow," he said and turned for the door.

But before he could leave, she grabbed his shoulder and urged him around.

Then she kissed him.

"What was that for?" he asked.

"I don't know," she replied. "I guess I just felt like it."

"Well, you can feel like it anytime you want."

"Besides, my kisses are good luck, and I have a feeling you're gonna need it—whatever this hare-brained scheme of yours is."

Phil paused a moment, and took in the vision of her beautiful face. Don't turn into a sap, he commanded himself. "Like I said, don't worry about it. Talk to you tomorrow," he said and left.

The kiss tingled on his lips. *Yeah, I must be doing something right,* he thought. So *make sure you don't get yourself killed now...*

Sullivan lived in one of the big trailer parks just out of town; Phil drove straight to it. Hope Paul's an early riser. It was close to four-thirty in the morning when Phil pounded on the flimsy aluminum storm door.

"Who's that?" came Sullivan's rocky voice after a good five minutes of knocking.

"It's me, Phil."

"Who?"

"Phil. You know, your new driver."

"Whadaya want?"

"Come on, man. Open up. This is important."

With further grumbling, Sullivan undid several safety chains and opened the inside door. He stood there groggily, dressed only in boxer shorts. "What? Ya find that bastard Blackjack?" he asked.

"No, man," Phil said. "Sorry to wake you up, but this really is important."

"Yeah, bub, ya already told me that."

"I need to ask you something."

Sullivan's muscled chest flexed when he thumbed the sleep out of his eyes. "Ask me somethin'? What?"

"Well, I need to know which side of your face do you want me to bust first, the right or the left?"

Sullivan's beady, sleep-puffed eyes stared at him. "What the fuckin' hell you talkin' ab—"

Phil punched right through the flimsy storm screen; his fist slammed into Sullivan's big, wedgy face with a sound like a baseball bat to a heavy bag. Sullivan reeled backward, arms pinwheeling, and stumbled over a tacky armchair. He landed flat on his back.

Phil invited himself in. "Wow, Paul, great place you've got here. I love the Dart Drug furniture, and those carpet tiles?" Phil whistled. "I'll bet they cost you a buck a piece at least, huh?"

Sullivan dizzily tried to rise; Phil kicked him in the chest with his pointed boot. "Oh, by the way, Paul, your previous trepidations were quite on the mark. I'm a cop. And one more thing... You're under arrest for possession of and intent to distribute PCP."

Sullivan looked up from hands and knees. "A cop? You chump motherfucker. I knew there was somethin' fucked up about you."

"Congratulations on your perceptivity," Phil said. "And, let me make it perfectly clear—" Phil rammed the heel of his palm into the top of Sullivan's head—whap!—"that you have the right to remain silent"—whap!—"and anything you say will be used against you in a court of law." Whap! "You also have the right to an attorney. If you can't afford an attorney"—whap!—"the state will be happy to appoint one to you at no cost." With that, Phil picked up a flimsy, fiberboard coffee table and promptly broke it over Sullivan's head—

*crack!*

Sullivan collapsed.

Phil looked around. The place was a dump, but that's pretty much what he expected. Porno magazines were spread over the kitchen table; empty beer cans filled a plastic trash can. When Sullivan came to, he rose again on hands and knees.

"I got my rights, bub," he growled. "You can't just walk in here and assault me."

"Yes, I can," Phil said, and swept his pointed boot right up into Sullivan's belly. "Please pardon my lack of proper law enforcement protocol, but you know, it's a two-way street? I get great pleasure out of kicking the shit out of a dope-dealing scumbag like you. And you can tell the D.A. that I violated your rights till you're blue in the face, but who's he gonna believe? As for the bruises and, hopefully, broken bones, well...you should be more cooperative with the local constables, Paul. It's not nice to resist lawful arrest."

Phil then punched Sullivan in the side of the head so hard his knuckles hurt. Then he straddled Sullivan, and cuffed his wrists behind his back.

"Listen to me, Paul. I don't like PCP, and I don't like guys who sell it. You've been to the joint already, and I guarantee you, this bust will send you up for five to ten. I think the cellblock boys will be happy to see you again, wouldn't you say?"

Phil grabbed Sullivan's mussed hair and gave it a good hard twist.

Sullivan shrieked. "You can't do this, man! You're torturing me!"

"No I'm not, Paul." Phil gave Sullivan's hair another twist. "I'm 'interviewing' you, for relevant information concerning a local police investigation."

One more twist, and Sullivan was a ludicrous sight, squirming flat on his belly in his boxer shorts with his wrists handcuffed behind his back. "But there is one thing you should know, Paul," Phil went on. "There are times when I am mysteriously given to acts of leniency. In other words, you start running that ugly mouth of yours and tell me the stuff I want to know, then maybe, just maybe, I'll drop the distribution charge and see to it that you don't get more than eighteen months in the can. They'll drop it to nine if you show them some good behavior, Paul. So what's it gonna be? Nine months or ten years?"

Sullivan continued to squirm on his belly. "Why should I trust you?"

"Because to a lowlife, scumbag, two-time loser like you, I'm the most trustworthy guy in town." Phil laughed. "I want to know who your supplier is, and I want to know where he makes his product. But more than any of that, Paulie, I want to know about your competition, this other local supplier you and Eagle are trying to undersell."

Sullivan slackened. "I ain't tellin' you shit, bub."

"Aw, Paul, don't call me bub. Let's try to cooperate, huh? Who's that local dust supplier? Where's his lab?"

"Fuck you," Sullivan replied.

"Okay, be like that." Phil got back up, kneeling on Sullivan's back in the process. Sullivan shrieked again, then shrieked even more when Phil hauled him up by the handcuffs.

"Guess I'll just have to get what I want out of Eagle," Phil remarked, hauling Sullivan toward the door. "I'm taking you to jail now, that's right, in your boxer shorts. How do you like that… bub?"

Phil booked Sullivan into the county lockup, with an isolation request pending investigation—no visitors, in other words. He didn't want Paul telling Eagle or any other cronies that Phil was the law. Let him sit in the lockup for a week or so, he'll change his tune once he remembers what it's like to be back on the cellblock. And as for Phil's overall conduct—well, he didn't feel too badly about it. If he'd learned any-thing at all on Metro, it was this: When dealing with scumbags, you sometimes had to be a scumbag yourself. Nor was he wor-ried about Sullivan filing any brutality charges. The judge would take one look at Sullivan's rap sheet and laugh harder than Slappy White, and Sullivan knew this. Pretty soon that lesser-charge offer Phil had made would be looking better than a pile of ground round to a wolf that hadn't eaten in a week.

He was dog-tired when he pushed through the rickety front door at Old Lady Crane's boardinghouse. What a night, he thought. Then his heart skipped...

Just as he passed the stairwell, a figure stepped out.

"Phil?"

"Jesus, Susan!" he nearly yelled. "Don't sneak up on me like that—I was about to go for my piece!"

"My, aren't we jumpy today," she said. "I heard your car pull up, so I came down."

Phil let his heart return to its normal beat, then smiled. "Didn't mean to yell," he apologized. "But I'm getting so deep into the local dope circuit, it's making me edgy." Only then did he take full note of her. Her bright-blond hair was tousled, and she stood bare-legged and bare-foot, dressed solely in a long white night-shirt. Her blue eyes looked at him groggily; she'd obviously been sleeping, and this only reminded him of the ludicrous schedules night-workers kept. "It's almost ten a.m.," he joked. "Isn't that past your bedtime?"

"I couldn't sleep. I was too worried about you getting your ass shot off," she came back. "What happened with Sullivan?"

Again, Phil was flattered that she actually worried about him. What did that mean? "I busted him," he told her. "Come on, I'll fix us some coffee and tell you all about it."

She padded behind him to his room. "My room's hotter than a steambath. How about ice water instead?"

"Coming right up." He went to his cubby of a kitchen and plunked ice into two glasses. "Anyway, like I was saying, I went to

Sullivan's place and busted him on a distro charge. You should've seen how ridiculous the guy looked standing in front of the booking sergeant in his boxer shorts. It was great!"

"Did he give you any trouble?"

"Not after I broke the coffee table over his head." He gave her the glass of water, then they both sat down on his busted couch. "They took me on to drive for them, and Eagle verified that they're trying to undercut another dust distributor in the area—"

"Natter?"

"I'm sure," Phil said. "And they also told me their point people have been disappearing right and left, so that just verifies our suspicions even more. We were supposed to meet some drop-man named Blackjack last night, and the guy never showed. I'm convinced now. Natter's putting contracts out on anyone trying to move dust on his turf."

Suddenly Susan looked distressed. "Phil, you're getting too close too fast, aren't you? This is really getting scary."

Phil wasn't sure what she meant. "How so?"

"How so? Natter's hitting the outside competition, Phil, and with you driving for Eagle, that makes you as big a target as any of them. If they catch you with Eagle, they'll kill you."

"And if I flash my badge—"

"They'll kill you anyway."

Phil shrugged at the undeniable reality. "I've been doing stuff like this for years. And I'm very careful."

"You better be," she whispered more to herself than to him.

It seemed strange, the way she was acting, but by now it was occurring to Phil very clearly that something was up. As always, her plain, honest beauty was tuning him up. Here she was, in an old nightshirt, her hair mussed, and her eyes puffy with fatigue, but she still seemed more beautiful to him than a thousand centerfolds. She's gorgeous even when she's a mess, he thought. He could tell she was braless beneath the nightshirt, and probably pantiless too, judging by her obviously conscious effort to keep her legs closed. Any other guy, he knew, would be making a move now, but Phil also knew that Susan was not a woman men made "moves" on; she didn't live by typical social games and sexual tactics. He'd like nothing more right now than to take her to his bed and make love to her. But...

"You look tired," he said.

Her sleepy blue eyes fluttered. "Yeah, I guess I am. Getting used to midnight shifts is harder than I thought. Anyway, what's your next step with Eagle?"

"I'm supposed to meet him tonight at Sallee's. He doesn't know that Sullivan's busted—I'm betting that he'll think the guy 'disappeared' like the others." Phil grinned. "I can't wait to see his reaction."

"What did Mullins say about you busting Sullivan?"

"He—" Phil's train of thought collided with a brick wall. "Damn it! I'm supposed to be keeping him posted on this, and I haven't even told him yet. Be right back."

Phil rushed to the den and dialed the station. The last thing he needed was the county detention center calling Mullins and asking him about the jurisdictional processing of a prisoner he didn't even know had been arrested.

Fortunately, Mullins was at his desk when he called, and Phil gave him the rundown.

Mullins, once Phil explained his plan, was ecstatic.

*At least I'm making things happen,* Phil told himself. *Hope it works out.*

When he came back to the main room, Susan was asleep on the couch. He didn't want to wake her; she'd been up for hours, worrying about him. So he put her legs up and turned off the light.

Before he went to bed himself, he went into the bathroom to take a quick shower. And while he was showering...

Susan, nude now, came into the bathroom. She didn't utter a word when she got into the shower with him.

# TWENTY-ONE

Ah-no-prey-bee...
  *Ona-for-blood...*
Gut shuddered.

The dream-words siphoned round his head. His eyes bugged open. He felt cold and hot at the same time; he felt drenched in sweat yet dry as pumice.

It was always dark in here, and the darkness was his nemesis. It seduced him with its comfort, then dropped the memories into his lap like freshly severed heads.

The darkness whispered the dream-words again and again as he lay helpless and churning...

But they weren't really dream-words, were they?

*Ah-no—*

They were real...

*prey-bee...*

The hideous face, like a cracked mask, was always there, hovering in the dark. Day or night, asleep or awake—it didn't matter.

It was simply...always...there...

Gut shuddered fiercer this time.

He peed his pants again.

The screams were there, too. How could he forget them? And how could he forget what they'd done to Scott-Boy?

*Christ...Scott-Boy...*

"Fergive me, God," he whispered.

It had to be God, sending demons after 'em for their sins. Gut knew they'd done terrible things, all the razzin' and dope-sellin', sellin' all that shit ta kids just ta turn a buck. Not ta mention all the rape and throat-cuttin'. He'd rucked plenty of guys for their green, and he'd laughed right along every time Scott-Boy busted some chick's coconut with that hickory pick handle of his.

*We deserved it.*

Yeah, that was fer shore. He and Scott-Boy, they had done some down-an'-dirty things all right, and now God was gonna fix their wagons fer it, an' He was gonna fix 'em so they'd never roll again. Tears streamed down Gut's blubber face, glistening like slug trails. Aw, shit, God, I'se really sorry fer all the razzin' we pulled an' all the splittails we fucked with, an' all them poor folks we hooked on the dust so's we could git reg-ler scratch out of 'em. Yeah, God, I'se really shore's shit sorry fer it all.

It was a fine time ta get religion. But maybe God had fergiven him 'cos, if not, wouldn't He have let the same thing that happened ta Scott-Boy happen ta him, too?

Oh, yessir, Gut remembert what they up and done to Scott-Boy. One thing he remembert expressly was how one of 'em got ta whittlin' the flesh offa Scott-Boy's fingers like he was just plain whittlin' bark off a pine switch…

Gut's sweat turned rank as dead fish gone belly-up in a swamp. He felt grimy in his layin'-down-goin'-nowhere-sheer-fuckin' terror, like somebody had throwed him smack-dab in a shithole and made him roll around in it fer awhiles.

And the memory of the face hovered.

*We give you this day your daily flesh.*

Yeah, ol' God had sent demons.

Thing was, Gut reckernized one of 'em.

Yessir.

He shore's shit did.

Phil's alarm went off at 4 p.m., another unwelcome reminder of his queer night hours. He turned irritated in bed, then noticed the unfamiliar warmth of the sheets on the other side.

Then he remembered the rest—

*Susan…*

She'd slipped into the shower with him. Neither of them said a word. Her gesture should've surprised him, but it didn't. It was nothing like that at all. Their attraction to each other was self-evident, so perhaps he even, in some unconscious way, expected something like this.

*Oh, jeeez…*

Beneath the cool torrent, they touched each other as if they'd been lovers for years. The water cascaded; her denuded beauty shone like a beacon. They alternately kissed, sudsing each other with the foamy soap. Their tongues frolicked, their hands strayed through bubbles over each other's flesh.

She was so soft, so wonderfully warm. Her breasts squeezed against his broad chest as she slipped her arms tight about his waist to desperately draw him closer. The cool water turned hot the instant it hissed against her skin.

Her skin felt like fine, warm silk…

It was a dreamscape of sensation and cool rain. Of timeless kisses and wet, caressing hands. Of undistracted love. Phil was aware of nothing else in the world but her. This was his only world right now, a world of her beauty and his desire, a perfect domain where the only inhabitants were the two of them, and where the only sounds were their ardent breaths, their moans, their gasps, and their sighs, and the endless hiss of the water.

Dripping wet, they hauled each other from the shower. They kissed and fondled and stumbled across the hot room and fell onto the bed in one another's arms.

She was beautiful. He'd always known that, but never in his life did he fully understand the meaning of the word until now. It was so much more than her body, so much more than her gleaming blue eyes, her damp silver-blond hair, her face. It was everything ineffable about their being together like this.

His passion became palpable. His passion delved into her, explored her every inch. His hands ranged over her perfect skin as a novice sculptor might touch a masterpiece. He touched and kissed and licked her everywhere, from her eyes to the tips of her toes, to her most secret and private places. Her ardor gave; second by second she opened herself to him.

But first, before he demonstrated his passion most fully, she stopped him, whispered into the crook of his neck—

"Phil. I—I need—"

"What?" he asked, trailing his tongue up the sleek, damp slope of her throat.

"I need to know something…"

"What?"

He kissed her, tasted her, reveled in her.

"I need to know…if you're still in love with…with…Vicki," she finished.

"No. I'm not," he promised her, and it was no lie. If he was in love with anyone, if he ever could be in love with anyone, it was with Susan.

"I swear," he said.

They made love for hours. It was beautiful. She explored him as he explored her, in every manner thinkable, by every position they could devise. Time and time again, they spent themselves with one another...

But—

Phil, now swathed by the fervid memories, felt around in the bed.

*Where is she now?*

Did she leave? Did she go back to her own room while he slept? Or—

*Oh, no.*

Had he talked in his sleep? It was something he knew he did. It was something past lovers had made him well aware of. All too aware.

Had he muttered Vicki's name in his sleep?

*Jesus, don't let it be so.*

He couldn't imagine it.

Despite the happenstance of the other night, Vicki meant nothing to him compared to Susan. He still cared about her, yes, he still wished her well and hoped that she could shed her addictions and make something good for herself, but...

He didn't love Vicki. He knew that.

*I love—*

He got up, wrapped a towel around his waist, and rushed out of the bedroom, then sighed and leaned gratefully against the wall.

There she was, back in the long nightshirt.

*Thank God.*

She sat placidly at his cheap little desk in the den, her legs crossed. She was reading.

Phil came up from behind, kissed her on the neck. "Good morning," he said. "Or I should say, to those of us on night shifts, good afternoon."

She kissed him back very matter-of-factly, as though it were something commonplace, something expected. Something purely and honestly natural.

"What are you reading?"

"These books you got out of the library," she said. "They're really interesting."

"Yeah, I know. I was reading some of them last night. It's bizarre, but a little too technical for me; a lot of that genetic stuff went right over my head."

"It says here that there are inbred communities in some parts of the world that are hundreds of years old. They're rural or mountain settlements, completely cut off from the rest of the world for centuries. And it makes for a completely isolated gene pool. The inbreeding becomes so intensive that normal births almost never happen. It mentions one settlement, somewhere in Russia, where there hasn't been a normal birth since the early 1800s."

"And it's all exponential," Phil remarked from what he remembered reading himself. "Not only does the rate of normal births decline the longer the gene pool remains isolated, but the genetic defects become more severe. One of those books has pictures, but don't look at them if you're squeamish."

Susan clearly wasn't. She turned to the book with color plates. "Look at this, red eyes. Just like the Creekers."

"Evidently, red eyes and jet-black hair are typical genetic signs of prolonged inbreeding," Phil told her.

"Prolonged," Susan repeated in a low murmur. Then she glanced up at Phil. "I wonder how long Natter's Creeker clan have been inbreeding among themselves."

"Who knows?" Phil replied. "Maybe centuries."

Eagle looked haunted when Phil met him at the bar.

And Phil knew why.

"Hey, Eagle." Phil ordered a beer from the keep, glanced back at the stage to spy a trim, long-legged blonde doing splits. "You ever get ahold of Blackjack?"

"No, man," Eagle morosely replied. "And lemme tell you something else. I haven't been able to get ahold of Paul either."

"Don't fret it. He probably just went out somewhere."

"All fuckin' day? When he knows our points are waiting on that pickup? This is serious biz, Phil. I tried to get Paul on the phone for hours, and there was no answer. So then I went to his place…"

"Yeah?"

"The whole joint was busted up, looked like there'd been a riot in there."

Phil smiled to himself.

Eagle went on. "His truck was there, but he wasn't. What do you make of that shit?"

"Doesn't sound too good," Phil said, sipping his Bud. "But maybe we're worrying a little too soon."

"Shit, man," Eagle objected. "I told you, his joint was wrecked. Shit layin' all over the place, furniture busted."

Don't worry, it was crummy furniture. "I catch your drift. Blackjack disappears, and now Paul disappears."

"I just don't like it—And Paul's a big guy, strong as an ox. Probably took four or five guys to drag him out of there."

Phil smiled to himself again. No, just one. "Well, look," he suggested. "There's no point in us just hanging around here doing nothing. Have you been by Blackjack's place?"

"No, I only tried to reach him by phone."

"All right, then let's drop by, see if his pad's busted up like Sullivan's. And, who knows? Maybe the guy'll be there. Maybe this isn't as bad as we think."

"Yeah, I guess it can't hurt."

They left Sallee's and hopped into Eagle's pickup, then followed the hot night north up the Route. "So where's Blackjack live?" Phil asked.

"The boonies. He's got a shack up in the hills."

Phil cranked down his window, let the breeze sift his hair. But as hard as he tried to keep his mind on business, the more his thoughts kept trickling back to Susan.

Do I love her? he asked himself. It took all of about a half-second to conclude that he did.

*Does she love me?*

Well, it might take a bit more than a half-second to determine that.

*But at least I've got my work cut out for me.*

They'd made love one more time before he left, slow, lazy love right there on the floor of his den. Each time with her was better, and each time he looked at her, or even thought about her, the more beautiful she was.

*My God, it just occurred to him more powerfully.* I really am in love...

"Keep an eye out," Eagle instructed. He'd just turned up another long dirt road through the woods. The headlights pitched back and forth over interminable ruts. "We're in hillfolk country now. They don't take too kindly to folks driving their land."

"Blackjack's hillfolk?" Phil asked.

"Sort of. And he's big and nasty, so if it turns out that he is there, don't cross him."

"Got'cha."

Phil didn't know anything about this guy Blackjack, but whether he was in or not, knowing where he lived was something he could follow up on later, and if Blackjack really had been whacked by Natter—all the better. Phil could go through his place on his own, and maybe find an address book or something with more names and info. Best of all, busting Sullivan was keeping Eagle on pins and needles—the guy looked absolutely paranoid behind the wheel—and the more discreet pressure he could keep on Eagle, the better.

*I'll get what I want eventually,* Phil felt sure.

The roads narrowed as they progressed, and the woods grew denser and darker. They passed a couple of old shacks and lean-tos, and several ragged trailers up on blocks. Mucous-like spiderwebs hung like glistening nets in the trees; every so often the headlights picked out the orange glints of possum eyes. Creepier still was the mist; it had rained earlier, but the rain had just been a quick drizzle. Now the hot night sucked tendrils of fog out of the damp woods. It wafted up like steam.

Suddenly, everything looked remote, unearthly...

And Phil began to feel weird.

He knew what it was. The decrepit scenery was triggering memories, taking him back...

To that day. And—

The House.

"Hey, Eagle," he asked, wiping sudden sweat off his brow, "how's your Uncle Frank doing?"

"All right. He retired. Moved to Florida." Eagle cast him an odd glance. "I'm surprised you even remember him."

"Oh, I remember him. And the spook stories he used to tell us. Remember? He was always warning us not to go into the woods, that there were 'things' in the woods that kids shouldn't see. And remember what we overheard him saying one night? You remember that story?"

"Which story? Frank had enough bullshit to fill a couple of fifty-five-gallon drums."

Phil rubbed his face. "You know. The story about the big old creepy house way back in the woods—"

"Oh," Eagle livened up. "The Creeker whorehouse."

"Yeah. You believe it?"

"You're shitting me, right? It's just an old local legend. Frank liked to push that one 'cos he liked to scare the shit out of us."

And Frank did a good job.

"So you never really thought it could be true?" Phil queried.

"Maybe when I was a ten-year-old snot-nose punk, but not now."

"But it *could* be true, couldn't it? I mean, what's so unheard of about it? Christ, Natter's got Creeker girls stripping at Sallee's. And they're all hookers, too. Wouldn't it make sense that they'd have a house to work out of somewhere?"

"And you must be smoking dust," Eagle laughed. "Those girls are roadside whores, Phil. They turn their tricks in the parking lot. The Creeker whorehouse was just a bogeyman story, that's all."

"I don't know." Phil was sweating profusely now; he was jittery. His voice filtered down. "I think I saw it once."

Eagle gaped. "Now I know you've been smoking dust. What, you're telling me you saw the Creeker whorehouse?"

"Yeah. At least I think I did. It was back when we were kids. Remember how we used to prowl the woods every day when school was out?"

"Sure," Eagle said. "Shit, we'd find all kinds of stuff in the woods. Old shotgun shells, beer, porno mags."

"Right. And there was one time when you got grounded for beating up on your brothers, so I went by myself that day. And I got lost…"

# TWENTY-TWO

Yes, ten-year-old Phil Straker got lost...

The woods were a tangled maze, as terrifying as they were mysterious in their heaped detritus, skeletal branches, and dense hanging vines. Then he'd stumbled upon the little Creeker girl, her big red eyes staring at him through ribbons of black hair. Phil was afraid at first—he could see her deformities: the misshapen head, the uneven joints, and the wrong number of fingers and toes. Plus, he'd never forget what Eagle had told him—that the Creekers had teeth like Kevin Furman's bulldog, and sometimes they'd bite you if you got too close...

But that was stupid. Phil could tell right off that this girl, though he hadn't seen her teeth, wasn't going to bite him. His fears dwindled away in seconds. She was like him; she seemed fascinated. In chopped speech, with her fallen hair puffing in front of her mouth as she spoke, she told him her name was Dawnie.

Then the voice cracked out of the woods, calling her home, and she quickly ran away.

But Phil didn't want her to leave. So—

He followed her.

And was lost again in minutes. The dank woods seemed to swallow him whole. The sun beat down through the trees like a hot hammer; sweat drenched his Green Hornet T-shirt till it stuck to him. As his Keds crunched on through the brush, bugs buzzed around his face and shoulders, biting him as he vainly swatted at them with frantic hands.

And just as he feared he'd never get out, the forest opened up into a clearing where high sun-baked brown grass rustled in a dead, hot breeze.

And that's when he saw the House.

*Holy poop!*

The big rickety three-story farmhouse sitting up on hill. Veins of gray wood showed through cracked white-wash, and the missing shingles on the steeped roof reminded him of Mrs. Nixerman's missing teeth. The high black windows looked back at him like eyes...

*It's haunted,* he felt sure. *It's a haunted house.*

It had to be. It was the creepiest house he'd ever seen in his life, and if ever a house had ghosts, this was it.

This must've been what Uncle Frank meant. This house had to be one of the "things" ten-year-olds weren't supposed to see.

So Phil did what any ten-year-old would do.

He went up to see.

The steps creaked under his Keds when he hiked up to the front porch. He could barely see anything through the screen door, just clunky shapes and murky darkness.

Then he tiptoed to the first window and looked in...

The sun baked down on his back as he leaned over further to squint. At first he couldn't make out a thing, just more clunky shapes. But then his eyes began to pick things out: a big old couch, a cane chair, paneled walls and framed pictures hanging.

But—

No ghosts.

*Aw, poop,* Phil thought in the ultimate childhood disappointment. *There ain't no ghosts in there. It's just an old house. Nothin' at all to be scared of—*

Phil shrieked high and mighty when seven little fingers tapped on his back. He probably jumped a foot in the air, turned, then landed bug-eyed on his feet.

Dawnie was laughing; Phil felt like a wimp.

"You—you live here?"

"Yuh-uh-yeah," she said.

And when she'd been laughing, Phil noted with more disappointment that she didn't have teeth like Kevin Furman's bulldog. She had just plain old regular teeth like everyone. Eagle was full of poop.

"They-uh-now goan," she said.

"Huh?"

"Goan."

Goan, Phil thought. Gone. She must mean that her parents were gone now.

"Come-up-on," she said.

"Huh?"

She gestured him away from the window with her finger. "Come on. In-ah-side. Grot, er, got's sunipin' ta's show-ur ya."

Phil translated. She wanted him to come in the house. She had something to show him.

But what?

Part of him didn't want to go—this was a Creeker's house. She might have big ugly Creeker parents who'd want to whup him, thinking he was fixing to do something bad to Dawnie, like maybe even raking her like that girl Eagle told him about.

Yeah, Dawnie's parents might whup him bad, or worse…

After all, they were Creekers.

Nobody knew Phil was out here, even Phil himself didn't know where he was. All he could see were the girl's big ugly Creeker parents chasing him around the house with big sharp teeth like Kevin Furman's dog. But then he thought, Don't be a little wuss. She just got done saying her parents are gone. And, anyway, she's kinda neat…

"They goan. Come on."

Phil followed her into the house. He stopped a moment and noticed the brass knocker on the opened front door. It was the strangest thing. The knocker was a face, only the face didn't have any nose or mouth. Just two big blank eyes staring back at him.

"Commer-on, now. Don't be scairt. I'se-uh tole ya, they'se uh-goan."

They'se-uh goan, Phil mimicked in thought. Can't hurt to just go in and look around. He could tell Eagle he'd been to the haunted Creeker whorehouse, that he'd gone inside. Then Eagle and his other friends would think he was cool.

The front room wasn't that much different from his aunt's. Regular furniture, chairs, a big wooden highboy in the corner, and a grandfather clock. It was just a little older, that's all. He followed Dawnie up the stairs to the left. The stairwell was dark, and the hall upstairs was even darker. But this made sense 'cos he'd heard Creekers, like most hillfolk, didn't have electricity. "Where we going, Dawnie?" he asked on the landing. "We going to your room?"

"Naw," she said, facing him. Again, he noticed her boobs; they were little but sticking out real nice through the old sundress she wore, and actually she'd be kinda pretty if it weren't for the messed-up hands and feet.

"Foller uh-me."

Then she took him by the hand and led him up another, even darker, flight of stairs.

Jeez, it's hot, he thought. Twice as hot as outside, and a lot more muggy. Once they got on the third-floor landing, Phil was so hot he felt like he was cooking. Up here was a smaller hall; more old framed pictures hung on the walls, but they were too dark to see. The only light came from a small, high little window at one end, and then he noticed a line of lights—tiny white dots shooting from each door in the hall.

Keyholes, Phil realized.

Dawnie seemed winded with some weird kind of excitement. Phil could see the grin behind the black ribbons of hair.

She squeezed his hand.

"Wanner, uh, wanner-see-um?"

"See who, Dawnie?"

"Er-um, my-um sisters?"

Her sisters? Phil didn't know about this. He didn't know if he wanted to meet Dawnie's sisters. What if they were real messed up and ugly? What if they didn't like him?

And what would Dawnie's sisters be doing up here in all this darkness and heat?

Her hand was hot and moist. She squeezed his own hand harder.

"Wanner, uh, wanner-see-um doin' it?"

Doing what?

All of a sudden, Phil didn't like this. He could get in trouble. He wasn't even supposed to be here, and he didn't even really know where he was.

He wanted to leave.

But Dawnie pulled excitedly at his hand. Phil wanted to pull away, but for some reason he couldn't.

She took him to the first door.

"Git-er on down," Dawnie said and put her hands on his shoulders.

Phil knew what she meant. She wanted him to get down on his knees.

*She wants me to look in the keyhole.*

Phil knelt as her excited hands on his shoulders pushed harder. The bright light from the keyhole blazed on his face.

Dawnie's hand nudged his head.

"Look-it. Looker-on in-nair."

Phil felt woozy, kinda sick. He hadn't felt good for the past coupla days, and right now he felt real bad. His stomach quivered, and even though it was so hot, he suddenly shivered against a chill. He knew he was coming down with the flu or something, or maybe some stomach bug he got from eating his aunt's awful stuffed peppers.

Plus, he was scared.

"Hey, Dawnie, I'm not feeling too good. I better get on home now."

But Dawnie wouldn't hear of it. Her fingers tightened on his shoulders, and she nudged him again.

"Go-on. Look-it."

The keyhole blazed.

Chills coursed up his back.

Then ten-year-old Phil Straker took a deep breath, put his eye to the keyhole—

*Jesus Jesus Jesus!*

—and looked in.

Eagle seemed duly amused by Phil's recital of the story. "Yeah? So what did you see?"

"I don't know," Phil foolishly confessed, his elbow propped out of the truck window. "That's the last thing I really remember, kneeling down and looking in that keyhole. Sometimes I think I remember more, sometimes I dream about it, but the only stuff that comes to mind are just little pieces, glimpses of things, like a hand or a foot, or part of a face in the shadows. Anyway, next thing I knew, it was a couple days later. I was in bed with a hundred-and-four fever."

Eagle laughed. "Ya probably didn't see anything; ya probably just dreamed it all on account of you were sick."

"Yeah, maybe you're right," Phil said, but he didn't really believe that, even though the doctor said that fevers frequently caused hallucinations and morbid dreams. Phil knew he could never prove it, but he also knew that the whole thing really had happened and that the House—

Phil blinked hard.

The House was real.

*I just wish I could remember. I wish I could remember what I saw in that keyhole. Not just the glimpses I've dreamed about. Everything. Why can't I remember it all...*

"Time to forget about your haunted Creeker whorehouse," Eagle said. He pulled the truck up another rutted, narrow road, and stopped. "We're here."

Blackjack had a little hovel of a cottage with clapboard shingles. It sat jammed back into the woods amid a bed of high-reaching weeds and gangling vines.

Strings of mist from the previous rain floated off the ground.

"Wasted trip," Eagle cited. "His truck ain't here. I knew something happened to him. I'll bet you and Paul were right. Somebody put a hit on him."

Phil peered through the moving mist. "Keep your shirt on. You ever think that maybe it's just that his truck blew a gasket, and he's got it in the shop? And look." Phil pointed out the window. "That back window—there's a light on."

"Blackjack's bedroom. Well, maybe the fucker is home after all. Come on."

They disembarked. The night sucked up the heavy chunks of Eagle's truck doors closing. The mist parted as they moved forward, swatting at mosquitoes and gnats. Phil seemed to inhale the thick fog, the air's humidity sopping him at once. Pulsing nightsounds throbbed from the woods which backed the shack.

Eagle began to rap on the front door but stopped when the door, ajar, swung open. "Shit, now I know he's here. No way Blackjack'd leave his place with the door open. He's got guns and shit in here."

"Guns?" Phil asked with some concern.

"Yeah, so we better announce ourselves good and loud." Eagle stuck his head in. "Hey, Blackjack, you here? Don't shit a brick. It's me, Eagle."

They waited a moment. The shack responded with silence.

"Blackjack! Come on, man, wake it up and shag ass. It's Eagle, and I got our new driver with me."

Nothing.

"Must be asleep or stoned," Phil guessed.

"Yeah, come on."

They edged inside. The place was a dump, but it wasn't wrecked. "At least there's one good sign. Ain't all busted up like Paul's joint. Wait here. I'm gonna go check out the bedroom."

Phil nodded, glancing around. I've seen better-looking shit-houses, he reflected of Blackjack's interior decorating tastes. He crossed his arms, waiting, but then—

*What?*

Some sound, ever-faint, seemed to slowly leaven itself into his ears.

*What is that?*

A hum, etchy yet so slight he could barely detect it. It seemed to originate off to the right.

The kitchen, he realized, noticing old enamel-white appliances standing in the dark.

Phil walked over, looked in.

The shifting hum rose.

Phil's hand padded up the wall and flicked on the light.

His stare locked downward...

"I don't believe this shit, man," Eagle complained, coming up from behind. "The fucker ain't here."

"Yes, he is," Phil croaked.

Then he pointed down to the fly-covered corpse sprawled across the kitchen floor.

"Dream On" by Aerosmith ended Vicki's set amid a rowdy cannonade of applause. Sure, dream on, she thought beneath her best "dance-face." Dream forever—

*Dream till you're dead.*

She could swear Sallee's walls actually shook, they were clapping so hard. It sounded like a storm. And when she stepped down through the stagelights and endless, moving sheets of cigarette smoke, she always felt the notion that she was stepping down into hell.

Maybe I really am, she considered.

She took a final bow, then left the stage and the noise and the crowd behind her, perhaps in the same way she'd left her dignity and self-worth behind her so many years ago—with a cold turn of her shoulder.

Druck stood at the entrance to the back room, a deformed sentinel in overalls. Vicki could feel his warped gaze sliding down her naked back as she quickly passed and slipped into the dressing room. She noted a trickling sound the moment she entered; it was coming from one of the toilet stalls. Someone douching, she guessed at once. One of the Creekers. Cody forbade the Creeker girls from using condoms—hence the necessity to douche. The rednecks paid more to forego protection. What did they care? Men couldn't get pregnant, and were at much less risk of contracting diseases. There'd only been a few occasions when, servicing a special client, Cody had ordered her to not use condoms, but on those nights she'd been too coked up to really care. She got tested every two months at the county clinic and had so far tested negative. It seemed a miracle, considering the extent of her prostitution before she'd married Natter. Anything for a line, she thought in utter grimness. She'd done things she couldn't believe...

The stall door opened and, as predicted, one of the Creeker girls emerged, immediately looking down when noticing Vicki there. The Creekers treated Vicki with an almost queenly respect; they were afraid of her. After all, she was the king's wife now. The girl, who only had one arm, limped past and out the door, her black hair lifting in her wake.

*Jesus...*

Vicki knew the Creekers were powerless against Cody's exploitation of them. Still, she subtly despised them. The Creeker girls were an ultimate reminder of the depraved backwoods underworld that Vicki's life now tightly revolved around.

They reminded her of her own powerlessness against Cody Natter. They're retarded and deformed and terrorized, she thought. At least they have an excuse.

*But what's mine?*

She knew there were no excuses. She had no one to blame for the wreckage of her life but herself.

Dozens of one-dollar bills stuffed her tip garter, along with a few tens and twenties. It all went to Cody, just like her trick money. She knew he made a fortune off her, and God knew how much he made off the Creekers. She transferred the cash to her purse, then, as she did every night after her last set, turned to face herself in the mirror.

It was an accuser's face that peered back, or a ragged Doppelganger's. Her red hair didn't shine like it used to, and her green eyes had lost some of their emerald luster. Crow's feet encroached, with the tiniest threadlike lines. At least my boobs aren't sagging yet, she indelicately noted of her bare, thrusting bosom.

But what of the rest of her?

The truth compiled every day. Her lean, nimble physique was a little too lean now, and beginning to show signs of depletion. Sometimes, when she woke up, she looked absolutely emaciated. The coke stole not only her vitality but also the simple common sense that she should eat better. Each day of her life took another little fleck away.

And the flecks were adding up.

*Yeah, I'm starting to really look beat,* her thoughts informed her reflection. *Pretty soon I'll be lucky to pull a couple five-dollar blowjobs per night.*

Not much of a destiny.

And what would Cody do then? There was so much she had seen, so much she knew...

She tried to think of a time when her life hadn't been in so many pieces. She knew when it was: during her engagement to Phil. She'd been a different person then; she'd had a real future, and real ambitions. Where had it all gone? To hell, she thought. To hell in a handbasket and straight up my nose. The diamond pendant glittered between her breasts—Phil had given it to her a decade ago. For the past few nights she'd been wearing it again, but—Why? she wondered. Did she think that he would notice? And so what if he did? Phil's own life, it seemed, had taken the same fall as hers; he was hanging out with Eagle Peters now, a known dope runner. He said he was doing dust. And the other night? I was just another fuck, like I always am. She must be out of her mind thinking that he could somehow save her from Natter. Why would he even want to? she asked herself in steepening self-hatred. My whole life is in the pits...

She'd never even bothered telling Phil the real reason she'd married Natter. He'd never believe it; it would just sound like the typical self-pitying bullshit of any whore. It was best to simply let him think what anyone else would think: that she'd married Natter for convenience, for free coke and fewer tricks. Those were parts of the reason, but the main reason was that Natter, in exchange, agreed to pay for her father's heart-valve operation. She'd bartered her flesh, and now Cody had his prize. It was almost medieval.

Her father had died a few years later, but at least her effort had given him some extra life.

No, Phil's necklace was nothing more than a dead icon, another reminder as to how flagrantly she'd let her whole life slip away from her.

Then another reminder reared.

"Damn it!" she whispered aloud when she reached into her purse and withdrew the tiny vial. It was empty.

The vial was an icon too, a perverted censer by which she worshipped her own demon. She was enslaved, and it was hard to clearly remember back to the time when she wasn't...

Rap-rap-rap! the hard knocks resounded on the door. Oh, God damn it, she thought. She knew who it was; it was Druck. And just when things were looking like she wouldn't have to turn any tricks tonight. At least being married to Natter had one benefit: he only reserved her now for higher-paying clients, which amounted to two or three tricks per week instead of five to ten per night. Having as his wife the highest-priced hooker in the club was Cody's prestige, like a pimp's "top-drawer" girl. The other girls provided the standard grist for Natter's mill, and the Creeker girls, of course, catered to the kinkier clientele. Vicki was on a pedestal in a sense. The Queen of Sallee's, she thought. Cody Natter's fuck trophy, the grade-A prime of the redneck underground...

*Rap-rap-rap-RAP!*

"What, Druck?" she nearly screamed through the door.

"'Scuse me, Miss Vicki," the halfwit voice came back. "But ya about done in there?"

"Yeah. Why?"

"Cody wants to see ya."

"What for, for God's sake?"

The slow voice behind the door paused. "Don't rightly know, Miss Vicki. But ya best git finished up 'cos he been waitin' on ya fer awhile's now."

"I'll be out in a minute," she replied, all the bite gone from her words. Yes, she knew. One last glance in the mirror, and she nearly broke out into tears.

Who did she hate more? Natter, or herself?

She swiftly put on her jeans and blouse, and left.

Druck waited outside, cracking his strange double thumbs. "Yessir, yer shore lookin' mighty perdy tonight, Miss Vicki."

"Where's Cody?"

The smile on the warped face looked like two fat worms lain together. "He's on back in the office."

Druck's uneven red eyes gazed at her bosom. The smile squirmed. His gaze felt like a molestor's hands freely kneading her breasts.

*Scumbag.*

She went down the hall, her stiletto heels ticking, and entered the back office. At once she noticed two of the less-defected Creeker dancers, nude save for their g-strings, standing against the wall. Their ebon-haired heads were bowed as if in the presence of a deity.

Which, in a sense, they were.

Cody Natter sat at the desk.

"So lovely, so beautiful," came his familiar, creaking voice. "And how was your night, my love?"

"Peachy. Druck said you wanted me for something."

Natter sat half-cloaked in darkness, which somehow made his twisted visage even more terrible. "Merely a minor arrangement; it shouldn't take too long. But there are three gentlemen who would very much like the pleasure of your company."

She looked aghast. Three bigshot rednecks, no doubt, chock full of cash from a recent dope deal. "Aw, Cody, come on, I don't do groups anymore. I hate doing groups."

"Well, certainly I'd never expect you to engage upon such a task on your own. You'll have some assistance." And with that disclosure, Natter's dark blood-red eyes looked across to the two Creeker girls.

Vicki gaped at them, then gaped back at Natter. "What? Them?"

Natter's crooked brow rose. "What of them?"

"They're *Creekers!*"

The room fell silent. Vicki knew she shouldn't have said it, but it slipped out. And there was no taking it back.

Natter stood up. He seemed to do so in increments, more or less unfolding to his nearly seven-foot height. The dark office corner released him; he began to walk forward.

"Cody, I didn't mean it," she rambled. "I—"

His long, three-fingered hand blurred, reached out, then snatched her throat.

And his voice seemed to flow, like a brook full of dark water. "Yes, my love, you are right. They're Creekers. But then...so am I."

His hand felt like an iron cuff. His face was hideous, a gaunt framework of pocked and lined flesh, the enlarged head and uneven ears. Lumps could be seen beneath graying-black streams of hair, protrusions of his cranium.

And, of course, his eyes.

The huge blood-red eyes...

"And..." The eyes slid down to the V of her blouse. "What have we here?"

The long thumb and forefinger of his free hand plucked up the pendant about her neck.

Oh, no, Vicki thought.

"Who gave you this, hmm?" queried the cracked voice.

"Yuh-you did, Cody," she lied.

His lips stiffened. "I did? Are you sure?"

"Yes, yes, don't you remember? You gave it to me before we got married."

"Hmm. Well." He jerked the pendant away, snapping the tiny gold chain. Then, right before her eyes, he rolled the gem and mount between his fingers. Eventually the mount broke, and the diminutive diamond fell to the floor.

His big booted foot ground it into the dust.

"Then I guess I'll just have to buy you a better one."

This secretly infuriated her, like everything else in her life. His eyes slid back up to hers, boring in like drill bits.

"You have a job to do now. Are you going to continue to make a nuisance of yourself, or are you going to do as you're expected?"

Something happened then, something dangerous. Some remote part of her psyche seemed to snap like a dry, tiny twig. Her terror shook her, and the deeper she stared into the corrupted face, the more she saw the ruination of her own life. A simple wave of his stone-like hand, she knew, could send her to the hospital.

He could snap her neck at will.

But suddenly, if only for a mad, exploding moment, she didn't care.

"You son of a bitch," her throat rasped the words. "You want me to be in a six-way orgy with three redneck dope peddlers. I'm your wife!"

"Indeed, you are." His grasp about her throat tightened. "And why is that? Tell me, my love. Why are you my wife?"

By now she couldn't answer. Her eyes began to swell forward as her husband's twisted hand exerted more pressure against her windpipe and the arteries leading to her brain.

He answered for her. "You're my wife only because I allow you to be. Yes? Am I right?"

Vicki's fear returned in just one beat of her heart. She forced herself, trembling, to nod in the affirmative.

Natter's black voice flowed on. "Yes, you're my wife. But there's something else that you are, yes? And what is that?"

The cuff of Natter's hand lifted, squeezing tears out of Vicki's eyes like water from a rag. Her heart squirmed in her chest...

His hand was lifting her off her feet.

She gasped, choking to get the words out. "I-I'm a—"

"Yes?"

"I'm a, I'm a—"

"Hmm? Tell me, my love. You're a what?"

"I'm a whore!" she finally hacked out.

The claw-like hand released her. Vicki fell to the floor.

"You're a whore," he repeated. He loomed over her, dizzyingly tall. "Yes, a whore. You always have been, and you always will be." Then his voice receded to its absolute darkest pitch. "Now go and do what it is that whores do."

Vicki wheezed air back into her lungs, coughing. Suddenly Natter was leaning down.

"But one more thing, my love. Isn't there something you need?"

Vicki squinted up, her head reeling. She'd barely heard what he said.

*Something... I need...*

"Hmm?"

His misshapen hand opened right before her face.

Her eyes widened.

She gulped.

In Natter's queer palm lay a baggie full of cocaine.

# TWENTY-THREE

"Jesus Christ, man," Eagle observed. His eyes looked peeled open. "The guy's been skinned."

"It's a tough piece of work," Phil said.

"Shit, who knows how much we missed 'em by."

"We didn't miss the guys who did this; they're miles away by now, Eagle. Ain't no way they did this here."

"How do you know?"

"Take a look, man."

The corpse lay sprawled, scarcely even resembling a human. It was the same job they'd done on Rhodes. The thing at their feet appeared coated with clotted blood, its complete surface showing sinuous crimson muscle. Flies, hordes of them, pecked over the corpse.

"There's no blood," Phil told him. "If they'd done this here, there'd be a lake of blood on the floor. There's almost nothing here. The guys who did this, they did it somewhere else, then brought Blackjack's body back here and dumped it."

Eagle straightened out; he looked confused. "But that don't make no sense. Why go to the trouble? Why didn't they just bury him somewhere, or dump him in the woods where he'd never be found?"

"Why do you think? They want him to be found," Phil said.

"Why?"

"To send a message out, man. The people you're dealing against know what you're doing. They left this here so you would see it, and get the gist quick."

"To lay off," Eagle said.

"That's right. They want you off their turf, and they left this little reminder here to give you good reason."

"Christ, man." Eagle backed out of the kitchen, dizzied by the sight. "This ain't my ballpark. I'm just a small-time dust runner; I ain't into this shit. I mean, look what they did to Blackjack. They fuckin' skinned him."

"Yeah," Phil agreed. "And we're next. We're in a stew pot of shit, and it's just about to start boiling. What are we gonna do?"

"Boogie," Eagle offered. "That's what we're gonna do. Look, I was just trying to make a living, but this... Fuck it. It ain't worth it."

"Why don't we hit back?" Phil tried to egg him on.

Eagle looked at him as though he'd just been told that the Pope was Jewish. "Are you fuckin' crazy, man? Hit back? These people mean big-time business, Phil, or can't you see that? We try to hit back on them, we die."

Don't chicken out on me now, Phil thought. He needed Eagle to be pissed, to want to strike back. That was the only way Phil would ever find out the location of Natter's lab.

"And I guarantee they did the same thing to Paul," Phil lied. "You want to take this shit? We gotta fight back. We gotta hit your competitor harder than he just hit you."

"Hey, they didn't hit me, they hit Blackjack, and that's hard enough. I'm out of this business, as of right now."

"Come on, man. Who's the other supplier?" Phil dared to ask. "Let's show them who they're fucking with."

Eagle laughed incredulously. "Fuck you, man. Like I said, I'm just in this for the bread. I'd rather pump gas than have to deal with guys who'd do something like this. Come on. We're out of here."

God-DAMN! Phil thought. Each time he got close, it shot out of reach. If he didn't push Eagle, he'd never find the location of Natter's lab, but if he pushed too hard, Eagle would smell cop in two seconds.

Guess I'll just have to work on him some more, Phil concluded. Give it more time. Plus, there was always Sullivan. Perhaps by now the county detention center was loosening up his mouth.

"All right. Let's book."

The hideous buzzing of the flies faded behind them as they tracked back through the house. It sounded unreal. Phil tried to shake off the afterimage of the corpse. It was hard to fathom that the thing in there had once been a man.

Phil's mind wandered, over the sheer grotesquerie.

No man deserved to die like that, not even a dust dealer, not even the world's worst scum. Phil tried to technically contemplate the task. One of Natter's Creekers, perhaps even Natter himself, had actually sat down with a blade to flense away all of Blackjack's skin. How long had the job taken? Had the skin made a sound while being cut away? How long had the man been dead?

How could someone do such a thing?

The empty bungalow echoed their footsteps. Eagle opened the front door to leave, then—

"SHIT!"

—ducked just in time to miss the swoosh! of a small sickle. "Look out!" Phil yelled, then came another swoosh!

A big Creeker kid, late-teens and probably six-five, had been waiting for them just outside the front door. "Holy fucking shit, man!" Eagle screamed and ducked yet again. A third swipe of the sickle missed Eagle's scalp by a fraction of an inch, whereupon the sharpened tool's point—

*crack!*

—sunk into the wall.

Phil was already down on one knee, shucking the Beretta from his wallet holster. "Get out of the way!" he shouted at Eagle, who was bungling backward in total shock. "I got him!"

The kid, trying to tug the sickle from the wall, gaped back dumbly. Then—

*pop!*

His cleft head whipped back. Red eyes crossed as blood squirted from the shiny new hole in his bulbous brow. Then he collapsed.

Phil rose, lowering his pistol.

"Man, where'd you get that?" Eagle asked, astonished.

"It's my good luck charm. Now quit jabbering and let's get out of here."

"Yeah, yeah. Out of here," Eagle frantically repeated, and scrambled for the front door.

"Not that way!" Phil shouted and suddenly lunged. "The back!"

Eagle turned. "Whuh—"

From outside, a muzzle-flash erupted like a split-second of daylight, then a great shotgun blast exploded through the room. A ragged hole the size of a dinner plate tore into the back wall

Phil had pulled Eagle out of the doorway just in time. "Come on, come on!" They pounded toward the bedroom, while rounds from a pump shotgun tore up chunks of the floor behind them.

"Man, you said they weren't here!" Eagle screamed. "You said they were miles away!"

"Well, I guess I was fucking wrong!"

They dove into the bedroom, slamming the door behind them. More shots rang out, punching through the door panels.

"Holy shit, man!" Eagle was babbling hysterically. "Holy ever-lovin' motherfuckin' shit!"

Phil slapped him in the face. "Shut up! Get a hold of yourself!"

"What the hell are we doin' holing ourselves up back here?"

Phil slapped him again. "You said Blackjack had guns—help me find them!"

They turned the little room upside down. Rapid footfalls could be heard entering the house. "Hurry!" Phil kept his gun trained on the door while he yanked drawers out of the dresser with his free hand. His heart felt like it was skipping beats.

Eagle tipped the bed mattress off the box spring, then slid off a sheet of plywood. "Here, man!"

*The motherlode!* Phil thought.

The box spring had been cut out, like a hollowed book. Inside lay a cache of guns—pistols, shotguns, rifles, and even a couple of sub-guns—plus ammunition.

"Dig in!" Phil commanded. "Just grab something and start shooting!"

Eagle picked up a 9mm Browning. "It don't work!" he screamed when he pointed it at the door and squeezed the trigger. Phil took it from him, cocked it, and threw it back.

"Now it works!"

Eagle, with grit teeth and closed eyes, discharged the weapon at the closed bedroom door. The gun coughed out fourteen rounds, to the extent that Phil's ears were ringing.

"How do like that, ya fuckers!" Eagle celebrated.

Then a single massive shotgun blast blew the door out of its frame.

"How you like-uh dat, white trash boys?" an unearthly voice queried in response.

Then three more shotgun blasts ripped into the room, pulverizing the plasterboard behind them.

We're definitely in some shit, Phil thought. He tossed his Beretta .25 to Eagle, who squeezed off its remaining four shots at the hole in the door. The shots sounded miniscule compared to the shotgun, and Creeker laughter rose from the outer room. When they laugh at your gun, you know you're in big trouble, Phil realized. "Come on, man, come on!" Eagle prompted, his hands shaking. "They're coming down the hall, I can see 'em!"

Meanwhile Phil was busying himself with a MAC-10 machine-pistol. The 30-round clip felt loaded; he snapped it in the mag well, then fumbled for the charging handle.

"Come on, man! Don't you know what you're doin'?"

"Can I help it I ain't Gun Digest!" Phil cracked back. He wasn't very familiar with the weapon, but finally he was able to snap the charging handle back. Then—

"Shit, I can't find the fuckin' safety!"

"Oh, man, hurry!"

Eagle ducked. Two more shotgun blasts volleyed into the room, backed by what sounded like pistol fire. The room vibrated.

Then two Creekers barged in.

"Oh, man, oh, man!" Eagle whimpered.

Both had great bulbed heads, enlarged jaws, canted teeth. The one with the shotgun held the weapon with hands that were but thumb and index finger. The other one, who quickly reloaded a Smith revolver, had what appeared to be two knees on his left leg and a right shoulder which dipped down nearly to his waist.

And through shags of coal-black hair, their crimson eyes burned at Eagle.

"Hey-uh, blondie," one mouthed. "Where yer buddy?"

"We gonna's fucks you whens yer dead," the other enlightened. "Fucks ya sumpin' fierce, white-trash boy."

"An' eat-cha's then."

The Creeker with the shotgun was lowering his weapon to Eagle's head when Phil sprang out from behind the other side of the bed. Amid a terrifying sound like a lawnmower, Phil squeezed the MACs trigger.

The sub-gun vibrated in a way that was almost eloquent. The burst of .45 bullets caught the Creeker in the belly, then literally picked him up off his feet and pushed him back out into the hall, lines of blood swirling in the air.

Phil jerked his wrist, then squeezed off another short burst at the other Creeker. He danced jerking as big, meaty holes rip-stiched his chest.

"Phil!" Eagle shouted. "Behind you!"

Glass shattered; two shots whizzed by Phil's head. A third Creeker was climbing in through the window.

The MAC buzzed again, and blew the Creeker right back out. "Grab that piece!" Phil ordered, pointing to the revolver on the floor. "Follow me!"

Eagle foundered for the dead Creeker's pistol, then he and Phil tumbled out the window into waist-high grass. "Quiet, quiet," Phil whispered, holding the MAC at the ready. He quick-peeked around the side of the cottage. "It looks clear. I think maybe we got them all. Come on, fuckin' run like fuckin' hell to the truck and get the fuck out of here."

The front yard was wide open, which was good—less conceal-ment—but the moon shined bright, which was bad—it highlighted them as targets. Their feet beat down the tall grass as they tramped forward, each step dispersing swarms of gnats and other insects.

When they arrived winded at Eagle's truck, Phil checked the perimeter. Nothing. But—

"Awwww, shit—"

"What's wrong?" Phil snapped. "Get in and start this thing so we can get out of here."

"Awwwwwww, shit," Eagle moaned. He stood stock-still, star-ing. The hood of the truck stood partly open. Wires hung out like entrails.

"They trashed the truck, man…"

We're fucked, Phil came to the delightful conclusion. "All right, so we gotta run out on foot. Let's g—"

Suddenly a sound like metallic rain began to circle them—plink-plink-plink-plink!—and small holes began to appear in the truck's fenders like strange magic. "Someone's popping caps at us!" Phil shouted. "Get down!"

He dragged Eagle to the dirt. Christ, how many of them are there? His peripheral vision caught the white dots of muzzle-flash on the far side of the house.

A fifth Creeker was running toward them, firing a pistol.

Phil ripped another burst of .45 off the MAC…

The Creeker went down with a garbled howl.

"Got him!" Eagle shouted with glee.

Then a sixth Creeker, much taller and less coordinated, turned the corner and advanced on them, too.

He was firing a pump shotgun.

"Jesus Christ!" Phil complained. "What, did they charter a fucking bus!" And when he aimed the MAC and squeezed—

"Shit, man!" Eagle shrieked.

—nothing happened. The bolt locked open. The clip was empty. Phil swore under his breath. A mere few seconds had expended the MACs magazine. *I wish to hell these things would shoot for as long as they do in the movies!* He snatched Eagle's revolver and, using the truck as cover, drew a bead on the advancing Creeker. Steady, steady. This would be tough. Just when he'd acquired a decent target, the next shotgun round blew out the windshield. Another shot socked into the side of the truck, spraying pellets across the hood, then another tore through the passenger and driver's windows.

Phil sprang back up, aimed, fired.

The .38 caught the Creeker in the groin and dropped him, screaming, in the grass.

*God, I hope that's all of them.*

Getting out of here on foot would be hell, but at least Eagle knew where they were. Phil turned. "All right, man, now we run our asses off—"

But when Phil turned, Eagle wasn't standing there. Instead, he was lying there—

"Eagle! No!"

—gargling his own blood.

Frantic, Phil dropped to his knees. Eagle convulsed in the grass. *That last shotgun round,* Phil realized. It had blown through the passenger and driver's windows and caught Eagle high in the chest. Eagle reached up feebly, shivering. Bubbles of blood percolated at the holes in his chest as he tried to breathe.

Phil didn't know what to do. This was about the hardest type of wound to treat in the field. And moving him would be fatal. "Hang on, man," was all Phil could say.

"Aw, shit, they really fucked me over," Eagle's voice gurgled. He hacked up some blood, which looked like black syrup in the moonlight. "Can't move, can't hardly breathe…"

"Just sit tight," Phil implored. "If I try to carry you out of here, you'll never make it. I'll be back as soon as I can with an ambulance."

Eagle's hand shakily grabbed Phil's shirtsleeve. His eyes were glassing over. "Pop me, man. I'm fuckin' dyin'."

Phil knew he was right. Eagle would be dead in minutes, drowned in his own blood.

"You'll be all right, man. Just hang in there."

Blood bubbled out of Eagle's mouth with the words. "Kill me, Phil, I'm beggin' ya. Don't leave me alive...for them."

Phil stared down. "You're gonna be okay," he said, knowing it was a lie. "I got all the Creekers, so you just wait it out. I'll be back as fast as I can... But, look, Eagle, you gotta tell me something first. You gotta tell me where Natter's lab is."

The dying eyes gazed back up. "Natter? Lab?"

"Natter's dust lab. It's got to be out here somewhere. Tell me where it is, Eagle. Then I can pay them back for this shit."

"The...lab..." was all Eagle could reply with any coherence. A high, wet whistling sound ensued as his chest heaved. He mumbled some words unintelligibly, then twitched. The hand gripping Phil's sleeve fell away...

Then Eagle died.

Phil sighed. Poor fucker. An array of feelings collided: rage, sadness, confusion. Things like this shouldn't happen. Why did the world have to be so insane? Sure, Eagle was a penny-ante dust runner, a two-bit criminal who Phil was playing for a dupe, but he didn't deserve this. In spite of Phil's undercover role, and in spite of his unrestrained hatred of PCP, Eagle was still, in a way, Phil's friend...

"Goddamn it," he muttered.

*click.*

Phil's heart seemed to stop mid-beat. The click had sounded at his head. Someone cocking a pistol hammer...

Phil, still on his knees, dropped his own gun. Very slowly, his eyes turned up.

Yet another Creeker stood before him, with odd, knuckly double-jointed hands that seemed to wrap around the revolver he gripped. The right side of his skull possessed a swell large as a cantaloupe, and his entire head seemed to hang off a thin, extended neck. His nose sported but one nostril.

The hard steel tip of the pistol barrel nudged mockingly at Phil's temple...

I'm dead, Phil was able to contemplate. It was not an easy

surmise to make, but Phil managed to do so with a surprising sense of calm.

But the Creeker kid paused. The scarlet eyes, which seemed twice the size of normal eyes, peered down at Eagle's corpse and the massive, bleeding chest wound.

"Skeet-inner-to," the kid said. "Ona-prey-bee."

*Creeker jibberish,* Phil realized. The words oozed thick in their defect. *But why doesn't he just kill me now?*

Then the weird red eyes moved back to Phil's face. The gun, a Smith .38, wavered.

Mannona, the word suddenly drifted from the kid. And then another word: Onnamann.

Phil's thoughts seized in a sudden static. He blinked. What eventually occurred to him was this: he hadn't heard the words in his ears—he seemed to have heard them in his head.

The kid's red eyes stared at him.

What's he waiting for? Phil thought, but he didn't think for long. He used the extra second to his advantage and quickly snapped his hands up. The disarm technique they'd taught him in the academy worked to a tee. His left hand grabbed the barrel, his right hand grabbed the Creeker's wrist, then, simultaneously, he pushed, twisting the gun right out of the kid's hand.

The kid's face went wide with astonishment—the disarm had taken less than a second.

Phil stood up, training the gun between the Creeker's crooked eyes. "Where's Natter's lab, you ugly fuck?"

Fat lips like tumors parted. The kid blinked.

"Mannona," he repeated. Then he lunged.

Phil squeezed off a single round into the kid's forehead. The back of his skull erupted, emitting a splat of gore which landed yards behind him in the high grass.

Phil stared through shifting gun-smoke. Goddamn. What a fucking night....

Then he turned for the path and jogged away.

# TWENTY-FOUR

"You were supposed to be fucking careful!" Mullins leaned forward over his desk and bellowed. "You could've gotten yourself fucking killed!"

Phil shrugged. "Hey, this ain't Mr. Rogers' Neighborhood. I'm working undercover on a PCP case. Shit happens."

"Yeah, shit happens. Well, your shit almost stopped happening!" Mullins reseated himself. Somehow, he looked fatter when he was mad. He seemed to tick behind the desk, an irate Jabba the Hut in a police suit.

It had taken Phil till well-past dawn to find his way out of the woods. Then he hitched back to Sallee's for his car and made it to the station about a half-hour after Mullins came in, walking up, as always, from the convenience store so his car wouldn't be seen. Obviously, the chief was not too pleased upon learning of last night's bullet-fest at Blackjack's shanty.

"Are you all right?" Mullins finally got around to inquiring.

Phil, for the first time, sipped some of the chief's noxious coffee. It tasted like bilge, but after what he'd been through he didn't really care. He needed something—anything—in his system with a little kick. "Yeah, I'm all right. Still a little shaky, though, but at least I wasn't hurt."

"Yeah, and you're goddamn lucky, too. So what else are you trying to tell me? You're telling me you killed three or four Creekers last night?"

Phil frowned, slumped in his chair. "More like five or six."

"Jesus Christ," Mullins exclaimed, peering at him. "Who do you think you are, Wyatt Fucking Earp?"

"Believe me, Chief, I'm not too happy about wasting all those Creekers, but it's not like I had much of a choice. It was a regular firefight out there. They were all over the place, and they had enough hardware on them to start their very own armory show."

"Shit," Mullins grumbled. "I wanted to keep all this out of the papers for as long as I could. But with you blowing six of them away like a one-man killing machine, I guess I gotta call county Technical Services and have them pick up the bodies. After the job you did up there, those county fuckers'll ask all kinds of questions."

"Save yourself the hassle, Chief," Phil pointed out. "You can bet Natter had all the bodies removed within an hour. And when I was jogging out of there, I could see a fire start up on the hill."

"They burned Blackjack's place, you mean."

"Yep, and I guarantee you they took all their dead out, too. No bodies, no shack, no evidence, no nothing. Probably just a whole lot of spent brass which the county won't give a flying fuck about because none of the Creekers have their fingerprints on file."

"You got that right. And Peters, you sure he was dead when you left?"

Phil gulped at the recollection. "Dead as dead can be. He took a shotgun blast full in the chest. Died in minutes." Phil's thoughts darkened further. "I guess I feel pretty shitty about it."

"Shitty? Why? The guy was everything you hate. We oughta give those Creekers a trophy for putting that asshole six feet under. Saves the state big-time tax dollars. He was a scumbag PCP dealer."

But was that really it? Was there no gray area? "Sure, Eagle was a criminal. But he was also a friend, a guy I grew up with, you know?"

"Oh, boo-hoo. You need a hanky for your tears?"

Fuck you, Phil wished he could say. Part of the reason he's dead is because of me. It was a strange concoction of feelings; Phil really didn't know how he should feel.

"Only thing that pisses me off about the Creekers killing his dope-dealing ass is it cost you your only good tie to Natter's PCP net," Mullins said. "It took you weeks to get where you were. What are you gonna do now?"

"I still got Sullivan to lean on. The county's putting him in general pop. Give him a few weeks there, and he'll start singing like a canary."

"Yeah? Well, let me tell you something, Phil. We ain't got a couple of weeks. I can only keep a lid on this shit for so long. It's too bad you couldn't get Natter's lab location out of Peters before he kicked the bucket."

"I tried," Phil lamented. He didn't feel very good about that, either. Pressing a guy for info as he lay dying in the dirt. "But he died before he could say anything. And that last Creeker too..." The imagery of the scene reemerged in his head. "It was really strange. He kept repeating this word: Mannona, or onnamann, or something like that."

"Creekers talk garbage all the time. Half of 'em can't talk at all. Their brains are all scrambled from all that family fucking they do out there in the boonies."

"Yeah, sure, but it was also pretty weird—I had a gun to this kid's head, and he still lunged."

"They're retards, Phil. They're all a bunch of inbred crazies. And you can bet your ass before Natter sends them out on a job, he's got them dusted to the gills. You've seen what PCP does to people's heads. Turns 'em crazier than bedbugs in a whore's mattress."

It was another legitimate point that Mullins made, however ineloquently.

"I just don't know what the fuck you're gonna do now that Peters is dead. Who else have you got to sap info off of? No one."

"Relax, will you?" Phil requested. "I'm doing the best I can, which—and pardon me if this is offensive—is a lot better than before I came on."

Mullins nodded smugly. "Go ahead, rub it in. I ain't arguin' with ya. You're right, with you we're closer to Natter's dust op than we've ever been. But what good is that gonna do me—or you, for that matter—if you get yourself killed?"

"I'm not going to get killed, Chief. Trust me."

"Okay, killer. But tell me this. What's Susan gonna think when she hears about your little chopping party in the woods last night? Tell me that."

Phil looked crookedly back at Mullins. It, too, was a good question, but—"What do you mean, Susan?"

Mullins guffawed, slurping coffee and spitting tobacco juice at the same time. "Like they say, with age there's wisdom, right? Don't bullshit me. You and Susan got something going; I can tell just by looking at her. She's got big-time hots for you, boy. And you got the same for her, and don't even think about telling me otherwise."

Was it that obvious? Phil almost wished it were so. But Mullins had made a sound inquiry. Susan would raise hell if she knew how deep Phil had gotten into this mess. And if she found out about the firefight last night...

"So how about doing me a favor, Chief? How about clamming it up to Susan about this?"

"I hear ya," Mullins said, smiling. "And why don't you do me a favor, huh?"

"What's that?"

"You look like death warmed up on my grandma's wood stove. Go home, all right? Get some fucking sleep."

Good idea. Phil got up. "Thanks for the coffee; remind me to never drink it again. I'll call you tomorrow."

Phil made for the door. But before he left, Mullins stopped him with a fat wave of his hand.

"Oh, and Phil?"

"Yeah?"

"Tonight when you're on the job?"

"Yeah?"

Mullins chuckled. "Try not to kill more than ten people, huh? Would ya do that?"

Phil drove home numb. Morning sunlight glared like a great blade—an annoying scimitar—across the windshield. Only now were the realities sinking in. He'd killed men last night, a lot of men. Eagle had been killed.

And he'd nearly been killed himself.

All that adrenalin left him hungover now. He felt jittery, dry-mouthed. Two pinpoint headaches buzzed behind his eyes as he drove the Malibu down the Route, and he could swear his heart was still skipping beats in the aftermath of split-second terror.

When he parked at the boarding house and got out, he instinctively glanced up at Susan's window. Her curtains were drawn. She's asleep by now, he realized, and this depressed him. He wanted to sleep with her, not to make love, just to...sleep. After the frenzy of last night, he didn't want to be by himself.

*I want to be with her,* he thought sappily.

Should he go up to her room right now and knock on her door? Should he wake her? Would she mind?

It didn't matter; Phil never got the chance.

Just as he was about to go up the stairs to her room, the faintest sound wisped from down the darkened hall.

A moan.

Phil turned.

Something sat huddled right beside his door.

Susan? he stupidly thought. No, it wasn't Susan.

The huddled figure moaned again. When Phil realized it was Vicki—and that something was very wrong—he ran down the hall to help her.

He knelt down; her hand reached out.

"Good God, Vicki. What happened?"

She was only partly conscious when he helped her up. Her hair was disarrayed, her clothes were torn, and when Phil looked at her face—

*Oh, Christ, no...*

—he could tell at once that she'd been beaten.


"Calm down," Phil said, gingerly daubing at the cut on her forehead. "It's not as bad as it looks."

Vicki flinched for probably the hundredth time. "That hurts, Phil!"

"Hey, I ain't Dr. Kildare, the alcohol is going to sting a little—"

"A little? Jesus!"

"—but you don't want it to get infected. So pipe down and let me do this," Phil finished. There hadn't been much blood, and the bruises weren't too severe. It was easy, though, to see what had happened. Yeah, somebody gave her a pretty good knocking around, he observed. But why?

"How did you get here?" Phil asked, next applying a Band-Aid over the small cut.

"I walked," she said.

"All the way from Sallee's?"

She nodded groggily.

"That's some haul." Phil sat down on the edge of the bed while Vicki lay back on the couch holding a cold wet rag over her eyes. "How do you feel? Are you dizzy? Confused? Are you seeing double or anything like that?"

"Just tired mostly," she murmured and sighed. "It was a long night."

I guess it was. For you and me both. "Yeah, well, come on. I better take you to the hospital."

"No, no—"

"Vicki, it's a good idea. You could have a concussion or something."

"I don't have a concussion," she complained rather testily. "I just got slapped around a little, no big deal. Just—" She sighed again. "Just let me lie here for a little while. Is that okay?"

"Sure," Phil said. Actually, it wasn't okay—what if Susan found out she was here? What would he say? How could he possibly explain it? But he couldn't very well throw her out. Something serious had happened, and Phil wanted to know what. *I'll just let her calm down a little,* he decided. *Susan had classes this afternoon before work. She can sleep on the couch till Susan goes to school. Then I'll figure out how to get her out of here.*

"So," he got on to the next question. "What happened?"

"It's a long story, Phil. You don't want to hear it."

"You're right, I probably don't, but tell me anyway. Did your husband do this to you?"

She relaxed back on the couch with her feet up. Her jeans looked scuffed. Her blouse had been ripped open; she feebly clasped it together with her hand but not very effectively. Phil could see almost all of one of her breasts.

"Since I married Cody, he's kind of held me in reserve," she said. "He stopped making me turn regular tricks."

"He made you his top-drawer, in other words," Phil suggested, remembering how things worked on the street when he was with Metro. Pimps got prestige by "marrying" their most marketable women and charging more for them.

"Yeah," she affirmed. "He'd save me for the bigger money tricks. Anyway, last night after my set at Sallee's, he wanted me to do a six-way with three guys and two of the Creeker dancers. I had no choice. If I didn't do it, Cody would've beat the shit out of me."

"So who did beat the shit out of you?"

She paused as if to quell something. "Christ, you should've seen these guys, they were three bikers who ran dust north of Waynesville. Some friends of Cody's. They just came off a big drop and were loaded with cash. Things got out of hand pretty fast; they were all smoking flake and doing coke at the same time."

"Bad combination," Phil said.

"Tell me about it. Anyway, these guys were kinks, and they started beating up on the two Creeker girls. Cody doesn't mind so long as they don't bust them up too bad. Lotta guys pay extra to rough them up. But these guys—shit. They got to beating up on the two Creekers like really hard. So I started to pitch a fit, and when they wouldn't stop, I tried to leave."

"So it was the three bikers who beat you up."

"No," she said. "It was Druck. He slapped me around and threw me right back in the room. Told me I shouldn't embarrass Cody in front of his friends."

"Jesus," Phil commented. Then he took the mark. "So how is it that Cody's friends with out-of-town dust dealers?"

She shrugged. "They spend a lot of money in the club."

"That the only reason?"

"Yeah. Why?"

Was she lying? Was she hiding something? Phil couldn't tell. Maybe she doesn't even know that Natter's the main dust supplier in the area. "I don't know," he eventually said. "It just seems strange."

Vicki let out a quick, cynical laugh. "The whole thing's strange, Phil. Christ... I could tell you things you wouldn't believe."

"Try me."

"Just forget it, okay? I don't feel like talking about it right now."

Phil looked at her. *So maybe that means she'll feel like talking about it later,* he considered.

"You know something, Vicki? You're flushing your whole life down the toilet with people like that. Being married to Natter, working in his club. You're just a curio to him, you know. You're just status."

"I know." She laughed humorlessly again. "The top-drawer whore. The White Trash Queen of the Creekers."

"So why don't you do something about it? That whole Creeker scene is crazy. Why don't you leave Natter? Go somewhere else, start over and try to get your shit together?"

"Phil, you don't even know what you're saying. If I did that..."

"What? He'd send people after you? He'd kill you if you left him?"

She made no reply.

"Well, let me tell you something, he's killing you right now, and you don't even realize it. The only way you're ever going to make your life better is to get away from him."

"I don't need a lecture, Phil," she said wearily.

"You need something," he pressed. "As long as you're running with Natter and his crowd, you aren't going anywhere but down."

"Don't you think I know that!" she almost yelled. "Don't you think I know what's happened to me! My whole life has been shit since the day you left town ten years ago!"

"Calm down," he said. "I just want you to start thinking about things a little more, about what you're going to do with your life. And you can't blame me for your problems. Yeah, I left town, that's true, but I'm not the one who puts coke up your nose and makes you turn tricks at a strip joint."

"I know," she said much more quietly.

Phil got off her case and let her collect herself. Then he asked, "So where was Natter last night when all this shit was happening with the three bikers?"

"He was out. Somewhere—don't know."

*Yeah, well I think I do,* Phil felt sure. *I think maybe your darling hubby was sending his Creeker boys out for a little party in the woods. Killing Eagle. Trying to kill me.* But, of course, he couldn't tell her anything about that...

He let more silence pass, looking at her. He felt helpless. She wasn't part of his life anymore; nevertheless he hated to see her like this. He hated what Natter was doing to her. But what could he do to help her?

Nothing, he concluded. The only person who could help her was herself.

"Look, I'm really sorry about dumping myself here," she said. "I didn't know where else to go. I better leave now."

"Stay here," he said. "Sleep on the couch. Get some rest for now. You can figure out what you're going to do later."

"Thank you," she whispered. Her voice was trailing away. "Thank you..."

Then she was asleep.

Phil turned off the light, drew the shades, then quietly undressed and got into his bed. In minutes, he too was fast asleep.

And dreaming.

# TWENTY-FIVE

"Look-it, look-it," Dawnie urged, hunched behind him and pushing at his shoulders.

Phil's ten-year-old eye opened wide over the first keyhole. What he saw at first was just a stark, white glare; his eye, going from the hot dark of the third-floor hall to such glaring whiteness, needed time to adjust. But eventually his vision focused, and he could see.

He could see what was inside the room...

It was like a hole in the wall to hell.

In the room lay a sunlit bed. It was big and white. And on the bed lay some weird kind of motion Phil couldn't figure out at first.

Shapes.

Shapes the color of skin.

One shape was a bearded man with a big hairy belly. He had long hair and was buck-naked.

"Suzie, Suzie," he was saying.

Then Phil noticed the other shape on the bed. A woman—

"Suzie, Suzie..."

She had hair on her head that was blacker than Phil's aunt's fire hearth. Her skin was whiter than their front yard the time last winter when it snowed.

Then Phil realized what she was doing to the fat, bearded man.

*Jesus to Pete!*

Her head was positioned between the fat man's legs. It was going up and down, and what she was doing, exactly, was—

*Jesus to holy Pete!*

—she was sucking the fat man's thing. Her mouth was going up and down over it, slow at first, then faster, then real fast.

Just like Eagle said they do. *She's trying to suck out his baby-juice!*

Then more of the scene came into focus, and Phil almost

upchucked when he saw the rest...

The woman had a butt and hair and boobs just like most women. But it was what she didn't have that hit Phil in the face like someone's big fist.

*She ain't got no arms or legs!*

She had stumps but that was it. The stumps ended where her elbows and knees should be.

"Suzie, Suzie..." Phil jerked his face away from the keyhole.

"Neat-uh, huh?" Dawnie said.

It was not neat. It was gross.

But it all added up. It was just like what he and Eagle had heard Uncle Frank talking about that night they stayed up late to watch The Alfred Hitchcock Show when the lady killed her husband with a frozen leg of lamb and then cooked it for the police.

This was a whorehouse.

A Creeker whorehouse, where men paid to do it with Creeker girls who were all messed up on account of their fathers did it with their sisters and their mothers did it with their brothers and stuff like that.

It messed up their genes.

Dawnie tugged at his Green Hornet shirt, pulling him toward the next door. Phil didn't want to see stuff like this anymore, but something made him put his eye to that next keyhole anyway. He couldn't help it. It was like a ghost or something grabbed the back of his head and made him look.

A big naked man was tying a girl up on the bed with rope, stretching her out. Then he began to crack a leather whip across her thighs and belly.

*Crack! crack! crack!* went the whip.

It left marks on the girl's skin that were so red. Almost like she was bleeding...

She was crying and shivering.

Then the man's thing went up...

And when the girl lifted her head to look at him, Phil saw that her head was huge.

It was big as a watermelon!

"Here, here-uh," Dawnie said next. She was pulling him to a door on the other side of the hall.

"No, Dawnie, I don't wanna look no more," Phil begged her.

But Dawnie didn't seem to care what Phil said, and she was

strong, stronger than most girls. She pulled him over and slammed him back down to his knees before the next door.

"Look-it."

Phil's head was hurting bad, and he was sweating so much his Green Hornet T-shirt was fully wet but still he felt cold and shivery. His stomach felt bad too, worse than the times in the past when he'd eaten his aunt's stuffed peppers. His head felt lighter than a birthday balloon.

"Look-it…"

Inside the room another man had his face between a girl's legs. She had a big black plot of hair there, and the man looked like he was licking at it. Phil couldn't understand why anyone would want to put their mouth on the same place a person goes to the bathroom, but this man was doing it sure as hell and making more noise than heifers eating. The girl's white legs went up into the air. Phil could see her feet. She had what looked like ten toes on each! And her hands were the same way, more fingers on 'em than two people, and they were running in and out of the man's wiry hair.

Then Phil noticed her legs…

He couldn't do anything but stare.

One leg was surely a foot shorter than the other, and it didn't have no knee. But the other longer leg looked kind of like it was coiling in the air, and Phil soon saw why.

The longer leg had three knees.

The girl was laughing. She seemed to like the man putting his mouth on the place where she went to the bathroom.

And then the man's face came away.

Phil looked into the sprawl of hair…

"She's got two baby-holes!" he shrieked.

"Shhh! Shhh!" Dawnie panicked. "I'll'se get whupped if they'se know we'se lookin'! Nanc'll let that there fella do all that ta me-uh if she's knowed I seed!"

But it was too late. Phil's face trembled as his eye remained over the keyhole.

"What was that?" the naked man asked, jerking his head toward the door.

"Oooo, Dawnie must-uh be lookin' at us," the girl on the bed said. She was grinning, leaning up to look right at the keyhole.

And when she leaned up, Phil saw something else.

He couldn't help it…

"Dawnie! She's got six boobs!"

And she sure's bullpoop did. Six of 'em, three on each side, and each one had a big nipple on it the size of the top of a can of beans, only they were stickin' out real far and were real pink. Dang! She's got herself six boobs! he repeated in thought.

But when he looked up at Dawnie, she didn't look too good. She looked like real scared all of a sudden, and then Phil noticed that the front of that crummy dress she wore turned dark in the front.

*She done peed herself,* he realized.

And Phil knew that people only peed themselves when they were real scared...

The door swung open.

Phil shrieked, and Dawnie was crying real hard, blubbering like and stepping back.

Phil couldn't move.

"What we got here, huh?" the naked man asked. He grabbed Phil by the hair and lifted him up, chuckling. "You part of the deal, boy?"

Phil wailed.

"You wanna come on in with me an' Nanc?"

The man's breath smelled like his aunt's when she'd been drinking, and his belly jiggled when he laughed. "Maybe a good cornholin' would teach ya not ta look in on folks."

Phil tried to jerk away but couldn't. The naked man just grabbed his hair tighter and kept on laughing.

It was a whole lot of madness going on in the same moment: the naked man cackling, Phil wailing, Dawnie blubbering and peeing herself.

Phil barely noticed the sound of bedsprings.

Then another sound:

*thah-THUMP, thah-THUMP thah-THUMP...*

It was the whore-girl.

She had climbed off the bed, and now—

Phil's stomach shrank.

—she was walking toward the doorway.

Only she wasn't really walking; she was kind of hop-shuffling. The foot on her short leg dragged while the one on her long, three-kneed leg kind of lifted real quick, then snapped forward—THUMP!—and landed on the floor. Her black hair tossed in swaying strands; her head bobbed. Phil could see those blazing red eyes of hers get brighter as she approached.

*thah-THUMP, thah-THUMP, thah-THUMP...*

Her shoulders pitched back and forth, and each time she took another noisycrutch-like step, all six of her boobs bounced around fierce on her chest.

The naked man cackled. The whore-girl thumped forward.

Then it was Phil who peed his pants.

Her red eyes felt like spikes sticking into his face. "Hey-uh, boy. What'cha peein' yerself fer, huh? Scairt?"

Phil wanted to scream, but his throat felt locked shut. "Yeah, he's a'scairt, ain't he-uh, Eddie?"

"Shore is. Little fella peein' away like a reg-lar racehorse," the naked man who held Phil by the hair said and cackled some more.

Then the whore-girl cackled, too, worse than the man. The cackle sounded like a flock of big catbirds picking at a dead possum in the road.

"Ay-uh, an'yer's real cute, boy. Wannas come in an' let Nanc suck yer thang? That like ya think, boy?"

Phil was shivering like he was buck-naked in the dead of winter. Then the girl's weird ten-fingered hand slowly reached out—

"No!" Phil cried, head shaking and eyes pinched shut.

—and trailed tickling down his face. It felt like a bunch of big beetles crawling there on his cheek.

Phil thought he might die...

But then the whore-girl turned real fast and clopped out into the hall.

Toward Dawnie.

*thah-THUNK, thah-THUNK, thah-THUNK...*

"No-uh, Nanc, pull-eeese!" Dawnie cried.

"What-choo doin' bringin' boys in hee-uh!" the girl yelled, pitching forward. Her hand swept up and—

*ka-Crack!*

—smacked Dawnie in the face so hard she fell down. The girl's hand flailed up and down, then, smacking away at Dawnie's head like it was a tetherball.

"Nev-uh, nev-uh! Girl so dumb you! Nev-uh bring no one up hee-uh!"

*ka-CRACK, ka-CRACK, ka-CRACK*

"Yer daddy gonna so bad whup ya, but ain't's be gonna much left of ya after I'se through…"

It was horrible. Now the girl was not only slapping Dawnie, she sat right on her stomach, pinning her to the floor, and was punching and choking her. "Bringin' boys up hee-uh—crazy you? Bet you's fuckin' him, were yas? Girl-huh, were yas?"

"Stop it! Leave her alone!" Phil shouted. "She didn't do nothin'!"

Then Phil peed some more in his pants, peed till there was nothing left in his insides.

Other naked Creeker girls on the floor, who must've heard all the noise, one by one opened their doors to look out. A girl with a bunch of belly buttons, a girl with a humped back and arms hanging down almost to her feet, a girl with no neck and no mouth. Also the girls he'd already seen through the keyholes: the one with the big watermelon head and whip-marks on her thighs and stomach. And the girl whose arms and legs were just stumps that ended where her knees and elbows should be. She edged out into the hall on all four stumps and jabbered something…

And at once the hall was full of sounds: mish-mash words, cackling and laughter, and dogs barking.

All that sound seemed to press against Phil's head. He'd never been so terrified in his whole life…

The whore-girl climbed off of Dawnie and clopped toward Phil, and then that big weird ten-fingered hand of hers reached out and snatched him by the collar of his Green Hornet T-shirt.

"Get you-uh outta hee-uh, boy," she said.

Then, in a split second, she opened her mouth and bared her teeth at him.

Big crooked fang-like teeth, like a dog's.

Phil screamed high and hard, pulled away till his shirt tore to ribbons, then ran for the stairs faster than he'd ever run in his life…

# TWENTY-SIX

The afterimage remained:
        The teeth.
*Jesus God...*
Jagged fangs, just like a dog's or a wolf's.

Phil kicked the sheets off his bed. He leaned up in the dark and sighed heavily. Another dream, he thought. They're wearing me out...

This was an understatement. The dreams drained him. He felt hungover and exhausted now, mentally sapped and as physically devitalized as if he'd just dug ditches for six hours.

The dreams were boring into his mind, piece by piece unearthing what had happened that day twenty-five years ago. And there was one thing he was sure of—

There were still a few more pieces.

Why couldn't he remember?

*Do I even want to remember?*

Phil didn't think he did.

Vicki was still asleep on the couch, tossing fitfully. Her red hair lay across her face like a crimson drape, and she seemed to mumble things in her slumber. The room was stiflingly hot; sweat shined evenly as lacquer on the V of skin that her blouse exposed. Phil slipped into the bathroom and took a quick, cold shower, but as soon as he stepped out, he was burning up again. With a towel about his waist, he went to his dresser, was about to reach for some shorts, when--

*"Nuh-nuh-no!"*

Phil turned and looked quizzically at Vicki. Her eyes squeezed shut against her sleep, and, evidently, against a nightmare. At least I'm not the only one who has them, Phil considered.

"No, pleeeeeeeease..."

Indeed, Vicki was dreaming up a storm, tossing and turn-ing in the torment of her own mind. Phil wondered what she was dreaming about, but then he thought he had a pretty good idea, considering what had happened to her last night.

"Ona... Ona," she murmured on.

Phil's eyes narrowed.

"Skeet...inner..."

He peered at her.

"Ona...prey...bee."

*What?*

Phil leaned closer, studying her.

Then, very clearly, and with her eyes shut so tight her face dis-torted, she whispered:

"Mannona."

Dream jibberish? Phil wondered. But...

The word sounded familiar, and now that he thought of it, so had the other words she'd mumbled.

*Onn. Ona.*

*Skeet-inner*

*Ona-prey-bee.*

And, especially:

"Mannona," the whisper came off his lips.

Phil felt momentarily adrift.

Then it dawned on him. *Last night. The ambush at Blackjack's.* Now he remembered. *That last Creeker kid, he'd said the same words, right before I blew him away.*

Yes...

Phil felt sure of it.

What did the words mean? Or did they mean anything? Was it part of the Creekers' sublanguage? Most were clearly deficient in verbal skills—

"Mannona," Vicki again whispered in her sleep.

Then she sprang bolt upright and screamed.

"Jesus Christ, Vicki!" He rushed to her, to try and settle her down. The scream had rung out like a siren, and shocked her awake. Phil leaned over, gently jostling her by the shoulders.

"Vicki, Vicki, are you okay?"

Her eyes were frozen open, bloodshot. She shivered where she sat and just stared...

"Vicki?"

"Oh...oh, God," she muttered and finally came out of it. She numbly pushed her hair back, her eyes fluttering. Phil could actually see a vein in her neck beating manically.

"Are you okay?" he asked again.

"Yeah. I—"

"You must have had yourself one hell of a nightmare."

She paused, catching her breath. Her hand came shakily to her bosom. "I did. It was...awful."

"I guess so. You screamed so loud you probably woke up every stiff in Beall Cemetery."

"Sorry," she wavered. She shook her head, rubbed her eyes. "I have nightmares like that all the time."

"What was it about?" Phil asked.

"Nothing, nothing—"

But Phil wasn't even thinking. He should've been.

Because a moment later the door swung open—

"Phil, are you all right?" a worried voice rushed. "I heard someone scr—"

Susan stood in the open doorway.

Awwwwwww, shit, was the only thing Phil could think, standing there agape with just a towel around his waist.

The next two or three seconds seemed like two or three years. Plenty of time for Phil to curse himself up and down. Goddamn it! How could I be so goddamn STUPID! How could I have left the goddamn door UNLOCKED! Meanwhile, Susan just stood there. The expression on her face showed worry, confusion, and disbelief, all percolating at once. Then the expression hardened. She glanced at Phil, then at Vicki, and then at Phil again.

Then she said, none too quietly, "Fuck you!" and turned around and ran back up the stairs.

Phil ran after her, ludicrously holding the towel around his waist. "Susan, wait!" he yelled.

"Eat shit!" she yelled back, thumping up the steps ahead of him. "Eat lots of shit!"

"Would you please wai—" Phil began, then barked "Jesus!" as he stubbed his toe on one of the uncarpeted stairs.

He heard Susan's door slamming shut on the landing above.

The entire house shuddered.

Phil limped the rest of the way up, feeling about as low as a typical snake belly. What could he say that wouldn't be a foolhardy cliché? He could hear himself now. *Susan, let me explain!* Or, *it's not what you think!* If he said anything like that, it would prove an even worse insult to her.

Pathetically, he asked himself, *How do I get myself into messes like this?*

No answer was forthcoming.

"Susan?" he said, rapping gently on her door. "Please, open the door and at least let me talk to you."

"Fuck off!"

"All right, you're really mad now, I understand that. So how about if I come up a little later when you cool off?"

"Blow yourself!"

"Tomorrow, then. Okay? Can we talk tomorrow?" he all but pleaded.

"If I ever see you again, you lying son of a bitch," she shrieked from the other side of the door, "I'll kick you in the balls so hard they'll pop out of your ears!"

Phil took a forlorn step back from the door.

*Well,* he thought. *I guess that means no.*

Vicki, of course, was gone when Phil went back to his room. *I guess she knows a bad scene when she sees one.* He couldn't blame her for the mishap—he could only blame himself. Susan had told him weeks ago that any sound in his room traveled up to hers through the heating duct. He felt scorned; he hadn't even done anything wrong.

*So what else is new, Phil?*

Right or wrong, though, common sense told him that nothing he could say could salvage things between him and Susan.

It wasn't even 6 p.m. when he was dressed and ready. But ready for what? *Eagle's dead—he was my closest lead, and God knows where Vicki is.* He'd have to start from scratch again, go back to the club tonight, and try to cultivate the trust of another denizen of Crick City's underworld.

It would take weeks.

But there was still one person he could work on...

He drove the Malibu to Millersville, to the county lockup. He flashed his ID, then signed his gun in with the block sergeant. In a few minutes, Paul Sullivan was brought to the interview room in handcuffs.

Phil sat with his feet up on the desk. "Hey, bub, how's it going? I'll bet you thought it was your Aunt Millie coming to visit, huh?"

"Fuck you," Sullivan grumbled.

"Believe it or not, Paul, you're not the first person to say that to me today. Oh, and I really dig your wardrobe. Brooks Brothers?"

Sullivan sat down, dressed in bright orange prison utilities. "How come I got moved out of PC to general pop?"

Generally new inmates were kept in protective custody for five days, for in-processing, before being moved into the general prison population, but it had been at Phil's request that Sullivan was transferred immediately. And Phil noticed something else: Sullivan had a black eye and new bruises on his face. "You can thank me for that, Paul," Phil told him. "A sociable guy like you, I figure you'd appreciate the company of your fellow convicts. And with that handsome mug of yours, I'll bet you got a lot of fans already."

"Motherfucker," Sullivan replied. "Half the chumps in there hate my guts. I get in half a dozen fights a day."

"It's called socialization, Paul. Let me ask you something. Does the word mannona mean anything to you? Or prey-bee? Or skeetinner?"

"Naw. But it sounds like Creeker talk."

"And how would you know that? You know a lot of Creekers?"

"Naw, man, but, you know, they're all over the place, and a lot of the whores at Sallee's are Creekers. I hear 'em jabberin' all the time. Coupla years back, me and Eagle ran flake with some hillfolk out of Luntville, pretty much the same as Creekers 'cept they ain't all fucked up from inbreedin'. They told us all about the shit the Creekers were into, scared shitless of 'em. Said the Creekers were cannibals and shit like that, and they got some weird religion."

Phil raised a brow. "What do you mean? What kind of religion?"

"I don't know, why the fuck should I care? But these hillers also said the Creekers, since they can't talk right, they kinda got their own language. You been to Sallee's, you've heard 'em jabbering that shit."

This just proved more of what Phil already suspected. Sullivan's familiarity with the way Creekers spoke only verified some kind of proximity to them. And it was also pretty obvious that he was hiding something.

"You been a liar and a scumbag all your life, Paul? Ever think you might want to do something with your life besides be a lying, ugly, redneck, dope-dealing piece of shit?"

Sullivan grit his teeth. "Man, if I wasn't in these cuffs, I'd kick your cop ass up and down the wing. I'd dance on your fuckin' face, bub."

Phil leaned forward and smiled. "Oh? Well, you sure weren't doing a whole lot of dancing the other night when we had our little party in your luxurious abode."

"That's just 'cos you didn't fight fair."

Phil laughed. "Bill me for the coffee table."

"Go ahead and laugh, bub. At least I got ya back, blowing your cover all over fuckin' town."

"Blowing my cover, Paul? And how did you manage that?"

Sullivan mustered a smile, which made the wedgelike face even uglier. "You think you're pretty smart, slapping that bullshit no-call order on me. So ya wanna know what I did?"

"What's that, Paulie? I'm dying to know."

Sullivan's smile came to its peak, like a curved gash in a slab of tenderized steak. "I had one of the guys on the block call Eagle."

"Oh? And this colleague of yours talked to Eagle?"

"Well, no, but he left a message on Eag's answering machine, and spilled the beans about you."

Crafty fucker. Phil leaned back, chuckling. "Well, let me tell you, Paul, unless they got an answering service at the pearly gates, that's one message Eagle's never gonna get."

Sullivan's face pinched. "What you mean?"

"Eagle's dead. And so is your buddy Blackjack. We went out to his place last night, and Blackjack was lying there looking like something in the fresh meat rack at Safeway. Then some Creeker kid blew a hole in Eagle's chest big enough to drive your big piece of shit truck through."

"A Creeker?"

"That's right, Paul. We got set up, there were six of them waiting for us. And I'm sure it breaks your heart to see that I got out alive."

"A Creeker," Sullivan quietly repeated.

"One of Natter's boys. I smoked all of them. A tragic waste of some worthy humanity. Guess none of them will make it to Harvard now, huh?"

Sullivan's cockiness quickly grew drained of its edge.

His shoulders slumped. Phil could tell the guy was worried now.

"All right, you want me to talk, I'll talk. But you gotta get me outta general pop and back into PC, and you gotta drop the distro charge."

Now we're getting somewhere. "I'll think about it," Phil baited. "But you gotta give me something now."

Sullivan's big, unpleasant head nodded. "Awright. We'se been workin' through a new flake lab outta Lockwood. New guys. Some backer from Florida and an egghead labman just out of stir from the federal can in Bradford, PA. The regular supplier jacked the price, and the rednecks went nuts. These rednecks out here, they go through flake and dust like kids buyin' cotton candy at the fuckin' carnival."

"An eloquent simile, Paul," Phil remarked. "So you got with these new guys and decided to corner the local market, undersell the group turning out the old product."

"Yeah."

"What was the deal?"

"It was me and Eagle running point with Blackjack and Jake Rhodes and another guy named Orndorf. They'd drop the product to us, and we'd take it to the distro runners, a couple of whacks— Scott-Boy Tuckton and some fat kid named Gut. They were the replacements."

"Replacements?"

"For the other distro runners. There were a bunch of 'em, but they all disappeared. Like I told you the other night. But Gut and Scott-Boy, they disappeared too, I don't know, a month ago, so me and Eagle were running the product to the distro points ourselves. That's why we took you on to drive." Sullivan sputtered. "Dumbest-ass thing I ever agreed to. Usually I smell cop a mile away."

"I stopped using deodorant—that way, I'd smell just like you." Phil whipped out a pad and jotted down the names. "Okay, Paul. Good boy. Now give me the loke on your lab."

"Shit, man!"

"Come on, Paulie. You don't want to miss the cellblock shower, do you?"

Sullivan glared. "They'll know it was me who dropped dime on them!"

"No they won't, Paul. They'll think it was Eagle or Blackjack or any of the other guys in your operation who disappeared. For all your supplier knows, those guys are in the joint, too. I'll even put the word out that it was someone else; I'll say I heard it was Blackjack. They'll believe it because nobody even knows Blackjack is dead." Phil tapped his pen. Sullivan was small-time on a losing streak; Phil wanted the big fish, Natter. Give him a deal, he decided. Get what you really want. "You know what PBJ is, Paul? Probation before judgment? That means you don't do time. Give me what I want, and if it all checks out square, I'll talk to the state attorney's office. I'll tell them that you've been a good citizen, cooperating fully with the police, and I'll get you PBJ'd. You're out of here in forty-eight hours. You leave town, you leave the state, no one knows where you went. All you gotta do is see a probie officer once a week wherever you go. And you know what you could even do? You could start all over again, Paul, get a real job, a real life, live like a real person for once. Who knows, you might even like it. It's got to be better than sitting in the slam, making dust runs, and sweating bullets every night not knowing when the other guy might have you in his crosshairs."

Sullivan's heavy jaw set. He was chewing his lip, thinking.

"It's a good deal, Paul, and it's either that or you get to sit in this stone motel for the next five to ten years. But don't worry—I'll send you a fruitcake every Christmas."

It was fun putting the squeeze on a guy like Sullivan.

"Time's a'wastin'," Phil quipped. "Keep me waiting, and I might just have to go shake down some other dust dealer and get what I want out of him."

Sullivan swore under his breath. "Awright, shit. Who else I got to trust?"

Then he gave Phil explicit directions to his supplier's lab operation.

"Outstanding, Paul. I knew you were a good guy deep down. But there's one more thing I want, and you know what it is."

Sullivan looked at him, incredulous. "The fuck you talkin' about? I just handed you the works, ya motherfucker!"

Phil idly shook his notepaper. "This is penny-ante, Paul. What I want more than any of this nickel-dime shit is the location of Natter's lab."

"I don't know nothin' about Natter," Sullivan said. "Just that the ugly Creeker runs whores out of Sallee's."

"You're pulling my dick, Paul. Here I am giving you the best present of your life, and you're bullshitting me again. That's no way to show gratitude, is it?"

Sullivan slammed his handcuffed wrists on the interview table. "You're the one bullshitting, ya fuck!" he yelled. "I knew this was a crock! I just dropped the whole operation in yer lap, and now you're not gonna give me shit!"

Phil didn't flinch, though to himself he had to admit that Sullivan's outburst was a bit intimidating. Sullivan was a big man. *You know, Phil,* he considered to himself, *if he broke out of those cuffs, you'd be in a world of hurt. I don't see any coffee tables here.* "Let me put it this way, Paul. This shit here—" Phil held up the piece of notepaper, then crumpled it up and tossed it over his shoulder; he'd already committed it to memory, but the gesture seemed very dramatic—"it doesn't mean squat to me. I couldn't care less about a bunch of pissant punks like you—I want Natter's lab, and if you don't give it to me, I'll make sure you do the full ten big ones with no parole." Which, of course, was way beyond his power as a police officer, but Sullivan didn't know that. So why not pour on a little more? "Shit, Paul, I'll even lie to the judge; I'll tell him that I saw you kill Blackjack. Then you go up for fifty."

Sullivan's face turned beet-red; it was a terrifying and nearly inhuman visage. The muscles in his forearms flexed, showing puffed, dark blue veins, and his massive chest threatened to tear open the orange prison shirt. "You can't treat me like this, ya motherfuckin' cop! We had a deal!"

"What deal?" Phil said, and smiled like a cat.

Yes, indeed, it was fun putting the squeeze on a guy like Sullivan, but there was one problem with someone like this. They weren't exactly stable. And Phil found this out the hard way when Sullivan, handcuffs notwithstanding, leapt up, kicked the table over, and plowed into Phil's chest.

"Ho, boy!" Phil fell backward in his chair. Sullivan was all over him, snapping his cuffs as he grabbed for Phil's throat. *Never mess with mad dogs,* he remembered his aunt telling him once. *'cos you'll only make 'em madder, and they'll git ya.* Well, this mad dog was definitely gittin' him; Phil thrashed under Sullivan's dense muscled weight. "Guard!" he yelled, but by then Sullivan already had his throat, and the sound that came out was little more than a loud rasp.

"So ya like fuckin' with people, huh, bub?" Sullivan inquired, wringing Phil's neck like a sponge. "Let's see how ya like this!"

Through warped vertigo, Phil noticed that his opponent's face more resembled some sort of a kid's devil mask. The other night had been different; Sullivan had been half-asleep, and Phil had enjoyed the element of surprise—not to mention the coffee table— but now the guy was so wired-up mad Phil couldn't even get a punch in.

Whap! whap! he heard just when he thought his neck would break.

The weight lifted. Phil squinted up to see two county detention officers dragging Sullivan off. A third officer calmly re-sheathed his nightstick. "You all right?"

"Yeah, yeah," Phil said and clumsily rose to his feet. Meanwhile, the other two guards had Sullivan face-first against the wall and were re-cuffing his hands behind his back. "Put a collar on that guy," Phil said. "Don't let him get out of the yard."

"This punk's been nothing but trouble since the minute he got his ass thrown in here," the guard remarked. "Say, you're bleeding a little. You want to go to the infirmary?"

"Naw," Phil said, wiping a handkerchief at a small cut on his lip. "Sorry about the hassle. How'd I know he was gonna go berserk?"

"Happens all the time."

Phil walked up to Sullivan, who was now chicken-winged in front of the other two guards. "Think about it, Paulie. You got no one else to play ball with."

"Go ahead and take a shot if ya want," one of the detention officers said. "What's funny about us prison guards is we got really bad vision."

"No, I think I've fucked with him enough today. You can take Mr. Sullivan back to his suite now."

"You fuckin' cops are all alike," Sullivan growled as the guards tugged at him. "One day I'm gonna bust your head."

"Paul, by the time you get out of here, you'll be so old you won't be able to bust an egg. I'll let you sit a few more days in general pop, then maybe I'll come back and see if you're ready to have another chat."

"What the hell is wrong with you?" Mullins asked, gawking from behind his desk. "Last night you get in a shootout and wind up killing six Creekers, and today you're getting your ass kicked by prisoners."

"Not kicked," Phil corrected. "Royally kicked. The guy went bonkers. I was playing with him, sure, and not exactly telling the truth about some things, but he went schizo on me. Took three screws to pull him off."

"And the fucker didn't give you the loke on Natter's lab?"

"Nope. He gave me everything but. I already called the county tac team; they'll be checking out that other lab. But as far as Natter goes, I struck out."

"He'll never spin on Natter," Mullins said. "If he does, he knows Natter's people will be waiting for him the second he walks out of the pokey. And he knows what they'll do. These other guys—they're lightweights, and guys like Sullivan ain't afraid of lightweights. But Natter and his Creekers?"

"Different story," Phil agreed. "You're right. I didn't even think that that could be the reason he squealed on his own outfit but not Natter's."

Mullins scanned Phil's notes which he'd uncrumpled before he'd left the lockup. "Good work. I can't wait for the county to bust this new lab."

"Natter'll probably be pretty happy about it, too," Phil observed. "There goes his competition. But we still gotta get him." Oh, yes, he thought. It was personal now, or perhaps it had always been. All he had to do was remember what Natter had done to Vicki, not to mention having Eagle killed. And then there's always me, he reminded himself. Only now was he fully realizing how close he'd come to getting killed last night.

"Sullivan said something weird," he pointed out next. "I asked him if he knew what those words meant—"

"What words?" Mullins asked, replenishing his bloated jowl with chewing tobacco.

"Those weird words the Creeker kid said just before I blew him away. Sullivan didn't know what they meant, but he did know they were Creeker words. 'Creeker talk' he called it."

"Just proves Sullivan knows more about Natter's people than he's letting on."

"Yeah, I know. But he said something else, too. He said that the Creekers were cannibals."

"Wives' tales," Mullins suggested. "I been hearin' shit like that since I was a kid. It's stuff our daddies dreamed up to keep us in line. 'You don't shut up and go to sleep, the Creekers'll come and get ya.'"

"Yeah, sure, local legends and all that. I remember some of those stories, too. But Sullivan said one more thing that was pretty specific. He said the Creekers have their own religion."

Mullins expectorated into his cup. "Oh, you mean they ain't Catholic?" he attempted to joke.

Phil gazed blankly out the window. It was getting dark now, the smudged panes filling up with twilight. Their own religion, he recited. In the black sky, stars shone like swirls of crushed gemstones.

*I wonder what it is they worship.*

"Ona," the Reverend voiced to himself.

His voice was a black chasm, incalculable, endless like the night. The Reverend wore raiments just as black. Just as incalculable…

The shadow stirred in the corner. The Reverend could feel the miraculous heat, could smell the exalted stench.

*Oh, how long we've waited,* his thoughts wept in joy.

Ages.

No, a hundred ages.

He thought of things then, beautiful things. He thought of the recompense of all the truth of history. Of a time when the slaves would be freed of their fetters, when they would be praised instead of reviled, glorified instead of cursed. He thought of a time when he too would walk with his brethren through the holiest dark channel-works, amid the savory smoke of burning human fat and steaming blood, to gladly pay homage, and to eat. A time when he too, and all of them, would pull the flesh off the bones of the faithless, sink deft fingers into their wide open eyes, and strip their skulls of their pitiable faces. Their screams would ring out like the sweetest madrigals. They would inhale their blood and scarf their unchaste flesh forever and ever.

Yes, the Reverend thought of the most wondrous things.

*Ona…*

The Reverend bowed, then fell to his knees, his arms red with blood to the elbows.

*Soon, your time will be upon us.*

And from the stygian dark, his god looked back at him and smiled.

# TWENTY-SEVEN

"Hi," Phil said.

The station door slammed. Susan trudged in, a knapsack full of her school books tugging at her arm.

"Need some help with those books?"

"No." She dropped the sack at the foot of her desk, then sat down at her commo console and prepared for work.

"How was school tonight?"

Susan frowned at him. She wasn't biting on the cursory small talk, but then Phil never really guessed that she would.

"What are you doing here?" she asked.

"Talking to the chief." He shuffled his feet, looking down. He felt like a little kid sent to the principal's office. "Then I thought I'd hang around awhile, wait till you got in."

"Why?" Susan sniped, checking the hot sheet and county blotter.

"Well, I think we should talk."

"About what?"

Phil looked down at the floor. *This was a lost cause before it started. Christ—women are so unforgiving.* He didn't know what to say then. But at the same moment a notion struck him very keenly. *Forgiven? Wait a minute, Phil—don't be a schmuck. What do you have to be forgiven for here? You didn't do anything WRONG!*

So against his better judgment, he mustered an unfounded gall:

"I didn't do anything wrong!" he yelled.

Her expression seemed to recoil.

"Go ahead, make a face!" he yelled again. "Give me the cold shoulder! Treat me like dog shit! Do whatever you want, honey, but tell me this. What did I do wrong?"

"You didn't do anything wrong," Susan calmly replied, paging through her code book. "It's a free country. You can do anything you want. You don't have any obligations to me just because we went to bed. That certainly doesn't mean we're involved."

"Well, pardon me if I'm just stupid, but I kind of thought that we were involved."

"You thought we were involved?" She gaped at him. "Well, then I guess we both have drastically different definitions of the word."

"What's that supposed to mean?"

She gaped at him again. Phil didn't like it when she gaped.

"Doesn't involvement imply some kind of monogamy?" she asked.

"I didn't cheat on you!"

"Oh, I see. I hear a scream coming from your room," she went on, "so I come down to see if you're all right, and what do I find? I find monogamous Phil, with a bath towel around his waist, leaning over a prostitute."

"I didn't sleep with her!" Phil yelled.

"Oh, then what did you do? Tell me, Phil. What do guys with towels around their waists do with prostitutes? Play chess? Read the Sunday Post? Discuss the vagaries of quasi-existential dynamics?"

"I didn't have sex with her," Phil nearly growled.

"Oh, okay. You didn't have sex with her. But you can have sex with whoever you want, Phil. That's not my point."

Phil felt like a pressure cooker about to blow its seam. "What is your point?" he asked as calmly as he could.

"My point is you lied to me."

Silence.

"How did I lie to you?"

If looks could kill, Phil would be dead now, a dozen times over. Her eyes leveled on him. "Before you and I did anything, I asked you, didn't I? I asked you if you were still involved with Vicki. And you said no."

"And that was the truth!" he yelled.

"So what was she doing in your room with you standing there with a towel wrapped around your waist?"

"She had a problem," he said. "She got beat up, and she needed a place to sleep."

"So you thought your bed would suffice?"

"She slept on my couch! I didn't touch her! And I just got done telling you—I didn't have sex with her!"

More silence, but it was not a contemplative kind of silence; it was a mocking one. "So you're telling me," Susan asked, "that, since you've been back to town, you haven't slept with her?"

"I—" Phil began. If there was one thing he could never do, it was lie to her. If he lied, he was as phony as the phoniest guy on earth.

"Well," he admitted, "I did once. But not today. It was last week—before you and I even went out."

She seemed to sit in a dull shadow generated by her own anger and disappointment. It made her bright-blond hair less bright, her blue eyes like ruddy stones. Her voice sounded just as ruddy when she said, "I'd have to be out of my mind to believe a load of crap like that."

"Susan, you've got this all wrong—"

She mockingly glanced at her watch, then looked up at him again. "Oh, you're still here?"

Phil turned and went out the back through Mullins' office. Why flog a dead horse? *She'll never trust me in a million years,* he realized. *I fucked it all up—good job, Phil. I wonder what else you can fuck up today.* He could scorn himself forever, but that would not change the fact that there was nothing else he could do.

*Clank!*

Out by the back driveway, Phil looked to his left. The door stood open to the old lockup, which Mullins had converted to a supply room. *He must be in there now,* Phil deduced, noticing both the patrol cruiser and Mullins' own sedan still in the lot. *Probably getting more coffee and Red Man.* Phil strode on toward his car. It was back to Sallee's, to start all over again now. The low moon shone pasty yellow, just rising over the top of the station. Cricket sounds throbbed steadily.

Phil turned again, much more abruptly this time, at yet another sound coming from the old lockup.

The sound of breaking glass.

It was probably nothing—*The chief probably dropped a coffee pot*—but Phil thought it best to investigate anyway. What if it wasn't Mullins? What if someone was actually breaking in? *Yeah, the rednecks around here are even stupid enough to bust into a police supply room,* Phil considered.

The building stood merely as a drab cinder block edifice about the size of a typical trailer. Phil entered cautiously. A single low-watt bulb lit the dusty hallway. Another door stood open at the end. Phil decided not to call out; in the event that someone was burgling the place, the element of surprise would work greatly to his favor.

He walked very quietly to the next door, peeked in, and—

*What the hell is this?*

—noticed at once that this was no supply room. It was what it always had been. A jail.

Three barred cells lined the wall. The first two were empty. Mullins bent over before the third, picking pieces of glass off the floor.

"Ya fuckin'A-hole dimwit. Ya busted a perfectly good glass," Mullins griped.

But who was he griping to?

"Hey, Chief?" Phil spoke up. "What gives?"

Mullins glared up, his fat, round face inflamed. "What the hell are you doing here!" he shouted.

Then Phil saw why his chief was acting so guilty. In the third cell, which Mullins claimed had been empty for years, sat an unshaven, overweight young man.

A prisoner, Phil realized. Mullins had a prisoner in here all this time and never told me... "For shit sake! I was gonna tell ya!" Mullins insisted.

"Yeah, right, just like you were gonna tell me about how for the last six months you've been finding mutilated bodies all over god-damn town!" Phil was so mad he was shaking. "Yeah, you were gonna tell me, Chief, only you didn't! Christ, you never would've told me if I hadn't found out on my own!"

"Phil, you're jumpin' the gun here. Let me ex—"

"Goddamn, Chief! Everything you tell me is a crock of shit! And now this—" Phil extended a hand to the third jail cell. "You tell me you haven't used the lockup for anything but a supply room, and now I walk in and see you've had a prisoner in here all along! What the hell's going on?"

"Well, if you'd shut up and quit yelling a minute and let me fuckin' talk—"

Once again, Phil couldn't help but feel totally betrayed by his boss; this was the third or fourth time Mullins had oddly withheld information from him. Red-faced, then, he jerked his gaze into the cell. "And who the hell is this guy anyway?"

"His name's Gut Clydes," Mullins said. "Just another local punk selling dust and raising hell. Came in here one night all wired up and crazy, saying he'd been attacked by Creekers."

"Creekers?" Phil asked, as astonished as he was outraged. "This fucking guy was attacked by Creekers, and you wouldn't let me question him?"

"He said he was attacked by Creekers," Mullins corrected. "Don't believe a word of it—he was hallucinatin', the fucker could barely walk, he was so high on dust."

"No, I weren't!" exclaimed the guy in the cell. "And it's true, it was Creekers that jacked us up that night. And it was Creekers who killed my buddy."

"Shut up, ya A-hole," Mullins replied, "before I kick ya straight into the county can. Probably what I shoulda done in the first place."

"What did you charge him with?" Phil asked.

"Nothing. I'm just lettin' him dry out for a while."

Phil rolled his eyes big-time. "Chief, you can't just keep a guy in jail without charging him and filing with the DA for an arraignment."

"Shore I can; this is a personal matter. I'm not charging the kid on account of his daddy's a friend of mine. Figure I'll let him dry out in there a while, and hopefully the fat punk'll learn his lesson. Besides, he don't want to leave—don't believe me, go ahead and ask him. And I didn't bother tellin' ya about him 'cos I wanted to wait till he'd gotten his head straightened out before I let you question him. Shit, for a week he wasn't talkin' nothin' except the craziest load of malarkey you ever heard, and he ain't much better now."

None of this sounded right, but it was beginning to occur to Phil that nothing Mullins said ever sounded right. True, chronic PCP users frequently required several days or even weeks to detoxify enough to regain their mental coherence, and it was also true that they frequently hallucinated. But at this precise moment that didn't matter much.

"You think I'm bullshitting you, don't ya?" Mullins challenged, his steely eyes leveling.

"Yeah," Phil said. "I think I do."

"Why would I do that?"

"I don't know. I don't know what to think any more."

"All right," Mullins grumbled. "The fucker's crazier than a possum in a shithole, but don't take my word for it. What do I know, I've only been the fuckin' chief around here for thirty fuckin' years. Go ahead and question him, then you can tell me about all the great reliable information you got out of the guy. Go ahead, go ahead, waste all your time—see if I care." And with that final objection, Mullins huffed out.

Phil turned on another light and peered into the cell, to get a closer look at its occupant. The kid sat dejected on his cot next to a metal sink and toilet. Jeans, sneakers, baggy T-shirt, and a belly on him that rivaled Mullins'. Long, stringy brown hair dangled at his shoulders, and he obviously wasn't given to shaving with any regularity. Just another fat, going-nowhere redneck, Phil suspected. But his name, Gut, rang a quick bell—one of Sullivan's point runners, one of his "replacements."

"So, Gut, what's your story? How long you been in there?"

"'Bout a month, I guess. It ain't bad. Chief Mullins, he brings me in food three times a day, decent stuff from like the Qwik-Stop and Burger King, and takes me ta the shower ever so often."

*Qwik-Stop and Burger King*, Phil mused. *All the daily nutritional requirements for a growing boy.* "Is it true you don't want to leave here?"

"Well, yeah, it's true."

"Why's that? Why's a kid your age want to sit in jail?"

Gut ran a hand over his face, looking down between his feet. "I figure if I stays in here long enough, they'll ferget about me."

"Who's they, Gut? The Creekers?"

"Yeah." The kid gulped at the sound of the word. "The Creekers."

Phil sat down on an opposite bench. Typical. Drug-induced paranoia. A common trait among chronic PCP-users. "And what's this you say about them killing a buddy of yours? Would that be Scott-Boy?"

Gut looked up from between his knees. "Howdja know that?"

"I know a lot of things, Gut," Phil said. "I know you've been driving drop-off points for some new dust lab backed by some money guy from Florida. I know you guys have been trying to take the local dust market from the regular supplier. And I know you've been working with Eagle Peters, Paul Sullivan, Jake Rhodes, and Blackjack."

"Shit, man. Who's been walking all over me?"

"Don't worry about it. All those guys? They're all either dead or disappeared. Your competition has been hitting them all, and they've been doing a damn good job. You should've seen Peters and Rhodes. Sullivan ever tell you why he took you and Scott-Boy on to drive points?"

"Naw. Why?"

"Because everybody they had doing the job beforehand disappeared. And there's one more thing I know, Gut. I know that it's Natter and his Creekers who're making the hits. He's been using Sallee's as a distro point. I want you to tell me where his lab is."

Gut looked suddenly perplexed, or just stupid. "Natter? I don't know nothin' 'bout Natter. Paul never told me exactly who we were selling against."

Jesus, not this shit again, Phil thought. "Come on, Gut, don't bullshit me. It's nice and safe in there, but I don't think you'd like the county slam. You ever heard the term 'boy-pussy, cell-block bitch'?"

"I swear, man. I don't know nothin' 'bout Natter dealing in flake. All I knows is it was him who had the Creekers do the job on Scott-Boy."

"You saw Natter kill your buddy?"

"He was there. I knows it was him 'cos I seed him with my own eyes. At first I weren't sure on account of I was so shit-scared. But once I got out of there and turned myself in to Chief Mullins, I realized who it was. It was Cody Natter."

Phil took a time out, to control his excitement. *This was too easy. Five minutes ago I didn't have a case, and now I got an eyewitness who can testify that he saw Natter perpetrate a drug-related murder. Guess I got up on the right side of the bed today.*

"But it weren't fer running flake that the Creekers jacked us up," Gut continued, staring out from the darkness in his cell. "It was Scott-Boy, see? We picked up this chick hitchin' that night— Scott-Boy had a mind to give her a goin' over, ya know, we was out rucking. But it turns out this chick's a Creeker. So's Scott-Boy's got her in the truck gettin' ready ta do her, and all's a sudden there's Creekers all over the place, and they'se haul him out and slit him open right there in the dirt. It was, like, fer sackerfice or somethin'."

Phil's face drooped as he looked back through the cell bars. What the hell is he talking about? "Gut, you're telling me the Creekers killed Scott-Boy as part of a sacrifice?"

"Yeah," Gut replied with no reluctance—and, it seemed, with no lack of belief. "Cody Natter, he's pure evil, see?"

"Pure evil?"

"That's right, the evilest man I ever seed. Them Creekers, they worship themselves a demon, and it's to this demon they sacker-fice folks."

Phil shook his head. "How do you know this, Gut?"

"I know it on account of 'cos Natter, see, he come in here and told me."

"Wait a minute, wait a minute, Gut," Phil caught him up. "You're telling me that Cody Natter came into this jail one night and told you this stuff about sacrifices and demons?"

"Er, well, it weren't like he came in here phys-ick-erly." Gut, then, pointed to his temple. "He come inta my head, see? Most ever night. Sometimes while's I'se sleepin' and sometimes not. And he whispers ta me and shows me things, in my head. He shows me this demon, and he shows me hade's place. Says he's got hisself a special place fer me down there once he gits me."

*Oh, for Christ's sake,* Phil thought in disgust. *There goes my eye-witness right out the window. I can see him sitting up on the stand testify-ing and then telling the judge that Natter comes into his head at night and shows him demons.* Phil despondently put his face in his hands and rubbed his eyes. "You know, Gut, that shit you do really fucks up a person's brain."

"What shit ya talkin' 'bout?"

"Dust, Gut. Flake. PCP. It's fucking horse tranquilizer pro-cessed through paint thinner and industrial solvents. It causes irreversible brain receptor damage."

"Aw, but ya got it wrong. I ain't smoked flake but maybe twice in my life, and that were years ago. Didn't like it, so's I never did it again."

*Yeah, right, and the Pope shits in the woods.*

"Now I ain't sayin' we weren't movin' it. What me an' Scott-Boy did, see, was we used ta wait behind bars at night and jack guys out fer their green. Scott-Boy, he had hisself a pair of brass knucks that'd do a zinger on the biggest of fellas. And we went on doin' that some, when the pickin' was ripe, but, see, we could make lots more scratch faster by running drops fer Sullivan and Eagle. Folks buy the shit right up, any town you can name from here ta Lockwood. Big money ta be made. 'A'course, I knows now all that shit we pulled, either ruckin' or working fer Sullivan, was bad. And I also know that's why Natter wants ta git me, to send me ta hade's place where I'll have ta pay fer my sins. See, what he plans to do is snatch me when I get outta here, and then he'll take me to the demon."

Phil groaned. Why does this shit always happen to me? Why do I always get the live ones? So far, nothing jibed. Every time he got close, his leads turned to garbage. It was almost like this case had put a curse on him.

"It's part of their religion," Gut said.

Phil's thoughts stalled a moment. Religion. What had Sullivan told him at the county lockup?

Something about the Creekers' religion...

But that was ridiculous. Mullins was right: Gut was obviously suffering from a PCP-related psychosis. Cranzier than a possum in a shithole, you ain't kidding, Chief. Nothing Gut said could be deemed reliable. He wasn't fit to testify, and never would be.

"Thanks for your time, Gut," Phil got up and said. "You sure you don't want me to let you out of there?"

Gut flinched at a sudden pang of fright; his belly jiggled. "No, man, please. I ain't safe nowhere's else. Please don't make me leave."

"All right, Gut. You want to stay in there a few more days and get your head together, that's fine."

"Ain't nothin' wrong with my head. I know it all sounds crazy, but it's true."

"Sure, Gut. Later."

"And you best be careful, man. Don't go messin' with Natter and them Creekers, or else they'll be doin' the same job on you they did ta Scott-Boy. They'se be sacker-ficin' you to that there demon."

"I appreciate your concern, Gut, and you can be certain I'll keep it in mind." Jesus, just what I need, another whack, Phil thought. Aren't there enough eight balls in the world?

Phil began to walk out, but before he made it to the hall, a single word sounded behind him:

"Skeet-inner."

He stopped, stood a moment. The word nailed him in place. He walked back to Gut's cell.

"What does that word mean?" he asked very slowly.

"That's what they calls the demon," Gut replied. "I thinks it's sort of a nickname, 'cos it's got another name, too."

"What's that?"

"Ona," Gut said.

# TWENTY-EIGHT

S keet-inner, Phil thought. Ona.
He drove the Malibu down the Route, the two words hanging like vapor in his mind. They wouldn't go away.

A demon.

Phil didn't believe in demons, but he definitely believed there
were lots of people who did. The country was full of whacked-
out cults that worshipped the devil—you read about them in the
papers every day. And a lot of these cults incorporated drug-use in
their rituals, and also sold drugs to finance their activities.

Before he'd left the station's jailhouse, he'd asked Gut about the
other words he'd heard. Mannona. Onamahn. Prey-bee. Where
Sullivan had dismissed them as "Creeker talk," Gut had indeed
verified them as still more designations regarding the Creekers'
religion...

It could all be meaningless, but then again, everything Phil
found out about Natter and his Creekers would lend a better
understanding of them. And the more he understood them, the
closer he could get.

Except when all my leads are either crazy, clamming up, or
dead, he reminded himself. Starting from scratch would be a pain
in the ass, but there was no other alternative. He'd have to go back to
Sallee's and try to cultivate more low-lifes, get back into the scene.
Still too early, though, he realized when he looked at his watch. The
denizens didn't generally start coming in till midnight or so.

To kill time, he went back to his room and read more in the
books he'd gotten from the library. One text did indeed mention
a frequency among inbred communities to participate in non-
Judeo-Christian systems of worship. This, of course, stood to reason: in their sheer isolation, such communities and settlements
had no exposure to more popular religious beliefs. They existed
and developed within their own spheres of influence; therefore, it

made sense that their theological beliefs would develop on their own, too. Most of these religions, though, were nature-oriented, or revolved around self-made superstitions. Many actually were rooted in guilt-syndromes; in other words, the inbreds believed that the "gods," through birth deformities, were punishing them for their sins. And those born non-defected were frequently given higher social status; sometimes they were even worshipped themselves as semi-gods, as proof of forgiveness. The book, however, made no mention specifically of demonological beliefs.

In time, Phil's curiosities took him back to the more technical text, the one with photoplates. Again, his most immediate observation came when comparing the book's most extreme examples of inbred defectivity to the most extreme examples he had seen himself among Natter's Creekers. The enlarged heads (hydrocephalus), lengthened bone structures (endo-acromegaly), and cleft skulls (cranial bivalvism or "split-head syndrome") were all well-known traits of congenital inbred birth defects, all caused by hypersecretions of pituitary growth hormones. Also common were crimson irises, additional or missing fingers and toes, even extra limbs (adulterated biamous appendagalus). But it was the extent of these extremes that struck Phil right off.

The textbook depictions were minor in comparison. He understood that the more actively inbred the community, the more grievous the defects. And this could only mean that Natter's Creekers had been inbreeding for a very long time.

Next the text delved deeper into causal aspects of inbreeding. Initially, parental or sibling reproduction presented only one chance in about nine of producing a defected offspring. But it was exponential. After generations of incestuous reproduction, a community's gene pool became so corrupted that normal births were rare. The text gave examples of several such communities which hadn't known a normal birth in decades, yet—quite futilely—these same communities would inbreed even more actively on the false assumption that the more births they achieved, the greater the chances of a rare normal birth.

God, this stuff's dense, he thought, reading on in the lamplight. Some of the words hurt his eyes just to look at.

Here was an oddity: homeoaxial transfective deflection—What a mouthful, Phil thought—a congenital syndrome where a person displayed horrendous defects while remaining possessed of

absolutely normal reproductive genes. And here was another oddity, the kicker:

"Hierarchal savantism." Phil had skimmed this description
the other day, but now he read it carefully. One more commonality
among inbreds. By some chromosomal fluke (which was termed
homotopic genetic inversionism), some were born with grievous
physical defects but normal if not brilliant minds, and these persons often became the community's leaders...

Natter, Phil thought.

At midnight, he embarked for Sallee's.

The notion of religion continued to peck at him. Were the
Creekers really an inbred cult that worshipped a demon? And
were they actually sacrificing people in some sense of appease-
ment, or in some plea for forgiveness? And if so:

Was Natter the "priest" of the "sect"?

Phil shivered. The entire idea shed new light on Natter's possible motivations. *Maybe he's more than just a pimp and a drug lord,*
Phil considered. *Maybe he's also some crackpot cult governor urging his
followers to commit murder...*

He parked in the back of Sallee's; the lot, as usual, was jammed.
Concussive music hit him in the face the second he walked through
the door. "Highway to Hell," the speakers thundered. Cigarette
smoke burned his eyes; the strobe lights flashed. Up on stage an
ungainly blonde scarred by tattoos was demonstrating the dex-
terity of her pectorals, flexing them to the beat, which made her
breasts jump up and down as if jerked by unseen strings. Then she
flung herself to the top of the brass stage-pole and spiraled all the
way down, a human corkscrew.

Don't worry, honey, you'll make the Olympics next time. Phil
pulled up a stool, and in less than a second a draft was placed
before him. "Ya never get here early enough," the keep complained.

"Don't tell me, I missed Sting whipping Ric Flair's ass."

"Ain't no way in hell the Stinger'd whup the Nature Boy. To be
the man—"

"I know...you gotta beat the man."

"You're catchin' on," the keep smiled. "But you did miss
Ravishing Rick Rude winning back his U.S. title from that putz
Ricky the Dragon Steamboat."

"Them's the breaks. Seen Paul or Eagle?" he asked to gauge a
reaction.

"Nope, not tonight," the keep replied immediately. He obviously knew nothing. "Can I interest you in a hot dog?"

"Maybe later." Phil shook his head to himself, then turned when the crowd's applause grew riotous. The tattooed blonde had stepped down, and in her place stepped Vicki.

More bad thoughts. He hadn't seen her since being "caught" by Susan, which probably hadn't been the most comfortable situation for Vicki. Yeah, he reflected sourly. I'll bet that really made her day.

The jukebox chunked on to the next song, and Vicki commenced with her set, flawlessly as ever. Her red hair glittered in the fracturing light; her high, large breasts swayed with her movements. Even now, seeing Vicki close to naked before a roomful of uncouth rednecks didn't exactly leave him overjoyed. And worse was the way she discreetly shot quick glances at him during her act. Yeah, she still loves me, he could plainly see. I better get out of here. He slapped cash on the bar and made for the back room.

Druck, ever the Creeker sentinel, stood by the door with his arms crossed, a meld of colors from the strobe roving his enlarged head.

"Hey, Druck," Phil greeted.

"Hey-uh."

"Can I get in back tonight?"

"Shore," Druck said.

"Kinda muggy tonight, ain't it?"

"Yeah."

"Seen Eagle or Paul?"

"Naw."

A real motormouth, yes, sir. Druck pushed the door open with his two left thumbs, and Phil walked through.

The back didn't seem as crowded tonight, not that he could see a whole lot in the darkness. The weird music churned in the air while light churned as well up on stage. "He-ah, come," a soft voice whispered, then a hand queerly took hold of his arm. Phil couldn't help but note that the single hand possessed only one finger, though the finger itself, by means of six or eight additional joints, was nearly a foot long; it coiled about his arm. A bosomed Creeker waitress with a grossly recessed forehead led him to a table. She wended through the semi-circle aisle with the aid of a tiny flashlight. But when Phil sat down and ordered a beer, he noticed that she'd been holding the flashlight with a thin, stunted "accessory" arm, small as a baby's, sprouting from her armpit.

*Jeeeeze…*

These sights, along with what he'd read not an hour ago, depressed him further. He glanced around to survey the audience now that his vision had acclimated. Shit, hardly anyone here. Then he glanced up to the stage…

The dancer appeared normal. Beautiful. Sleek-white in nothing but a frilled, lemon-yellow g-string. Glossy straight hair, black as pure obsidian, shimmered past her shoulders and covered her face like a smooth, silk veil. Hour-glass figure and lustrous white skin. Her legs were perfect, and her breasts—Perfect, Phil recognized. High and full, centered by pink, defect-free nipples. But the back room, he knew now, existed to accommodate those whose tastes were significantly bent: kinks and slobs who got off on the misfortunes of the handicapped and the defected. Phil noticed no extra fingers or toes, no warped head, crimped spine, multiple navels, or "accessory" limbs. *What's she even doing here?* he wondered. *There's not a thing wrong with her.* When the stage lights upped a little, Phil was able to see the number on her garter: 6.

And that gave him an idea.

He finished his beer, paid up, tipped the waitress, and went back out to the hall. Druck was still minding the door.

"Hey, Druck," he said. "I think I'd like to spend a little time with that last gal, number six."

Druck's swollen head nodded. "Uh-yeah. Purdy one, ain't she?"

"Sure is. So what's the deal?"

"Fifty fer a half."

Fifty bucks for a half hour must be what he means, Phil realized. "Square," he said. Then he discreetly slipped a fifty-dollar bill into Druck's twin-thumbed hand.

"Just ya go on out an'wait by the side door now," Druck said. "Name's Honey, an' she'll do ya right. Give her a few ta get ready."

"Okay, man. Thanks."

*Yeah, Mullins would love this, his star undercover cop soliciting a prostitute at a strip joint,* Phil joked to himself as he exited the club. But, no, he had no intention of soliciting sex from the girl. What he planned instead was simply a little discreet talk. *Drop a few hooks, slip in a few questions, see what I can get out of her.*

And perhaps she could even tell him what some of those strange words meant.

*Skeet-inner. Mannona,* he reflected. *Prey-bee. Onnamann.*

Of course, it might be all for nothing; most of the Creekers had serious speech impediments and could barely talk coherently, and some couldn't talk at all. But he wasn't making any headway in the club, so this seemed the next logical step. He had nothing to lose—except fifty bucks, he reminded himself.

As instructed, he waited by the ill-lit side door. The big road sign flashed, painting one side of his face in garish reds and yellows. The moon peeked at him from the tree line on the other side of the road, and the night's humidity seemed to suck the sweat out of his pores.

Then—

Phil turned.

The side door clicked open, then clicked shut. The girl stood before him in flashing silhouette.

She wore a red satin robe now. She stood there a moment. Her face remained occluded by the shiny black hair; she seemed to be looking at him through sliver-like black gaps.

"Hi," Phil said.

She opened the satin robe, fully nude beneath it.

"Got you's yer car here?" she asked in a strained peep of a voice.

"Uh, yeah," Phil faltered in reply.

"Well's then, come on," she said.


*No one believes me,* Gut lamented. *They all think I'm done plumb crazy.*

The darkness seemed almost gelatinous; only a slant of light coursed in from the bare bulb on the outer room's ceiling. Sometimes Gut could look into that darkness and gander the same things he saw in his mind every night. Awful things…

But at least here, in the jail, he was safe.

It was hard to keep track of time; it was hard to keep track of anything. But Gut would just as soon sit here and rot than leave 'cos he knew full well once he did that he was finished.

*They'd do me just like they did Scott-Boy.*

He never really slept now—he just dozed off every now and then and was jerked awake each and every time. By Natter's evil whispers, and by the hideous things he showed him in his head. Natter's wrecked face always seemed to hover just outside the bars, all squashed like something run over in the road, them dry puffy lips barely moving, them big blood-red eyes staring at him. Sometimes Natter'd scratch on the wall, and other times Gut thought he heard him tapping on the glass of the jailhouse's only window with those long kinky fingers of his. Gut, Gut, the whisper creaked like old wood. Look...

And Gut looked. He had no choice really. And Natter would say fancified things too, while Gut was looking, like, Such blessings, Gut! Such epiphanies! and Behold my promised dominion, little one. Upon some future time, it will be your dominion, too... And that's when Gut was forced to look into that place.

It was a horrible place. Smoking canyons of rock, miles deep. There was never a sun, just a big warped black moon shining its black light over blacker hills and lakes-yes, lakes, like giant steaming pools of tar, and Gut could see things in those lakes. He could see people. And then he saw other things that weren't people at all, but monsters. The monsters would pull people out of the lake and put a rucking on them like ta make the stuff he and Scott-Boy did look like two kids playing paddycakes. These monsters would bust open folks' heads like they was melons under Scott-Boy's big-ass hickory pick handle, and they'd yank off arms and legs likes they was wings on flies. They'd slice folks' bellies open and haul out their kidneys and livers and stuff and play catch with 'em, and they'd pull people's faces off like they was rubber masks only they wasn't masks at all, they was the folks' real faces. One time he'd seen one yank a fella's spine right out his asshole. They'd chop folks up into big piles of chunks and then walk around in the piles. Once he saw one suck some fella's insides right out his mouth lickety-split and swallered it all right down neat. And as for havin' themselves a nut—well, these ugly monster dudes got ta layin' dick on gals—and fellas, too—in a bigtime way. They'd stick their peters inta any hole they seed fit. Shit, one of 'em twisted a fella's head clean off and fucked his throat, and another time Gut saw one bite a hole in a gal's belly and get his rod off in the hole, and a whole lotta super gross shit like that...

And the whole time, Gut knowed full well what it was he was a'lookin' at. Sure as shit, yes, sir, he was lookin' smack-dab right down inta hell...

*Yeah,* he assured himself yet again, *but I'm safe in here. They can't get me in here...*

And that's when he noticed the two figures step out of the shadow by the doorway.

Two Creekers...

They peered crookedly into the cell, inbred red eyes sunk into their bulbed heads. One's face seemed jawless, the other had no ears and just a pit for a nose.

"You can't get me in here!" Gut yelled.

The two Creekers tittered and smiled. Then the jawless one advanced, jingling the keys to the cell door.

"What's this?" Phil asked. "This right here?"

"Huh?"

"This tattoo," Phil said, and pointed. His finger daintily touched her flesh, which felt moist and very soft.

It looked crude, primitive, burned onto the milk-white skin of her upper left arm. Probably homemade, he realized. Did it with ink and needles herself. The tattoo, tiny as it may have been, clearly depicted a horrifying face whose mouth was crammed with jagged teeth. Two stubs modestly sprouted from its head.

Horns, he realized.

"It looks like a demon. Is that what it is, Honey? Is it a demon?"

"Deem-nom," she attempted. The mispronounced word sounded like a child talking with a sore throat. Her shining hair remained hanging in front of her face; she smelled slightly sweaty. Only a few wedges of blinking light from the road sign seeped into the car. The girl elected not to answer Phil's question—if she'd understood it at all—but instead slid over right next to him.

The bench seat's springs groaned as Phil, in reaction, slid away a few inches. "Honey, listen..."

At once her perfect hands touched him, one rubbing his neck, the other sliding to and fro along the inside of his thigh. "Blow job, ya want?" she asked. Then her hand slid directly over his crotch and squeezed.

Ho, lord! Phil thought and immediately jumped in the seat. He took her hand away and placed it in her lap. "Listen, Honey, I just want—"

"Fuck me, ya wanna then, huh?" she presumed. "Everwhat ya want, s'okay," and then she reopened the satin robe and let it slide off her pretty shoulders. Suddenly Phil was looking right at her perfect bare breasts. Jesus, he thought, and promptly gulped. "No, Honey, that's not what I want either," he said and pulled her robe back up over her.

"Oh-uh," she murmured. Then her head bowed in a pause. "Hit me ya wanna, I guess."

Phil shook his head. The girl's plight was just another exercise in despair. She thinks I want to beat her. "Honey, I don't want to hit you, I don't want to hurt you. I don't want to do anything except talk."

"Talk?"

"That's right, I just want to talk to you for a few minutes."

She peered back at him through her raven hair, as if in complete confusion. "Hit me no?"

"No, Honey, I won't hit you." The whole thing was so sad when he contemplated what life must be like for her. Though no deformities were noticeable, she was still one of Natter's Creeker whores: kink fodder. Probably gets slapped around every night, he realized. Tied up, beaten, you name it. "Let's just talk, okay?"

"Talk I-uh good-no, er no good," she peeped.

"You talk fine. I can understand you fine." He wanted to set her at ease; he didn't want her to be afraid of him, or think he was just another sick redneck slob who wanted to use her. "But first, let's get all this hair out of your face," he said calmly, and then he reached across and pushed her hair back.

And nearly shuddered.

Be cool, he ordered himself, and then quelled the urge to recoil. Once he'd pushed her hair back, her deformity was manifest.

At first she seemed to have no face at all; he was looking at her left side, and her face was—

Nothing, he saw. Featureless, No eyes, no mouth, no nose. Just...skin.

Then she turned her head toward him. Jesus, he thought, and it was a dry, inhuman thought. Nature had pushed her face all the way over to the far right side of her skull: tiny mouth, tiny nose, two tiny red eyes all existing in a narrow strip running from her right temple to her chin...

"Ugly me," she wisped. "I know."

"No, you're not, Honey," he said. "You're just different."

"Iffer-dent."

"Yeah, you're different, that's all, and there's nothing wrong with that." But these words of consolation were hard to form looking at her. Here was proof of what a monster nature could be. It was difficult for Phil to absorb all at once.

She tied the sash of her robe and quickly brushed her hair back in front of her face.

"What about you wanna talk?" she asked.

Crickets trilled in his ears, backed by the bizarre words he remembered. "I want you to tell me about...Ona," he said.

Suddenly the silence seemed to ooze from another world. Phil thought he could hear the girl's heart beating.

"Ona," she said.

"Tell me about Ona. It's a demon, isn't it?"

"Ona," she repeated. Then her hair-cloaked face turned to him—she seemed about to speak.

*Holy—*

Phil didn't have time to complete the thought. Shadows jerked and fluttered, maddeningly fast. At once his door was yanked open; misshaped hands reached in and hauled him out of the car. Can't get to my piece! he realized; one guy had Phil's arm twisted behind his back, and another had him in a half-nelson.

Creekers.

Phil's captors held him up on his feet beside the car. The more Phil struggled, the tighter they gripped him. Two more Creekers pulled the girl out and shoved her forward.

Then another figure advanced, a huge figure...

"Welcome to our world," a voice intoned. The voice was resonant, heavy as lead. "How do you like it?"

Phil squinted up. Standing before him, tall and still and frightfully gaunt, was Cody Natter.

"Tell these fuckin' apes to—let me go!" Phil shouted.

"In time. But first, I understand you've been making some inquiries about my proud family, hmm?" Natter's cracked face turned toward the girl. "Tell him, Honey. Tell our friend here about Ona."

The girl, still backed by two Creekers, shivered in Natter's presence.

"Go on, Honey—"

Then one of the Creekers put a buck knife in her hand.

"—our friend wants to know." Natter was staring intently at

the girl, his smile like a canyon gouged across his face.

"I-uh-yuh—" the girl muttered.

"Go on."

"I—"

"Go on."

Natter held his stare.

The girl raised the knife, croaked, "Ona-prey-bee," then—

"Noooo!" Phil screamed.

—dragged the knife so deeply across her throat that her head fell back as if hinged. She collapsed to the gravel immediately, blood pouring from the wound freely as water from an open spigot.

"You motherfucker!" Phil exclaimed, wincing at the downward pressure on his neck. "You ugly sick Creeker son of a bitch!"

"Really now," Natter chuckled. "I should think a police officer would be more politically correct."

I'm made, Phil realized. "Who fingered me?"

Gravel crunched. Natter laughed softly as another figure stepped out of the bank of shadows.

"Hey, bub."

It was Sullivan, his beady eyes fixed, his grin cocked.

"How the hell did you get out of jail?" Phil demanded.

Sullivan pinched Phil's face between his fingers. "Well, see, bub, that no-call order you slapped on me didn't wash with the public defender. He got it pulled. So I gave Mr. Natter here a call, and we had a nice long talk. And he was kind enough to post my bail."

"Natter, you asshole," Phil said. "Sullivan's the one who's been cornering your dust operation."

"My 'dust' operation, oh dear," Natter replied. The permanent smile seemed to appraise Phil with hilarity. "So you're the best that Mullins could summon? Such a sad state of affairs for our local law enforcement contingent."

"And, bub," Sullivan added, squeezing Phil's face harder, "I owe you a couple, and I think I'll pay ya back right now."

"Don't be a fucking id—" Sullivan rammed his fist into Phil's solar plexus. All the breath in his chest exploded out his throat, and his knees gave out.

"Hold him up. Lemme take a few more pops."

Phil was hanging by his elbows; his two captors hoisted him back up where his face was suddenly on the receiving end—

*whap! whap! whap!*

—of Sullivan's fists. Each blow jarred Phil's brain.

Then he fell to the ground.

His vision wobbled, his head reeled. Spitting blood, he managed to raise himself to hands and knees, and gasp, "You assholes, I'm a fucking cop, you can't do this to a cop!"

"Oh, but we can, my good constable," Natter informed him. Then—

*crack!*

Sullivan kicked Phil square in the chin. Phil's upper body snapped back, flipping him completely over in the gravel.

"No witnesses, bub," Sullivan said, wiping his hands.

Phil was close to passing out. He wasn't seeing stars, he was seeing galaxies. Footsteps scuffed around him in the gravel; chuckles and crisp laughter fluttered like birds. I'm losing it, Phil thought...

The Creekers picked him up and threw him into the car. Sprawled on the front seat, he sidled over, limp. He sensed more than saw Natter's big warped face leaning over.

"Go home, officer. And don't come back."

"Yeah, later, bub," Sullivan added. "Hope ta run into ya again sometime. Let's make it soon."

"But before you leave," Natter went on, "don't forget your prize. It's well earned."

More shuffling. More chuckles. Then a squeal...

A sudden weight landed on Phil's back. Someone else had been tossed into the car. The figures were walking away, their laughter fading. Eventually Phil was able to lift himself up. He turned his head, drooling blood, and saw that the other person they'd thrown into the car was Vicki—

*Those sons of bitches...*

And he could also see that she'd been beaten considerably worse than he had been.

# TWENTY-NINE

Somehow, Phil managed to drive back to his room; he didn't know how he was able to do this—instinct, perhaps. He'd practically had to lug Vicki down the hall. Blood dripping from her mouth left a trail along the floor. But—

Aw, no, he thought once he got her inside and had the door locked. His consciousness tripped around in his head like a rummie about to stumble and fall.

Eventually, and before he could tend to Vicki's wounds, he did indeed fall.

He fell into the cloaks of his past…

He was ten years old again, on the stairs of the House and running for his life. He'd just seen the whore-girl's big doglike teeth, and that was all he needed to know that this was the last place in the world he should be. His sneakered feet pounded down the stairs, his torn Green Hornet T-shirt hanging in flaps. Then he stopped short—

Halfway down the steps, he saw the figure.

It was a big figure, big as a wall, and it was just standing there, blocking his way out.

It stood in shadow, backlit. He couldn't see any features, just its shape, and just that it was big.

"Young man," it said, "curiosity is a commendable trait, but I think you and I have some talking to do."

Phil ran back up the stairs, his feet pacing with his heart. When he turned back right, he saw the whore-girl standing there cockeyed and grinning, and the fat guy holding Dawnie, and he was grinning, too…

So he turned again.

And raced back up another set of stairs to the next floor.

He was so scared he couldn't think. All he could reckon was the necessity of getting away from the giant figure on the stairs

And running up those stairs was like running through a swamp, it was so hot and humid.

*A window,* he thought mindlessly. *Find a window and climb out!* Never mind the long drop…

On the next landing, darkness seemed to swallow him. Yes, he was in the guts of the darkness, and its heat seemed to shimmer. Suddenly he was so hot he thought he would pass out, or maybe even die. He shuffled along, frantic, blind, his blood racing through his veins like a siren. Then his hands landed on something—

A doorknob.

He turned it and fell inward…

His breath blurted out as he landed on his belly. The bare wood floor felt damp and nearly too hot to touch when he pushed himself up. Threads of sunlight glowed through closed shutters. What…is this? he thought. It was just a room, sure, but—

Something was wrong.

Like the rest of this house, and the people in it, and the things that happened here, there was something wrong with this room. He knew it, he could feel it in its throbbing dark and in the thin white lines of sunlight pouring through the shutters' seams. He could feel it like breath on his neck.

Then he opened the shutters—

It wasn't movement that caught his eye. Instead, it was the sensation of sheer bulk, or perhaps it was breath on his neck all along, because when he opened the shutters and let the light blaze in, he knew there was something else alive in the room.

But Phil was too busy screaming to figure out what it was.

The door burst open. Figures clambered in: several of the whore-girls from downstairs, and several other men he hadn't seen, Creeker men with big melon heads and humped backs and crooked eyes. One of them held Dawnie in front of him, with a big three-fingered hand clamped over her mouth.

Phil crawled to the corner, screaming himself nearly into shock. He was helpless, limp, staring…

Then another figure entered the room—the giant man from the stairs.

His face was hideous in the sunlight. It looked squashed and filled with crevices, with two red Creeker eyes that looked bigger than Phil's fists.

"So the curious little boy has taken a liking to our sister," the voice rattled in the dark. "We have many sisters."

Every red eye in the room, then, turned to the corner opposite Phil. Phil couldn't scream anymore; he could only shiver, sweat, and stare at the bulkish, glistening thing that sat there on its side...

It sat in the dark, the sunlight streaming in front of it. There was little to describe...but a little was enough.

Long, thin, crippled limbs. A roughened, tubby torso. Two oval holes for eyes, and a giant warped head the size of a feedbag. Its skin—pocked, spotted, and gray, like a slug's—seemed smeared with some lumpy clear jelly. Shags of ribbony black hair hung in damp ropes nearly to the floor, and when it opened its mouth— a great thin slit a foot long—teeth like rows of carpet blades shimmered.

*Ona...*

*Skeet-inner...*

*Ona-prey-bee...*

In dumb horror, Phil realized that he wasn't hearing the words in his ears. He was hearing them in his head.

A tearing sound, a thin, wispy shriek. One of the Creekers ripped Dawnie's dirty dress off her body in one stroke and threw it aside.

*Onnamann, us-save...*

Mannona, come...

The giant man from the stairs stepped forward, the crevices in his squashed face like gouges in clay. His voice rattled:

"We give you this day your daily flesh..."

Dawnie shrieked a final time as she was thrown into the corner with the thing. Suggestions of limbs reached out, hands more like feet, with clusters of foot-long fingers. Dawnie was quickly pulled into the darkness.

Then came a wet gnawing sound. And then—

*thump!*

Dawnie was thrown back out onto the floor.

The sunlight blazed. It wasn't Dawnie anymore, just the vaguely human shape of what was left of her. Radiant wet scarlet limbs askew on the floor. Scalped, faceless now. A tiny wet red body.

Fully and completely skinned.

The giant man's hand reached out and down like a descending vulture. He hauled Phil up, and then his dark voice grated: "Go now, boy. Run away fast." The red eyes drilled into Phil's face. "But we'll see you again someday."

"Phil? Phil?"

*pap-pap-pap*

"Phil?"

Repeated slight slaps to the face revived him. His eyes felt glued shut; when he opened them, he actually heard a peeling sound, and then realized that it was blood that had sealed them shut. He looked up at Vicki's blurred face, which seemed to swim above him. His consciousness corkscrewed.

He muttered one word: "Ona."

Did she scowl at him? The word seemed to put a pike in her expression. "You were out longer than I was. Are you all right?"

"I think so. Christ, that fucker Sullivan hit me hard."

"You were dreaming," she said.

Dreaming. Was he? Or was I remembering? Leaning up from the couch, he told her the whole story, twenty-five years late. About that day. About Dawnie, and the House, and the things he'd seen in it. "When I got back to my aunt's house, I had a bad fever. I was laid up for days, didn't know anything. The doctor came over, and I told him the story, and he told my aunt that I was hallucinating."

"You weren't," Vicki said.

Phil contemplated that, reserving comment. He looked at her. Her face was bruised, there was blood crusting her red hair, and her clothes were torn. He also noticed that some of her teeth were missing.

"They raped you, didn't they? I mean, before they beat you up and brought you out to the car?"

Very hesitantly, she nodded. "There were so many of them," she eventually murmured. "They were taking turns with me. They were all laughing while they were doing it."

"Don't talk about it," he said. "It's best not to even think about it. Look, I'm gonna check you into the hospital, then I've got some things to take care of." Oh, he had things to take care of all right. First, Sullivan, then Natter. And fuck the judicial process, he told himself. Why bother? He was going to tend to this himself.

"Don't take me to the hospital," she pleaded. "You don't know Cody. He'll figure that's what you did, then he'll send someone. You don't understand these people. They'll sacrifice themselves for him. He'll send someone to kill me. Just let me go with you."

What could he say? She's right. "Okay. Let's go."

He helped her up, and aided her down the hall and back out to the car. He had lots of questions, but he didn't want to pour them on all at once, not after what she'd just been through. "Let me ask you something, Vicki. How did Natter know that I'd seen you?"

"Watchdogs," she told him. "He had Creekers following me. They must've seen me come here... I'm sorry."

"Don't worry about it, it's not your fault." Watchdogs, huh? he thought. Well, I'll be putting a leash on them, and fast. It was close to two in the morning. He drove the Malibu down the Route to the station. "Shit!" he exclaimed when he pulled into the lot. Mullins' car wasn't there, and neither was Susan's.

Phil needed backup. And he needed guns.

"I gotta find some hardware," he said. "Come on."

In Mullins' office there was nothing, just file cabinets full of papers, and an equipment locker hung with junk. He tried calling Mullins, but there was no answer. No answer at Susan's either. And just as he hung up the receiver, the phone rang...

"Yeah?" he answered, wiping sweat. and blood off his brow.

The ancient voice creaked like an old house in the wind. "Didn't I tell you, all those years ago, that we'd see you again someday?"

*But we'll see you again someday,* his memories echoed.

He'd known the minute he regained consciousness that the giant figure from his childhood and Natter were the same...

And Natter's voice, now, rattled on. "An incentive, perhaps? Yes."

"What are you talking about, you fucker?" Phil yelled into the phone.

"There's someone here," Natter guttered on, "who'd like very much to talk to you." The line crackled, the pause seemed to last hours. Then:

"Phil?"

Phil's heart dropped. It was Susan.

"Phil, they have me!"

"Where are you?"

"They're doing...horrible things to me!"

Phil needn't imagine. "Tell me where you are!"

"Phil, don't come here! They'll kill you—"

Her voice was pulled away, and Natter's returned. "Incentive enough? Or…perhaps not. Listen, lawman."

A scream shot through the line. Phil winced.

"In case you're curious as to the cause of that scream," Natter told him, "I'll have you know that your good friend Mr. Sullivan just cut off one of your paramour's nipples with a pair of roofing shears. But perhaps you need even more incentive. Yes?"

"Stop it! I'll do whatever you say!" Phil yelled.

"Listen."

"No!"

Another of Susan's screams shrilled through the line.

"That," Natter said, "was the entirety of the breast. Your friend Mr. Sullivan really is deft with a knife."

"Hey, bub," Phil heard next. "Come on out. Let's party!"

Phil's emotions collided. He could picture what they were doing to her. And the only other thing he could picture was killing them all.

"Natter, you there?"

"Indeed."

"Don't hurt her anymore. I'll come out there. Just tell me where."

"Ah, a test. Think." Natter chuckled. "You know."

"No, I don't know! Tell me where you're at!"

"Little boy. You remember."

Click.

"Goddamn!" Phil shouted and slammed down the phone.

"They have Susan, don't they?" Vicki asked.

"Yeah. Why? Why did they take her? Why do they want me to come there when they could've killed me earlier at Sallee's?"

"I don't know," she said.

"Come on!"

They raced outside to the lockup. Maybe Gut, the prisoner, would be able to tell him something. And maybe Mullins had some guns stored there.

But he wilted when he trotted into the room of holding cells.

Gut had been…

Gutted, Phil observed.

He'd been hung by the neck from the cell's ceiling, his large abdomen drooping open like fat white lips from a spine-deep knife slash. His innards lay in a pile at his swinging feet.

He pushed Vicki out into the hall before she could see it all.

"Go down to the end of the hall and check out the storage room," he directed. "Look for guns, ammo, anything we can use for weapons. Hurry!"

Distracted, she did so, and Phil went back into the cell rows. Gut's cell door was unlocked. Who unlocked it? And when he looked closer, he noticed a scrap of paper pinned to Gut's chest.

Phil squinted through the bars.

WE'RE WAITING FOR YOU, someone had written on the note. In blood.

*Christ, they planned this whole thing. But why?*

He didn't waste time. Several more lockers lined the block. Phil rummaged through them all but found nothing in the way of weapons. What kind of a fucking police station is this? he outraged to himself. There wasn't a gun to be found. Like a fucking gas station with no gas! All he had was a puny .25, but he'd need a lot more than that for the undertaking he foresaw. A shotgun at least, and a couple of 9mm's would be nice. But in the last locker, in a box at the bottom, something caught his eye. He picked it up...

My God, he slowly thought.

It was a framed black and white picture, like something taken at a graduation, yellowed with age. Two men, in police cadet uniforms, stood smiling for the camera, their arms draped about each other's shoulders.

Phil couldn't believe what he was seeing.

One of the men was Mullins.

The other was Dignazio, the guy who'd set Phil up on the Metro scam.

"I just pulled up out front," came a voice from behind him. "Didn't want you to hear my car. Pretty nifty job they did on Gut, huh? It was me who gave 'em the keys."

Phil turned to face Mullins, whose bulk filled the block entry. The chief's fat hand was filled with a Colt .357.

"You set me up," Phil said stonily. "You had Dignazio kill that kid and plant the illegal rounds in my piece."

"You got it."

"Why?"

"To get ya back. Me and Dignazio, we been friends since we got out of the academy. I asked the guy a favor, and he did it. And me and Natter—well, we ain't exactly what I'd call friends, but we've always had an agreement. He runs his whores out of Sallee's and gives me a cut for lookin' the other way."

"And I guess he gives you a cut for looking the other way on his PCP network, too, huh?" Phil suddenly felt certain.

Mullins' big, bulbous face grinned at the remark. "Jeez, Phil, you must'a left your brains back at Metro along with your career."

"What's that mean?" Phil asked.

"Natter ain't got no PCP network."

Phil peered through his own confusion; he stood in an instant fog. No...network? Suddenly the revelation made sense: in all of his investigative work, he actually had found not one iota of evidence to suggest that Natter was dealing PCP. Just heresay, just lies. Just...Mullins, he realized.

"You've been lying to me the whole time. You've had me looking for a PCP lab that doesn't exist. You made the whole thing up."

"That's right, partner," Mullins admitted. "And you fell for it hook, line, and sinker. I know you've had a hard-on for PCP since Metro, so after I had Dignazio shit on you, I figured the quickest way to get you to take a job here was to make up some bullshit about Natter running dust. Shit, Natter ain't never run dust. It's all just been a bunch of cowboys like Peters and Sullivan and those guys, workin' for a couple of labs out of town."

"But...the murders—"

"Oh, sure, there've been murders for a long time, that part wasn't BS. Natter and his Creekers have been offing people for as long as I can remember. It was part of the deal. I looked the other way on that, too. And when time started to get short, I told him to start hitting local dust runners 'cos that way you'd be more likely to believe the whole story in the first place."

Hook line, and sinker, Phil thought. He's right. *Yeah, it all made sense now, all except one thing.*

"Why? Why?" he asked, utterly confused. "Why go to all that trouble? It almost sounds like you were trying to lure me back to Crick City."

"Something like that. It'll give ya something to think about on our way to Natter's."

"Oh, so you're going to deliver me, is that it?"

"Might as well, I'm here." Mullins waved the gun toward the exit. "Drop your piece on the floor, and don't try anything."

Frowning, Phil took out his pocket .25—his only weapon—and tossed it aside.

"Good boy. Now come on. You've got some driving to do."

Mullins kept his distance as Phil approached the exit. Shit, I'm had, Phil thought. He could try a disarm, but the chief wasn't close enough; making a move would get him shot. His only chance was a distraction...

And at the same moment, Vicki walked in. "Phil, I couldn't find anything in the storage—"

Mullins, taken by surprise, turned at Vicki's voice. Then Vicki shrieked. It was all the distraction Phil was going to get, so he took his chance, spun back, and hit Mullins across the bridge of his nose—crack!—with his right hand. With his left, he grabbed Mullins' gun.

A round went off; Phil flinched at the massive concussion. Next the two men were on the floor, wrestling. But Phil had the gun, and he shoved its blue-steel barrel under the chief's jaw. "Give it up!" Phil growled, but Mullins only struggled further, his own hands pawing at Phil's.

"Don't!" Phil yelled.

BAM!

The magnum discharged, bucking fiercely once in Phil's grasp. Cordite stinging his eyes, he lay still a moment. Mullins, however, lay significantly more still, his face agape. When the smoke cleared, Phil got up and saw that the chief's bald pate had been replaced by a ragged, pulpous crater. A fantail of brains plumed from the man's head across the shiny tile floor.

They took Mullins' souped squad car; it was more reliable than the Malibu, plus it had a pump shotgun in the dash-lock, and several revolvers which Vicki awkwardly loaded as Phil drove.

"Listen," Phil said. "Earlier, when I told you about what happened to me as a kid, you said it wasn't a hallucination."

"It wasn't," Vicki grimly replied. "It's all true. And that word you said when you came to—'Ona'—"

"What is it? It's a demon or something, right?"

"It's something they worship. It's their god."

Their god, Phil reflected as the Route wound through another bend. A demon...

"I don't know all the details," Vicki went on, "but the story goes like this. The Creekers have always worshipped a devil, a male devil named Onn. For hundreds of years they made sacrifices to it—incarnation sacrifices…"

"Yeah?"

Vicki's words darkened. "Well, supposedly, a long time ago, one of their rituals succeeded."

Phil's gaze saw little past the windshield. *Am I supposed to believe this? She's telling me that the Creekers incarnated a demon…*

"Their goal, for all that time, was to add the demon to their bloodline. They considered this to be the ultimate blessing. According to the story, Onn mated with the least defected Creeker girl in their clan."

"And then gave birth?" Phil guessed.

"Yes."

"But to what?"

"To Ona, the female inbred of the demon and the Creekers." Vicki paused. "That thing you saw when you were ten."

Phil fell silent again, driving without direction. So many queer ideas were wafting through his head, he didn't know what to think. "But they also call it 'skeet-inner'—"

"That's its nickname," Vicki said. "Most of the Creekers can't talk right—it's called dyslalia—like dyslexia, only with words. When they say skeet-inner, they're really saying—"

"Skin-eater," Phil deduced, and with the deduction came a crushing weight of contemplation. Rhodes, those other cowboys on the death reports, and Dawnie, he remembered. They were all skinned. "So the murders weren't really murders. They were sacrifices."

"To Ona," Vicki affirmed. "It's symbolic. Consuming the appearance—the skin—of the unflawed. The Creekers consider themselves cursed by their inbreeding, so they pay homage with sacrifice victims. It's the Creekers' gift to Onn, by providing uncursed flesh to Onn's inbred daughter. And the Creekers have been reproducing with it for generations."

Phil thought about it, gripping the wheel. It was just too crazy. "I don't believe it, Vicki."

"How can you not believe it? You've seen the Creekers, you've seen how deformed they are. You ever seen any other hillfolk as defected as the Creekers?"

"Well, no," Phil admitted.

"Most of them don't even look human, and that's because part of their bloodline isn't human."

Then Phil thought back to the books he'd read. She was right, at least in part. The worst-case examples in the photographs of typical inbreds weren't nearly as genetically defected as most of the Creekers he'd seen. The consideration chopped through his head. Creekers. Inbred. With a demon…

By now he didn't know what to believe. The only thing he was sure of was this: *Natter and his Creekers have Susan, and they're going to torture her to death unless I can find them.*

"Okay, so you're telling me that Ona is real, fine. Then the House must be real, too."

Vicki nodded.

"Tell me how to get there," Phil said.

# THIRTY

"So many years, so many ages," he whispered.

Eternity, he thought.

Years were grains of sand sifting through his fingers.

Multitudes had gladly given their blood, their lives.

Onn, he thought. And blessed Ona.

"Unto you we bow forever..."

Redeemer. Sanctifier. Holy father, holy daughter.

The visions sang to him; they always did. Entrails routed shone briskly from the bellies of the unfaithful. Blood squeezed from the heads of the unsaved. Screaming faces clawed at till they were screaming plops of pulp. Soon, yes, the cursed would become the blessed, the damned would rise to the dark heights of the absolved.

Soon they would go on, shed of their curse, enlightened instead of deprived, one with their master.

Forward into the new nights of a new age, perfect instead of corrupted, no longer in turmoil but in bliss...

Natter, the Reverend, opened his eyes upon the hot, starry night. His old, blotched skin felt new and young now. His ancient mind felt aglow. His savior whispered blessings to him.

The moon shined on the crags and furrows of his disfigured face. His triple-jointed hands opened to the sky.

"So many years, so many ages."

Time was no longer short.

Instead, the time was upon them.

# Thirty-One

"They're also telepathic," she said.

"What?"

Vicki shifted in the passenger seat, her red hair flowing about in the warm breeze from the window. "Ona," she said. "And Cody too, and some of the stronger Creekers. You can hear them in your head."

Phil scowled. "That's a load of—" But then he stopped. Wasn't that what Gut had told him? That Natter talked to him at night, in his head? And showed him visions? Even Phil himself had to acknowledge it. Twenty-five years ago, at the House, and just the other night when he and Eagle had been ambushed. He'd heard words, hadn't he?

*In my head.*

"Just tell me how to get to the House," he insisted.

"You don't believe it, do you?"

*I don't know what I believe,* he told himself. "Look, I don't want to hear any more about demons, all right? I got enough to worry about." That much was true. Like, how was he going to get Susan out? *If she's not dead already,* he added. And *since Natter was expecting him, and anticipating his motives, the House would surely be a fortress of armed Creekers. And all I've got to fight back with is a shotgun, three pistols, and a drug-addicted prostitute...*

"Just keep heading down the Route," Vicki instructed. "I'll tell you when to turn."

The night seemed crammed down onto the road; the mangy tree line on either side funneled them through each winding bend. Every so often the headlights caught the glimmers of possum eyes in the woods, which reflected red and reminded him all-too-keenly of the Creekers' crimson stare. "Tell me about the House," he said. "What, it's just a whorehouse?"

Vicki smiled without humor. "Sure, sometimes it's a

whorehouse. And sometimes it's a slaughterhouse."

She's high, Phil dismissed. "Come on, tell me something I can use."

"The girls at Sallee's, most of the time they'd just turn their tricks in the parking lot, in cars and trucks. But sometimes, if there was a high-paying john, or one of Cody's friends wanted a girl, he'd let her take the trick back to the House. And then there were other nights..."

The rest of the words seemed to drift out the window.

"What?" Phil asked testily. "Other nights, what?"

"Cody would pick certain victims—"

"What do you mean, certain victims?"

"Drug dealers mostly, from the surrounding towns, the kind of guys nobody asks questions about when they disappear. And if anybody did file a missing persons report, Mullins would bury it, or stonewall the county cops. That was part of Cody's deal with Mullins—Mullins took a cut to throw the county off track about any bodies that were found. The other part of the deal was Mullins let Cody run hookers out of Sallee's as a lure."

"A lure?"

"Yeah, like I was just saying. A john would buy a girl at the club, then she'd take him back to the house. But that's where the trick ended."

Phil glanced at her. "I don't follow."

"Cody would have some Creekers waiting, then they'd over-power the john and sacrifice him to Ona."

Phil still couldn't believe this, but then he couldn't deny how well the pieces fit. All those murder victims found. All drug dealers from nearby towns. All regulars at Sallee's.

All skinned.

Then another word emerged into his head: Skeet-inner, he thought. Then: Skin-eater

"Turn here," Vicki told him.

Phil slowed and steered the cruiser onto a road that was little more than a rutted path twisting up into the woods. Like skeletal fingertips, the ends of branches reached out and scratched deeply into the cruiser's paint. Mullins won't complain, not now, Phil reminded himself. The sound, as they traveled farther up, was worse than nails on slate. And the cruiser's wheels rocked over the road's ruts so much that Phil's teeth began chattering.

Several more turns onto even narrower roads took them into

a no-man's land of vines, brush, and hugely knotted trees. They passed rotting timber-falls; foxfire glowed green on slime-laden logs; networks of spiderwebs glistened between drooping bows. The hot air smelled sweetly putrid.

*All these roads, all these turns. Christ, no wonder I couldn't remember the way.* The woods were a labyrinth now, the road a juddering maze to nowhere.

But then another road opened to moonlight. An unkempt field, high with dying grass and weeds, swept to their left. And to their right—

Phil recognized the hill, which rose upward against the forest belt.

And there it stood, before the hundred-foot oaks and bare in the moonlight, the abode of his worst nightmare.

The House, he simply thought.

His eyes felt glued to it.

It had changed little from what his memory offered: graying whitewash, narrow windows, a slightly sagging roof. Decrepit. Worn down by the weight of age but somehow still standing.

"Turn off your lights!" Vicki whispered.

Phil cursed himself, then quickly switched them off and cut the engine. Suddenly the air was alive with throbbing night sounds, gently deafening, gracefully chaotic. The heat bore down, seemed to press against his face.

Something was calling him, his past perhaps, or the fears he'd kept buried for the last twenty-five years. Something was in there. Right this instant. He wasn't sure what, but somehow that didn't even matter. A demon, or a cult, or just a bunch of crazy inbreds—it was more than any of that. Something powerful, and something equally insane.

Waiting for him.

He grabbed the Remington pump, then stuffed a second pistol into his pants. The third he gave to Vicki. "Wait here."

"No way!" she objected. "You're crazy if you think I'm going to sit here by myself."

"All right, then, come on, but stay behind me and keep quiet."

They both got out. Phil, feeling like a vagabond mercenary, wiped sweat off his brow and stuffed loose ammo into his pockets. Then he clipped a flashlight to his belt and motioned Vicki to follow.

A dirt path wound around some trees up the hill; suddenly the moonlight blared at them. Perfect targets for these hayseeds, he realized. *Some Creeker with a long rifle is probably scoping us right now.* He leaned low and quickened his pace with Vicki in tow, moving in a rough zigzag. Sweat drenched them both when they got to the top of the moonlit hill. They ducked by the side of the house.

Phil leaned against cracked siding, staring down the hill at nothing. *This is suicide,* came the bald and very sudden thought. *We don't stand a chance, we won't make it ten feet past the front door. I'm gonna wind up getting us both killed…*

Vicki's hand touched his shoulder. "Are you all right?"

*There are probably fifty Creekers in there…*

"Phil?"

Phil turned slightly; his stare lost all focus. *You must be out of your mind. Take Vicki, get back in the car, and drive away. Go somewhere, anywhere. Start again, and live…*

Just as he considered throwing in the towel and abandoning this madness, a high scream from one of the upper windows shrilled into the night—

Susan's scream.

*They're torturing her, they're tearing her apart—*

"Come on," he said. "We're going in now."

Lightly but quickly, he crept around to the front and mounted the wood steps to the porch. All the windows were vaguely dark, but he detected the faintest fluttering orange light from within. *Candles and oil lamps,* he realized. *No electricity.* "Anything that moves," he whispered to Vicki, "shoot it."

Shotgun at the ready, he stepped to face the front door, then paused. The strange brass knocker—a blank face bereft of features save for eyes—stared back at him. He remembered it, from all those years ago. A face from his past, beckoning him now. But there was another face from his past, too, wasn't there? Natter's face—

And that was one face Phil couldn't wait to have in his sights.

The door stood slightly ajar, and it creaked appropriately when he pushed it open and aimed the Remington. Several candles flickered; it took Phil a moment for his eyes to adjust, then another moment to digest what he was seeing…

"Good God," he murmured.

There were indeed Creekers waiting for them. Several waited

right here in the foyer. But none of them were armed.

And none of them were alive.

Five or six of them lay in a heap on the threadbare carpet which was now just a sponge of wet blood. Knives lay on the floor too, having recently fallen from limp hands. Their swollen heads hung off their necks at impossible angles to show grisly gashes cut deep across their throats...

*They all killed themselves,* Phil realized.

Vicki gasped behind him. Phil stepped in. He spotted more bodies lying in the halls to either side, all pale in death, all throat-cut. What in God's name... Each room off the hallways, too, were now death chambers. And when he'd finished checking all of the rooms on the first floor, he realized there must be over thirty dead Creekers total. All suicides.

It was hard to fathom so many dead bodies at once. Phil felt winded, and Vicki looked like she was about to pass out. "Come on, we gotta check the next floor," he said.

The stairs were a slow waterfall of blood, and once they got to the second-floor landing, they saw more piles of bodies, more slashed throats, more dead-staring crimson eyes and twisted death-grins. "Why are they doing this?" he muttered to himself.

"I told you, they'll do anything for Cody," Vicki whispered. "Suicide is the ultimate homage to their god..."

He stood in ragged shock in the hall. More candles flickered about the heaps of disfigured and bukge-headed bodies. Homage? Phil thought. More like madness, sheer and total madness.

"Mannona!" a voice shrieked. A figure wheeled out of the dark, a Creeker. Phil brought the shotgun to bear and fired. Half of the Creeker's head flew away in chunks. "Onnamann!" shouted another flawed voice, and then another Creeker, with a bivalved head, limped quickly out of the flickering darkness. Phil fired again. The blast caught the inbred square in the chest and carried him halfway down the hall. Then—

*Holy shit!*

Every door in the hall flew open, and a legion of Creekers converged on them. Vicki fired ineptly behind him, screaming, as Phil emptied the shotgun into the approaching mass. Bodies fell only to be replaced by more. Then Phil whipped out his two pistols, pinpointing and dropping targets one after another in a hail of concussion and muzzle-flash. He managed to reload twice in the melee, firing repeatedly, the guns bucking in his hands, and more inbreds fell like hinged ducks in a shooting gallery. When he was done, a lone overalled Creeker with a cleft face grinned at him, raised his arms, and said, "Mannona!"

Then he lunged.

Phil's final shot caught the marauder in the eye and dropped him.

Gun smoke filled the hall like tear gas. Now a deadfall of bodies lay at his feet. I just killed twenty or thirty people, he realized, but by now the shock had worn away, to be replaced by some stoical kind of complacency. None of the Creekers had been armed, yet they'd attacked anyway. Again, it didn't make sense. They'd willingly, even gleefully, lunged to their deaths.

More proof of Natter's evil.

"Where is he?" he asked, tasting cordite. "Where's Natter? He's upstairs, isn't he?"

Vicki, blood-spattered and gore-flecked, nodded. "In the upper room," she said.

Natter had gone to all this trouble to get him here, and had sacrificed all these people, but—*Why?* Phil asked himself. He had to know now, no matter what the risk. He reached into his pocket for more bullets but found none. He didn't even care. He took Vicki's hand, stepping over bodies, and made for the next flight of steps.

Then, not in his ears but in his head, Natter's voice grated like stones.

*Yes! Up here, little boy...*

The narrow stairs creaked underfoot. The heat grew stifling, but Phil was oblivious. He felt oblivious to everything now, to blood, to violence, to killing. He was cauterized, immune. He didn't know what he was walking into, and he didn't care.

The memories hovered. He walked directly to the door at the end of the cramped hallway. Opened it. Stepped in.

Only moonlight lit the room, from the open shutters. Four black corners and a block of tinseled light.

*I told you we'd see you again someday*, he heard in his head.

Phil glanced at each of the room's stygian corners.

*Yes, little boy, we've been waiting...*

"Where's Susan!" he erupted. "If she's dead, I burn this whole place to the ground and all you ugly fuckers with it!"

This invective was answered with a low chuckle. *Not many of us left to burn, hmm? You're quite handy with a gun.*

"You killed those people, Natter!" Phil railed. "You ordered them to kill themselves! You sent them to their deaths."

*No, rather, I sent them to paradise. The time has come; we've all suffered long enough. They are in paradise now, which is where they deserve to be. Tonight our travails are at an end. Tonight our curse is lifted. Tonight we start anew.*

The darkness, now, seemed to coagulate; Phil felt he was standing in a grotto with the moon, like a spotlight, casting an aura about him.

Welcome home, the voice croaked.

"This is a hell house, it isn't my home."

*Oh, but it is. We've waited a long time for your return.*

"What do you want?"

*You.*

"But you had me earlier in the parking lot at the club. Why didn't you take me then?"

*Because there were still a few things you needed to remember, weren't there? Hmm?*

The dream, he realized. The final part of my childhood memory. He gazed cockeyed into the dark. The last piece of the puzzle. "You can't know when and what I'm going to dream," he protested.

*I know lots of things about you, Phil.*

*Because I'm your father.*

"Bullshit."

*Think about it, son.*

He did then. The darkness focused. Orphaned as an infant. Raised by an "aunt." Could it be possible?

"But I'm not a Creeker," he said. "There's nothing wrong with me. I'm—"

*You're what?*

Phil's mouth opened, but no words came out.

*You're perfect.*

"We're both perfect, Phil."

But it wasn't Natter who'd said it. He recognized the voice at once.

"Susan?" he said, squinting.

Moving very slowly, Susan emerged from the dark. But she was fully dressed, smiling softly.

Unhurt.

"I thought—"

"That they were torturing me, raping me, killing me?" she finished. "If you didn't think I was in danger, then you never would've come."

A trick, he realized. *All this time she's been one of them.*

"And, of course," she added, "that wouldn't be any way for them to treat your sister."

*My...sister?*

"You should have read those books a little more closely, Phil," she said. "We're both Creekers, but we're perfect. It took a long time for our father to breed us. Trial and error, for ages."

Then Phil thought back to the books about inbreeding.

The more intensively inbred the community, the more astronomical the chances of an undefected birth. One chance in thousands, he remembered. And Susan and I are it.

"We're living proof, aren't we?" Susan said. "No red eyes, no black hair, no physical deformities. We're the offspring the Creekers have been trying to produce for a hundred years. But—" She took another step closer. "Too bad for me I was born a woman. The progenitor has to be male."

The Mannona, Natter said.

"You," Susan said. "Haven't you realized that by now? It's you."

Then Phil remembered what Vicki had told him about Creeker speech—dyslalia—how spoken words were inverted. Skeet-inner meant skin-eater. Ona-prey-bee meant praise be to Ona. And now:

"Mannona," he said in a voice that was dark as the room. "And Onnamann."

"The Man of Ona," she translated.

Me, Phil thought.

The darkness seemed to hush.

The moonlight radiated.

Phil's heart slowed.

"We're hybrids," Susan informed him.

Vicki had mentioned that too, hadn't she? Hybrids. *Ona,* she'd said. The female inbred of the demon and the Creekers. Most of the Creekers don't even look human. Because part of their bloodline isn't human...

And what had Natter said, just moments ago?

*Tonight we start anew.*

Something thunked to the floor. Phil stared down. It was Vicki's head—cleanly severed—just dropped from Susan's scarlet hand.

Poor little whore, Natter's black voice remarked.

"The whole thing, I'm sure you realize now," Susan said, "was a set-up. To lure you here at precisely this time."

"Why?" Phil asked dryly.

"It's generational."

"What is?"

*The fertility of our god,* Natter answered.

"Skeet-inner," Phil whispered. "Ona..."

*The thing you saw when you were ten,* Vicki's dead words echoed now.

Two more figures—Druck, and another male Creeker, grinned as they came out of the obsidian dark. But they were dragging a third figure by—its elbows.

The figure was naked. Bound and gagged.

The figure was Sullivan.

Watch, Natter said in Phil's head.

Druck, with his double-thumbed hand, raised Sullivan's head by the hair. Then he chuckled.

Then he shoved Sullivan into the room's darkest corner.

Phil couldn't see anything; it was too dark. But he could hear sounds, and the sounds were familiar. A wet, slavering sound. A sickly, wet grinding like ravenous animals at a trough...

*We give you this day, your daily flesh...*

And next:

*thump!*

The dark corner seemed to eject what remained of Sullivan: a skinned, glistening-red corpse.

And only now did Natter himself surface from his own darkness, just a deformed face in a black robe and black hood. "My daughter," he said. "Now you, too, must go on your way."

Susan shed her clothes, then turned her succulent body to face Phil in the moonlight.

"You're our saviour, Phil. You're the one. You should feel honored to serve our god in such a way."

Phil could only stand numb and look back at her.

"And someday, brother," she finished, "I'll see you again, in paradise."

Then Susan, with no reluctance, stepped into the deadly dark corner and disappeared, where, within moments, the skin was eaten off her flawless body, and she was spat back out onto the floor.

"My son, my god." Natter's face seemed awed now in its deformity. "A few of us will remain, to tend to your needs. You will be the father of a new and holy race. A perfect race. The answer to our prayers for all these years. The answer to our call and to our duty."

Druck and the few remaining Creekers left the room. Then Natter slowly backed away. His disjointed hands raised high. His great scarlet eyes closed, and then his malformed face lifted.

"Praise be to you, my son," he said in the deepest piety. "Praise be to the Mannona…"

Then Natter, the Reverend, was gone.

Phil's eyes fixed on the corner. He could just barely see it now, just a trace of what he'd seen more completely all those years ago.

He was looking at his heritage, at his predestination, at the real reason he'd been brought into the world.

*To make a new world*, he realized.

His entire life up to this point had all been a lie. Only now did the truth shine plain to him. It was here, his true reality, right there in the corner, just a few yards from where he now stood.

And from that same abyssal and holy corner, another voice seeped into his head. It was a beautiful voice—

A woman's voice:

*My lover, my husband, my son*, it said.

There was a cosmic ringing in his ears, and unfathomable visions swimming behind his eyes. Visions from the lowest places of the earth…

*I've waited so long*, the voice wept to him. *But now we will always be together.*

More vague features formed. The corrupted, bent limbs, the demonic face and razor-toothed slit for a mouth. The petite nobs of its warped forehead, its high, full breasts, and the faintest glimmer of its sex.

*My love! It's our wedding night*, it rejoiced.

Phil stared, agape.

*Come to me now.*

Behind him, Phil heard the tiny click as the door was finally locked.

# ABOUT THE AUTHOR

Edward Lee is the author of over 50 horror, fantasy, and sci-fi novels, and dozens of short stories. He has also had comic scripts published by DC Comics, Verotik Inc., and Cemetery Dance. A great number of his novels have been reprinted in Germany, Poland, Italy, Romania, Greece, Russia and other countries. He is a Bram Stoker Award Nominee; his Lovecraftian novel INNSWICH HORROR won the 2010 Vincent Price Award for Best Foreign Book (Austria), his novel WHITE TRASH GOTHIC won the 2018 Splatterpunk Award for Best Extreme Horror Novel, and in 2020 Lee won the Splatterpunk Lifetime Achievement Award. In 2009, the movie version of his novella HEADER was released by Synapse Films; several of his novels are currently under option. Lee is a U.S. Army veteran and lives in Seminole, Florida.

Curious about other Crossroad Press books?
Stop by our site:
http://store.crossroadpress.com
We offer quality writing
in digital, audio, and print formats.

www.ingramcontent.com/pod-product-compliance
Lightning Source LLC
Chambersburg PA
CBHW031552240626
47153CB00002B/474